Girl in a Blue Dress

LONGLISTED FOR THE MAN BOOKER PRIZE 2008

'Fabulously indulgent Victoriana . . . a lovely, rich evocation of the period that rises above the faintly damning "historical fiction" label with its complex characterisation and silky prose. It also seems apposite – a neat rendering of a celebrity marriage with all the pressure and expectation that courting fame invites. Wag hopefuls take note – anyone who belongs to the public can never really belong to you' *Observer*

'A fine work of imagination and compassion that offers up other ways for us to understand a popular genius and those who loved him' *Telegraph*

'In this clever act of biography and fiction, Arnold brings him exuberantly alive: the entertainer, the raconteur, the Wonder Dad – always brightly dressed, captivating and magnetic, ready with a joke or a silly face. Alfred Gibson, as Dickens is called here, was a ferociously controlling man with boundless energy and an insatiable appetite for affection' *Washington Post*

'Gaynor Arnold's deep understanding of human relationships marks out this story of a strong woman in an age when women weren't perceived as such' Erica Wagner, *Times*

'With Gaynor Arnold's *Girl in a Blue Dress* the Birmingham indie house Tindal Street Press confirms its magic touch' Boyd Tonkin, *Independent*

'With his manic energy and flamboyant waistcoats, Gibson is a Dickensian character – and no wonder, for Arnold's inspiration for her wholly absorbing novel lies in the complex married life of Charles Dickens and his wife, Catherine' *Daily Mail*

'Arnold's knowledge of Dickens is impeccable, and she uses fiction to give Mrs D what she never had – a chance to interview her husband's mistress, and reclaim her beloved children. Beautifully written, entirely satisfying' Kate Saunders, *Times*

'*Girl in a Blue Dress* is exceptionally well controlled in its playing of past against present' William Palmer, *Independent*

'In its quiet way it chips away at the image Dickens wanted to leave posterity. One puts the novel down with a sense of justice, belatedly, done. And very readably done' *Financial Times*

'Arnold balances contemporary clarity with a real sense that the reader is immersed both in the Victorian world and the novels of Dickens. She vividly conveys a time when social convention demanded Dorothea be the perfect helpmate. And as the widowed Dorothea gradually comes to terms with the fact she could never have lived up to Alfred's fantasies of family life, her story makes for reading you cannot put down' *Metro*

'Arnold demonstrates fiction's capacity to imagine the truth behind the facts and so performs a service for the ghost of Catherine Dickens which no biographer, in the absence of further documentary evidence, could' *Sunday Times*

Girl in a
Blue Dress

Gaynor Arnold

First published in September 2008
by Tindal Street Press Ltd
217 The Custard Factory, Gibb Street, Birmingham, B9 4AA
www.tindalstreet.co.uk

This edition first published February 2011

2 4 6 8 10 9 7 5 3 1

A CIP catalogue reference for this book is available
from the British Library

ISBN: 978 1 906994 15 0

Typeset by Country Setting, Kingsdown, Kent
Printed and bound in the UK by CPI Mackays, Chatham Kent

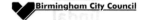
Birmingham City Council

For my mother
a great storyteller

1

My husband's funeral is today. And I'm sitting here alone in my upstairs room while half London follows him to his grave.

I should be angry, I suppose. Kitty was angry *for* me; marching about the room dementedly. *They couldn't stop you,* she kept saying. *They wouldn't dare turn you away – not his own widow.* And of course she is right; if I'd made an appearance, they would have been forced to acknowledge me, to grit their teeth and make the best of it. But I really couldn't have borne to parade myself in front of them; to sit in a black dress in a black carriage listening to the sound of muffled hooves and the agonised weeping of thousands. And most of all, I couldn't have borne to see Alfred boxed up in that dreadful fashion. Even today, I cannot believe that he will never again make a comical face, or laugh immoderately at some joke, or racket about in his old facetious way.

I have tried to keep cheerful. I have sat at the piano in my brightest frock, playing 'The Sailors' Hornpipe' until my fingers ached. I have wept too, loud and long, but I cannot let Kitty see me weep. She will come soon, I am sure. And when she is here, I shall need all my strength.

At last, the doorbell rings, and in seconds Kitty is in the room. She has an immense black veil, a heavy train running for yards behind her and jet beads glittering all over. 'Oh, you should have been there, Mama!' she cries, almost knocking Gyp from my lap with the force of her embrace. 'It's completely *insupportable* that you were not!'

I pat whatever part of her I can feel beneath the heavy folds of crape and bombazine. I try to calm her, though now she is here – so strung up and full of grief, so pregnant with desire to tell me all – I am far from being calm myself. My heart jitters and jumps like a mad thing. I dread to hear what she has to say, but I know of old that she will not be stopped. She is near to stifling me too; her arms are tight, her veil is across my mouth. 'Please, Kitty,' I gasp. 'Get up – or you will suffocate us both! Sit down and tell me all.'

She stands up, starts to wrench off her gloves. 'Sit down! *Sit down?* How can I *sit down* after all I have been through? Oh, he might almost have done it on purpose!'

'Who? Your father? What can he possibly have done now?' Yet it would not surprise me if he had managed to cause some kind of mayhem. Alfred always hated funerals, and would not be averse to undermining his own. But I do not see how even *he* could have contrived such a thing from beyond the grave.

'It's all his fault! Oh, Mama!' She throws her mangled gloves on the table. 'As if it's not enough that we've had to share every scrap of him with his Public for all these years, but no, they had to be centre stage even today, as if it were *their* father – or *their* husband – who had been taken from them!' She lifts her veil, revealing reddened eyes and cheeks puffed with weeping. 'Oh, I cannot bear it!'

So it is the Public she inveighs against; that is nothing new. 'Oh, Kitty,' I say. 'It is hard, I know, but you must allow them their hour of grief.'

'Must I? Really, Mama, must I?' She takes out her handkerchief. It is silk with a black lace border and I cannot help thinking that she must have outspent her housekeeping with all this ostentation. She dabs at her eyes as violently as if she would poke them out. 'You'd have expected, wouldn't you, that after giving them every *ounce* of his blood every *day* of his existence, at least they'd let him have some peace and dignity at the end?'

'And didn't they?' My blood runs cold; all kinds of grotes-querie fill my mind. 'For Heaven's sake, child, what did they do?'

'They were like lunatics, Mama.' She takes an angry turn around the curio-table, nearly knocking it over. 'It was *insupportable.*'

I do not understand. Even the most cynical of his critics would not have begrudged him a decent funeral. 'Lunatics?' I say. 'Was there really no respect?'

She pauses, shrugs reluctantly. 'Well, I suppose there *was* at first. I even thought how patient they'd all been: men, women and children standing six foot deep, even though it had been raining for hours. Everyone still and silent, save for the sound of the carri-age wheels, and the shufflings and sighings and doffings of hats. But the moment we turned away from the park, some desperate wretch ran out and started pulling at the heads of the horses, crying, 'No! No! Don't leave us!' And then it was as if a dam had burst, and the crowd was a great surge of water, flowing every-where. It was terrifying, Mama! The horses were rearing, feathers floating in the air. I thought we'd be turned over and trampled to death. Trampled by his very own Public at his very own funeral – how fitting that would have been!' She glares around the room, as if daring the furniture to disagree with her.

So that is all; simply some over-exuberance of the crowd. But she is not used to it, of course; she never had to run the gauntlet of the savage masses in America all those years ago, when I'd had to cling to Alfred's arm as he cleaved through them, smiling as if it were nothing in the world to be pulled about by strangers who thought you belonged to them, body and soul. 'Poor Kitty,' I say. 'How dreadful for you! And yet your most fervent wish is that I had been there too; I think that is not quite kind.'

She looks a little chastened. 'But it was your *right*, Mama,' she says, sniffing loudly. 'You should have insisted. It is a matter of principle. You should not have allowed Sissy and the others to win again.'

'Oh, I am not interested in winning or losing,' I reply – although as the words leave my lips I know it's not strictly true; I was once prepared to win at any price, especially with my proud and pretty sister. But it's too late now, and none of Kitty's raging will make one iota of difference. And if by staying home I avoided being overturned and trampled upon, I can only be grateful.

I look at her sumptuous frock, her extravagant train, her acres of beading, and her very fine, long veil; only the mud around her hem spoils the theatrical effect: 'But you seem undamaged, Kitty. Surely the excitement of the Public cannot have been so *very* bad?'

'You think I exaggerate?' she exclaims, casting herself into the fireside chair. 'Well, you can ask Michael. He was in the carriage with Alfie and me. If he'd not kept hold of the door-handle, we'd have been pitched out on the road! And if I hadn't clung to the curtains, I'd have cracked my head against the windows or been knocked to the floor! There was such a monstrous *surging* ahead of us that I would not have put it past them to have laid hands on the coffin itself.' She wipes her nose defiantly. 'He would really have belonged to his blessed Public then!'

I am distressed at her ordeal, but I want to laugh too. And I see Alfred in my mind's eye, throwing back his head and roaring with mirth. But poor Kitty sees only the disrespect. 'I'm sure they did not intend to frighten you, Kitty,' I say. 'They were simply expressing their grief.'

'Grief? Well, it was a strange kind, then! It seemed more – oh, I don't know – as if they were some kind of savages and he were some sort of *god*! In Piccadilly they actually pelted the carriages with flowers; at the corner of Pall Mall they chanted his name and pressed his books to their hearts as if they were holy icons. Ladies fainted and had to be carried away by the dozen. Gentlemen lost hats and gloves – and even boots.' She shakes her head vehemently.

I smile to myself: urchins and pickpockets must have had a fine time.

'I don't know how they had the gall – taking it upon themselves to wail and sob as if they were widows – when his real widow wasn't even there!' She leans forward and sets about the fire, wielding the long poker as if she would stab the coals to death. She is all anger; but I can see that she has clearly relished the drama of the day. Why else is she so sumptuously decked out in all the finery of sorrow, the elaborate mourning she knows he hated so much?

'It doesn't matter,' I say, taking the poker away from her. 'The funeral was not for my benefit; it was for theirs. And you saw how much they loved him.'

She turns on me. 'Only because they didn't *know* him. So many times I wanted to push down the carriage window and shout out to them that he was a cruel, *cruel* man. Cruel to his wife, and cruel to his children! And yet you sit here so calm and docile! Aren't you *angry* at the way he used you? Don't you want to howl up to Heaven at the unfairness of it all?' She looks as though she will lift up her own head and howl, but instead she gets up and paces a path between the fireplace and the door, her train catching around the chair-legs and the sofa-ends as she turns and turns about.

I knew she would taunt me with complacency; it is her constant theme. Yet, God knows, I have been angry, and jealous, and sorry for myself. But such emotions only feed on themselves. It is not Alfred's fault that things happened the way they did. 'I will not speak ill of him,' I say. 'And I trust *you* will not either. Especially today.'

'Well,' she says tartly, 'I cannot promise that. After all, it's such a relief to be free from him. I may find it impossible to hold myself back.'

'What do you mean – *free*?'

'Don't pretend you don't know what I mean! Don't say you don't feel it too – knowing we shan't have to bow to his opinion on every blessed thing! Doesn't it fill you with a wonderful sense of liberty?' She spreads her arms in a theatrical gesture, the beads along her bodice shivering in unison. 'When I think of all I've had to endure, I'm almost glad he's gone.'

I cannot endure hearing her say those things, even though I know she doesn't mean them. 'What nonsense!' I say. 'You wouldn't be weeping this way if you were glad; and you wouldn't be nearly so angry. Your father was a wonderful man – one of the most wonderful men that ever lived – and you know it.'

'Oh, yes, I know it. We all know it. We couldn't get away from *the One and Only, Yours Truly, the Great Original.*'

She may speak sneeringly, but I feel the tears starting to my eyes as I hear those famous sobriquets and see his laughing face come before me again. I must keep steady though; the poor child has had a wretched time. She's cold and muddy, and I need to see to her. I push the tea tray forward. 'Have some tea to warm up, dearest. Have a little cake, too. Wilson went for it this morning; it's very fresh.'

She hesitates; she is always tempted by food. She takes off her bonnet and veil, wipes her nose on the silk handkerchief, and pours herself some tea. Then she settles herself snugly on her favourite footstool by my chair. After a while, when the fire has warmed her, she speaks again. She is more composed now: 'Every one of the shops closed early, you know. They had black curtains up too, in so many places. And the blinds drawn all along the route. Every man I saw had an armband.' She reaches to take a slice of cake.

'You see, he *was* a Great Man, Kitty. You should be proud of him.'

She doesn't answer. But I know she is proud of him. Kitty was by far his favourite child. She munches away at the cake: 'So, Mama, what will you do now?'

'*Do?* What do you mean?' I am horrified. I have always hated change, and this past week has brought me change enough. I cannot think that more would suit me.

'Well, I trust you won't stay cooped up in this dingy set of rooms any more. It hardly becomes the widow of such a *Great Man*.'

'And what do you suggest I do instead? Move in with you and Augustus?'

She stops eating, flushes red. 'Well, of course you may. You are always welcome. But that's not what I meant —'

No, it was unfair of me to say that. She thinks I am unaware of how Augustus treats her. Out all day and sometimes far into the night. She wouldn't want me to witness his neglect at first hand.

'I simply meant that you are more independent, now. You don't have to think about whether His Greatness would approve of what you do. All this —' she flings her arms around like a veritable Indian goddess '— was what *he* wanted; what *he* thought fit. Every blessed chair, every cushion, every plate and cup and cake-stand! Now you can do anything you choose. You could take a cottage in the country. Return to Chiswick, perhaps? The air would be better for you. And I could still come and visit.'

'I find the air quite well enough where I am, thank you, Kitty.' I glance around at the red plush curtains, the easy, old-fashioned chairs, the Turkey rug, the walnut piano; and I appreciate for the thousandth time how he had such a tremendous instinct for other people's comfort. I falter, however, as I catch sight of my music on the piano. The page is open still at 'The Sailors' Hornpipe' and I feel his arm, so firm around my waist, as he propels me around my parents' parlour at breakneck speed. 'I think I shall never move from here,' I tell her. 'I like it, and I'm used to it. And on the contrary, it makes me happy to know that he chose "every chair and cushion and cake-stand" himself.'

'He gave you all the old things he didn't want any more,' she retorts. 'Why don't you admit the Truth for once?'

'The Truth?' I look her in the eye and sigh. 'You mean, of course, that I should agree with *you*?'

'Not necessarily.' She tosses her head and the slivers of jet at her ears do a macabre dance. 'But now he's no longer here, you don't need to be loyal. You can admit it all now, surely.'

'Admit what, Kitty dear?' We have been over this so many times.

'Oh, Mama! Admit that he never gave you anything but heart-ache. And children, of course,' she adds sarcastically.

I won't have that. 'If I have had heartache in my life – and God knows I have – your father was not to blame for it. He gave me everything I have valued. If blame there is – well, it is the fault of circumstance.'

Kitty glares. 'Circumstance? Oh, of course,' she says, starting to pleat her handkerchief with angry movements of her fine, active fingers. '*The One and Only* cannot be wrong. *Yours Truly* remains forever above reproach.'

She means to provoke me; but I know her of old, and will not be drawn. 'You may pretend to think ill of him, Kitty, but he has always shown a proper regard for me: I have these comfortable lodgings in a nice part of town, with Mrs. Wilson to look after me – and Gyp, too, to keep me company.' Gyp barks as if he ack-nowledges the memory. He is old and fat, as I am, but still affec-tionate. I laugh and tickle his nose.

Kitty won't have it. 'He gives you a *wretched* apartment in a *wretched* area of town. With one servant, and no carriage – and a dog with a foul temper. A fine arrangement!' She springs up from the little stool, but she forgets the weight of the train she is wearing and staggers a little against the fender, making the fire-irons crash into the grate.

I want to smile – but I have to hide it. Kitty can't abide being laughed at, any more than a cat. 'Mrs. Wilson cooks and cleans for me,' I say. 'I need nothing more.'

[8]

'But you never venture out. You're like a hermit. Or a ghost of the past, wandering around the room in the dark. Expecting him to 'turn up', perhaps?' Kitty brushes the coal-dust from her skirt and turns to pour more tea.

'I'm not at all like a hermit. I see *you*. I see O'Rourke.'

'Michael? Oh, but he's so thin, and old, and unexciting! He was like a *skelington in a suit* today. You might have thought he was the corpse himself got out of the coffin!'

'Kitty! How can you say such a thing?' (But I can't help smiling to myself: Kitty is always so wickedly apt.) 'If it were not for Michael I don't know what I would have done these ten years.'

'Don't you? I cannot imagine what he's done for you, other than be two-faced about the whole affair!'

'Two-faced?' I am a little angry with her now. 'Why do you persist in saying that? He's been my advocate with your father on every little matter: the rent, the bills, the laundry —'

She rolls her eyes.

'And he's always been most faithful with the books. He gets me every new edition straight from the press.'

'Does he, though?' She looks at me dully.

'Yes, I think I'm the first person in London to lay eyes on them.' I cast a glance at the dark red line of Alfred's novels in the bookcase across the room, some of them so battered that they are about to fall apart. 'I still read a chapter every day, you know, Kitty. And when I finish each book, I start another. And when I finish them all, I start at the beginning again. When I read, I can hear your father talking to me exactly as if he were in the room; when he used to rush into the parlour, pen in hand: *What do you think of this, Dodo? Does this make you laugh?*'

'Or cry.' Kitty stands by the fender, punishing it with her boot.

'Indeed,' I say. 'He was a master of every emotion. I knew that from the very first day we met.'

As I speak, I can see it. My bedroom, with its casement window opening upon the garden; the balmy weather; the fragrance of the lilacs drifting in; the growing dusk as I stand quietly folding sheets and bolster-cases. I am completely and utterly content. Every day is tranquil, full of family affection. Every evening I can be sure Papa will come home at seven sharp, and equally sure my two little sisters will rush to greet him, pulling his hat and cane from his grasp, and making him sit in a chair while they chatter about their lessons, their games, and what they have seen on their walks.

In those days, on summer evenings, it was our habit to sit together in the garden before supper. And after supper, Papa would read to us in the drawing room, or we'd gather round the piano to sing before Alice and Sissy were sent up to bed. So I had no reason to think that particular May evening would be any different; or at least not different enough to give me a moment's pause. I suppose I heard the usual click of the gate as my father passed through. I suppose I heard his footsteps coming up the garden path in the usual way. And if I heard some quicker, lighter footsteps alongside his – and I cannot swear I did not – it was of no significance to me. After all, my father often brought home unexpected guests who had to be smiled at and played to. If there *was* such a personage lurking below, I was in no particular hurry to make his acquaintance. So I carried on folding and stacking the linen, making sure the edges all came together neatly, that the corners were well-turned.

And then something happened. I can hardly describe it, though I have tried again and again. It was the way the scent of the lilacs and the sound of a clear, cheerful laugh drifted in through the window at exactly the same moment. I could hardly tell the sound from the scent; yet each entity seemed completely entrancing and divine. I stood in the middle of the room with the bed-sheet in my hands as if all my senses were in suspension. Yet all the time I could hear my father talking quite normally outside, and I picked out the words 'Alfred Gibson' and 'supper'. And then the stranger laughed again and I realised that I was trembling – no, more than trembling: giddy. And faint. And hot and cold all at the same time. I was in a complete state of confusion, and yet that confusion was more delightful than anything I had ever known. I lost all sense of reserve and rushed to the window. I think if it had been required of me I would have waded through oceans to see the owner of that wonderful laugh. As it was, I could just see the top of my father's head as he called into the house. 'Dodo,' he said. 'There is someone I want you to meet.'

Even if I'd wanted to, I could *not* have answered him. I was transfixed by a vision: the figure of a young man standing perfectly still in the spilling lamplight below, dressed in an eye-catching way I knew was not quite gentlemanly – a scarlet waistcoat, a sky-blue coat, and slender trousers of a buff that was almost yellow. He had voluptuous long hair, far too wayward and rich for a man; and deep brown eyes, too wayward and rich for anyone. They shone like stars. His whole face seemed illuminated.

I'm sure I didn't make a sound, or even a movement; but he looked up suddenly as if he knew *exactly* where I was. And he smiled. And bowed. He walked backwards to bow; he bowed in the middle of the lawn, an extravagant, theatrical bow – very quick, yet very low. I could not take my eyes off him. He was a complete wonder. He was standing in our garden in Chiswick. And he was coming to supper.

Of course, my father looked up too, calling out in his usual affectionate way: 'Ah, there is my Swan! There is my Loveliest of Girls!'

And I called out desperately to stop him going further, lest the stranger would expect a beauty and be disappointed. 'I am coming,' I said as loudly as I could manage. 'I am coming!'

I truly cannot imagine how I contrived to get down the stairs, my legs were so tremulous. I must almost have slithered down, as running water finds its level. My skirt seemed to rise up and float around me and all the while I could feel my face burning ever brighter. When I reached the newel-post at the foot of the stairs, I clung to it as if I would collapse without it. Our maid, Nancy, stopped at the dining-room door with the extra knives and forks in her hand and looked at me, her eyes round with surprise: 'My! You look as if all the blood's gone to your head, Miss Dodo,' she said. 'I'd sit down for a spell if I was you. Get your nice complexion back.'

So I settled my gown, pressed my hands against my cheeks, and waited for my gasping to subside before stepping into the drawing room. The long windows were open, and I could see the garden stretching back, clots of blossom white in the twilight, a hazy blur where the dark hedges met, a hint of high brick wall and the dim shape of the wicket gate. The scent of the lilacs was so rich, I could almost taste it.

My mother and father were sitting outside, but there was no other person with them. I thought for a moment that I must have conjured up some kind of vision, and that there was no such being in the world as the radiant Mr. Gibson with the bright clothes and the wonderful laugh. Then I saw him. He was lying in the middle of the lawn. He had his arms spread, his eyes closed. For a second I thought he might be ill, or even dead. My blood seemed to stop in my veins. But then Alice and Sissy tiptoed forward, fingers on lips, and I realised with relief that they were in the middle of a game. But Mr. Gibson's stillness was amazing; he showed no flicker of life; then, at the very last moment, when my sisters were emboldened to come close, his hands shot out as if they were pistons and entrapped their ankles. And at the same instant he opened his eyes wide and showed his teeth like an ogre. They screamed, and I screamed too, from relief and delight and the general wonder of it all – the young man lying there with such an air of abandon, his poet's hair spread out on the lawn, his yellow trousers and sky-blue coat given up to grass stains, his dignity compromised so thrillingly.

But as soon as he had caught them, he let them go, resuming his apparent slumber in an instant, and they came at him again, giggling and holding their breath. But this time he contrived to miss them entirely, rolling about the lawn with great energy and animation, and somehow managing to grasp at the hem of my gown as I stood looking on. 'Aha!' he cried out, tugging the muslin so I had to move towards him, until I was standing right over him. Then, without warning, his other hand reached up and caught me firmly by the waist, pulling me so close that my bosom was almost touching that astonishing waistcoat of his. 'What's this, what's this?' he cried out, his eyes still fast shut. 'Not Miss Alice, I swear.' He fumbled a little at my bodice. 'Nor Miss Cecilia either. Good Heavens, something *Even More Delightful*!'

Then he opened his eyes and looked straight up at me. Such a bold and inviting look, yet so full of laughter! From that moment I was completely lost. Indeed, a minute more, and I would have been in his arms on the grass. But he was already jumping up, letting go my skirt, and bowing: 'Miss Millar, if I am not mistaken! Dear Miss Millar! Can I ever hope to be forgiven? Over-excitement, I'm afraid. A fault of mine when in the company of Young Persons. But if you knew my remorse, Miss Millar, you'd forgive me. I'm struck to the Very Art, indeed I am!'

I don't know how long I would have stayed looking at him – for ever, I think. But Papa came towards us, laughing and rubbing his hands: 'Dodo will indeed forgive you, my good sir. She is the kindest girl in the world – and the prettiest, although she doesn't like me to say so.' I blushed and shook my head. Although I possessed the blue eyes and golden curls young men were supposed to admire, I'd always felt that I was too soft and sleepy-looking to be appealing; I'd always wanted to be one of those dark, lively girls with darting eyes and vivacious manners. So I could feel my cheeks flaming afresh as Papa introduced us, saying that his new acquaintance was a writer of plays, and a young man of whom he had great hopes, and that he had been pleased to help him with a little 'pecuniary advancement'. 'I am sure that it will lead to great things, great things,' he said. 'And the first great thing is that Mr. Gibson's play is to be performed in Stepney a mere week on Friday. He has invited us all to see it. And, moreover, Mr. Gibson will be taking a leading part.'

Mr. Gibson smiled at me. 'I am very ugly,' he said.

'Indeed you are not,' I protested.

But I was too hasty. I blushed as he added, 'In the part, Miss Millar. I am very ugly in the part. I have no end of hair and eye-patches. It's capital stuff.'

✤

Gyp interrupts my reverie, jumping off my lap and waddling towards Kitty, who is staring deep into the fire. 'Well, you say he was master of every emotion,' she says. 'But it was all for the Public, not us. Sometimes I think the most wretched pauper on the street knew him better than I did.'

'How can you say that? You were always his favourite, Kitty – always at the centre of his heart.'

'So everyone says!' She frowns ferociously. 'But what good did that do me? Even that very last day, I had to wait my turn. And then he actually –' She rests her forehead on her hand as she leans against the mantelpiece. 'Oh, I hate him for it, Mama! I *hate* him!'

She is always saying how much she hates him. The poor child confuses hatred with anger and pain. And with love, too, of course. She wants so much to talk about her father but she has no one to confide in. Except me. Yet whatever I say seems to anger her more.

'How can he have done it?' she cries. 'He knew I was waiting. He was expecting me, after all. He had clocks; he had that wretched pocket-watch of his – and you know how he could guess

[14]

the time almost to the second. He needed only to open one door – *one door* – and say a kind word to me. He could have explained that he was busy. He could have given me a kiss and asked me to wait an hour or so, as any reasonable person would. But he wouldn't – or at least he didn't. So Mrs. Brooks was obliged to sit and make me endless cups of tea, and I had to listen to her going on about the price of sugar and boot-blacking, while she knitted pot-holders by the yard. Sissy and Lou didn't show a fin. They were apparently Not At Home, but I could hear them opening and closing doors, whispering and laughing. It made my blood boil.'

I feel for her. I too remember that house with its background of stifled sounds, that sense of being unwelcome and faintly ridiculous. 'They treated you shabbily,' I say. 'But don't blame your father for that. You know how it was when he was writing.'

'Yes, that's what I mean, Mama. That's exactly what I mean. Everything revolved around *him*. He never considered the rest of us.' She is up and walking about again; she has his continual nervous energy. 'And don't try to excuse him. Don't tell me how *good* he was. Don't tell me that he paid for my clothes and piano lessons and singing lessons – because I know it. I was his child after all; he was obliged to. And don't for Heaven's sake say he *wrote* for my benefit because we all know he wrote to please himself. And his blessed Public, of course.'

She circles the room, then sits down, staring gloomily at the carpet. 'You know, don't you, that I almost went away without seeing him? I'd got up to go at least three times, but Mrs. Brooks kept saying, 'Wait until five o'clock, my dear!' so I stayed. But when five o'clock came, and no sign of him, I was so cross I put on my bonnet and shawl. Mrs. Brooks had gone and I was buttoning my gloves to go too. Then –' She stops. She chokes, her voice full of tears. I want to put out my hand and take hers; I want to share that moment with her; I want us to grieve together as a mother and daughter should. But Kitty won't look at me. She doesn't want my compassion.

She struggles on: 'They say he couldn't have spoken, let alone called out – but I heard him, Mama, I swear I did. "Kitty!" he said. "Kittiwake, come quick!" He sounded so desperate, as though he needed me so much – yet I still knocked on the door for fear of interrupting him!' She gives a dry laugh that doesn't cover the sob beneath. 'And then, even when I was in, I thought I'd made a mistake. He was in his usual place facing the window, his back to me. Everything was as it always was. Then I saw that he was – well, not sitting quite as straight as usual and that his arm hung down a little awkwardly. And then I saw that his pen was rolling on the floor.' Her voice breaks. 'Even then I hoped he might be having one of his *little jokes* and in an instant he'd be up, laughing and making me feel a fool. But once I saw his eyes, I knew it wasn't a joke. He was staring ahead, seeing nothing; but breathing in a rasping kind of way. I didn't know what to do, Mama! I shook him, I think. "Papa," I said, "it's Kitty. I've come to you."' She swallows hard. 'I tried to lift him – but he was as heavy as wood. I could only manage to lift his arm, and hold his face against my shoulder. I whispered to him, some nonsense or other. Then there was that dreadful rattle in his throat. And I knew, Mama, I *knew*! And then the rest of them came running in. There seemed to be hundreds of them, laying hands on him, pushing, pulling, screaming, wrenching him away from me. I was dragged out of the room. Can you believe it – dragged out! I'll never forgive Sissy for that. Never!'

I close my eyes. I cannot bear to think of his last agony, to know that other hands closed his eyes, washed his body, dressed him for the grave. But I have always expected to be shut out, whereas Kitty has hoped otherwise. She turns on me as if I am to blame. She would rather I *were* to blame, I know. 'How can he have done that! How can he have kept me waiting until it was too late! How can he have died almost in front of me? Three hours I waited, Mama. *Three hours!*' Her voice becomes angrier. 'Why did he have to slave away anyway? He was rich enough to keep us all in clover without putting pen to paper ever again. He could have done exactly as he pleased – and taken tea with me every afternoon for a month! But he still set himself those ridiculous deadlines as if he were the most junior of struggling hacks! As if he were paid by the word. As if his life depended on it.'

'Because it had, once, my dear. You know that. And as with many habits formed when we are very young, he couldn't rid himself of it. You know, even when we were first married and enjoying a modest success, I'd often find him late at night, fretting over the accounts: *Prepare for the workhouse, Dodo. I cannot make ends meet.*'

'Well, since none of us was ever obliged to don pauper uniform and drink gruel out of metal mugs, he must have realised that that particular danger was past.' She wipes her eyes defiantly.

'No, he always feared that one day his ideas might desert him and his money would dissolve. It was always at the back of his mind – even *that* day, I daresay.'

'It's ridiculous. Augustus says he could have bought up half London.'

'Your husband knows nothing and understands less,' I say sharply. 'He doesn't have a notion of what your father suffered in his early days, how for years he would wake up night after night, convinced that we were all reduced to bare boards with the furniture gone. The wonder was, Kitty, that he could turn all those anxieties into such marvellous prose.'

She jumps up again. 'Oh, prose is all very well. You can control prose. And his prose children did what he wanted them to do. But he was never so passionate about his real children – or his wife, for that matter.' She paces about the room, colliding with the furniture. 'He treated you so *badly*, Mama! How can you forgive him?'

'Many a woman has been treated far worse.'

'What kind of reasoning is that? He did what he *had* to; what the law of England demanded; what common decency dictated; and to placate his precious Public. Not an inch more!' She looks around pointedly. 'And how could you have let him condemn you to such a *chicken-coop* without a fight?'

Poor Kitty, she can only see how *she* would have felt in my place. She would have fought harder than I did, no doubt. And been even more miserable as a result. 'This place may be small, Kitty, but Papa is always here with me. As soon as I open his books, I can hear the cadences of his voice as clearly as when he used to read aloud to me in front of the fire – the villain Botterby, or the Amazing Madame Delgardo. I can hear and see his characters as *he* used to hear and see them. I can see him gesture, and grimace, and alter his voice. And I sit in the chair with tears of happiness running down my cheeks, although there is no one to wipe them *with his big bright Genleman's Kerchief as what belonged to the Custard of Peru.'*

Kitty shakes her head. She thinks I am a case beyond redemption. And yet she was the most romantic of our children; the one who slipped her silken arms around his neck and willed her enchanted childhood to go on for ever. But today, everything about her is sharp, hard, black and glittery. She gets up and ties on her bonnet. 'I'm going, Mama. It's late.' She flashes her dark eyes at me. They are so like his.

If only she'd listen. She'd understand the meaning of love then. But I fear Augustus has spoiled her heart for ever. 'Come, Kitty,' I say soothingly. 'Come and sit down with me. Let us reminisce as we used, mother and daughter together.'

She hesitates, unties her bonnet, then chooses the old chair in the corner, one she used to sit in as a child. 'Very well,' she says. 'Start with that first evening. Remind me how my dear Mama fell in love with the One and Only.'

2

'*That* first night,' I tell her, 'your father made me laugh so much, I felt quite lifted out of myself; as if I were floating somewhere near the ceiling. And he looked at me so intently that I thought he must care for me a little. After supper, he sang 'O Mistress Mine' while I played the piano, and then he danced a hornpipe – such clever steps – while Alice played. At the end, he caught me by the arm and held me close to his scarlet waistcoat, his arm tight around my waist as he jigged round the room. I felt the beating of his heart as we danced, and was sure he could feel mine. His shirt smelt of lavender, his hand was dry and warm. He whirled me to a standstill, while the room turned and turned around us – and I thought that if I died there and then, I would have no regrets. He kissed my hand when he left and said he would always remember that night. "You're a capital dancer," he said. "A man could dance with you for ever, Miss Millar. A man could be under your spell and dance and dance to the Very Death!"'

Kitty says nothing.

'I didn't know what to make of him, of course. The young men who usually came to dine didn't lie on the grass or prance around the furniture. They didn't clasp me to their bosom or make declarations of love with their eyes. I went to bed that night in a fever. I even kissed the hand he had kissed, and imagined how it would be to be married to such a man. The next day a short note came to thank my mother for a 'splendid evening' and for the company of her 'three lovely daughters'. Sissy and Alice were delighted to be mentioned, but there was no special word for me.

I was in torment, Kitty. Everything about my life seemed to have changed. I couldn't believe that folding linen, sewing, and press-ing flowers could be all there was to do. I couldn't imagine that *Alfred Gibson* would spend his time sitting at home, quiet and content. I knew he'd be out lighting up rooms all over London, his arm around the waists of eligible young women who danced with divine skill and sang like divas – clever women; pretty women; women who knew the ways of the world and how to fascinate young men with dazzling waistcoats and dark eyes. I have to confess that I contrived a terrible hatred of them all. Up until then I'd believed my Mama when she said that a sensible disposition was worth its weight in gold, but now I wished I were possessed of more fascinating arts. I longed for wit; I longed for a greater knowledge of the world; I longed to know what I should do to make Alfred Gibson love me.'

I look at Kitty. She still does not speak. But she does not interrupt either, so I go on.

'You can imagine my feelings when the time approached for our trip to Stepney: soaring hope on the one hand, enormous dread on the other. To tell the truth, I was so at odds with myself that I found fault with everyone, particularly with my Papa, who took to teasing me about the very thing I wanted to know. When I asked him if Mr. Gibson was a good writer he merely laughed and said, "Oh, he's very comical. Light stuff, of course – well, you've seen him – but a way with words, yes, a way with words." I asked what he knew about his circumstances, but he was exasp-eratingly vague: "The same as any other young clerk, I suppose. That is to say, on the poor side of adequacy. Although he appears to have a good tailor and an endless supply of fine waistcoats. But a legal clerk doesn't earn enough to hire a hall and bear all the expenses of a public performance, so I am his benefactor in this instance. However, I hope to recoup my outlay. I understand the House is sold out."

'I must confess that my heart sank. A clerk! Like Timothy Smallwood who worked for my father and had frayed cuffs and darned mittens and no prospects. "But you think he will get on?" I asked. "That he could do great things in the future?"

'Papa looked at me and said, "Dorothea dear, I hope this young man has not turned your head. It would be most unwise to encourage him. Most unwise. His circumstances are – unstable. He has a headlong nature."'

Kitty breaks in: 'Yes, yes, we know all about your father's misgivings. Go to the night of the play.' She is impatient as always, but I indulge her.

'Well, as you know, your father was a triumph. We all rocked with laughter. But in the midst of our mirth he suddenly stopped dead and made us shiver with horror. Then he made us laugh again. The hall was hot and crowded and bright with the limelight – and some of the young clerks had been drinking but he held them in the palm of his hand. Such silence – and then such roars! You would not have believed it.'

'Oh, don't forget I saw him do it. He'd come home and boast about the number of ladies who had fainted at 'The Bells'. And he'd stand there and recite it for me all over again.' She takes up his attitude: '*And the bells ring on, sparing no tenderness for little Dick Crawley as he lies upon the gravestone in the churchyard below. They do not know him, and he does not know them. He is insignificant and small; he is lost and alone. Alone, Ladies and Gentlemen! Alone in the greatest metropolis of this great country of ours. And though the bells ring out with all their might, Dick cannot hear them. He is beyond hearing. He is beyond sight. He is beyond pain. He is beyond all the tribulations of this earth. He is dead.* And he'd sob, Mama! There in the middle of the drawing room! How he felt for his own writing! How he felt for little Dick Crawley! More than for any of us!'

She's wet-eyed, though, and I ache to comfort her. 'Come here.' I pat the stool beside me. 'Come to your mother.' I would go to her, but getting up from the chair is difficult for me now. And Gyp is fast asleep.

She turns away abruptly. 'No. This is all foolish, Mama. It does us no good. I have wept enough today; I cannot squeeze a single drop more.' She gets up. 'Anyway, I am expected at home.'

'*Are* you?' I look at her directly.

She drops her eyes. 'People may be calling.'

'Not at this hour, surely.'

'So many people spoke to me, Mama. So many strangers . . .'

'Yes. I can imagine that. Your father's life touched everyone; people we didn't know and won't ever see. Many will want to pay their respects. But no one would intrude upon your privacy *today*.'

'No, I suppose not.' She is irresolute for once.

'You could stay the night.' I am reluctant to ask her, for she has always refused in the past, but today, wrung out as she is, I feel she may not have it in her to resist. She hesitates, and, knowing once her mind is made up there is no going back, I add quickly: 'We can be cosy together, just as in the old days. You can send a note to Augustus. Wilson will see it's sent.'

She nods, and for a moment she is my eager little girl again. She heads for the writing-desk in the corner. It's the one he bought for a shilling from a pawn-shop in Camden Town, the first piece of furniture we ever had. He stood it next to the window in our parlour at Mrs. Quinn's, pens ranged neatly along the top, paper set ready. He'd sit at it for hours, by turns writing and looking out of the window. His unruly hair would fall forward, and time after time he'd push it back as he raised himself from his seat to spy out what was happening below. Then finally he'd jump up and throw his pen down and say we'd both needed a breath of air. *Come on Dodo, get your shawl. Let's have a lark!* And he'd find it for me before I could call to mind where I had left it, and he'd be bundling me up in it and pushing me ahead of him down the narrow stairs before I could protest that the dinner would be spoiled.

And now Kitty sits at the same desk, her black skirts awkwardly crammed into its slim kneehole. Her attitude is so like his, head held slightly to one side, fingers holding the pen quite high up so that the ink does not stain her fingers. But Kitty lets her pen rest. 'I think Augustus may not be at home. I believe he intended to dine at his club.'

Poor child. She can see the empty rooms, the unlit fires, the careless servants. I cannot help it: I must speak. 'Kitty dear, what can be so important that it takes him away from you now? Today of all days? He should be with you. It is his duty.'

I regret the word 'duty' – and indeed she is on me in a flash: 'Mama, it is not his character to be *dutiful*. I did not marry him for *duty*. Augustus and I allow each other to follow our own inclinations and don't impose upon each other, thank the Lord.' She glares at me. 'I've had enough of being under the thumb.' She puts down the pen, crumples the notepaper in her hand and throws it into the fire: 'I need not write. Augustus will do as he pleases.'

'That much is evident. And he does nothing to please *you*.'

'And you can see that, can you? From the wretched apartment where you meet no one? Where you have hidden from the world for ten years? How dare you make judgements?' She almost overturns the desk as she rises to her feet, her face red.

'I try not to judge. But I see that you are lonely, Kitty, and it breaks my heart. I always had such hopes for you. And so did he.'

'Oh, no. He had no hopes. Except for me to stay in thrall to him. That's why he never wanted me to marry.'

'You're wrong, Kitty. He knew you were young and headstrong. He was merely trying to protect you from adventurers.'

'Well, he should know all about that. After all, what was he when he met you? A nobody! No money, no prospects, no family to speak of. He was an adventurer if ever there was one! And you ignored your father in order to marry him, in the same way I did!'

It's true, of course. I can hardly condemn her behaviour when mine was much the same. Once I'd seen Alfred that fateful night, I was determined to have him. I had never before been so determined about anything. So before our foray into Stepney I did everything to make myself desirable. I knew nothing of the world, but I knew that every young gentleman I had ever met had remarked on the beauty of my eyes and complexion. But I'd also noticed that after this initial salutation, they had allowed their eyes to stray to my bosom, which seemed to be a source of great fascination. So I took out my needle and altered my best blue gown so that the bodice dipped a little lower; and when the evening of the outing came, I got Nancy to lace it as tight as she could. When she had finished, it was difficult to breathe, but the effect in the glass was gratifying. Finally, she pinned up my hair with an ostrich feather, and I put on my pearl necklace to offset the whole effect.

I was, admittedly, too grand for Stepney, and when we went backstage after the play, everyone stared at my finery. Alfred was still in his stage costume, although he had removed his wig and false beard. 'Ah, Miss Millar!' he said, as we squeezed through the low door into a small room with a quantity of candles burning on every surface. 'Take care you do not set your fine blue gown alight – or I should be obliged to douse you with water and roll you on the ground till you were quite put out!'

Alice and Sissy giggled. My parents looked rather taken aback. But he did not seem to notice, and continued in his extravagant way: 'Well, dear sir and Benefactor, what did you think? A little rough-and-ready for such sophisticated theatre-goers as yourselves, I daresay?'

'Not at all. It was excellent. Excellent. Very droll and so forth.' My father had regained his composure, was smiling around as if the play, the dressing room, the candles, and Mr. Gibson himself, were all his own work.

'We all laughed *so* much.' Alice was shy of him now, half-hiding behind Mama's gown.

'*I* was frightened when the young man turned into Captain Murderer.' Sissy, more forward as always, approached the rough table at which he sat, and started to finger the paints and powders that were so enticingly laid out in front of him. Suddenly he caught her hand in his, his face contorted: '*Don't touch the pretty paints, my child — or I'll eat your heart and lungs alive!*'

Sissy jumped back. Then he laughed, his face unfolding into its usual cheery look. 'Like that, you mean?'

Sissy turned bright scarlet. Tears started from her eyes. I took her by the hand and said sternly, 'You have frightened her, Mr. Gibson. She doesn't understand that you were acting a part. She is only a child.'

He looked at me in his observant way. I felt suddenly embarrassed by my blue silk, my pearls, my low-cut bodice, as if my intention were all too clear to him. He inclined his head. 'Indeed. You are right.' He turned to Sissy. 'Miss Cecilia, I apologise. And as a recompense, would you care to see what I have here —' He lifted his hand to his ear and suddenly there appeared a bonbon wrapped in pretty paper. Sissy's eyes shone with desire, but she wouldn't take it from him. He laid it on the table. 'And what have we here?' A second bonbon appeared from his other ear. He laid it next to the first. 'They are yours, little ladies. But you must claim them for yourselves. If we see things we like, we must claim them, mustn't we, Miss Millar?' His direct look again. I felt my face more aflame than all the candles.

But he had already turned from me and in an instant was deep with Papa about receipts and costs and all manner of business things. Alice and Sissy snatched the bonbons as quickly as if they were treasure from a sleeping dragon, and hid themselves behind the swirl of my skirts. Mama, fanning herself with the playbill, said the low-ceilinged room was too hot and airless for her, and she would wait for us in the carriage. 'Good evening, Mr. Gibson,' she said. 'It has all been very novel. Very novel indeed. But the children are far too excited. They are not used to such outings. I'm afraid if I do not take them away now, they will never sleep.'

She ushered them back through the door. I did not follow. I was afraid that if I did, my acquaintance with Mr. Gibson might end abruptly here in this cramped room with its roaring candles, cracked looking-glass and strange greasy smell. Papa could not be relied on to promote our connection; I had to be bold for myself. I let my shawl slip a little lower over my shoulders, and put my head on one side. 'Have you written *other* plays, Mr. Gibson?'

'I am half-way through another, Miss Millar. It's steaming along nicely.' He applied a handful of white grease to his face with a flourish, leaving only his dark eyes visible. Then he wiped his face with a cloth, swiftly taking away the black lines that had aged him so convincingly.

'And is it another comedy?'

'Tragi-comedy, Miss Millar. I like the scope for rhetoric.' He opened his eyes wide, and laughed his loud, cheerful laugh.

'And will we be able to come and see that too?'

'By all means. That is to say, if it is ever put on in public. I rely on your good father, my excellent Benefactor, in that respect.'

'And will you enable Mr. Gibson to put it on, Papa?'

He rubbed his hands. 'Well, indeed. We'll see, we'll see. One step at a time!'

'Oh, Papa, you must!' I grasped his hand and gave him my most earnest look.

Papa laughed. 'You have an excellent advocate here, Mr. Gibson. I cannot resist her.'

'Indeed, who could? An angel in blue, with eyes to match. Miss Millar, I am in your power.' And he sank to one knee.

But the reality was that I was in his. And, sadly, he did not seem serious. But I pressed my advantage. 'Then will you call again at our house for supper? This day week, perhaps?' I could sense Papa's disapproval at my forwardness, but I felt reckless.

Alfred laughed. 'I should be delighted. Although you must promise not to exhaust a poor clerk with your wild dancing –'

'With *my* dancing, Mr. Gibson?'

'Indeed. Do you not remember? The Scottish reels, the polka, the hornpipe? You would not let a man rest!'

'I remember the wildness seemed to come from *you*, sir.'

'Not at all! You were '*La Belle Dame Sans Merci*'! Wasn't she, Mr. Millar?'

Papa frowned. 'She was my usual lovely Dodo. The kindest, sweetest girl in the world. And not to be trifled with. Now, Dodo, we must be on our way.' He took me by the arm. 'Mr. Gibson, I give you good night.'

* * *

'Well?' Kitty says. 'You do not answer my question. Was Papa not an adventurer?'

'Not at all,' I say. 'He was merely poor. And *my* father was simply trying to protect me, knowing I'd had a soft upbringing and hardly knew how to manage my ribbon allowance, let alone feed a whole family. But all fathers suspect their daughters' lovers, I imagine. Including yours.' I turn and smile at her.

'Oh, Mama, I am sure you are right. Augustus has many good qualities, believe me.' She comes and plants a kiss on my cheek. Gyp wakes and shakes himself. I ease him down upon the rug and suddenly Kitty is taking his place, depositing herself and her heavy complement of petticoats upon my lap, clasping her arms around my neck, laying her cheek next to mine. I have so longed to be close to her, I hardly dare to move. We sit, silent, watching the coals flame and fall until it is quite dark outside and Wilson comes in to light the lamps. She starts when she sees us thus entwined.

'Sorry, madam. I didn't realise Mrs. Norris was still here. Beg pardon, miss.' She stands, a little flustered – two grown women embracing on a chair.

[27]

'That's all right.' Kitty gets up, smoothes down her skirts. 'I've decided to stay the night.'

'Yes, miss – madam. And will you be wanting supper?'

'What culinary delights can you tempt me with?'

'I don't know about *curinaly*. But there's cold mutton and potatoes. And I've done some soup.'

Kitty pulls a face. 'I suppose that will do. Have you any wine, Mama?'

That's Augustus's influence. But I don't generally keep wine. Apart from the tonic variety Dr. Phelps prescribed after Ada was born. 'No,' I say. 'You'll have to make do with water.'

'There's a flagon of stout in the kitchen, miss, if you're so inclined.' Wilson's lighting the lamps, and at last it feels as though the long day's almost over.

'Very well, I'll have some of that.' Kitty turns to me, suddenly alert. 'They had hot punch at the house, to warm us up. It was not a patch on Papa's, though.' She looks round in a distracted way. 'It's a pity we can't make some now.'

I feel cheered at the thought. 'Maybe we could. It's not difficult. Oranges, lemon, brandy . . .'

'But you have no brandy, Mama.'

'No.'

'And no oranges neither,' adds Wilson, on her way out. 'I'd have got some if I'd a known we was having special treats.' She shuts the door, pointedly.

Kitty laughs, rolls her eyes and mimics Wilson's voice and manner: '*If I'd a known we was having special treats, I'd a gorn and laid down and died.*'

I put my fingers on my lips. Wilson is a good creature and I don't want her offended. But Kitty is so sharp in her observations I cannot help but laugh. 'You could have written characters, you know. You have his talent for it.'

'Could I? He never thought so. He never encouraged me.'

'That's not true. He was always proud of what you wrote. He'd bring things for me to look at. He'd say, *That child's a marvel! An Infant Phenomenon!*'

'Babyish stories and poems! Silly little plays. Nothing as I grew older.'

'And *were* there things you wrote as you grew older?'

She colours. 'No.' She was too busy rebelling to spend time with her pen. 'But he stopped me doing everything I wanted to. I could have been an actress. But he said the theatre wasn't a life for a lady. While all the time he was –'

'Let's have supper,' I say, pushing myself up from the chair. 'And go to bed early. We are both tired out.'

⁂

Kitty makes a good supper and downs the glass of stout that Wilson brings her. Then she asks me to play for her, and I do – although she is the better pianist. All those lessons, that endless practising! She stands behind me now, her hands on my shoulders, and we sing the old favourites, all the choruses from Christmases past when we were all together. When we retire, she is so exhausted she can hardly undress herself. I help her off with her clothes as if she were a child – although when she was a child it was somewhat simpler. Now she has such layers and accoutrements, such panels and streamers!

'Don't you think you've over-reached yourself with all this – extravagance? Your skirt has enough petticoats to stand up on its own.'

The skirt indeed *does* stand up unaided, as if there were a third person in the room, standing guard at the fender. I lay the veil and the bonnet on my ottoman and try to collapse the skirt so it can dry before Wilson takes a brush to it tomorrow. There's mud up to six inches all around the hem; the funeral carriages must have churned it up. I finger the dead, dull crape. It's ugly, and it's made

Kitty ugly – a thing he'd never have wanted. *Black extinguishes the spirit,* he'd say. *It makes women into walking mausoleums.*

Kitty doesn't counter my remark; she's almost asleep on her feet. I struggle with the hooks of her corset, and as my fingers touch her spine I realise how thin she is. Even as a girl, I was never thin. *A buxom beauty,* he called me when we were first married. He said my body was the softest in the world. But now there is far too much of it. Kitty, by contrast, looks half-starved.

She falls into bed as if insensible. I remove my own clothing slowly, but without help. I keep my laces loose, so the matter is accomplished easily enough. I find myself eager for the sheets, for the presence of another human being. For the first time in ten years my bedfellow will be someone other than Gyp. I am aware of a need I have not admitted to myself that almost overwhelms me as Kitty turns and snuggles deep into my bosom. She says, 'Mama, you are so vast, I shall get lost in you,' and goes to sleep in an instant. But even in sleep she stays tense, brittle. From time to time she twitches and gives a moan, just like her father. Who had also said he wished to lose himself in me.

3

The doorbell rings at nine o'clock. No one respectable calls this early. I am dressed and having my breakfast, but Kitty is still asleep. I hear a voice on the stair; it is Augustus.

'Hallo, Ma. Kit here?' he says in his unceremonious way as he pushes through the door, hat in hand. He is still in evening clothes, but looks rabbity and stained.

'Good morning, Augustus. Yes, of course she is. Where else does she have to go?'

'She hasn't been home all night.'

'No. And neither have you. I daresay it's only now that you are aware of her absence.'

'I was away from home, yes. She knew that.' He throws down his opera hat, picks a plum from the bowl on the table and bites into it. 'But it don't do to leave the servants in the dark. I was called for, you know.'

'How inconvenient.' I cannot believe that I once thought him handsome. In the morning light his long whiskers are sparse and gingery and he smells of tobacco-smoke and whisky.

'It *was* actually, Ma. *Very* inconvenient.'

'May I remind you that Kitty's father was buried yesterday? She needed human company last night. As did I.'

He has the goodness to be taken aback. 'Well, yes. Sorry. My condolences and all that. But you can't say you're a normal sort of widow-woman. Any more than she is a normal daughter. You both hated the Great Man when he was alive.' He sits down opposite me in Kitty's place and starts to help himself to tea and toast.

'I certainly did *not*. And I think you'll find Kitty didn't either.'

'Well, she made a good show of it. Anyway, I went to the Abbey, didn't I? Kept up appearances. Didn't let the home contingent have it all their own way. And what a fracas that was! All that shouting and sobbing. Enough to give a man a headache for weeks. And then they went and put O'Rourke and Alfie in the carriage with her, and stuffed me in with some strange ladies at the back. Mind you –'

'I don't want to hear.'

'No.' He laughs. 'Anyway, she's wanted now. Lawyers and such.'

'She's asleep.'

'Then be so good as to get her up, Ma.' He mimes the action, as if I am stupid and don't understand English. The reek of whisky is intense across the table. His eyes are bloodshot and unreliable.

'There's no hurry, Augustus. I don't believe he's left her anything. Except perhaps his books.'

'There must be a fortune *somewhere*, Ma. All that beavering away as if his life depended on it. And she's his eldest.'

'And I'm his wife. But he cut us *both* out, if you recall.'

'Well,' he says, tucking into the remaining kipper, 'he may have cut you *in* again. He always was a rum cove.'

⚜

Rum. That's what my father had thought, although he put it more genteelly. *Headlong,* he said. *Unstable.* On the carriage ride home from Stepney that fateful night he'd admonished me for having made a spectacle of myself. 'You surprise me, Dodo. Setting your cap at that poor young man.'

'I only invited him to supper, Papa.'

'That is not quite all, Dodo.' He looked at me sternly.

'Heavens! What else did she do?' Mama looked up from cradling my sleeping sisters. 'Nothing unladylike, I hope, Dodo.'

'No, Mama. I simply spoke to him about his plays.'

'She encouraged his propensity to extravagance, Esther. You know, the smiles, the glances, the kissing of hands, the going down on one knee and so forth. The whole panoply of effects.'

Mama laughed. 'He is very dashing, Oliver. He rather takes one off-guard. But there is no harm in him.'

'On the contrary, the young man is full of his own importance and may believe he has a chance with our daughter. It is unfair of her to encourage him.'

I had to speak out. 'But he *does* have a chance with me, Papa! He is the most brilliant and clever man I have ever met! But I fear he is too fascinating to be bothered with a simpleton such as me!'

'Dodo! What has come over you?' Papa's voice was sharp in a way I had never heard before.

'She's in love,' said Alice, opening one eye, then falling asleep again.

The carriage jolted on, and we all sat as if stunned.

And now Augustus gets up, cramming the remains of toast into his mouth. He looks more petulant than ever, his lips sensuous and weak as they close over the food. 'Where is she?'

'Don't disturb her, Augustus. She's tired.'

'Thank you, Ma, but I'll do as I damn well please with regard to my own wife.' He never spares with his oaths, even in front of me. He starts for the door.

I am horrified. 'That is my bedroom. You cannot go in there.'

'*You* fetch her, then.' He stands aside, watching me belligerently.

'Let me finish my breakfast at least.'

'I'm a busy man, Ma.'

'*Are* you?'

The question annoys him, and he whirls round. He meets Wilson coming in with fresh tea and collides with her. The pot nearly empties itself on him. For half a second I hope he is scalded, but he has sidestepped nimbly and the tea spills on the hearthrug instead. He mutters, 'Why don't you damned servants look where you're going?'

'I believe I *was* looking, sir. I believe it was *you* as turned suddenly. It's easily done.' She puts the pot on the table and bends to attend to the stain. 'But you're all right. It'll come off with a rough rag and a bit of elbow grease.'

'This is a mad⁄house. I'll take Kitty and go.' His hand is on the doorknob of the bedroom.

'No.' I get up. 'I'll wake her. Please sit down.'

I cross the room in front of Wilson, who has risen from the rug, her face a little pink. 'Well,' she says, 'this is the first time we've seen Mr. Norris in I don't know how long, isn't it, madam? But I'm glad to see he's made hisself at home.' She starts to clear his plate. It's carelessly piled with the kipper carcass, the stone from the plum, the crusts from the toast. She looks at it with distaste. 'Shall I re⁄lay the place?'

'I doubt Mrs. Norris will be breakfasting. Mr. Norris is in a hurry.'

'Yes, madam. Then I'll come back and see to that stain before it sets.' She sails off.

'That's more insolence than I would take in *my* house.' Augustus slumps into the armchair, his long black legs stretching over half the hearthrug.

'But it's *not* your house, and Wilson is an excellent woman.'

He takes out a cheroot. Then he looks at my expression and puts it back again: 'I see you don't care for tobacco smoke, Ma.'

'Indeed not.'

'The Great Original was partial though, was he not? I seem to remember that. In the good old days when we were *bosom pals*.' He smiles sarcastically.

'He knew the time and place. And it wasn't at nine o'clock in the morning in someone else's breakfast room.'

He laughs. It's true, of course, that he and Alfred were once friends. An unlikely coupling: Alfred already at the height of his powers, famous and well-esteemed, a family man and doer of good works; Augustus a young man about town with more money than sense, no interest at all in literature and certainly none in good works. He had other interests though. It was he who introduced Alfred to the Turkish baths, to the smoking clubs, to the Chinese opium houses. Alfred was tickled: *Such a marvellous propensity they all have for lying about and doing nothing in particular.* But the novelty soon palled. Alfred could never be idle for long.

I open the bedroom door. Kitty is lying as I left her, her hair spread over the pillow. She'll never wear a nightcap. Alfred wouldn't either. And he'd undo mine as soon as we were in bed. And my nightgown: *Come, Dodo, don't be all trussed up like a Christmas turkey. Let me feel your hair. Let me feel your skin. Let us be in a state of nature.*

I bend over her. 'Kitty?' She sleeps on. I can hardly bear to wake her. In fact I won't wake her. I sit on the coverlet and watch her sleep instead. I don't know how much time passes, but next thing the doorknob is rattling and Augustus is in the room. He is too tall, too hard, too black against the fans and feathers, the pressed flowers, the heaps of letters done up in ribbon. No man has set foot in here, until now. Only Alfred, in his silver frame on the mantelpiece, has even gazed on it.

'You haven't made much progress, Ma. Looks as if all those things he said about you were true.' Augustus leans against the wardrobe, grinning.

'Kitty needs to sleep.'

'She can sleep some other time. *I* need her elsewhere. And I'm her husband.'

'You remember that now?'

'Come, come, Ma. Let's not quarrel. One quarrelsome parent is more than enough.' He moves to the bed, bends over Kitty.

'Wake up, Kit. It's your Ever-loving.' He shakes her, quite hard, his arm dark against the sheets.

I close my eyes. I don't like to see him touching her. I am not a prude – I couldn't have been married to Alfred and been a prude – but there is something coarse about Augustus that makes me anxious for my child. I suspect he may go further than is right; he may even be brutal. God forbid that it is true – but I fear Alfred knew a good deal more about his erstwhile friend than he ever said. Of course I don't blame Kitty for wanting to be passionately loved, and prepared to act rashly in pursuit of it. In that one thing we are not so different. Indeed, when I stood in that hot dressing room with all those candles burning around me, and Alfred smiling at me, I felt as though my whole body was alight with joy. I was so excited I could hardly think. Only the thought of never seeing Alfred again – or seeing him only too late when he was promised to another – could have made me speak in such a forward fashion.

But a supper invitation was one thing; the prospect of anything else was out of the question. My rash admission of admiration had put my parents on their mettle, and when they saw how enraptured I was at the prospect of the visit (and I could not conceal my joy; I carried a smile on my face that nothing could diminish) they made it clear that I could neither encourage nor accept the attentions of this *amusing but unsuitable young man*. Of course, I agreed to do and say nothing untoward. I would have agreed to almost anything as long as I could see Alfred Gibson again.

We were all sitting in the garden when he appeared at the gate. He seemed even brighter, even more wonderful than before. He was wearing a yellow waistcoat, a cherry-coloured top-coat, and trousers of a very neat cut. He had also acquired a silver-topped cane. He advanced up the path and made a low bow, holding his hat over his heart. We all smiled, and Mama graciously indicated the chair where he should sit next to her. But before he could do anything, Sissy, in her peremptory way, began tugging at his hand, trying to pull him down upon the grass: 'Play that game again! Play that game!' This time he would not be enticed. He withstood her efforts laughingly, then, throwing down his hat and cane, grasped her suddenly to his waist and made her stand with her feet on his. 'Hold tight!' he shouted, as he began to dance with her around the lawn. Sissy gripped his arms and grew redder and redder as she strove to keep her little slippered feet attached to his fast-stepping, shiny boots.

'Slower!' she demanded between breaths. 'Mis—ter Gib—son, slower, please!'

'Impossible!' he shouted, taking a wide turn at the walnut tree. 'There is only one pace for a waltz, and it is FAST!' He whirled her around so wildly that her legs and feet swung out from his body like the sails of a windmill before he brought her to a sudden stop. She stood for a moment, then cried, 'Again!' and tried to scramble back on his feet.

'No, Miss Cecilia, you must not be selfish. I think it is Miss Alice's turn.' He held out his hand to Alice, who was sitting quietly in a wicker chair, pretending to read a book. She shook her head.

He smiled. 'No, indeed. Miss Alice is too grown-up by half for such roughness. Miss Alice wants a proper dance. A Military Two-step, I think? Allow me.' And he approached her respectfully, bowed and took her gently by both hands, and before she knew it she was two-stepping down the garden path with him as he called out instructions – *Turn, step, side forward, back! Excellent!* At the end of the path they stopped. He bowed again, and kissed her hand, very nicely, so that Alice blushed. She was only my twelve-year-old sister, but I was jealous. I let my eyes fall, concentrating on my needlework, working the line of green satin-stitch to fill the oval shape of a leaf. In seconds he was back again, but

I could not meet his troublesome laughing eyes, not with my mother and father chaperoning my every look. I could see only his boots as he stood before me, and the first six inches of those neatly-fitting trousers: 'And what is your pleasure, Miss Millar?'

My pleasure? My heart was pounding so much I was astonished that my voice came out so coolly. 'I should like you to be still and sensible for a moment, Mr. Gibson. Before you wear yourself out.'

'Miss Millar puts us right! A man cannot always be capering about with the ladies. A man must be still and sensible.' He sat down next to Mama and affected a pose of thoughtfulness, chin on hand. Everyone laughed. I felt foolish and struggled to think of a witty response, but it was not (and still is not) my forte. Anyway, on this occasion, I was too excited to think.

At supper (where he was placed across the table from me, wedged in between Sissy and Papa) I asked him how his new play was coming along. He told us it was almost finished, and that in the manner of Shakespeare it was 'comical-tragical-historical-pastoral'.

'What is it about?' said Mama as she helped us to ham and cabbage.

'Love, Mrs. Millar.' He spoke airily as he passed the plates around in an accommodating manner. 'It's the only subject for a young man. Young men, you see, are so apt to be struggling in the throes of the same-said mortal passion.'

I couldn't help myself. 'Surely,' I said, my eyes fixed on a water-colour behind his head, '*you* are not struggling in the throes of mortal passion yourself, Mr. Gibson?'

'Every day, every minute, every second. Can you doubt it, Miss Millar?' He laughed delightedly.

'Indeed I can.' I allowed my eyes to rest on his. 'I doubt, Mr. Gibson, that you are serious about anything.'

He looked at me steadily: 'Then you are very wrong, Miss Millar. I am the most serious man on earth.'

I was in such turmoil after that, I could hardly eat my supper. I could hardly hold my knife and fork to eat it with. Indeed, I hardly knew I had a knife and fork. Or a plate. Or a glass. I could only see the vivid face, the shining eyes. I could only hear the thrilling voice. It seemed as though all at the table were silent save him. And that we were content for it to be that way; captivated, enthralled.

⚘

Kitty is awake now, shaken into life by Augustus. She stares at him, at the room, at me; tries to make sense of it all. Then a look of pain crosses her face. She has remembered. Then: 'Augustus, what are *you* doing here?'

'I was got up, for my sins. You're needed, apparently. The will's being read. Eleven o'clock sharp at Park House. They are all going, the whole pack of 'em. We need to be there, to protect your interests.'

'I don't want anything!' She stares defiantly from the pillow. Augustus responds by pulling the sheets away, exposing her naked legs and the dark smudge of hair beneath the rucked-up night-gown. He sees it, and hesitates. A look passes between them. I push him aside: '*I'll* dress her, Augustus. You can sit in the parlour. We shan't be long.'

'No, I'll wait.' He stations himself on the ottoman and grins. 'A man can watch his own wife *en déshabille*, I hope, Ma? I've got nothing else to pass the time.'

I fumble Kitty out of bed and sit her in front of the wash-stand. The water in the jug is tepid now, but I help her wash her face and arms. She sits doll-like, letting me move her at will. Augustus leans back and watches as if we are at a play, or some-thing worse. Kitty said he has brought back paintings from Paris – women in their underwear, at their toilette. I think of that now as I watch him sitting and smiling.

We haul the stiff mourning clothes back over her thin body. Wilson has brushed them, but they still reek of black dye, some of which comes off on my hands as I lace her up. She ties on her bonnet and veil and turns to Augustus. 'I'm ready.'

He takes her arm with exaggerated courtesy. 'Farewell, Ma. We'll let you know if the Great Man has left you his second-best bed.'

'Augustus!' Kitty turns sharply to him. I am grateful for her concern for my feelings, although I do not want or expect that anything material has been left to me. My memories are far more precious.

⚘

After Kitty has gone, I sit and gaze at Alfred's photograph. They say he aged badly at the end, ravaged by hard work; but in this picture he is still youthful-looking, still wavy-haired and handsome, though he stares at the camera in a curiously lifeless way so at odds with his natural manner. I tilt the frame towards the light. He's wearing his velvet smoking jacket and has his cheek resting on one hand, a pen in the other. It makes him look full of *gravitas*; whereas in reality he was high-spirited and animated, and liked nothing better than to don a turban and a length of embroidered cloth in order to become *the Amazing Abanazar* at our Christmas festivities. He would rig up a crimson curtain half-way across the drawing room and after supper he'd appear from behind it in a cloud of green smoke – *abracadabra!* – making us all jump, even though we'd been expecting it all along. Then he'd show us his top hat – empty – and he'd get Louisa and Eddie to hold it, one each side, and he'd draw out oranges, lemons, bonbons and tiny trinkets with amazing speed. Then he'd make silk scarves change colour as he pulled them from his pockets and flung them into the air. And he'd find pennies in the boys' shirt-collars and in the girls' pinafore-pockets that they absolutely *knew* hadn't been there before. And at the end he'd disappear in a golden shower of

[40]

confetti that would sparkle so in the candle-light that we'd really think we were back in the Arabian Nights.

I never knew how he did the magic, although he said his father had taught him tricks, standing him on a table in ale-houses when he could barely walk. But Alfred was so quick and slick he might have done it as a profession. *If the writing dries up, Dodo, I may take to the street corners after all. And you may take the plate round in a Punchinella skirt and high-laced boots, and collect the takings!* He adored the applause, the laughter, and was good nature itself. And the children adored him back. They couldn't have enough of him. After the magic was over, they'd sit on his lap and cluster round his chair as he made up wilder and wilder stories. And they'd hang on his arms three or four at a time as he polka'd round the room. And they'd laugh, just as Alice and Sissy had laughed, when he played Blind Man's Buff and caught their sashes and coat-sleeves as they circled around him, bumping and shrieking.

I shall never forget those wonderful Christmases.

I sit on the bed and open one of my caskets. I take out a letter and unwrap it from its silken ribbon. His first one. I cherish it above all else, and it's become fragile with re-reading. I look at the dashing script and remember my feelings when Alice had first given it to me, taking it from her pocket with exaggerated secrecy: 'From him, for you.'

'For me?'

'Of course.' She'd stood gravely, holding it out. 'He put it in my hand when we were dancing. Don't you want it?'

'Of course.' I'd snatched it from her, and ran up to my room, my heart in my mouth.

It was a single page, folded into eight.

My Dearest Miss M,
I hope you'll pardon this unconventional method of relaying correspondence, but your dear Papa has intimated that should I be so bold as to initiate

*any communication of any kind with his beloved daughter (written or un-
written, verbal and oral) he would be obliged to sever all transactional bonds
with Yours Truly — in short, he'd give me no more money.*

*However, much as I revere your father, I cannot comply with his wishes.
Because some things take precedence. Things of the heart take precedence.
And my heart is in a state of mortal dread. Dread that I shall lose sight of
your lovely eyes, and the sound of your sweet voice. Dread that you will be
taken from me or will give your heart to another. Dread (the worst) that
you may not care for me at all.*

*O, Dorothea, you are already more dear to me than I can say. I lie
awake and think of you in your blue silk gown and wish only that you were
in my arms. I am very forward, I know; maybe you do not care for a legal
clerk with no money and only Hope to offer you — but I do not think so. I
think I have felt your pulse race as mine has done; I think I have seen your
colour rise. In short, I am confident enough to believe my feelings are returned
and to write in a way which, if I were not so confident, might cause us both
embarrassment and pain. If I am wrong, I will drown myself in the Thames
and feed fishes for ever and a day. But say I'm right. Say I'm right, sweet
Dorothea. Whisper it on the night air. Tell it to your pillow. Write it in
your reply.*

    Yours in agony,
    Alfred Gibson

*Should you be minded to reply, there is a loose brick in the garden wall, near
the postern gate, where a letter may be snugly accommodated. I shall walk
out from London every day this week to see whether I am a condemned man
or a blessed spirit.*

I could hardly believe he was serious. I thought I might be deluding myself, mistaking his meaning, taking as truth something
only intended as fun. I read it over and over, and then over again.
It *was* a love letter. It deserved — it needed — a reply. I hardly cared
if I was making a fool of myself. Better to be a fool than to be

regretful for ever. So I wrote that very night to tell him how much I returned his affection. I probably said too much. I feared, once it had left my possession and was sitting under its damp brick, that I had indeed said too much. But he replied the day after that in a frenzy of jubilation, exclamation marks all over the page, and I knew I had done the right thing.

Over the following weeks, our lovers' letter-box was much in use. Only Alice knew of our correspondence and sometimes I had to entrust her with the letters, as Mama, seeming to sense something in the air, was forever finding complicated tasks for me at home, listing every item of silverware in the pantry, tidying the china cupboard from top to bottom, or picking and drying great quantities of herbs for the kitchen.

Alice took her responsibility seriously, swearing never to tell a soul, not even Sissy, who was as sharp as a case of knives. She kept a lookout as best she could, contriving to slip through the gate at least once every day without Sissy noticing. She always placed the letters deep in her apron pocket and never gave them to me until we were safely in my room. She would blow the brick dust off them, and give them to me solemnly with a little curtsy. Sometimes I would read bits to her. She was very young, but I so wanted to talk about him, to have him admired the way I admired him. She'd listen, then say things such as: 'You're so lucky, Dodo, to have such an ardent lover. And he's so funny too. Do you think you will get married, or be star-crossed for ever? Do you think Papa will change his mind? Or will you elope to Scotland and live in romantic penury?' Once, she told me she'd met Alfred marching along the roadside, swinging his cane, muttering to himself 'in funny voices'. Once she'd encountered him by the wall as he exchanged the letters – 'and he pretended to be a pirate and to capture me for my treasure. He held me so tight I thought I'd scream and Mama would hear us, but I didn't scream, Dodo, and he said I was ever so good and gave me a penny.'

I always hoped I would catch sight of him too, and once or twice I imagined I saw a flash of coloured waistcoat among the trees, but I was probably mistaken. When I read his letters, though, it was almost as good as being with him. His life seemed extraordinarily full – the 'daily grind' at Webster and Potts where he was *compelled to write out in a fair hand things that had nothing else fair about them – bills and contracts, codicils and wills. Wills! Let me not talk of wills! Such injustices are perpetrated there, my love. Let you and I have nothing to do with them.* He spent his evenings at the theatre with the other clerks, Tom Treadwell and Jeremiah Links, booing or cheering from the gallery; and the rest of the time he was at his lodgings *scribbling away in the worst draught there ever was – that keeps my candle guttering so much I can hardly see to write. But write I must. The Muse is demanding. And so is my need for cash. A romance, a tale of horror and a humorous sketch so far this week.* He wrote to me every day, page upon page, and I wondered often at his capacity to keep up the correspondence. It was a long walk to Chiswick – and although he often got a ride with the carter, he seemed to walk it once a week. I jestingly asked him what it was all costing him in shoe-leather. He replied that he was 'never happier' than when out walking, had an excellent cobbler who heeled and soled boots for sixpence a pair – and to top it all he had earned five shillings for selling a story to a gentlemen's magazine. *Five shillings!* he wrote. *This is the start, my love. The opener. I am scribbling so hard my fingers are blue to the knuckles and my face is adorned with ink blots as if I have a gloomy kind of chickenpox. But if I am recognised, then the time is only round the corner when I shall be independent and we can declare our intentions! Your parents will come round, I am sure. They are the dearest people and cannot – will not – stand in our way. Jack shall have Jill; nought shall go ill! Believe that, dearest, won't you?*

I was not so sure. Papa in particular had been adamant that Mr. Gibson and I should have no further connection, but as the days went past, he and Mama seemed to relax their vigil. One day, at breakfast, reading out a review of Mr. Macready's *Hamlet*, and getting into general conversation about theatrical matters, he favoured me with one of his old, fond looks: 'Well, Dodo, it seems our thespian friend Mr. Gibson has not troubled us any more with his attentions. It seems he is a young man whose affections are inconstant in the extreme. No doubt he is courting some other young lady even as we speak. You understand why I cautioned you in the matter.'

I, too, feared the extravagance of Alfred's declarations. In spite of the devotion that gushed from his letters, I could not rid myself of the fear that somehow he was trifling with me. It might suit him to believe himself in love now, but what of the future? What true attraction could I, Dorothea Millar, have for such a man? I was ordinary, timid, and only middling pretty even when decked out in pearls, feathers and an immodest dress. As I read his letters I became even more aware that I was indeed only one among many young women who seemed to fascinate him. He was not secretive about them. Indeed he seemed anxious that I should know all about them. There was Maria the Spanish dancer he had *once half-fallen in love with, her face is so severe and her limbs so damnably active in every direction*, and Madeleine the seamstress who lived downstairs at his lodgings and, it would seem, shared the deepest confidences of her heart. *She was jilted, you see, Dodo, and every mention of love or marriage sends her into a positive tempest of tears which Yours Truly does his best to stem, but how many handkerchiefs can a man give away and still satisfy the needs of his nose?* And there was Nellie, the aspiring actress who had played the lead in Stepney, and was *the most excellent young lady with the blackest of eyes and most rosy of cheeks and such a sweet voice that I must write a whole prologue for her to show it off.* And Flora the pie-shop cook, *who bakes the very best meat pies in the world and who goes about it with such neatness and with such a smile that some of the deliciousness of her person must surely get into the pies.* Every time he wrote there seemed to be new companions, new objects of his interest. I hated them all. They could smile at him with their eyes, hold on to his arm in the street, or dance tightly clasped in his arms. I was a blue silk Rapunzel locked up in my Chiswick tower. I contemplated running away to London and throwing myself on his mercy, but I had no money and no idea of where to go. I'd never gone to town unchaperoned, and every day the newspapers gave accounts of riots and mayhem in the streets. So I didn't dare.

Then came the terrible time when one of my letters was not collected, and no letters arrived from him in return. Two, three, four weeks went by. 'Perhaps he is ill,' said Alice, sensibly. But I didn't believe her. I thought it was as I had feared; he had fallen out of love with me as quickly as he had fallen into it. I had to know.

'Have you received the manuscript of Mr. Gibson's new play, yet?' I ventured to ask Papa.

'Indeed, no. In fact I've heard nothing of Mr. Gibson at all. Once he was on my doorstep every day, now he has disappeared into thin air. You see, Dodo, the man is not to be relied upon.'

'Yet you said he would do great things. Now, because I admire him, you have changed your mind!'

'A man is entitled to change his mind – as much as a woman!' He laughed. 'If the play is good, however – if it is ever finished, indeed – I am prepared to help him. I have helped many a young artist, as you know; I feel it behoves me as a man of business to pass on a little of my good fortune for the general betterment and so forth. But such benevolence does not extend to letting him pay court to my dearest of girls.'

My mother stopped pouring the tea, paused with the pot in mid-air. 'I think you exaggerate, Oliver. The young man has done nothing more than be a little attentive.'

'It's the thin end of the wedge, my dear. Dodo is not at all worldly. She doesn't understand flirtation. When she gives her heart she does it completely. A young man of that sort is best kept out of her life. I was foolish to bring him to our house, and now I must try to put things right.'

Poor Papa! His idea of putting things right was to distract me into a new love. He had no idea how appalling such an idea was to me, how my whole soul revolted at the thought of another lover. But he would not be dissuaded. Enter my cousin George. 'Such a nice young man,' said my mother, admiring a miniature portrait he had sent from Coventry in advance of his real self. 'Come, Dodo, do look. Don't pretend indifference – you know you liked him a good deal when you were both children.' So I looked, and duly admired his even features, remembering that he had been kind to me in the long summers we had spent together in his father's house, and how he had climbed trees to show me birds' nests, and had taught me how to blow snatch-grass and catch tadpoles. But I told Mama I had no interest in marrying him – or any other man who was paraded before me. I said I was not ready to marry. 'You must at least be courteous,' she said. 'And you may find once you meet him that you will change your mind.' I knew I would not, but I had no wish to be rude to my cousin. So I was courteous in the extreme. We strolled along the riverbank and remarked upon the weather and the changing landscape, and the fine quality of the houses being built on the road into London. We said 'please' and 'thank you' as we passed the dishes at supper, and smiled nicely at each other as we sang duets in the drawing room afterwards. It was all very dull compared to the frantic dancing and laughing with Alfred. Even Alice and Sissy could observe the difference as they lolled about the cushions, watching us closely for any sign of a kiss.

'Has she another suitor?' I overheard him asking my father as they sat together in the garden about a week after his arrival.

'No, my dear sir. Why do you ask?'

'Only I sense, Uncle, that she is – elsewhere. She treats me with a sort of pity, as if I have no chance at all. I have much to offer a young girl – so when I meet such indifference, I wonder if there is a previous attachment. I would not press my case in such circumstances.'

Papa lowered his voice. 'There was a young man, I admit. Dorothea rather lost her head over him. He was unsuitable in the extreme. Very headlong. And with no means. We discouraged her and I'm glad to say she has given him up.'

'I'm not sure she *has* given him up. She's grieving for him, I think. And I've no wish to persuade her against her will. I have not asked her to marry me, and I shall not do so. I shall go home tomorrow. And I advise you to speak to Dorothea about the real state of her heart.' And when he went, he pressed my hand so kindly I really wished I could have loved him after all.

Papa did not attempt to speak to me about the 'state of my heart', although he looked at me curiously from time to time, as if trying to discern my thoughts. I tried to pretend I was the same daughter who was always ready to sit on the arm of his chair, to stroke his hair as I read to him, or to laugh at his jokes. It was hard to disguise my feelings, though. My spirits were leaden. If he made a joke, I could not stop thinking of Someone Else and what jokes *he* could tell – and how I'd probably never hear one from him again. If I tried to smile, my lips trembled. Food made me feel sick. I could hardly bestir myself to comb my hair in the mornings, and I wore the same frock day after day. The once-pleasant routines of household life were now suffocating. I longed for any chance to leave the house, even if it were only to sit around a cake-stand and sip tea with neighbours; or a trip to the haberdasher's for silk thread or ribbons.

What I lived for was our outings to town. Papa adored the theatre, and liked to escort Mama and myself at regular intervals, one on each arm like a dancing major. I had no great belief that I would see Alfred on these outings, but I wore my blue gown in hope every time, and once in our box, I would nervously turn my opera glasses towards the back rows of the gallery, my throat dry with apprehension. Would I see him there with Nellie or Maria, paying them the attentions he should be paying me? In the intervals I'd scan the turbulent crowds at the refreshment tables, my heart leaping at the sight of each young man with a fancy waistcoat or long wavy hair. There were plenty of them, busy taking glasses of champagne to eligible beauties, or handing them into carriages at the end of the evening. But the one young man I was looking for was nowhere to be seen. I concluded Alfred was indeed too busy with some new object of interest. He had abandoned me, and I must bear it.

After a while, I tried to persuade myself that I should marry George after all. He was kind and had shown a delicacy of feeling, and I might well come to love him in time. It was simply a matter of putting Alfred's bright eyes and passionate words completely out of my mind, of forgetting him as he had clearly forgotten me. But even as I tried to persuade myself, I knew I could not do it. Alfred already inhabited every real part of me. He had spoiled me for anyone else. I lay in my bed in the room under the eaves where I had first heard his voice, and imagined I would die a spinster.

I still looked in the post-box, although its emptiness mocked me day after day. 'You never know,' said Alice, who would never believe anything bad about Alfred, and who kept her faith in him when I had lost mine. She would look at me so hopefully when I put in my hand, and then so despairingly when I shook my head: *Nothing.*

It was a particularly grey November day when I stepped out through the gate for yet another purposeless walk. The loose brick had its usual look, with a curl of ivy hanging mockingly over it. But this time my fingers encountered an obstacle. I could not believe it; crisp new paper. I snatched it out. There it was – his dashing writing with the long loops and flying t's! I opened it there and then, careless of who might be watching.

He had been ill; very ill. He had not been able to write, let alone make the journey to Chiswick. He had been delirious. He had suffered agonies in a rheumatic fever – but was in a worse agony of anxiety that I had misinterpreted his silence. *What must you have been thinking of me? It has been such an agony for me not to be able to read your sweet messages of love, to repeat each word and phrase a hundred times – but a worse agony to think you have imagined me, even for a second, to have grown cold in my love. That love burns as brightly as ever. That love lights up my life. That love will never die. Say, my dear Dodo, that you are still mine and that you will be mine from now on, for ever and ever. You are my Centre, my true Being. Without you my life is without meaning.*

I feel a tear roll down my cheek as I read. This is what they don't know. This is what they don't understand.

Wilson is standing in the doorway. 'That's right, madam. For all he wasn't as he should have been, it's still a great loss.'

I turn on her: '*Not as he should have been?* Why does everyone want to speak ill of him? Make him less than he was – now he isn't here to defend himself?'

'Beg pardon, madam. I didn't mean to speak out of turn. But Mr. O'Rourke is here. Shall I say you are indisposed?'

'No.' I wipe my eyes. Wilson's an ignorant woman, for all her common sense. 'Tell him I'll be along directly.'

Michael O'Rourke has been my most faithful friend. Such a shy young man he was when Alfred first brought him to our rooms in Wellard Street: 'Look who I've encountered on the stair! Michael Flaherty O'Rourke, Esquire – a fellow toiler in the vineyard of literature. He has the third floor back and is in want of a chop for his dinner. Dorothea, can you rise to the occasion?'

Alfred was always bringing people home with him. He loved the house to be full of talk and laughter, although he must have realised that it is difficult to turn two chops into three, or make a slice of cheese miraculously bigger. I always had to pretend I wasn't hungry.

O'Rourke is standing on the hearthrug now, with Gyp fussing round his feet. He is all in black save for an amber pin in his cravat. He has crape round his hat. 'Dorothea, my dear!' He holds out his hands.

I take them. They are cold, a little blue. His heart is not strong. 'It is kind of you to call again, Michael. I am so grateful for all you do for me.'

'No, it's not *kind* – don't say that. Our friendship is more than kindness, surely? And I wanted to make sure you're – well, you know, still bearing up.' He looks at me so gently that my eyes begin to fill again. I allow myself to lay my head on his chest. He smells of camphor.

'Oh, Michael. You understand that the fact that he and I had our differences doesn't mean – ' I can't go on.

'I know.' He kisses me on the forehead. We stand together on the hearthrug for a long time. I can hear his breath coming in laboured bursts, but he says nothing more. His silence speaks to me, though. In all that has happened, O'Rourke has been my only true advocate and supporter.

Gradually I find my voice. 'It's strange, Michael. For ten years I've dreaded this moment – '

He nods. 'So have I, my dear.'

'I've always thought I wouldn't be able to bear it, that I would be felled completely or go mad. But now it has come, and I find that I am still here; walking and talking and being alive. And I realise what I would never have thought: that our separation has, in its own way, been kind to me. Part of me has got used to his absence. Otherwise I'd be worse than Kitty, flinging myself about the room and wailing like a banshee.'

'Yes,' he says, with a sad smile. 'Time drips its comfort bit by bit. You and I both have reason to know that, but Kitty, poor child, feels the loss in a single stroke. She was in a dreadful state at the funeral; I never saw anyone so white.'

'She said *you* were kind to her, though.'

'Well, Augustus was useless. Insisting on some sort of precedence. Getting on his high horse. Absolutely reeking of whisky.' He shakes his head again.

'She came back here, you know. She stayed the night.'

'By Jove, did she?' He brightens. 'That's good – for you both.' He releases my hands. 'Do you mind if I sit down?'

We both sit, as we always do, one each side of the fire. I notice how thin he has become. He was always lean, but he is hunched now, his shoulders almost against his ears. However, he has still the same shy smile.

'Augustus was here too,' I say. 'This morning. Straight from Lord knows where. They've both gone to the house. The will: I understand Kitty may benefit.'

'And what about you?'

'You know what about me, Michael.'

'I thought he might change his mind.'

'Did you? When did he ever change his mind? Anyway, I don't need anything. It's different for Kitty. I hope he has left her enough to keep Augustus satisfied.'

He tickles Gyp with his fingertips. He thinks for a while, then asks, 'Has she said she's unhappy?'

'Oh, she'll never say so.'

'Stubborn like him, then?'

I nod, and we both smile. 'Oh, I nearly forgot.' O'Rourke starts to ferret in his coat and brings out an untidy bundle of letters. He hands them to me. 'Nobody at Park House had taken the trouble to send them on.'

I thank him. I'm surprised at the number. Dozens, I think, all with the black borders Alfred hated so much. I put them on the table next to me. 'I'll read them by and by.'

'There'll be a lot more. Hundreds, I shouldn't be surprised. You're still his widow, you know.'

'Even if I don't look the part?'

He eyes my bright dress. 'You still won't wear black?'

'No.'

'Tongues will wag.'

'No one sees me.'

Wilson comes in with the tea tray. 'I'll have to be getting some more tea from the grocer if we keep on having Dozens of People calling.'

'Heavens, Wilson,' I say. 'It's only been Kitty, and Mr. Norris, and now Mr. O'Rourke.'

'Well, Mr. Norris spilt some, and we was running low before that so, if you don't mind, I'll slip out to Mr. Collins for a shilling's worth while Mr. O'Rourke is here to keep an eye on you.'

'Do, Wilson. I can pour.'

'Like the old days.' O'Rourke smiles across the hearthrug. 'I think I must have drunk you out of house and home when we lived in Wellard Street.'

'You were always most welcome. Alfred said he wrote best when there was company present.'

'Good Grief, yes. He used to astound me – the way he'd sit at that desk scribbling away, then suddenly looking up and throwing some remark into our conversation that showed he'd been following it all along. And then turning and putting his head down and carrying on from the exact place his pen had stopped – without the slightest need for reflection.'

'Oh, that was when he was writing *Miggs*. With the other books it wasn't so easy. Many a time he was up half the night in the most desperate of tempers.'

'To be sure.' O'Rourke takes his tea – weak, with no milk. He refuses the aged bun Wilson has brought in which is making its third appearance in the parlour; Kitty has eaten all the decent cake. 'He used to tell me how you helped him; how you'd keep him company night after night. *Dodo in her nightgown, tending the flame of literature.* How I envied Alfred then for having such a lovely and devoted wife!'

'Not lovely any more,' I say with a laugh. 'Old, wrinkled, and expanding in every direction.'

'Beauty is in the eye of the beholder.' He looks at me rather too long.

I look down. 'Don't be *gallant*, Michael. I cannot bear it.'

'I'm sorry.' He clears his throat and takes a sip of tea. 'But I want you to know that if there is anything you need, anything at all . . . I am at your service, as always.'

'Thank you, Michael. I know that.'

Gyp starts to bark, showing interest in the stale bun. I break off a piece, feed it to him. O'Rourke laughs wheezily: 'That dog is spoiled.'

'Well, I've had no one else to love these ten years.'

'No one to love? What about – well, what about Kitty?'

'Kitty won't let me love her. And the others show no interest, not even Alfie or Lou. Whereas I doubt I'd recognise Eddie or Georgie if I saw them in the street. As for Fanny – well, it's hard to love truly someone you've never known.' I look sideways at him: 'I don't suppose any of them asked after me?'

He shifts his gaze; I know what that means. He knows I know, and shrugs slightly. 'I'm sure it'll be different soon. Things will take time, though. Don't give up hope.'

'No. I never give up hope.'

⚬

It was hope that kept me alive through the whole time that Alfred and I conducted our secret engagement. He was always optimistic that things would turn out well, and I, in turn, was so infected with his optimism that we convinced each other in a kind of *folie à deux* that we would be together within the year. I took courage from the fact that he was now selling stories for a guinea a time and that the publisher had asked him for a series of comical pieces that could, if satisfactory, be serialised for three months. *IF satis-factory!* he had written. *My dear Dodo, they do not know the full capacity of Yours Truly, the Great Original, the Lightning Lampooner, the One and Only. But they WILL!!*

If he was determined as a writer, he was determined as a lover too. Six weeks after his illness, he frightened me by resolving to make a declaration to my parents. *I cannot go on in this way. I have to be with you, Dodo. I need to see you, hear you, feel you, smell you, taste you. In fact, I want to gobble you up in your entirety, like the Big Bad Wolf, no matter what entreaties you make, however much you flail your little white arms in the air. So I shall be bold. Faint heart never won fair lady, and faint heart won't win her parents either. I shall write to them. I shall come and see them. Be strong. If the One and Only can't convince 'em, no one can.*

I thought he was mad, but I could not restrain him. And I too wanted that taste, that smell, that touch. I trembled merely to think of him; and the idea that I might never see him again, never have him hold me close, was awful to contemplate. Supposing he should become ill again? Supposing he should die?

'Young Mr. Gibson has written to me,' my father announced at breakfast shortly after Alfred had made his impetuous decision. 'He wishes to be heard "on the subject of my eldest daughter". Well, Dodo, what do you think of that? It's a bit of a bolt from the blue, but I shall despatch him swiftly. I shall interview him in the office tomorrow.'

'And where will you interview *me*?'

Papa looked taken aback. I went on, 'Don't *my* feelings matter? Didn't Cousin George urge you to speak to me? Why didn't you do so? Did you fear so much what I would say?' I could hear my voice, normally so calm and quiet, sounding shrill. Alice and Sissy ex-changed looks. Mama raised her eyebrows, but said nothing.

'I thought your interest in him had faded, Dodo. I wished to do nothing to revive it. You must realise any — liaison — is impossible.' Papa folded the letter and put it in his pocket with a decided air.

'I love him, Papa.'

'*Love him!* You hardly *know* the fellow.'

I longed to tell him about the letters, how I felt I knew Alfred Gibson's very soul — but I knew that to mention it now would mean disaster. So I retorted: 'I know him almost as well as I know Cousin George. And you would have married me to *him.*'

'George is family. Thoroughly respectable. What's this young man got to offer my daughter? A life on the stage? Cheap lodgings? Debt? And what kind of family does he come from? Really, Dorothea, it's quite absurd.'

'Perhaps he wants to explain all that, Oliver,' Mama broke in unexpectedly. 'You've hardly given the poor young man a chance. From the moment Dodo said she liked him, you've been set against him. You may be right about him, in fact you probably are, but give him a chance to state his case.'

My mother rarely disagreed with my father, let alone so vehemently, so Papa stared at her, nonplussed. Then he rubbed his hands together in an awkward way, and said, 'Very well. The ladies of the household get their way, as usual. I shall invite him here for Saturday at six o'clock. Never let it be said that I am not fair and so forth.'

When Saturday came, I couldn't turn my mind to anything for more than a few minutes at a time. Nancy laughed and called me a 'green girl'. 'You think you love this young fellow then, do you?' she said as she combed my hair. 'Well, there's nothing as good as a long engagement to put an end to flighty feelings, that's what Cook and me says.' She began looping my hair back, sticking pins in rather more forcefully than was required.

'Long engagement?' I stared at her in the glass. 'Who has mentioned that?'

'Well, it stands to reason. Your Pa won't do anything to upset his little rosebud, will he? But he won't see you married to a pauper neither. We reckon as he'll give young Mr. Gibson a bit of rope and hope he'll hang hisself. At least it'll show whether he loves you proper or whether he's only after your money.'

'But I have no money, Nancy.'

'You will have, when you marry. And I daresay the gentleman knows that well enough.'

'He does not!' I returned indignantly. 'He's never even mentioned it. He's quite indifferent to money!' But even as I said it, I recalled that, although he was always jovial and never downhearted, he *did* talk a great deal about his lack of funds, and how hard he had to work to make ends meet. I went hot and then cold. I saw him through Nancy's eyes, through my parents' eyes. It was indeed obvious what they would do: set impossible aims, place impassable obstacles in our way, thinking our love would break apart long before it came to marriage, that Alfred's ambitions would turn elsewhere. I pulled my head away from Nancy's hands. 'And who is caring about *my* feelings?'

'Oh, a young lady's feelings don't count in the big wide world. And anyway, you'll get over it, miss. He's only a man for all's said and done. There'll be plenty more where he came from.' Nancy pulled the strands of hair from the comb with a flourish.

I turned round from the glass. 'And that's where you're wrong, Nancy. There's no one in the least like him. He's the One and Only. And I won't let him go.'

She looked surprised at my spirited words. 'Well, miss, time will tell. Cook and I give him three months.'

I stared at her in the looking-glass and wondered if she – or Cook – had ever known real love. She could not have known anyone resembling Alfred and still remained so prosy and practical.

Alfred, true to form, turned up on the dot. When I saw him knocking at the front door, I was so overjoyed I thought I'd fall down in a faint. He was wearing a dark coat and a waistcoat of relatively sombre hue, no doubt to impress upon Papa that he was a serious and respectable suitor, and he'd obviously tried to comb his hair on the same principle, but it was still escaping around the brim of his hat. I quietly tapped the window-pane and he immediately stepped back and lifted his eyes to the window, giving me that inimitable smile. Any doubts I had completely vanished with that smile, and I blew him a kiss of encouragement, at which he affected to be mortally love-struck, staggering round the pathway clutching his heart. Moments later I heard his cheerful voice raised in salutation as Nancy ushered him into the study. I crept down the stairs, hoping to hear something; ready to be summoned. A long engagement would not be so bad, I reasoned. Alfred and I could withstand that – as long as we could see each other; as long as there was hope.

Within a quarter of an hour Papa was at the door announcing that if I'd like to come in, he and Mama had something to tell me. Alfred stood beaming by the fireplace and I was so overcome to be in the same room after all these months of letter-writing that I could hardly breathe.

'Well, Dodo, you have your way. At least you have some of it.' My father rubbed his hands. 'Mr. Gibson explains to us that he is starting out in a new profession, which, if successful, will perhaps make his prospects more encouraging. He has brought letters, commissions and so forth. There is much water to flow beneath the bridge, Dodo, but for the present, your mother and I are prepared to agree to an informal engagement for one year. *If* Mr. Gibson is then in a position to provide for you in a pecuniary and practical way, then we shall be happy to agree to a formal arrangement, and provide the necessary settlement. If not, you will go your separate ways.'

I could not believe it. It seemed too easy. Alfred must have worked his magic on them, too. 'Oh, Papa! I do love you so. And Mama!' I embraced them both.

'I hope you love *me* a little too.' Alfred's face looked positively luminous with joy. 'Unless I have a kiss this instant, I am likely to combust upon the spot!'

I felt suddenly shy. Our letters had been so passionate; we had imagined so much – but we had never exchanged a kiss. And now, my mother and father were looking on, albeit with approval. I moved haltingly towards him, but he was there first, sweeping me up in his arms, pressing his lips on mine. Warm, soft lips. Wonderful lips. My blush spread right down to my feet. He whispered in my ear: 'It won't be a year, Dodo. I can't wait that long.'

 5

O'Rourke has gone.

I have had lunch, and I now have the afternoon to fill. I finger the pile of letters on the table. One catches my eye: a coat of arms on the envelope. My heart jumps. I turn it over and over. It's a good hand, free and flowing. Black ink, a very deep border. I set it aside, but my eyes keep wandering towards it, and I am conscious of the time that may have elapsed since it was sent. I open it. It is dated two days after he died. It is short:

My dear Mrs. Gibson,

Allow one poor widow to offer words of comfort to another. Not that there is any comfort to be had in the terrible dark days after one's dearest helpmeet has been taken away. Much though one may try to console oneself that the loved companion is now in Eternal Bliss, one cannot help but selfishly wish he could be brought back, if only for a day — an hour even — to ease the suffering of the soul left behind. Mrs. Gibson, please believe the Queen when she says she understands your sorrow. She too was married to a brilliant Mind, to a wonderful Husband and Father. The Prince Consort had so much yet to give the world, as indeed did Mr. Gibson. When the Queen spoke to your husband not so long ago, he was telling her of his plans for the new novel. The Queen will be among the multitudes saddened by never being able to read it in full.

The Queen will be pleased to see you at Buckingham Palace next Thursday at three o'clock, to offer you her condolences in person.

Victoria R.

Thursday is almost upon us. I cannot go. I must find an excuse. I must plead illness, incapacity. But I know that the invitation is in reality a command. O'Rourke said Alfred could hardly walk when he had his audience; he had to stand for half an hour, nevertheless, nearly fainting with pain. 'She's a stickler,' he said. I am sure I cannot stand for more than five *minutes* before my head swims and I grow faint. I would make a fool of myself. I wish O'Rourke were still here to advise me.

There is a pounding on the front door. For one foolish moment I think it is the Queen, calling sternly in a coach-and-four to see why I have not replied to her letter. Then I hear voices and realise it's Kitty.

She shouts up the stairs: 'Mama! Mama!' Her voice has that injured tone I recognise so well from when she would run to me as a child, almost incoherent with the unfairness of life.

'What is it?' I ask, as she practically falls into the room. I look at her face and wonder what her father has done to her now. Can he be taunting her from the grave itself? Will their conflict never end?

'It's *insupportable*!' She is almost choking with anger.

'Sit down and calm yourself. I'll have Wilson bring a glass of water.' I reach for the bell.

'Water? Have you nothing stronger, Mama?' She is trembling. I wonder why Augustus isn't here to comfort her. No doubt he sloped off as soon as he could. As soon as he knew there would be nothing for him.

'Only Dr. Phelps's tonic wine. But you are welcome to it.' I go to the walnut medicine box and pour some into a glass. It smells not unlike brandy. I hand it to her.

She downs it in one gulp, shudders. 'This is *very* strong, Mama.'

'Never mind that,' I say. 'What's the matter? Has he left you nothing at all?' I am sorry for her if this is the case. It would be unjust. And, no doubt, all my fault.

'It's not so simple!' She throws herself down on the chaise

longue with dramatic abandon. 'After all the – oh, you know how he hated lawyers, Mama?'

'Oh, indeed.' Who could forget Elijah Farbelow and Janus Grabbitt?

'Well, he seems positively to embrace them now. His will is a legal masterpiece. Everything tied up, every eventuality foreseen. No omissions.'

No omissions. My heart beats a little quicker. 'Begin at the beginning, dearest. Who was there?'

As she speaks I imagine that grand house, that drawing room, those long windows, the sun filtering in, the will lying on the table. And I imagine each one of them sitting there as Kitty ticks them off on her fingers: 'Aunt Sissy, of course, Alfie and Caroline (with the child, Mama, such a sturdy little thing), Lou, Eddie, Fanny, Uncle Muffin, Bessie, Miss Brougham, Mr. Marshall and Mr. Hemmings. Me, of course, and Augustus –' she pauses, her voice a little lower '– and Miss Ricketts and her mother.'

I want to die. 'Miss *Ricketts*?' I can hardly say her name.

'Yes, Mama! Can you imagine? Both of them as bold as brass.'

I imagine them in brass, two vulgar little images, side by side. I want to strike them off their seats. I want to see them topple and fall. I want to see them lying on the floor with surprise on their faces.

'And Mr. Golding was so attentive to them. "Please sit here, Miss Ricketts. Or perhaps the armchair? Or by the window?" I made sure I was standing well away from them both.'

'Is she very pretty?' The words burst from me unexpectedly. I am surprised at myself. What does it matter now, after all?

Kitty shrugs. 'I refused to look at her, although I knew the mother was trying to catch my eye. She kept calling me "Miss Kitty".' She hesitates a little, then adds in a casual way, 'She looked well enough, I suppose. In *very* light mourning. Grey, edged with black. And a black velvet hat with the very *smallest* veil.'

[63]

I can see her. Young, with the sheen of a pearl. Slender-waisted. Elegant. Turning the head of old Mr. Golding. Jealousy snakes upwards from my belly. Then it is replaced by horror: 'He didn't leave all his money to *her* —'

'Oh no, Mama. That would have made a *scandal*. That would have upset his precious *Public*.'

'So tell me what it *was*, dear child. This is not a serial story.'

'He left me his books. He always promised me that. I don't know where I'll put them, though. Augustus says we've too many already. Dead stuff, he says.'

'And?' She can hold suspense as well as he did.

'Five thousand pounds. Each of us children gets five thousand pounds. And Aunt Sissy the same.'

'Sissy the same?'

'Yes. *To my very dearest sister-in-law, without whom I could not have managed these long years.* She looked extremely satisfied, I must say.'

I imagine the satisfaction on Sissy's neat, attentive face, and want to scream aloud — but I try to look happy for Kitty's sake. 'Well, that's so much more than you thought. Why are you so angry?'

'Because he has made her the co-trustee. We have to ask her for every shilling!' She takes out her handkerchief, and I note that she has dispensed with the black lace and has a good honest cotton one. 'And the way he's dealt with *you* — oh, Mama!' She shakes her head bitterly.

'I am mentioned?' My heart lightens, in spite of her tone. 'He's remembered me?'

Kitty looks down at her handkerchief. 'You are in a *list*, Mama. A list of all those to whom the annuities will be paid. You're there with Uncle Muffin, Bessie, Wilson, the Foundling Hospital, the Authors' Benevolent Fund — and Mrs. Ricketts.'

I begin to tremble. Mrs. Ricketts means, of course, *Miss* Ricketts — Wilhelmina Ricketts. In his Last Will and Testament, I, his wife, the mother of his children, am partnered in a list with

Wilhelmina Ricketts. This time I let go. This time I can't help it. I throw myself into Kitty's lap and start to sob.

'You see, Mama.' Kitty cradles my head against her bony black bosom. 'You see why I am so *incensed*. He takes care of the wife. Enough to avoid scandal. But not a whit – not an ounce – more. He is a *beast*!'

Yes! Yes! He *was* a beast to do that, to prefer her over me so blatantly. I sob fit to burst. Kitty rocks me, soothes me until I gradually subside. Then she helps me to my bedroom, makes a cold compress from a piece of flannel, presses it to my eyes. She is surprisingly gentle. I glance up at my looking-glass. Not only fatter than ever, but red-faced, ugly. He'd hate to see me now. He'd joke and pass it off with a laugh, but he'd hate it. I hate it myself. I'm not surprised he loved Miss Ricketts better. Why should he not love beauty? That was why he first loved me, after all. *You are so beautiful, Dodo. I'm the luckiest man in the world!*

He truly made me believe that, in those early days. During our engagement there was nothing he wouldn't do for me. He made me laugh when I was with him, and when we were apart, his letters made me cry with pleasure. Sometimes I'd read passages to Alice and Sissy, although there were other passages I kept to myself – passages that made me blush; that made me long for the day when we'd be married.

'Would you believe I am earning almost fifteen shillings a week?' he said one December day as we walked arm-in-arm by the river at Richmond, watching the wind sending shoals of dimples across the surface. 'Let us imagine we were married, Dodo. How should you propose to spend the princely sum?'

I had no idea. My head was completely empty of thoughts. I'd never had any reason to make proposals about money, and I could not imagine how to do it. A panic seized me. 'I don't know.' I looked around in desperation. 'A new pair of boots for you?' I hazarded. 'A waistcoat?'

[65]

He laughed. 'What an excellent creature! The most unselfish girl in the world! But be practical!'

Practical! My tongue clove to the roof of my mouth. I had always thought myself practical, someone with housewifely skills in darning and sewing and mending, in arranging flowers, and decorating a screen. But I realised suddenly that I knew nothing of importance.

'Well,' he said coaxingly, as to a child. 'What would we eat, dearest?'

I thought about the sort of things we had regularly delivered at the kitchen door: things wrapped in cloth or nestling in baskets. 'A joint of beef?' I hazarded. 'Some cabbages? A dozen eggs? A loaf of bread? Perhaps a quart or two of milk?'

'I see. And to cook all this delicious fare?' He stood smiling at me.

'A fire?'

'Indeed! And to keep the fire going?'

'Coals, I suppose. And firewood.'

'Excellent. At the advanced age of twenty, Miss Dodo learns to keep house!' He kissed me on the nose. 'And the rent? How much would that be, do you suppose?'

'I don't know, Alfred.'

'Of course you don't. Nor the cost of candles. Nor the laundry bill. Dodo, you are such a child. I shall need to take you seriously in hand or we shall end up in Queer Street.'

'Yes, Alfred. I am so sorry to be so useless and ignorant. I cannot imagine what you love about me.'

'Can't you?' He stroked my face. 'Dear Dodo, I love *everything* about you; I love your *whole life*: your house, your garden, your excellent parents, your little sisters. And most of all I love your dear Self, sitting in the middle of it all in a blue silk gown showing your very nice bosom – and stitching away with such an earnest look as if you have no idea of what you do to a man. It's all *quite perfect.*' And he stretched out his arms and wrapped his coat around me, so that we were cocooned together and all the warmth of his body seemed to be seeping into mine. And I didn't care that I couldn't add up or answer questions about house-keeping. I could think of nothing but the time when we would be truly together.

But of course it *did* matter that I knew so little and he so much, and that I was not as apt a pupil as he wished me to be. It mattered a great deal.

'I suppose I mustn't blame him.' I dab at my eyes with the flannel cloth.

'Why ever not?' Kitty rounds on me. 'I thought you were showing some proper feelings for once! He *is* to be blamed. *I* blame him, even if you don't!'

'Well, after all, I don't need a great deal of money. Enough to live comfortably. And I have that already.'

'In that case, why does Sissy need so much more?'

I try to find the reason. 'Well, she is still caring for the others,' I say. 'And she has the house and furnishings and servants to be responsible for. But it is wrong that he has given her such *power* over you all.' Indeed it is wrong. Unless she has changed, Sissy will exercise that to the last degree.

'Augustus says the same. He is consulting his legal people. It's monstrous that we should all have to go cap in hand to a mere *housekeeper.*'

She is too disdainful. Sissy was far more than that – and if she had not been, perhaps I would not be here, living in banishment, unable to say my proper farewells, to enjoy the comfort of all my children around me. 'And the others?' I ask. 'What do they think of Sissy's legacy?'

'Well, Lou thinks everything Papa did was marvellous, and Eddie simply smiles and whistles and shrugs his shoulders. And Alfie and Carrie bleat away saying it is only justice for all she has done. They've always been hand-in-glove with her, in my opinion. And now they have Lucy, Sissy thinks she can take over again, as she did with us. You should have seen her cooing and clucking.' She brightens. 'Lucy's an excellent child, though.'

'Is she?' It pains me to think I have never set eyes on my only grandchild. 'Perhaps I shall meet her one day.' I have pictured her, of course. I have pictured them all on the lawn at Park House, Alfie and Carrie laughing as they throw balls for the child to catch, Georgie in the hammock, Fanny playing croquet with Eddie, and Alfred sitting in the midst of them, his legs crossed, reading a book. And Sissy, of course, with Lou at her elbow, ready to dart off at her slightest request for more sandwiches or lemonade. 'How is Lou?'

'As cold as ever. Couldn't crack her face into a smile, even.'

'You two were always fire and ice.'

'She stuck a knife in me once.'

'*Louisa* did?' I am horrified. 'Why didn't I know?'

Kitty shifts, guiltily. 'You were ill; I didn't bother you. And I certainly wasn't going to tell *him*.'

'Whatever made her do such a thing? You weren't badly hurt?'

'Oh, no. It was nothing. Lou wasn't very strong.' Kitty laughs. 'And the knife was blunt. Bessie put ointment on it and bound it up. I still have the mark, though.'

I am shocked. 'Louisa was always such a *good* child.'

'Underhand, I'd call her. And very jealous.'

Ah, poor Lou. She would have seen the way Alfred looked at Kitty, the way he favoured her. When they were both on his lap, Louisa would always struggle to get closer, pushing Kitty to one side, snuggling up to his neck, burying her face in his neck-cloth, saying, *Papa, I do love you so.*

Do you, miss? he'd say. And he'd laugh and rumple Kitty's hair, saying, *And you, Kitty? Do you love me as much as Miss Mouse?* And Kitty, in her proud way, would never reply.

'What will Lou do now?' I ask. 'And Fanny? And poor Georgie, away at sea, still? What will they *all* do with themselves?'

'Carry on as before, I imagine,' she says tartly.

'Not in that great house, surely?' Without *him* there, entertaining the world to supper, what would be the point?

'Oh, it's to be sold to pay for the annuities. That's all laid down. Aunt Sissy has to find somewhere more modest, and lord it over a new set of servants.' She raises her eyebrows at me. 'Perhaps *she* at least will have the sense to go back to Chiswick.'

I ignore her. 'And Lou and Fanny?'

'They'll both go with her. Miss Mouse sticks to Sissy like glue.'

Miss Mouse; his pet name for Louisa. She crept about so quietly, never venturing an opinion of her own. She was Alfred's incubus – waiting on his every whim, fetching ink and paper, brandy-and-water. 'Poor Lou!' I say. 'She'll miss Papa so terribly.'

'As a doormat misses the shoe.' Kitty's up again, folding the piece of flannel over the edge of the wash-stand. 'It's her own fault. She and Sissy deserve each other.'

'You're very hard on them.'

'They are a pair of witches.'

'You shouldn't say such things. They are your sister and mine.'

'Yes, exactly. Weird Sisters. *Toil and Trouble.*' She croaks and makes a face like an old crone. She makes me laugh.

'And what about *you*, Kitty? What will you do with your five thousand pounds?'

'I don't have it yet. And I'm not sure I want it. Perhaps I shall distribute it amongst the Poor.'

I catch her eye in the looking-glass. 'Does Augustus feel the same?'

'He feels we should keep it – as a matter of principle.'

'I'm sure he does. As a matter of principle.'

She colours. 'At least he stands up for me.'

I begin to see why Alfred put the money in a trust; Sissy will never bow to Augustus's demands. 'Well, we'll have to wait, won't we? But is there nothing you would wish to do with it? Nothing you would like to have?'

She says nothing.

✢

All this talk of money! I have never valued it. Alfred said it was because I was brought up with it and took it for granted, whereas for him it was a constant anxiety. *Poverty gets in the blood,* he would say. *It's a disease you can't shake off.* He was always generous – ridiculously generous – to friends and strangers alike, but at the same time careful of every penny. All through his life he worked as if the bailiffs were about to threaten at the door. Even when he was earning thousands, keeping a carriage and a houseful of servants, and laying on dinner parties with a dozen courses, he would still check the butcher's bills to the farthing and make surprise sallies into the kitchen to ensure there was no pilfering from the tea caddy or wine cellar. He kept all the household keys himself on a big brass ring.

From the outset he had impressed my mother with his knowledge of household matters. 'I have to say your young man is a great manager,' she said some months into our engagement. 'He has all his expenditure under control. Nothing is unaccounted for. There are economies he has thought of that I would not know myself. Where has he learnt all this?'

'The School of Life, my dear,' replied my father. 'I understand his family fell on hard times when he was young. A very bad business, I understand. Very bad.'

Alfred had intimated as much to me, but I didn't know the details. He was very reticent where his family was concerned, although he'd told me he had a 'wonderful' sister, who lived near him in Camden Town, and a 'splendid' younger brother, who was in the Navy. His parents, he said, were retired to a cottage near

Dover. Yet all through our engagement he never once proposed our going down to see them. He said their accommodation was too cramped to admit our staying, and he was most adamant that they never came up to London. I began to think there was something shameful about his family that he kept them so distant from me. But one day he surprised me by announcing we were going to take tea with his sister Lottie.

Father took me as far as the Angel in the chaise, and Alfred met us there, promising to have me back at Father's office by six o'clock. We walked through the crowded streets until we came to an elegant milliner's shop, with three feathered bonnets in the window. I was so busy admiring them that I failed to notice the figure waiting in the doorway. 'Dodo, let me introduce my favourite sister!' Alfred proclaimed, sweeping off his hat in front of a small and energetic figure with a carefully-wrapped parcel in her hand.

'Your *only* sister,' she added with a laugh, taking my hand in a very lady-like manner. 'I am so pleased to meet you, Miss Millar. You are quite as pretty as Fred promised.'

'And why shouldn't she be?' interjected Alfred.

'Because it's well-known that you have an inclination to exaggerate, Fred.' She had bright, laughing eyes like his. She was very well-dressed, in the latest fashion, with a fur-trimmed tippet and matching muff. And she was very neat, clean and finished, exactly as he was.

As we walked briskly along to her lodgings, she told me what an excellent brother he'd been. 'I owe him everything. At one time I could only survive because Fred gave me an allowance. Left to myself, I should have been in a sorry state indeed. At such times you understand why women become desperate enough for anything, don't you, Miss Millar?'

I looked at her. I had never thought of women in such desperate situations. I could not believe that a woman as respectable as Lottie had either. I cast a glance at Alfred, but he was stepping out alongside us in his usual jaunty manner, as if in no way surprised by her words. I smiled to myself to think I had ever contemplated running away to London. How foolish I would have been standing on a street corner asking for directions from thieves and vagabonds, or being mistaken for a woman of easy virtue!

When we arrived at her lodgings – a sloping attic room, with a table, bed and chest of drawers all neatly arranged, and a canary in a cage – she put down the parcel and took my bonnet from me. 'You have not met our parents yet, I believe, Dorothea?'

'No, indeed. In fact I know hardly anything about them,' I said. 'Alfred is most dreadfully secretive on the subject.'

He frowned a little. 'Not secretive. One thing at a time, my love, that is all.'

'I'm simply a little apprehensive in case they won't like me.'

'They'll like you well enough,' said Lottie, bending to coax a brighter flame from the fire, before setting the kettle on top. 'But don't lend any money to them. Under any circumstances.'

It was a strange notion, to be thus warned about one's prospective in-laws. I shrugged my shoulders. 'I have no money to lend.'

Lottie looked sharply at me. Then at Alfred. 'So how will you manage, when you are married? I assumed –' She stopped.

I knew what she had assumed. 'Oh, Papa has promised a settlement. Provided we are engaged for a year, of course. I meant that I don't have any money *now*.'

She smiled. 'Give our parents no promissory notes, then. They think ahead.'

'Except when they need to, of course. Except when it matters.' Alfred's face had fallen out of its habitual cheeriness into an expression I had not seen before; an expression of deepest gloom. All his jauntiness seemed squeezed out of him, like forcemeat from a bag. I sat on the horsehair sofa next to him, not knowing what to say. Lottie seemed not to notice, or pretended not to notice.

She darted around, setting out cups, plates, a loaf of bread and some butter, a jar of jam. Then she unwrapped the parcel and took out a large cake, which she placed neatly on a china plate. Alfred looked at it and some of his cheerfulness returned: 'Ah! Seed cake! The very thing!'

Lottie laughed. 'Your favourite. I bought it from Parfitt's as a special treat. But you shouldn't keep Dorothea in suspense. Papa wrote to me only last week, saying how delighted they both were that you were engaged, and how they were looking forward to making your sweetheart's acquaintance. They are enchanted at the mere idea of her.'

'I am sure they *are* enchanted, Lottie. But it's none of their doing and, in the end, they are of no consequence. They will do as *I* please, this time.'

I was surprised at the hardness in his face, and the hardness in his tone. Then the kettle boiled, the tea was made in the pot and soon he was tucking in eagerly to seed cake, the smile back on his face. Food always cheered him up. Whenever he wrote about it, it always left him sanguine – flirtatious, even. I remember once when he was writing *Miggs' Tales*, he came up behind me and squeezed my waist and kissed my cheek, saying, 'I've given Old Tuppy the feast of his life. I am sending him on a picnic with the young Wendaways. There's a baleful, cold-eyed salmon on a silver salver, thirty pickled eggs in a jar, and a snooty footman in attendance!' And I'd laughed, and he'd squeezed me again, saying, 'So what have *we* got for supper then, Dodo? Why don't we broil some cutlets and eat them in front of the fire, licking the bones as if we were naked savages on the shores of Lake Titicaca!' And I'd asked him if there were really naked savages on the shores of Lake Titicaca, and he'd said he had no idea, but 'Have you never played the game of Make Believe?' and I'd shaken my head. And he said, 'Oh, Dodo, don't sit there so perplexed, as if someone has put an onion in your mouth. Imagine it. Imagine you are someone else, someone wildly different.' He could do it himself so beautifully, of course – immerse himself so instantly in a character. I could watch and listen to him for hours. 'But it needs two,' he'd say. 'You need to come along with me, Dodo. It's a joint adventure.' So, from the moment we were engaged, I had to set aside my homely ways and learn to experience new things. Starting with all the things Alfred already knew, and seemed to have known all his life. Starting with London.

As we had walked to meet Lottie, Alfred had been astounded that I did not know my way about the city, that my knowledge of the capital was confined to the Strand, Piccadilly and Covent Garden, and the high road in and out from Chiswick. 'London's more than that!' he said. 'It's a bran tub, Dodo – full of hidden delights – and sometimes things you don't expect! Things that pinch your fingers; things whose purpose you can't work out.' He couldn't wait to show me all the sights. 'Bring Alice with you! We'll have a capital day!'

6

Alice was very pleased to be invited to join Alfred and my-self in the jaunt around London. She wore her new felt bonnet and her best wool shawl in his honour, and spent hours crimping her hair. We set off from home early in the chaise, and met him at Blackfriars Bridge. 'I hope you both have stout boots,' he said as he handed us down. 'I can't have you stopping for sore feet. There is so much to be seen!'

He was as good as his word. We walked all day, Alice and I sometimes almost running to keep up with his cracking pace. 'Come now, ladies, don't dawdle!' he'd call, if we loitered for a moment to catch our breaths. Suddenly I was seeing the city as he saw it: the Temple and the Inns of Court with their quiet, muf-fled courtyards; the old city churchyards with tipsy tombstones dating back to the plague; the Thames, so much wider than at Chiswick and so much busier; all the ships docking and un-loading at the wharfs and the wherrymen rowing back and forth between them; the narrow streets with their beggars, orange-and-nut sellers, pie-men, bird sellers and crossing sweepers – and the even narrower alleys strung with sagging laundry and too filthy to set one's feet in. He pointed out all the houses where he had ever lived – a surprising number, in a surprising variety of locations. At one time, we passed the gates of the Foundling Hospital, and I said how sad it was for all those young women to give up their babies, and how sad for the children to grow up not knowing their mothers. 'Better than the workhouse,' he said, shortly, marching us on. As we passed under the walls of the Fleet Prison, we saw small children going in and out with bottles of beer and plates of food. Alfred stopped and stared at them, his face pale and rigid. Then he turned to me: 'Don't you ever get us into debt, Dodo, or I'll never forgive you.'

'No, Alfred,' I said, frightened a little at his emotion, his peremptory tone, the angry tears in his eyes. 'I am sure I would never land us in *prison,* however bad a housekeeper I am.'

'*Papa* would never allow it,' said Alice firmly.

'*I* would never allow it,' said Alfred, widening his eyes and raising his eyebrows in his Captain Murderer expression.

'So there is no danger, then,' said Alice, solemnly.

'You are right, little sweetheart,' he said, laughing. 'No danger at all.'

Finally, he said, he had a surprise. He took us to a small terrace of somewhat plain houses giving straight upon the street. Rather dirty and rather noisy, I thought. Carts clattered by continuously, and there were barricades and scaffolds at the end of the street where the new railway was being dug. I wondered why he had brought us there. 'It's to be our new home,' he said, which I thought rather premature. He seemed very pleased with it all, though, as he propelled me up a flight of six steep steps and began to knock on the brown door with a black iron knocker. 'Mrs. Quinn is an excellent woman,' he whispered. 'Although she does have more than the usual complement of chins and the very slightest odour of snuff. But she'll see to the linen and provide a girl to sweep and clean for only twopence a day. I think you'll find her kindness itself.'

'Mr. Gibbs!' cried out the woman who answered the door. 'What an elevating surprise! And is this your lovely fiancée? Mrs. Gibbs-that-will-be? Come in, dear happy couple and other young lady, please do.' And we went in, and stood like soldiers in a little square passageway until Mrs. Quinn moved her considerable bulk into the parlour and released the space for us to do the same. 'What an honour, my lady, to be offering lodgings to such as yourself,' she said, curtsying in the middle of the room, so we had to spread to the edges along with some stiff-backed chairs and ebony whatnots. 'Will you be so condescending as to take some tea?'

Alfred gave a slight nod in my direction, and I accepted her offer with a bow.

'EMMIE!' Mrs. Quinn bellowed, without moving from her spot in the centre of the room.

A tiny girl of about eight appeared in the doorway. 'Yes, ma'am.'

'Tea,' said Mrs. Quinn.

'Yes, ma'am.' The girl curtsied, disappeared.

'And some of that Madeira cake as is in the meat safe, if you please!'

Emmie reappeared. 'Yes, ma'am.' Curtsied again. Disappeared again.

'Emmie'll be doing your washing,' said Mrs. Quinn, confidentially. 'She's a good girl. Very quick. I got her from the Foundling Hospital.'

'She's very young,' I commented.

'Twelve or so, it's reckoned. But strong. You'd be surprised at how strong.'

She was one of the frailest children I had ever seen. And she looked nowhere near twelve. I glanced at Alfred. He was writing something in his pocket-book. He looked up and smiled: 'I'm sure she'll be of great use to us. To both Mrs. Gibson-to-be and myself.'

⁂

I see Kitty has cooled down now and is preparing to go, pulling on the gloves with the cut jet buttons. 'It's not that I want the money, Mama. It's that I don't see why *they* should have it. It's unfair. Well, Bessie of course, I don't mind that. And Uncle Muffin.

[77]

And Wilson. But why not Michael? Why not Augustus even? They were both his friends.'

'Yes, they were. But they crossed him. He never forgave that.'

'It's ridiculous, after all this time.'

'He had a long memory.'

'A very partial memory.'

'Yes. Don't you think *I* know that, Kitty dear?'

'Of course.' She comes over and puts her arms around my neck – the second time in two days. 'I am a selfish creature, aren't I? When I think what you've had to put up with.'

'Oh, don't feel sorry for me, Kitty. I consider myself lucky. Lucky to have known him. Lucky to have been loved by him. And I *was* loved by him, no matter what anyone says.'

'Oh, at the beginning, no doubt. You must have seemed a fairy princess, with your blue eyes and your golden hair and your idyllic life, tucked away in the country in the prettiest house that ever was. I'm not surprised he wanted to own you –'

What is the child on about now? 'I was not *for sale*, Kitty! It was an equal bargain. I loved him as much as he loved me.'

'Rather more, I think.' Kitty makes a wry face.

'I cannot weigh and balance these things, nor do I wish to. But I know he might have married any number of young women. Yet it was *me* he proposed to. And *me* he married. Even though it made for difficulties. Even though Mama and Papa did not approve.'

'I thought they liked him.'

'They did. They couldn't help it. He made Mama laugh, and Papa was very taken with his plays and stories. But they thought he was not serious enough for marriage. He seemed so boyish to them. Once he knocked at our front door wearing a sailor suit and carrying a parrot in a cage, pretending he had that moment walked off HMS *Trafalgar* and was looking for lodgings for the night.'

Kitty can't help a smile – although she has heard this story many times before.

'I daresay they hoped he'd fail to make his mark so they could extricate me from the engagement. Or maybe they hoped I would tire of him before the year was out. But your father was always impatient, and, as soon as I was one-and-twenty, he took out a special licence and we were married in secret at St. Martin in-the-Fields. Papa was so angry that he refused to give me my settlement. He said Alfred had betrayed him dreadfully.'

'Didn't he care if you starved?'

'He said it was up to your father to ensure I didn't. But then he relented and gave me twenty pounds a year so I could buy nice dresses and at least *look* like a lady. We'd expected two hundred pounds, so the difference was considerable, but Alfred said he wasn't going down on bended knee to beg for anything more. Not that he *needed* to beg, of course; within the year he was earning twice that much.'

'You were rich, then?'

'Well, not exactly. As soon as the money came in, it seemed to go out again. So many of Papa's family relied on him – Lottie, Muffin, and your grandparents. And you know how your grand-father was – money simply ran through his fingers.'

'Well, I *don't* know, to tell the truth. He was always perfectly agreeable to me.'

'Yes,' I say, 'to me, too. But he invariably contrived to enrage your father. That was amply apparent the first time we went to Dover. We were very newly-married then – a little over two weeks – and I sensed he felt it was now safe to introduce me. He was still uneasy, though, as we took the coach to the coast. He was very quiet, counting the milestones with a faraway look in his eye and scribbling away in his notebook from time to time, especially when one of our fellow-travellers started a comical tale about a valet and a missing pair of boots. I truly don't know what I expected when we got out. But an impressive gentleman in coat-tails and a tower-ing expanse of neck-cloth came darting out of the crowd, waving a silver-topped cane. He had a booming voice that carried over the clatter of the horses and the shouts of the grooms and stable boys: "Hallo, there!" '

'Oh, yes, that was Grandpapa! Always larger than life!'

'No sooner had he arrived than he began to take charge; to direct the porters in removing the luggage from the back, to help myself and the other ladies from inside, to assist an elderly gentleman from the top, to fasten up a dog that was rioting around, to make faces at an infant who had started to howl. He was like a ringmaster at the circus. "Sixpence for the coachman," he roared. "Three pence for the porter!" I saw Alfred dig into his pocket, and the next moment his father was handing out the tips with an air of largesse to one and all.'

Kitty laughs, but I remember how my main relief was that Mr. William Gibson was not only respectable but positively charming. 'And this delightful creature must be your wife!' he'd beamed, kissing my hand. 'Welcome to Dover! To the South Coast! To the Gateway to Europe! To the wide, wide world! And, of course, to our humble abode, where we hope you will not be too proud to spend a few weeks with Mrs. Gibson (Senior) and myself.'

'We are here for three days only,' Alfred told him, somewhat firmly. 'I have pressing work in London.'

'Ah, indeed. Yes. Pity. Perhaps Dorothea – if I may presume to address you in that way as befits your recent inclusion into the bosom of the Gibson family – perhaps you would care to stop longer? The sea air, you know? It is recommended. Alfred recommended it to us himself. Leave London, he said! Leave the smoke and grime! Leave all this –'

'Father, we are just married! Would you part us so soon?'

'My boy, I am at fault! In my enthusiasm for her company I forget the exigencies of married life, the demands of the honeymoon. I beg your pardon, Dorothea. Forgive an old man.' He chivvied us over to a dog-cart where a fat boy was lazing at the reins. 'Your conveyance, ma'am. *A poor thing but mine own.* Well, in fact not my own. Hired.' He helped me in and sat beside me. Alfred and boy lifted the luggage into the back. As we jolted off, he leant back with an air of complete satisfaction and said, 'Well, Fred. Is married life suiting you?'

'Yes, thank you, Father. We are getting along in a capital fashion. Capital. Dodo is the dearest girl in the world and an excellent wife. I only hope I can make her a good husband. A *reliable* husband.'

'No doubt of it, I'm sure; you have always been a *reliable* boy. He's been a good son, Dorothea. A very good son. We have not always been a family blessed with pecuniary advantage, but we are as close as can be – and I would take to task any man who would deny it!' He took Alfred's arm and pulled him towards him in an awkward embrace. Alfred raised his eyebrows at me in an expression of exasperation.

'Now, dear boy, before we enter the domestic portals, I have a proposal to put to you.' He then turned to me in a confidential manner. 'You see, occasionally, dear Dorothea, I am obliged to enter into certain transactions which – as is the way of the world – do not always come to fruition. It pains me to admit it. It pains my lady wife even more –'

Alfred held out his hand with a sigh: 'Give me the bills.'

'No, Fred. I cannot do it. I cannot accept such largesse. Not again. Not after all you have done. Not when you are so newly setting out on life's adventure. A loan, a mere five pounds. To be repaid when my investments take a turn for the better.'

'The bills,' Alfred said, still holding out his hand.

His father hesitated, then nodded. 'Indeed. You are very generous. Not a word to Mrs. G.' He pulled a sheaf of dog-eared bills from his top pocket. 'Excellent! Nevertheless, perhaps you could run in addition to a guinea for –'

'No, Father.'

'Perhaps Dorothea, in recognition of our new relationship — ?'

"By no means. Never. Ever. Do not ask her.' Alfred's eyes were blazing.

I thought Alfred was being unduly parsimonious. 'Please, Alfred,' I said. 'Don't forget I have some money.' He'd let me keep my twenty pounds to buy 'finery' for the wedding, and I still had quite a sum left.

Alfred looked at us both with a steely expression. 'Father — you must NEVER ask her for money. Dorothea — you must NEVER give him any. Is that understood? Any breach would end all communications between us.'

And that was the cause of the first quarrel I had with my husband.

⚘

'I've never really told you, have I?' I say to Kitty. 'What your grandmother asked me at that first meeting?'

Kitty shakes her head. 'I suppose she was sponging, too?'

'She was a trifle more subtle — but only a trifle. We were all out walking on the second day of our stay. The men were attempting to fly a kite on the cliff top and we were lagging behind because of the wind. She took my arm very tightly, telling me how delightful it had been to meet me. "And I hope that at some time in the near future we will have the pleasure of meeting your Mama and Papa too. They sound such estimable people." She came close and whispered to me: "I want you to know, Dorothea, that what you behold in me now is but a shadow of my former self. I was not always as I am now. I had Family. I had Reputation. I need not say that Mr Gibson — I speak of my spouse, of course — I need not say that Mr Gibson has many virtues. But an understanding of money is not one of them. I, on the other hand, can be relied upon to be both discreet and sacrificial. I do not open my mouth to complain. I do what I can. I sell my jewellery; I pawn the clothes

[82]

from my back. I am like the pelican with her young. But Mr Gibson is Inveterate. He cannot be held back. He has to Spend, just as water has to Run Down Hill. I have tried everything to keep us solvent. The result? Useless. The creditors are dissatisfied, the family is ruined, and our future is dependent on the goodwill of others."

'Well, Kitty, you can imagine that I was taken aback at all this. I told her that I was sorry to hear what she had confided to me and that Alfred had never intimated the extent of the troubles. Ruin was not a word he had ever used. At which she looked frightened suddenly and begged me not to say she had told me anything: "My son is very proud."

'"He is fearful of debt, certainly," I said. "When we once passed the Fleet —" At which point she stopped me, gripping me tight. "Do not speak of That Place," she said. "Never mention it — promise me." So I said I would say nothing about it unless your father raised the matter himself. And she thanked me, Kitty, saying she did not wish to intimate that Alfred was not a good son to his wretched parents. "Any differences in the past are now resolved, any threats in the past are now removed. The dear boy sends me a half-sovereign when he can, when he has sold some piece of writing. But the cottage does not pay for itself. Visitors — though welcome I need not say — are a Cost."'

I look at Kitty. 'So you see what a difficulty I was in, then. I couldn't help remembering how your Aunt Lottie had warned me about both your grandparents; and what your father had so solemnly required of me only the day before with regard to lend-ing your grandfather money. I was in a dilemma. It seemed only right to relieve the burden of our stay, but I was fearful of your father's anger. In the end, I told Mrs Gibson that I would speak with him on the matter. "I am sure we can help you," I said. She just clasped me tighter by the arm: "No Dorothea. Let this be between us alone. A sovereign, that is all." I remember her glancing at my brocade gown, my silk shawl, my kid gloves, and my new leather boots, and I felt guilty. A sovereign was nothing. So I opened my purse, fearful all the time that your father would turn round and spy me. But her hand was quick. The coin slipped into her reticule as if by magic.'

Kitty perks up. 'You went against him the first week you were married? I hope he did not find out?'

'Oh, Kitty, indeed he did. It was the occasion of our first quarrel.'

'Oh, Mama!' She looks cross again. 'Did you go and confess all like a green girl?'

'Well, he asked me point blank, and I couldn't lie to him.'

Indeed, I remember him pacing round the cottage bedroom, his hair awry, his waistcoat unbuttoned. "How could I have been plainer, Dorothea?" he'd said. "Tell me, how could I have been plainer?" I told him he could not have been, that the fault was entirely with me. "No, it is with me," he said gloomily. "To have brought you here. To have submitted you to it all." I tried to mollify him: "It was only a sovereign," I said. "And our being here is causing extra expense." He'd whirled round and fixed me with such a withering look. "Don't you think I have allowed for that?" he cried. "I have already given my mother more than enough. Please don't interfere in what you don't know."

Don't interfere in what you don't know! The words cut me to the heart. Only two weeks into our marriage and we were quarrelling! I had never quarrelled with anybody before. Even as a child I was always mild-mannered. I was even patient with Sissy, who was a very determined and strong-willed child. So I was shocked to find myself quarrelling with the person I loved most in the world, and to be the object of his displeasure. This was a new, cold Alfred, totally at odds with the man who had courted me so rapturously; who had been so tender with me on our first night together.

'You see, I didn't want to quarrel,' I tell Kitty. 'Not so soon in our married life, at any rate. So I told him I would do as he said.'

'He wins, as always.' She gets up; she is really going this time. But her eye falls on the Queen's letter. I had forgotten it; my heart turns over to think I must make some attempt at a reply. 'What's this?'

'As you see, it's a letter from Her Majesty.'

'The *Queen*? What is she writing to *you* for?'

'Why shouldn't she? Why shouldn't a widow write to a widow? She understands my feelings.'

'She's invited you to the *Palace*?' She has picked up the letter, and reads it quickly, turning it over as if there is some surprise to be found in it.

'Did I never teach you about private correspondence?' I ask.

'I'm sorry.' She puts it down.

'I cannot go, of course. I must find an excuse.'

'Must you? She's probably as lonely as you are.'

'That is very unlikely.'

But I wonder about it after Kitty has gone. I re-read the letter. I listen to the echo of her words and I see that she is indeed lonely. One does not have to be living in a small apartment to be lonely. A palace is no protection. Indeed it may be worse. People criticise so much. I've heard the world mocking the extremity of her grief. I feel a sudden fellow-feeling for her and I resolve to go after all. I pick up my pen to reply, then realise I have no mourning clothes. I cannot see the Queen without proper mourning; it would be an insult. It is not too late to order some, even now. But it is breaking faith. Never in my married life have I worn it. Not for my parents; not for our children.

I ring for Wilson. 'Do you think Miss Walters would make me a black silk dress by Thursday?'

'Black?' Wilson looks puzzled. We have had words on the subject.

'Yes, black. I have an audience with the Queen.'

'The Queen?' She stares, exactly as Kitty had.

'Yes. She has written to me. I am a person of importance, in *her* eyes at least.'

'But you've always said – *he* always said –'

'I simply don't wish to offend Her Majesty. And it is my choice what I do in this life.'

'Yes, madam.' She smiles. 'I'll send straight away. Silk, you say?'

'I am not wearing crape. I draw the line there. The Queen can think what she pleases about that.'

 *7*

'*The* light's going. Do you want me to turn up the lamp?'
Wilson has come back into the room and seen me reading
my letters.

'No, leave it,' I tell her. 'I want to think.'

'Very well.' She goes out, shutting the door behind her.

I've had to put on my spectacles. People write so badly these
days, I can scarcely make out the signatures: Mr. and Mrs. Clarence
Smiley – or Smithy; James and Mary – Whittaker, I think; Miss
Angela Boot – or is it Booth? They must think I remember them
so well that I can identify them immediately. But I can't; we met
so many people through all that long time we had together. And
towards the end, my recollection became poor. Many days I felt as
though I was walking in a kind of fog; seeing only outlines, my
hearing muffled. I'd be aware of Alfred pulling at my arm, whispering in my ear, *Come on, Dodo. Wake up. Show willing! Try for me,
darling, please!*

I did try. Of course I did. But there were times after each of
my children was born when I lost whole hours out of my day.
Often, I'd look down at myself and wonder how I had got
dressed and who had done my hair; and I'd look up at the people
around me and have no idea of the occasion that I was presiding
over. The faces around me would be indistinct. I'd see black ties,
white shirt-fronts, necklaces sparkling on décolletages; I'd hear
men's voices booming and ladies' voices chirping. I'd smile and
hope I wouldn't need to talk; that Alfred would carry all before
him, as usual.

Yet when we were first married, I was always eager for an outing. Every week Alfred and I were to be found high in the gallery at the Lyceum, the Haymarket or Drury Lane, watching Kean or Macready give us their Shakespeare heroes and villains. We'd applaud enthusiastically and wave our handkerchiefs till our arms ached. We saw the great clown Grimaldi, too, and the child prodigy Adele Smith dancing on points. And when we were too penniless to go out, I'd sit at the piano in the corner of the room playing Chopin. Although Alfred would listen to me for a while, he'd soon become restless; then I'd catch his eye and launch into one of the popular ballads that he loved so much: 'She Was Never Mine' or 'You and Your Sister'. And we'd sing them together – sentimental and comic by turns – until we were quite exhausted.

Those first few months in Mrs. Quinn's upstairs rooms were among the happiest in my life. We had little spare money and almost no furniture, but Alfred was so affectionate and such cheery company it didn't seem to matter. We might only have mutton stew for dinner – and not a lot of it at that – but he'd drape the small pedestal table with a cloth, lay it with knives and forks, and pretend to be the waiter, the cook and the diner all in such rapid succession that I ached with laughter.

My only regret was that he did not have quite as much time for me as I had hoped. I thought a new bridegroom would want to spend every minute he could with his bride. I forgot that, to make ends meet, Alfred had to push himself to write at every opportunity, even on our honeymoon. I got used to waking up and finding an empty space next to me, his pillow already cold. He'd be at work in his nightshirt, by the window, pen moving quickly across paper. The fire would be lit and the kettle on the hob, his clothes warming on the fender, his boots polished: 'Come here, Dodo,' he'd say, lifting up a page to the light. 'Listen to this!' And he'd read aloud and laugh at what he had written. 'You know, it's capital stuff, though I say it myself! I should be demanding twice the price. Indeed, I think next time I *will* ask twice the price! There's nothing as good as this being written in the whole of London.'

Nor was there. I was so proud of him, I'd come and put my arms round him. 'You are the One and Only.'

'And you are the One and Only's wife!' And he'd hug me close with his left arm while making amendments with his right, so that the paper shifted about and his quill spluttered. I'd feel his fingers through my shift, and my blood would leap.

'Won't you come back to bed, Alfred? For a little while?'

'Bed?' He'd look up at me. 'What a naughty creature it is! How it pouts its lips and displays its bosom! But it is half past seven already, and there is much to be done!'

And before I could set my things out for dressing, he'd have made the tea and fried some eggs and would be plunging his head into a bowl of cold water, splashing it all over his body, and drying himself vigorously with a towel.

His passion for washing surprised me. 'It's not natural,' my mother commented, when I joked to her about his twice-daily ablutions. 'He's not a navigator digging in the earth, for Heaven's sake. He's a gentleman, or trying to be so, at least.' But Alfred could not be distracted from his habits, and I loved the scent of clean skin and lavender that reminded me so much of that first evening together. And it wasn't only the bathing. Soiled shirts were discarded at once, undergarments perpetually in the wash. Little Emmie was always toiling up and down stairs to the wash-house, often with a penny in her hand to make her *extra special careful* with the clear-starching. She'd fold his shirts with reverence, sleeves behind the back, shirt front smooth, *exactly how he likes;* and he'd be delighted, and give her another penny and a sweetmeat for being such a good girl.

I was learning a lot too – how to shop, and how to cook. He'd propel me around the markets, showing me how to avoid bad meat and rotten fruit, and the costers who'd palm the small change.

His quick eye would see some bargain item – candle-snuffers, sugar-tongs – and in a flash, they were ours. I made many errors as I struggled to learn, but he'd shrug them off with a laugh: *Try not to set the food alight next time, Dodo – that is a shade more done than I care for! Not so much fat in the pan, perhaps!* He liked to see me with my apron on, though, poring over recipes with smudges of flour on my cheek, or sitting and mending by the fire. *This is happiness,* he would say, leaning back in the chair and surveying the whole scene with those bright eyes of his.

But he was not content with Mrs. Quinn's for long. His weekly stories – *Adventures of a Young Man with No Means* – had attracted much attention; he had a play in rehearsal about a comic servant and his master, which I thought very funny; and he was about to start some new stories – *Miggs' Tales* – for a monthly magazine. 'Another fifty pounds a year!' he crowed. 'We must find a better class of lodging, now – more befitting to the One and Only, don't you think?'

So after only three months of marriage, we were piling all our belongings – our brass bedstead, our chest of drawers, his desk and chair, my piano and a small Turkey rug – on a cart, and setting off for the superior delights of Wellard Street. Emmie cried bitter tears as she waved us off from Mrs. Quinn's doorstep: 'Don't forget me, sir! Don't forget me, will you?' Her thin little form was shaking with grief. And Alfred, his own eyes streaming, called back: 'Never fear, little Emmie. The whole world will remember you!'

No sooner had we moved, than *Miggs' Tales* became the most talked-about serial ever. Yet although the monthly numbers were sold out, and Alfred's name was on the lips of half London, he was afraid it might not last. 'Fame is fickle,' he said. 'I cannot rely on my writing alone. I have to have a steady income.' So he continued to work on newspaper articles – rising at six – before taking himself to Webster and Potts at half past eight, and then writing the next number of *Miggs* in the evening: 'I shall dissolve into ink, at this rate, Dodo – starting at my fingers and liquefying slowly until you have to catch me in a bucket and carry me around with you, like Isabella and her basil pot!' But he did not liquefy; rather he seemed to sparkle with energy. He would sometimes come home as late as ten o'clock, saying he'd been at his wanderings in the City, as far as Deptford or Greenwich or out on the Old Kent Road. *What for?* I'd ask. And he'd look at me with astonishment. *What* for? *For the love of it, Dodo. To see the sights, to meet the people, to suck it all in.* He had a new tale in mind already. The wandering of a poor orphan girl, born in the workhouse, sent out as a maid-of-all-work to a grim old spinster.

'Emmie?' I'd asked him excitedly when he told me of it. 'Is this the story of our little Emmie?'

'Emmie as she might have been,' he'd replied. 'Emmie who will find her mother and come into a fortune! Emmie who will become a lady at last!'

'But isn't that most unlikely?' I replied.

He paused for a moment. 'Is it? I find life is remarkable for its unlikely qualities; the way fortunes can change in an instant. The tide of the river flows in and out, Dodo. At some point the in becomes the out; the out, in. Thus the poorest child can become rich and famous; and the most abandoned, neglected and friendless urchin can discover himself to be a prince. That is the great thing, my love. See what has happened to Yours Truly in but a few months!'

I pointed out that he was not a bit like Emmie – that to my knowledge *he* had not been abandoned, neglected and left friendless; that he had had family and education and people who loved him.

A shadow passed over his face. Then he brightened. 'Of course you are right, Dodo. And above all I have *you*, dearest. The very sweetest pussycat of a wife. The very dearest, softest little woman in the world!' And he lifted me off my feet and whirled me into the bedroom and threw me down on the bed.

I protested: 'Alfred! The supper will be even more ruined than it is now.'

'Hang the supper!' he said, taking off his jacket and unbuttoning his waistcoat. 'I have a tastier morsel here!'

⚜

After only six months in Wellard Street we were on the move again. *Miggs' Tales* and *Little Amy* were running simultaneously. We had doubled our income and were beginning to mix in literary circles. We needed an entire house this time, and one, moreover, in a respectable area. He came back one day saying he had found exactly such a house in Channon Street. 'Room for your whole family and mine to come and stay, Dodo – and a study where I can be most furiously busy and hide from them all.' The house was indeed large – or at least very tall. It had three storeys and a basement. Best of all it had a nice flushing water-closet of which he was inordinately proud. 'We'll have the whole thing repainted,' he said, pulling me up the steep stairs and round the empty rooms. 'Bright colours,' he said. 'None of your drabs!' He ordered the latest cream-ware dinner service, he bought velvet curtains, bookcases, a new sofa, three new tables, candlesticks, and looking-glasses galore. To celebrate, we had a water-colour of us both done by his very new best friend Charley Evans, which cost us five guineas, and which we hung over the mantel in pride of place. I thought we looked very well together and almost cried with the wonder of it all.

It was at that juncture that Alice came to live with us. Kitty was on the way then, and Mama felt I needed a reliable companion during my confinement. I was delighted, of course. I loved both my sisters, and Sissy had always amused me with her stubborn determination and sharp-eyed view of the world and its inhabitants, but I had always favoured Alice's gentle companionship, and I now looked forward to the time we would spend

[92]

together. For her part, Alice was only too pleased to come and be helpful to me – and moreover to be in London, to enjoy the theatres and meet all the influential people we had begun to know. Alfred had been quick to make friendships, and a host of writers, painters, and actors – including the famous Mr. Macready him-self – came to our house and crammed into our first-floor drawing room, talking and laughing and drinking brandy-and-water. O'Rourke was a regular visitor, too, and always remembered to say something nice to me as I sat in the corner with my sewing. Alice was an asset at these times. Whereas I did not always know what to say when the men were talking of the Reform Act, the Poor Laws and so forth, Alice would ask some innocent ques-tion, and they would all stop and be kind to her, and explain in simple terms what they were talking about. 'Parliament's a shop of old fools, anyway,' said someone, once. 'We need a young per-son to sort it all out. A fresh vision. Let's hope the young Queen will do it!' And Alfred said he was sure the young Queen *would* do it – and he was quite in love with her already for being *about* to do it. And he lifted Alice upon the piano stool and they all laughed and held up their glasses, toasting *The Young Queen!* until Alice blushed to her very roots.

Alfred adored Alice. He could never praise her enough: *She is so sweet and grave, Dodo. I could not wish for a better or more graceful spirit in the house.* Much as I agreed, the words cut my heart a little as I wondered where my own grace and goodness had disappeared to, that he should admire them so much in her. Then, when she came to comb my hair and I caught sight of us both next to each other in the glass, I could see why: Alice was beautiful and dainty, with a cool, steady gaze – whereas I had become rather fleshy in my face and figure. When I looked at Alice, I could not but wish that I were fifteen again – or even nineteen and able to dance hornpipes around the parlour with a Certain Person until my feet ached.

The truth was that I did not welcome the child I was carrying. It had come too soon. It was changing me into a mother before I had had proper time to be a wife. It was transforming me from a girl into a woman. Sometimes I did not think Alfred liked me so well as a woman. He did not like to see me retch, or sweat, or toil up the stairs with my gown kirtled up and panting with shortness of breath. He would look away and laugh, talking of my *interesting condition* as if I had grown stout of my own accord, as an act of contrariness; as if he had nothing to do with it. Only O'Rourke took my part: *Dodo, you're a grand sight. Like a ship in full sail. Isn't she, Alfred?* And Alfred would say that if I walked into the bedstead one more time, we'd have a shipwreck, *and then, heave-ho me hearties, it'll be hard to get her afloat again!*

Of course, he worried continually about having another mouth to feed, saying he was working flat out as it was, and at this rate he was liable to drop down dead, pen in hand, before the child saw the light of day. I felt he almost blamed me for having allowed it. But what could I have done? 'It's not my fault, Alfred,' I said one day. 'It is the way of life. I couldn't prevent the baby, could I? Unless I prevented you too.' I could not help my voice quivering.

'It is too late, now, anyhow,' he said crossly. 'But perhaps we should use caution in the future.'

'Caution?'

'Well, I cannot afford to keep half London under my roof. Unless I write all day and far into the night. Which I am already damned near to doing.' As if to prove it, he picked up his pen and started to scribble in a furious manner.

'We are only talking of one tiny baby, Alfred.'

'Thin end of the wedge. Soon we'll have dozens of 'em – crawling all over the carpet, cramming themselves into cupboards, climbing the chimneys and lying about under gooseberry bushes. And all demanding silver spoons in their mouths.' He laughed, shortly.

'What can I do?' I asked.

'I don't know! Speak to your mother.' He went on writing.

'My mother! What could I possibly say to her?'

'Then talk to *my* mother, if you prefer.'

'Is it *my* business, then? Do I have to deny you? To deny myself . . .' My efforts to stop crying made me shudder so much I wondered if the baby could feel my distress through my flesh and bones.

Alfred stopped his frantic scribbling, dashed his pen down, and put his head in his hands. Then he rushed over to me and flung himself down at my feet in a movement so sudden that I nearly toppled over. 'I am sorry, Dodo. Please forgive me. I am a man distraught. I have taken on so much. The rent, the furniture, the servants. I am so afraid – in case I lose everything I am striving to build. Everything I – we – might be about to enjoy. I know it is not your fault, but you don't know what poverty can bring people to. You don't know what terrible sights I have seen around me, Dodo. And the children of the poor – such little wretches! Such half-starved, half-clothed wretches! God save us from ever bringing a child to that kind of life!'

I looked down on him with surprise. 'But we are so far from that, Alfred. How could that happen? You will never let us down. You are the One and Only. You will be an even greater success. I am as sure of that as of anything in the world. You have a great gift. Your readers love every word you write.'

His head rested against the unborn child. Tears flowed down his cheeks. 'You are right; I am morbid. I need you to keep me steady. I love you more than anything. When I am cross and peevish, remember that.' He put his hand on my stomach. 'And I love this Little One too. God bless her.'

He always said Kitty would be a girl.

I don't remember much of my confinement, except the pain, and a fat nurse who smelt of liquor when she bent over me to change the sheets. 'You'll be all right, dearie,' she said. 'I've seen many a lying-in and you're a strong 'un, with many more to come in the future, I don't wonder, if we're all spared, that is. But as I says to all my ladies, 'Who knows what the future holds? We are not privy to the secrets of the Lord. We shall know His Mind only at the End,' I says. 'At the Final Trump.' But in the meantime we must make the best of things. Take comfort where we can.' And she swigged at a little bottle she had in her pocket.

'Make her go away,' I asked Alfred when he appeared through the mists at the bottom of the bed, resplendent in a purple waistcoat.

'Who, my love?' he enquired. 'Not our little girl, I hope? Not our little Kitty.'

'Kitty?'

He held up the white swaddled bundle. The baby seemed ugly, with very dark hair; I found it hard to be interested in her. But he seemed delighted; 'She is like a little kitten. All soft and furry with her eyes closed tight.' He brought his head close to hers, and nuzzled her as a woman might.

'But we decided on Mary if it were a girl,' I said faintly. I was almost too tired to care. But we *had* decided on Mary. He couldn't change that.

He bent and put his free arm round my shoulders, bringing the child close. She opened one eye and stared at me. He said, 'But don't you think Mary is such a *very* plain name? And Kitty suits her *so* much better.'

I had no opinion; I could hardly see her. But I nodded my head, and he smiled. So Kitty it was. His entirely. His from the start.

'The midwife,' I said when my next wave of strength came back. 'Make her go. Let me have Alice.'

He frowned. 'Alice cannot manage on her own, dearest. She is too young, too delicate. Now don't be selfish, Dodo. Mrs. Pratt is very experienced. She comes with the best of testimonials from the very best bedsides in London, and will have you up and about in no time.'

I did not want to be up and about. I wanted to lie in bed for ever, not to have to make any effort at all. I started to weep, rolling about on the pillow, not caring how I looked, or who saw me.

'Now, now, you'll feel better when you have a fresh nightgown and your hair done; when you look pretty again. To be honest, my sweet, you do not look your best.'

I screamed at him: 'If I'm a fright, it's your fault – all yours! I never wanted this baby! I don't want her now! Take her away!'

'They gets like this, sir.' Mrs. Pratt pushed her way forward, taking the baby from him. 'It's something that afflicts 'em all, drab or duchess. Hysteria first, then Melancholy. And general hatred of the male person. It's soon over, but I suggest you keeps away for a bit. Let Us As Knows take charge.'

'No.' I clung to him, my eyes on a level with the shiny stuff of his waistcoat. I could see the purple silk was shot with red. It danced in my face. 'I'm sorry, I'm sorry. I didn't mean what I said. Don't leave me, Alfred.'

'I think, dear, maybe I should. You are overwrought. You need to rest. I'll see you tomorrow, when perhaps you will be more your old self. In the meantime, I have a Number to finish. My readers won't thank me if it's not done.'

'You are always thinking of them! More than of me! I hate your readers!'

'They are our bread-and-butter, Dodo. Without them, where would we be?'

Then he peeled my fingers away from his, and kissed me on the forehead. His sweet, fresh smell enveloped me, calmed me a little. 'Well done, Dodo.' He whispered. 'Well done.'

'Are you ready for the light now?' Wilson has come in again with the taper. She thinks it's unnatural to sit in the dark. I'll have to humour her, or she'll interrupt me all night.

'Yes, do,' I say.

'It's not good for you to brood, you know.'

'I'm not brooding.'

'What else do you call it, then? Don't tell me you're not thinking of *him*?' She bends to light the taper and starts to go round the lamps.

'I'm thinking about when Kitty was born.'

'Ah.' She stops a moment, then blows out the taper quickly.

'Do *you* have children, Wilson?' It occurs to me I have never asked her that. All these years and I have never known. But on the other hand, she has never said.

'Yes, madam. Or, rather I *did*. The Good Lord saw fit to take him.'

'Oh. I'm very sorry. Very sorry indeed.' I pause, wondering if I can intrude. 'How old, may I ask?'

'Ten, madam.'

Ten. A little man, almost. 'That must have been hard.'

'Yes, madam. It was. The hardest thing ever.'

'I lost children too, you know.'

'I know.'

Yes. Of course she knows. Everything about us has been public knowledge. He shared our life with them all – his Public – as if they were our intimates; so that Miss Booth and Mr. and Mrs. Smiley think they can write to me as if they know me.

'What was his name?' I look at Wilson again. I see her differently: a young wife, a gentle mother tending her only child.

'David. Mr. Wilson and I called him Davie.'

She has never before mentioned Mr. Wilson, although O'Rourke told me when he hired her that she was *a widow of impeccable credentials*.

'What was it?'

[98]

'The consumption, madam.'

'Yes. My little Ada . . .' I stop. After all these years, I cannot say her name without feeling overcome.

'I know. Mr. Gibson wrote about it so lovingly. It helped Percy and me so much. And when he wrote about little Tom Welby – you remember, the tide going out? And his soul going with it? Well, Mr. Wilson and I read it over and over. It was as good as the Bible, madam.'

'He would have been glad to hear you say that. All he ever wanted was to touch people's hearts.'

'And he did. He was a Great Man.'

'Yes. I thought you felt otherwise, though, Mrs. Wilson.'

'Well, I couldn't help seeing what he did to you. I cannot admire him for that, indeed not. But for his writing . . . yes, that was different.'

I look at her firm, sensible face. 'You knew what had happened between us? Before you came here?'

'Mr. O'Rourke asked if I knew how to keep my counsel. He said, "There is a well-known man and wife who have decided to live apart," he said. "They want it done without scandal. The wife needs a reliable servant. It will be a position of trust with a pension for life, dependent on that trust being unbroken." It was a very good situation and I agreed to the terms immediately. Then I asked if I could be so bold as to enquire who the lady was. And he replied, "It is a Mrs. Gibson." I was so taken aback, it was like a thunderbolt. I asked him if he meant the famous Mrs. Gibson, the wife of Alfred Gibson the great writer? 'Surely not?' I said.'

'You thought it unlikely, then?' I interrupt her.

'I thought it impossible. In fact, I began to wonder if Mr. O'Rourke were not making fun of me. But I could see in a moment he was not. "Why, sir?" I asked. "Surely they have the happiest of lives? What has gone wrong?" And Mr. O'Rourke said, "They cannot be reconciled. Don't ask me any more."'

'So what did you think – in your heart of hearts?' I'm eager to know.

She drops her eyes. 'Well, there's sometimes a lady in these cases, I believe.'

'And did you think there was one in mine?'

'I didn't know what to think. It wasn't my place to speculate.'

'But I'm asking you to speculate.'

'A lady was mentioned. Mr. Gibson mentioned her hisself, as I recall. But only to say it was untrue, and wicked to think so.'

'At the same time that he declared me a bad mother and a worse wife. Two untrue statements together.'

'I couldn't account for it, I admit. Not as how he said it had been going on so long – you being a bad wife and mother, I mean. After all, you'd borne him a child only eighteen months before.'

'Exactly. He could not have found me cold and indifferent then, could he? We'd had our differences, of course – who does not? I know I wasn't the wife he had set his heart on, the ideal woman he wrote about. But family men don't cast off their wives of twenty years because they are not perfect. There is almost always another lady in the case.'

'I don't think you should be telling me this, madam. It's not my business. My business is to look after you. What I think of Mr. Gibson is neither here nor there.'

'I want to know what ordinary people thought. What the great Public thought.'

'They believed him, of course. When he said as he was honourable and had behaved himself, they took it as the Truth.'

'Thank you, Wilson,' I say. She is right. Of course they believed him. Anything else would be out of the question.

'It's cold veal and ham pie for supper, when you're ready,' she says. 'And that mourning silk will be ready for a fitting first thing.'

I have always felt that much of the unhappiness that later arose between Alfred and myself started in some ways with the birth of Kitty. Perhaps the poor girl senses it; and our failure to develop proper mother-and-daughter feelings stems from some barely-understood instinct on her part that I hold her to blame. I do not blame her, of course – any more than I blame Alice for *her* unwitting part in it. Alice was completely innocent of any ill intention, yet when I look back, I wish with all my heart that she had never set her dainty foot in our matrimonial home.

I had so looked forward to having a companion who would approve of Alfred as much as I did, and allow me to talk about him as much as I wanted; so when Alice first arrived at Channon Street with her new cloak and bonnet and three boxes of belongings, I rushed down the stairs and embraced her as heartily as ever sister embraced another. I could not wait to show her the bedroom I had prepared for her, with its Nottingham lace curtains and extensive view over the chimney tops. She was delighted with everything, especially the vase of roses I had placed beside her bed and the two volumes of Sir Walter Scott that Alfred had put out for her perusal. She took them in her hands, trembling with anticipation: 'Oh, he is the best and kindest brother-in-law in the world!'

At first it was delightful. Alice and I were more than pleased to renew our sisterly affection, and Alfred seemed doubly delighted to find *two* young ladies ready to attend to his comfort when he finished work in the evenings. During the day, Alice and I had much opportunity to talk as we stitched the dozens of smocked gowns and tiny caps the new baby would need. We'd sit in the downstairs parlour so I could keep a weather eye on the servants and see to any tradesmen, and laugh about the days – not so far distant – when Alice had acted as our lovers' go-between. 'He used to frighten me, Dodo – in a delicious sort of way. I never knew when he would bob out from behind a bush or jump down from a tree, and what kind of person he would contrive to be when he did! But he was so in love with you, I could not understand why Mama and Papa did not simply shower you with gold and silver and send you off with their blessings!'

I knew why, of course. But I did not want to spoil Alice's innocent enjoyment of what she termed the *most romantic engagement ever* by explaining our parents' doubts and impediments. Alice never seemed to think ill of anybody and could never imagine that other people might not share her pure and charitable view of life.

But as time went on, and Kitty was born, I couldn't help noticing what a very firm favourite Alice had become with Alfred. He always spoke warmly of her, and looked at her with such soft affection whenever she came into a room: *Here she is, the little angel of the house – so quiet and cheerful and modest.* And I could not disagree with him even as I felt the pricking of jealousy within my bosom. Alice had the quick imagination he admired, and she was as eager to learn as Alfred was to teach. He'd lend her his favourite books and she would sit at his elbow and take notes very earnestly while he expounded on Hamlet's madness, or the character of Richard Crookback. They'd sit together for hours while I sat half-dozing in the armchair, listening for Kitty's cry; or pacing about the landings while she lolled red-faced and milky – and determinedly awake – in my arms.

Then he began to ask Alice to sit with him as he wrote, to hold his pens and sharpen his quills, as I had once done. *You know, Dodo,* he said, seemingly unaware of the criticism implicit in his words, *There is no one in the world who can be so still as Alice, no one so unlikely to disturb me with her presence!* And his fondness for her company extended beyond the domestic sphere. While I was obliged to rest at home, he began to take her out for walks and they would return with stories of what they had seen, laughing together as if they had a soul in common. Occasionally he took her to the theatre, saying, *Dodo is too fragile for tragedy, and liable to fall asleep by the second Act and disgrace us!* – and she'd take his arm so proudly, and he'd take hers so gently as they set out in their finery. And I'd think of my trip to Stepney in my blue silk dress and want to weep.

One night, as we undressed for bed, I felt I had to speak. 'You spend a great deal of time with Alice. Anyone would think you preferred her to *me*.'

He paused in the act of unbuttoning his shirt. 'Dodo, have you gone quite out of your mind?'

I said nothing.

'I cannot tell you what a very wicked idea you have allowed yourself to have. Wicked in the extreme.' He spoke in that very low, compelling way he had when acting a part. 'How can you even suggest such a thing? How can you even make such a comparison? Alice is a mere *child* –'

'No, she is not, Alfred. That is precisely the point. She has grown up. You can't play and flirt with her as you used to.'

He stared at me, his expression unreadable. '*Flirt!* What do you mean by that? Do you mean that I joke with her, that I pay her attention, that I admire her good nature and her beauty? I do all those things, I freely admit. But I do it all openly, as a brother would to a sister. Indeed she trusts me as one, and that trust is one of the most dear and precious things I have. How can you even suggest that I would *toy* with her in any way; that I would put her innocence in jeopardy? Alice of all people! Our own dear messenger who was so loyal and trustworthy through all those months of our separation!'

[103]

I felt myself redden with shame. And yet the sickening turmoil inside me had not diminished. I had expressed myself badly, as I always seemed to do when there was something important I wanted to tell him. What I had intended as a simple plea for him to pay me more attention had by some alchemy turned into an accusation against the sister I loved and the man I adored. Had he deliberately misunderstood me? Was there some unspoken fault he was guilty of and needed to defend? 'I don't mean to suggest anything wicked or wrong, Alfred,' I replied. 'It is simply that when I see you with *her*, you seem, well, you seem so happy. And when you are with *me*, you seem impatient. Not so happy.'

'Not so *happy*? How can you say that?'

I shrugged, unwilling to admit the seemingly foolish occasions of my jealousy. 'It's simply a feeling. I am mistaken, of course. I see that now.'

He softened then. He ran his hand through his wayward hair, seeming to reconsider: 'I am, I admit, a little overworked, a little distracted. Since I gave up at Webster's and have to rely on my pen for the whole of our livelihood, I have not given you as much attention as I should. But that you should assume from this that I am *unhappy* – and, moreover, that I am turning my attentions elsewhere – no, you are quite wrong.'

'But you are never too busy for *her*!'

'Alice makes so few demands, Dodo. Do you not see that?' He took both my hands and made me look into his eyes. 'She would fade into the background if we let her. And she so much likes to have books recommended to her, and to talk with me about them and ask my opinion. And I take on such tasks as a loving brother would, as I have done for my own dear Lottie in the past. That cannot be wrong, can it, Dodo? Even *you* must see that.'

I nodded.

'Good. Good. We are in agreement then.' He paused; then a thought seemed to strike him. 'I suppose it's understandable that you are somewhat inclined to strange fancies at the present, with the infant and so many new responsibilities. But never forget that you are my wife, Dodo. And the mother of my darling little Kitty. How could I not be happy with you? You have given me everything a man could want.'

'Have I? Have I, Alfred?' My heart almost burst for love of him.

'Oh, indeed you have. Oh, you silly little pussy, how can you doubt it?' He threw his shirt studs on the dressing-table and came to embrace me, his face full of tenderness.

I began to sob upon his open shirt. 'I *have* doubted it, Alfred. I have felt so ugly and clumsy. I feared that you have fallen out of love with me, and I have been so *very, very* miserable!'

He put his arms round me. 'There is foolish jealousy at work here, Dodo. And there is no reason for it.'

'You do not love Alice more than me, then?'

He stroked my hair. 'How can you even ask that question?'

'But you are *very* fond of her, are you not?'

'Of course I am! She is delightful company. And so gentle and good. Who could not be fond of her?'

'Perhaps you could not show it quite so openly, or with quite so much preference. And be a little nicer to me instead.'

'Am I not nice to you, Dodo?' He began to stroke my neck, my bosom. My heart jumped. It had been many weeks since he'd touched me in that way.

'Sometimes.' I could hardly speak for quivering.

'Only sometimes? Come to bed, Dodo. And I shall be *extremely* nice to you.'

I hesitated. 'What about – ?'

'Oh, I'm a reformed man. I adore babies. Let's have a whole houseful!' He began to undo my nightgown.

I stayed his hand. 'But I don't want to be stout and clumsy again. Not so soon.'

He stopped. 'How are we to manage, then? I am not made of ice. Nor, it seems, are you.'

'Promise you'll go on loving me however I look. Then I shan't care about anything else.'

'Of course I shall!' He laughed, and tickled me so that I laughed too. 'I promise I'll love you even when you are as fat as butter and crotchety as the devil. And imagining things that are not there.' He caught hold of me and pulled me down upon the bed. And I longed for him so much that I put aside any consequences and thought only of how lucky I was to have such a husband.

And indeed, only days after my foolish admission, he looked up over the tea things and announced, 'I've decided we need a nursemaid to help with Kitty. You are with her too much, I can see that. You need more time with other people, more time for enjoying society. Mary Evans was only yesterday asking why you did not come with me to Mr. Marshall's supper in Gough Row. "We hardly see Dorothea," she said. "Is she still unwell?"'

'She thinks me unwell?'

'Well, dearest, I have to say something when you are absent from every gathering. It seems insufficient to say that you are merely 'tired'.'

'You have never had a baby, Alfred, so you don't know how tired it's possible to be.'

'Don't I?' He raised his eyebrows and I realised that Alfred was, of course, quite as tired as I was. Shatteringly tired, with a novel coming out in numbers, and more and more articles in magazines and newspapers, and plans afoot to start a publication of his own. He sometimes fell asleep at his desk and woke up two hours later only to continue where he had left off. He was never at rest. Every day he drove himself with more work, more things to do. But somehow Alfred could transform himself and be fresh as a daisy in seconds, whereas I could only creep around with slow steps and heavy eyes, unable to imagine I'd ever be sociable again. 'You know, our Alfred's a bit of a Puritan where work is concerned,' said O'Rourke, who enjoyed an indolent morning as much as I did, sitting around in the upstairs parlour, talking about nothing in particular. 'If he were in Heaven, he'd be licking God's angels into shape right now.'

Having decided on a nursemaid, Alfred advertised and interviewed in short order; and a young lady called Bessie Jorkins was engaged to help me. She was tall and red-cheeked, and had brought up nine brothers and sisters in Kilburn. Alfred said she was exactly the kind of sensible girl we needed, and in no time she had organised the nursery, and organised Kitty as well. The child had never slept through the night for me, but she slept for Bessie. Every morning by eight, the bedclothes were out airing and Bessie was dressing Kitty ready for her walk in the park. At nine they departed, Kitty all clean and neat in the whitest of garments, and Bessie with her hair scraped back under her cap, and a warm grey cloak over her ample shoulders: 'It's the fresh air what tires them, ma'am. And I'll see she gets plenty! There'll be no more nonsense waking up all hours, I'll see to that!' The house was suddenly quiet from Kitty's mewling, and I could lie down and sleep all morning without interruption. And Alfred could work.

Gradually, I recovered. Alice and I began to go for short walks, and then longer ones; and she'd point out with excitement the inn where Boodles cheated an extra chop out of the melancholy waiter, and the street corner by the ballad-monger's where Mr. Mustard took a pistol to poor Miggs. If it rained, we played bezique and dominoes and she read to me from *The Vicar of Wakefield*, *Tom Jones* or *Northanger Abbey*. We talked about new gowns and bonnets, and planned trips to the theatre for when I was stronger. She was unfailingly kind and good-humoured and said over and over again how lucky she was to be living with her 'dearest sister' and the 'cleverest, most amusing brother in the world'.

'He thinks *we* are fortunate too. He is always praising you to me.'

'Is he? I can't imagine why. I'm so ignorant and tongue-tied.' She looked pleased, however.

'Well, you won't be ignorant for long. With all the education he's giving you, you should soon be able to write your own books. Do you find he's a good teacher?'

'Oh, Dodo, the best – the very best. Time flies past when he's talking. He's so different from Miss Prowse with her dull old verbs and gerunds.'

'And as for being tongue-tied, well – Mr. O'Rourke says that last week you actually spoke to him without being addressed. He was quite astounded.'

She blushed. 'I hope he did not think me forward. He is the kindest man I have ever met. Next to Alfred, of course.'

'He is indeed.' I paused, looking down at my sewing, wondering if I could hint at such a subject. 'He'd make someone a very good husband – now that he is making his way in the City.'

She looked startled. 'I hope you don't mean *me*, Dodo.'

'Well, would that be such a dreadful thought?' I looked up, teasingly. 'Or is there someone else you like better?'

She coloured. 'No, of course not. I'm far too young.'

Having been released from nursery duties, my first venture into society was a soirée at Mr. and Mrs. Hemmings' house in Chelsea. Mr. Hemmings was Alfred's new publisher. O'Rourke told me he had 'pretensions to grandeur', inviting all kinds of up-and-coming people to sup at his expense.

'Who will be there, Alfred? Anyone I am acquainted with?' I asked him as we dressed.

'Mr. Carlyle, the historian, is to be there, I believe, and Mr. Leigh Hunt, the poet, and Miss Amelia Brougham, the heiress,' said Alfred, tying an especially fancy neck-cloth underneath his chin.

'Oh, dear. I shan't know what to say to any of them.' I knew I would be separated from him at supper and that I would be forced to make my own conversation with these impressive strangers. In my anxiety I dropped my necklace and Alfred had to retrieve it from under the bedstead.

'The trick is to make *them* talk. Persuade Mr. Carlyle into talking about the French Revolution, or Miss Brougham on the need for charities among the poor. Then sit back and smile your beautiful smile.' He fixed the pearls around my neck with a flourish. 'There!'

I laughed. 'I don't believe it is that easy, Alfred. They may ask me questions, then I'll have to say *something* or they will think me a simpleton.'

'Ask them what *they* think is the best answer. They'll be too flattered to notice you haven't said a word. In fact they'll consider you the queen of conversationalists!'

I was surprised to find that Alfred was right. Luckily I did not have to speak to Mr. Carlyle, sitting sternly across the table behind a mass of glass and flowers. But Mr. Hunt was most amusing, and never at a loss for words, talking mainly, I have to say, about himself, and helping himself liberally to wine. Miss Brougham, addressing me across the corner of the table, was more serious. 'I must speak to your husband about my plans, Mrs. Gibson,' she said. 'I feel he is the kind of man who could give me disinterested advice.'

'What kind of plans, Miss Brougham?' I murmured, thinking she was dressed very plainly for an heiress. And she spoke plainly too, slowly and distinctly in the way of a schoolmistress, nodding her head for emphasis. 'I want to know how best to ameliorate the effects of poverty and disease among the working classes,' she said. 'It is shocking, is it not, Mrs. Gibson, that so many babies die before they are a year old? And so many young women turn in desperation from the right path? And so many fit men have no work? And so many families have nowhere to lay their heads at night? And that cholera stalks the streets?'

'Oh, yes! Indeed it is.' I'd heard the men talk, of course, Alfred in particular becoming very heated and angry about iniquities and injustices. And of course it was dreadful to think of all those hundreds of poor people.

'You see, Mrs. Gibson, I am fortunately endowed with more wealth than I need or could possibly spend. I wish to see it put to good use. Wide use. Efficient use.'

'Indeed. And my husband?'

'What better adviser than the author of *Miggs' Tales* and *Little Amy?* And *this*, too —'

She fished a piece of paper out of her reticule. It was a newspaper article: 'Why the Poor Law is an Ass'. It was signed 'Alfred Gibson'. I had never seen it before.

'I am sure he would be happy to help.' I looked up and caught his eye across the table. He was next-but-one to Mr. Carlyle, and had succeeded in making him laugh most heartily, so that he banged the table with his fork. The young lady who sat between them was apoplectic with mirth, and Alfred was doing things with a handkerchief and a glass of water that was making her laugh the more.

Miss Brougham's eye followed mine. I felt disconcerted. 'My husband is a great humourist,' I said. 'But that does not mean he is not serious at heart.'

'I am aware of that.' Miss Brougham smiled. 'He does not need defending.'

My memories of that night are burned into my mind. Not only because it was my first foray into company since Kitty's birth, but because of what happened afterwards. We did not stay late at the Hemmings'; I was still liable to become tired, and after only a half-hour in the drawing room, we took our leave, with much regret from the assembled company. Miss Brougham extracted a promise from Alfred to come and see her in Albemarle Street, and Mr. Carlyle and Mr. Hunt begged him to join them for lunch at their respective clubs. But while we waited for the carriage, Alfred suddenly became agitated.

'There is something amiss,' he said.

'What do you mean? How do you know?'

'We must get home as soon as possible.'

'Is it Kitty?' My heart was in my mouth. 'I should never have left her.'

'I don't know. I know only that something is wrong.' His face was rigid as iron.

He pushed me into the carriage and told the driver to put on all speed. We rattled crazily through the streets, and I longed to know the reason for his fear, but Alfred was so white-faced that I dared not speak further. As we turned into Channon Street, we saw the front door open, and Grace the kitchen maid standing on lookout. As we drew up, Bessie came running out, pale as paper. Alfred flung open the carriage door and was out in a trice, running past her up the stairs, a man possessed.

'Is it Kitty?' I cried, as I climbed down clumsily, catching my skirt on the carriage steps in my haste and ripping a long piece from the hem. I had to stop and tear it further to free myself, but I was so agitated, and my hands were trembling so much, I could hardly do it.

'No, ma'am,' said Bessie, breathlessly, as she stooped to help me. 'It's not the babby; it's Miss Alice.'

I have to admit to a moment of blessed relief that it was not my child who was the cause of the alarm, before the immediate renewal of anguish in knowing it was instead my sister. I took

Bessie by the arm as we hastened to the door: 'What's happened to her?'

'We don't know, ma'am. She went all pale and shaking. It's a seizure, we think. Joe's run for a doctor. We was looking out for him when you come. We sent a message to Chelsea too.'

I mounted the stairs to Alice's bedroom. Each step of the two flights felt like the side of a mountain. My heart was nearly bursting as I paused for breath at the top. The door of her room was open. He was sitting on the bedstead with his arms locked around her. Her head was drooping on his breast, her eyes were closed, her face was colourless. I stood by the door, panting. He made no acknowledgement of my presence, but held her as if she were a baby, repeating her name, over and over. Then a great shaking sob came from him, so violent that it went through his entire body, and by necessity through hers: 'Oh, my darling girl! Please don't leave me. I can't do without you!'

I stood there motionless. I thought I would faint – but whether it was at Alice's dead pallor or Alfred's groaning despair, I cannot say. Then there was a commotion downstairs. Footsteps coming up: a greatcoat, a leather bag, a smell of whisky, the doctor trying to attend to Alice, Alfred refusing to let go his hold on her. And all the time this dull pain, this terrible despair, these words echoing in my head: *My darling girl. I can't do without you!*

'Look, man, I must examine her.'

'She is gone. Leave her. You can do nothing for her now.'

'That's for me to decide, I believe.' The doctor lifted her eyelids and looked at her eyes, holding her wrist – so insubstantial it looked now – and waited. He frowned and shook his head slowly in my direction and I felt a terrible sense of disbelief. Then he took an instrument from his bag and attempted to look in her mouth.

It was too much for Alfred. He thrust the doctor's hand away in a fury: 'Enough, damnit! Leave her alone!'

'Come, sir! This is beyond sense. Not much point in calling a medical man unless you let him do his business. I need to certify the cause of death. I need to be satisfied.'

Alfred did not budge.

The doctor turned to me: 'The servants said the fit was sudden, ma'am. Did the young lady have a fever? Did she choke? Did she complain of pain?'

I shook my head. 'No, never. She was always well. She was well when we left her.'

'No history of fits, then? I need to be satisfied, or I'll have to refer the case to the Coroner.'

'No, she mustn't be mauled over.' Alfred's voice was thick with grief. 'You heard what the servants said. It was a seizure. Write that down. Seizure. *Seizure.* One word, that's all. I'll pay you five guineas, ten if you like. Do it, and leave your bill. Is that understood?'

The doctor paused, then, meeting Alfred's implacable look, said, 'I suppose the case seems straightforward enough.' And he turned and went down the stairs. Minutes later I heard the door bang. Alice continued to lie motionless in Alfred's arms.

I approached the bed tentatively. 'You should have let him —'

'What could *he* say that would make any difference?' He lifted Alice slightly, so her face was close to his. Tears poured down his cheeks, wetting hers in turn, so it looked as though she were crying, too. 'Oh, Dodo, she was everything to me.'

How could he say such a thing? To me, his wife? I told myself he could not mean it, that he was so shocked he did not know what he was saying. Yet as I watched him rock her in his arms, I knew he was never more serious in his life. It was as if I were watching a terrible living tableau of all my worst fears. I had to clench my teeth together to stop myself shaking. In desperation, I put my hand out to him. He did not take it; in fact I doubt he saw it, he was holding her so passionately. After a while he murmured thickly, 'Leave me with her. Leave me.'

I had to obey him, although it didn't seem right. I kept hearing his voice in my head: *My darling. I can't do without you.* Bessie and Grace were standing on the stairs, clasping their aprons to their faces. 'She's gone,' I said, forcing my voice out surprisingly loud. 'She's at peace.'

They both nodded, then started to cry. 'God bless her, she were such a good young lady,' said Bessie, wiping her eyes on her apron. 'Always so kind and helpful. I can't believe it, mum. I swear to God she were fine until nine o'clock. Then she said she felt faint and we – Grace and me – thought she had caught a fever walking out in the rain yesterday. She said she'd go and lie down, and I said that would be a good idea and I went to see to Kitty – not thinking nothing, mum.'

'And I goes down to see as Joe had done the boots proper, and to lock up the back door,' said Grace. 'And I'd that moment done it and cleaned round the sink and put away the dishes when Bessie comes running, saying Miss Alice has fell off the bed and can't talk . . .'

'And I send Joe to the Scotch doctor I knows round the corner –'

'And I gets a boy to take a message to you in Clarendon Terrace –'

'And I goes back to her and tries to get her back on the bed, but she's a dead weight and I can't lift her –'

'And I comes up and we both lift her, and try to get her to open her eyes. But she can't do it. Her eyelids are flickering, like moths. And I says she's too good for this world; that the Good Lord will take her –'

'Stop! Please stop.'

They stop, and look at each other. 'It's not our fault, mum. We did all we could.'

'Yes, I'm sure you did. You weren't to know.'

'The Master's taking it bad, isn't he?' Bessie indicated the sobbing coming through the bedroom door.

'He cannot bear to think of the death of a young person.'

'None of us do, mum. Although Miss Alice was pretty much grown.'

'Yes, but she was still a child to him.'

'It's being a writer isn't it, mum? That makes him feel things different?'

That must be it, I told myself. 'Yes, Bessie, that's why we shall all need to be very patient with him. Very calm and very quiet. Now go to bed and tomorrow we'll see what must be done.'

They went up to the attic, crying and whispering. 'It's *her* sister though, isn't it?' I heard Grace say. 'I shouldn't like it if my husband were carrying on like that, writer or no writer.'

I didn't know what to do. I sat on the stairs for a long time, looking at the jagged tear along the hem of my gown, and trying to put aside all thoughts of anger and envy, to think of the pity of it instead. Alice was dead: she would never see womanhood, or marriage or children. How mean and petty I had been to resent the brief moments of joy that Alfred had given her; the amusements he had afforded her; the glimpses he had given her of how it felt to be loved by a good, true man! And now, as if to serve me right, she was taken from me, and I would never talk with her again, or see her sweet face, or be the recipient of one of her many acts of kindness. I wanted to weep, to beg her forgiveness – but no tears came. In their stead was a kind of numbness, as the image of Alfred holding her tight forced itself upon me, over and over again: *My darling girl.*

A long time seemed to pass, and I began to wonder what was happening on the other side of the door. I got up and listened. No sound. So I seized the knob noisily and went in. He was on his knees at the bedside and Alice was lying on the counterpane. He had arranged her pretty silk gown so it spread out each side of her; and he'd loosened her hair and crossed her hands over her breast. He'd made her look exactly like an angel, and my heart nearly burst.

'Oh, Dodo, help me.' He held out his hand. And in the midst of my grief, my spirits rose to think he still needed me, and I went to him more gladly than I can say. His hand felt chill and trembling as he pulled me down next to the bed. We both knelt, side by side, my sister above us, as if we were worshipping her. As I gazed on her innocent, childish form, tears pricked the back of my eyes; and I felt my anguish reaching out and mingling with his. 'She was so very young and pure,' he said. 'I cannot endure it.' But as I gripped his hand, I felt something in his fingers. It was a lock of her hair, grasped tight.

'We both have to endure it, Alfred. It's hard for me, too. After all, I hardly thought to see my own little sister dead before me.'

'*Before* you?' He clutched me suddenly, his eyes almost starting from his head. '*You* won't die, will you, Dodo? *You* won't leave me on my own?'

I am ashamed to admit that, even in the midst of my sorrow. I felt a kind of joy. I embraced his shaking form with all my strength. 'I'll *never* leave you, Alfred.'

'You are a good wife.' And we embraced again, and I loved him so much at that moment that I resolved, as God was my witness, never to be jealous again.

Even as we knelt with our arms around each other, Kitty began to wail in the distance; and Alfred looked up, his face blank: 'What's that?' As if he had no recollection of her existence.

'It's Kitty,' I said hurriedly. 'Bessie will see to her. But we cannot stay here like this, Alfred dear. We must send to my parents. We must get in the woman to lay her out. We must call for the undertaker. And we must order some crape.'

'Crape?' A look of horror. 'No. Not for Alice. I absolutely forbid it. I want her buried in white with flowers all around her.'

I stared at him. He looked as if poised to drop senseless at the slightest opposition. So I kissed his forehead: 'Whatever you say, Alfred.'

[116]

He let go my hand, and taking Alice's curling strands of chestnut hair, he put his lips to them before placing them carefully in his watch case. His hand shook, and he could hardly do it. But as he struggled, I couldn't help noticing he was wearing her ring on his little finger.

'You have taken her ring, Alfred?'

'Yes. I shall wear it as long as I live.'

'That is so beautifully devoted of you,' I said, my voice trembling with the effort not to censure him. 'But don't you think Mama may want the ring herself? Or perhaps *I* should like it.'

'Your mother? No. I am sure she will not begrudge it me. And I know *you* would not, Dodo dear.'

I could see then that he was the tragic hero and Alice was the dead heroine, and I was simply standing in the wings. I knew at that moment it was useless to speak of my own grief. I knew it was in vain to hope that he would wipe my tears and cherish me and tell me I was not to blame; that my jealousy was not the cause; that Alice's death was not my punishment for having evil thoughts. I knew he did not see my anguish in the outpouring of his own. I could feel his massive grief filling the house, spilling out into the night. And I knew it would spill for ever into his books.

'*Miss* Walters is here.' Wilson announces the dressmaker. I can see her in the passageway outside. She is carrying a great parcel of cloth.

'Have her come in.'

Miss Walters is as thin as I am fat. She looks as if she could be blown down by the slightest breeze. But she is an excellent needle-woman and has made my clothes for many years.

'Good morning, ma'am. May I offer my heartfelt —'

'Yes. That is understood.' I hate speaking of my grief to strangers.

'But it was a most exceptionally fine funeral, was it not? All those hundreds of people. Thousands, perhaps, would you say?' She spreads her wares on the bed and unwraps them as she talks. I suppose she has a professional interest in funereal occasions. Per-haps she does not realise I was not present. Although she must wonder why I am ordering mourning attire so late.

'Thousands, indeed. But I am against ostentation in the matter of death. Indeed, I do not really approve of wearing black. It was Mr. Gibson's view, too.'

Miss Walters is astonished, although she tries to hide the fact. 'I see,' she says, although she clearly does not.

'However, I am bidden to meet the Queen, and must look the part.'

I watch for her response, and am rewarded. She looks up, eyes wide: 'The *Queen*, ma'am?'

'Yes. Tomorrow morning. So I am relying on you to have it ready in time.'

'Oh, indeed, have no fear. We'll have it ready even if the girl has to stay up all night. Now, Mrs. Gibson, do we need to be measured again?' She surveys me as if I were a building. 'Maybe the waist and bust. And the arms.' Her tape measure is out in a trice, and she is encircling my girth, bending my elbow, turning me round as if I were a humming top and jotting down numbers in the notepad that hangs from her waist. 'A *fraction* more since last time. But I have allowed for that.' She picks up a bodice, a sleeve, a yoke, places them against me, patting, pinning.

'I want it very plain.'

'No crape panels?'

'No crape at all.'

'No borders? No bands?'

'None.'

She is silent. I know what she thinks; that I show insufficient respect. Especially for one who is to see the Queen of England. But I shall only go as far as is necessary. I stand patient under her ministrations for ten minutes. The gown takes shape on me, tacked together with Miss Walters' fine tacking thread by Miss Walters' bony, pin-pricked fingers.

'How about a corded edge? Or some frogging? To give a little shape?'

She does not say that I have no shape, but I know what she means, and I have enough vanity to care. I don't want the flunkeys at the Palace to think I'm a fright. I give in. I've already compromised my position after all. 'Very well, Miss Walters. Edging cord and frogging. Nothing else.'

She makes a note, then gently removes all the pieces. Back they go into her brown paper parcel, along with her measure, her pincushion and her piece of chalk.

'As it's so plain, we should have it done for this afternoon. I'll send the boy with it before six.'

'Thank you. I appreciate your promptness.'

'Well, it's always short notice when it comes to mourning.' She purses her lips tight. 'Most people like to have it the same day.'

She bows and leaves the room in her quick, business-like way.

⚙

Of course I remember that same-day haste. The moment a death was announced, the hurry to get into black, the sudden transition from colour to gloom, the draping of the looking-glasses, the drawing down of the blinds. Although my parents were not strict in these matters, all three of us girls were in half-mourning for months when Grandmama Millar died. How I hated the horrible smell of the dye, the heaviness of the fabric – and how glad I was that we did not come from a large family! Some girls I knew seemed never to be out of black, as uncles, aunts, cousins, sisters and brothers all passed away in succession.

Although I had never seen Alfred in other than vivid colours, it had never occurred to me that he would not wear mourning for Alice. When he announced he had no such intention, I was shocked. But he was so adamant about the preposterousness of it all, and so eloquent about his reasons for breaching the 'hideous custom', that I decided to fall in with his wishes. I did not anticipate the dreadful scene that would arise on account of it only the day after Alice's death.

Mama had not noticed my lack of mourning at first. She and Papa had been too blurred with tears, too distracted with the shock of it all, as they crowded into the narrow hallway and climbed the stairs to Alice's room. And later, when we retired to the drawing room with its blinds down against the world, she'd seemed too exhausted to speak, lying back against the sofa cushions and closing her eyes. I did the same, my head aching and my ribs sore with weeping. Poor Sissy, conscious of the need to maintain decorum, but bored with the silence and stillness of the room, crept up and sat next to me, leaning her head against my chest and kicking her

[120]

legs against the edge of the Chesterfield – Alice's once-favourite doll dangling unheeded from her hand. As she did so, I was filled with the most awful grief to think that we three sisters would never again embrace each other, or share delightful sisterly secrets, and I suspected that, in her own way, Sissy was feeling the same. I hugged her close: 'Dear, dear Sissy! Don't fret, I'm still here.'

And she put her hard, thin arm through mine. 'Sing to me,' she whispered. 'Sing as you used to when you put us to bed.'

Our whispers drew my mother's attention. She opened her eyes, and as they lit on me, she was suddenly struck by my appearance. 'Is your mourning dress not ready, Dodo?' she said with some puzzlement. She and Sissy were, of course, already shrouded in black. Even the wretched doll was rigged out in sable satin.

I felt as though I had violated the family's grief by appearing before them in my light-coloured gown, but I answered boldly: 'I shan't be wearing mourning, Mama. Alfred disapproves.'

'*Disapproves?*'

'Yes. He thinks it a repulsive habit.'

She was silent. Shocked. Uncomprehending. 'Where does he get such ideas? It's a lot of foolish nonsense. It's all those *Radical* people he spends his time with – when he should be at home with his wife and child. Mourning is simply a mark of respect. Respect for our dear dead girl.' She leapt up and caught my hand, tears starting to her eyes once more. 'Oh, Dodo, I hope you will not turn your heart away from her memory!'

'Mama, you know I will not.' I started to cry again too. 'You know I loved Alice as dearly as any sister could.' But when I looked down at my gown with its cheerful pattern of leaves and flowers, I almost faltered in my determination. 'But I think Alfred is right, Mama. I think you should respect the Departed in other, more truthful, ways.'

'*More truthful?*' She rounded on me. 'Are you saying that Papa and I are *un*truthful in our observations of respect? Your poor dear father is consumed with the most dreadful grief. He has been hardly able to articulate a word, as well you know.'

I did know, of course. I had seen his face when he first saw her corpse, and had felt the thudding of his heart as he'd held me in his silent embrace. 'Oh, Mama, I am not blaming anyone. It is simply that −' I struggled to remember how Alfred had represented it to me '− it is simply Alice's *life* that we must think of, not her death. It is her sweetness, her goodness, her patience. When you see what lovely hymns Alfred has chosen, and what a fine inscription he has written for her headstone −'

'*Alfred's* been choosing hymns and inscriptions? *Alfred?*' She stared at me, aghast. 'I'm afraid, Dodo, but this is beyond anything. Alice is *our* daughter. Papa and I shall bury her how *we* wish. Alfred may be clever with words, and have half of fashionable London at his feet − but he has no say in this particular matter.' She got up to go, pulling a reluctant Sissy by the arm.

I was startled. When presented in that way, Alfred's actions did seem somewhat improper. But Mama did not understand him as I did. She had taken my innocent words of admiration and transformed them into words of blame. I felt a hot flush pulse through my veins. I loved my mother − never more than then, when we shared this terrible grief. Yet I could not let her speak of Alfred in that belittling way. I clasped her arm: 'Oh, but Mama, he is so *very* affected. You have no idea. Don't forget that Alice died in his arms; in his *arms*, Mama. The shock was dreadful; he is inconsolable.'

She gave me a sharp look. 'No married man has the right to be *inconsolable* over his sisterinlaw. What has been going on in this house, Dodo?'

I felt my colour rise the more. 'Nothing at all, Mama. Nothing wrong, at any rate.' How I longed for Alfred's facility with words! How I longed for him to be there with me to explain to her how chaste and honourable his affection was. But he was locked in his study and would let no one in.

'Indeed, I hope not.' She looked at me fiercely. 'I trusted you with her, Dodo. I trusted you to look after her. I never expected to come to your house and find her dead.'

'Nor did we!' I cried in a passion. 'Nor did we! We looked after her as well as could be. If only you had seen Alfred with her; how he always made sure she had something to do, or someone to talk to. Nobody could have been more careful of her – nobody! If you want to blame someone, blame *me*! Perhaps I over-burdened her without knowing – made her stay up too late or walk too far in the rain. But, Mama, please believe me, she was entirely well when we left home. She told us she was going upstairs to read the new book that Alfred had given her. She even stood on the doorstep and waved us off with that lovely smile of hers.' I started to cry as I remembered it all. 'Oh, Mama, don't you think I *wish and wish* I'd stayed at home? Don't you think I've wondered over and over again whether it might have been different had we been here?'

'I understand Alfred turned the Scotch doctor away. Why was that?'

'He didn't turn him away. She had already left us, Mama; Alfred simply didn't want her touched.'

'I should have liked her properly examined. By someone I trust – not some half-drunk incompetent willing to cover matters up for a guinea or two.'

'Cover matters up? What are you saying, Mama? *What are you saying?*'

'I wish to know –' She cast a look at Sissy, who was listening to everything with wide eyes, and stopped.

I realised she was overwrought and casting round for someone to blame, so I tried to hold on to the simple truth: 'She had a seizure, Mama. The servants saw it happen. That is all. What else could it be?'

'You take his side very stoutly, Dodo.'

'There are no 'sides', Mama! Alfred loved and respected Alice. He would never have done her the slightest harm. I can swear to that on my baby's life.'

She shook her head. 'You were always a trusting child, Dodo. Always ready to see the best in people. But there is wickedness, too, you know. Especially in men.'

I could hardly believe that she was saying this. 'But not between Alfred and Alice,' I cried. 'She was like his sister – or even his child.'

'He has his *own* child!' she snapped. 'Why did he want *mine*?'

The door burst open and Alfred stood there. Very pale, very dishevelled – and as angry as I have ever seen him. 'Is there no respect for the darling girl lying in the chamber above us? Why are voices raised?' He glared at us both.

'I understand, Alfred, that you have taken it upon yourself to choose hymns and inscriptions for Alice. Don't you think such things are best left to those closest to her?' Mama spoke quietly now. I could see she was frightened of his demented look.

'I want the best for her, that is all. The very best. Whatever I can afford – and more. But I shall do nothing either you or Mr. Millar disapprove of.'

'Well, we disapprove of these gaudy outfits, for one thing. I should like *Dodo* to show respect, even if you don't.'

'Respect!' He ran his hand through his hair and began to pace the room, throwing wild looks at me and Mama. 'Mrs. Millar, please do not believe I have anything but the greatest respect for Alice. A miserable paid Mute can wear black and drape himself in crape, snivelling into his handkerchief to order. But I am grieving for Alice in my *heart* – in the very depths of my heart! I am missing her presence every minute, every second. Her image is stamped on my heart for ever. She will always be with me, light and bright and lovely.' Tears ran down his cheeks afresh, and he bit his lip and turned away. 'Dodo can dress as she wishes. She is a free agent.'

Of course I was not entirely free. Caught between Alfred's wishes and my parents' disapproval, I compromised. I knew my feelings for my sister could not be measured by the yardage of crape I draped about my body, but there was a fitness in the traditional way of things that I respected. So, when the funeral came, I wore sober clothes and tied up my bonnet with a black ribbon. Alfred wore only an armband over his checked coat. The rest of the family were layered deep in black. The funeral was in other ways just as Alfred wanted it. Faced with his implacable grief, and the power of his will, my family agreed to his arrange, ments. My father was too ravaged to argue the case. 'In the end,' he said 'a funeral is a funeral. Let us not fall out with one another over details and so forth.' So Alice's coffin was draped in white, as Alfred had wanted, and the hearse was decked in wild flowers, as for a country wedding. The grave was newly-dug at Alfred's expense. No one else had lain there before, he said, and no one else should do so afterwards – unless, one day, it was him. For the headstone, he'd taken a line from Byron: *Snatched away in Beauty's Bloom – Alice Millar, aged fifteen.*

Alfred could not watch the coffin as it was taken down from her room, down the steep stairs to the street. But when we went down after it, he took a sprig of forget-me-not from the piled flowers on the hearse, and put it in his buttonhole with a kiss. We held hands tightly all the way to Chiswick, and his grip was so strong I thought I might cry out in pain. Then we walked in silence from my parents' house to the church where we had all worshipped for so many years.

I don't remember the service. All I was aware of was Alfred's ashen look. I did not go to the graveside, but Cousin George said he'd had to support Alfred as if he had been a sack of bones. 'I really thought he might jump in to join her. I have never seen a man shake so dreadfully with grief.' It was raining, and all the men came back with their hair streaming from standing uncovered.

Alfred's face was so wet, I could not tell which were tears and which was rain. That night he held me as desperately as if he thought *I* would die too.

'Do you believe in Heaven?' he asked, as we lay in the dark. 'Do you think we shall all truly meet again, Dodo? That all pain and suffering will be over?'

'I believe so, Alfred.' I knew only this answer would satisfy him, and for the first time that week he smiled.

'God bless you, Dodo. God bless you for ever.'

⚜

In the days that followed, although he went to his study every morning, he did no work. O'Rourke came and tried to reason with him; but he became agitated, and O'Rourke said he feared for his sanity. Lottie was summoned and tried to recall him to his normal spirits, but even she failed. 'If Fred is fixed on something, no one can deflect him,' she said. 'You will have to let him be, Dodo. He will come round in time. It is not in his nature to be sad for long.'

More days went past, and Mr. Hemmings sent word that the deadline for his monthly manuscript was fast approaching. Alfred sent back to say that he was very sorry but it would have to be missed; that he was not fit to think, let alone write. I feared that maybe he would never write again; that we would fall into debt and have to move out of Channon Street, and take poorer and poorer lodgings until we were back with Mrs. Quinn, only this time with two babies, and no means of supporting them. I began to understand his fear of the Fleet Prison, the Foundling Hospital, the Workhouse. I determined I would economise. I would give notice to Bessie. I would look after Kitty myself.

The morning after I decided this, I woke to find him gone, the pillow cold. I put on my dressing gown and crept down to the next floor. The study door was shut fast, but I imagined I could hear the scratch of a quill and the rustle of paper. I went back upstairs and dressed quickly, and took my breakfast in the drawing room so I could be ready to attend to him at a moment's notice. I occupied myself by embroidering pansies on the velvet slippers Alice had begun to make for him, continuing from where she had left off. It encouraged me to know that I still had my old accomplishment, even though Alfred would never notice or praise me for it. I stitched for a long time, thinking of them both; of that agonised cry: *My darling girl. I can't do without you!*

There was no sound from the study, except the occasional scrape of a chair, the faint tread of his footsteps as far as the window and back. Then I heard the front door bang and Bessie and Kitty return from their walk in the park. Kitty started to wake up and cry at being no longer on the move. I rose to tell Bessie to keep the child below stairs, but as I got to the landing, the study door flew open and Alfred shot out, pen in hand. He bent over the banister: 'Is that my favourite daughter exercising her lungs in the stairwell? Bring her up, Bessie! Let the dog see the rabbit!'

'She wants feeding, sir,' said Bessie from below. 'I doubt she'll settle till she's got some bread and milk in her.'

'Go and get it then, Bessie. Meantime, give the child to me!' He charged downstairs with his old enthusiasm, and came up again with Kitty in his arms. He caught sight of me at the drawing-room door, and smiled delightedly: 'Look, Dodo. See how she knows her Papa. See how she is transfixed by the Great Original, the One and Only.' Indeed Kitty was mesmerised by his face, with its big dark eyes, its shining features. She stared at him silently. Then, as he made faces at her – a whole panoply of contortions, eyebrows, mouth, chin – she began to laugh. And he laughed too; and I laughed, and a gurgle of happiness rose in me that things, after all, would be all right.

※

I didn't dare tell him I was with child again. I hoped that maybe I was mistaken, that the shock of Alice's death might have disturbed my functions. But in my heart I knew. How I wished I had sought advice earlier! Or that Alfred had. There was no possibility of approaching Mama now. She had decided Alfred was in some way at fault for Alice's death, and that my loyalty to him compromised me too. If it had not been for Sissy clinging so desperately to me, I truly believe she would have banished me from Chiswick altogether.

'You may come and see your sister whenever you wish,' she'd said to me one day after the funeral, as we sat watching Sissy – normally so active – lay out a game of patience at the card-table, her bright golden hair at odds with the dry, dark stuff of her gown, her normal high spirits subdued. 'She has already lost one sister; I would not have her lose two. You may sit with her here or take her for walks along the river. Alfred may visit *in your company*. But I can never – *will* never – let her loose in your household.'

I could hardly contain myself. 'You speak as if I am not to be trusted!'

'*You* may be, Dodo. But that husband of yours makes up his own rules of decorum.'

'You liked it in him once,' I ventured. 'That he was lively and didn't hold to convention.'

She seemed to colour a little. 'When he was a single young man it was excusable – attractive even. But he has responsibilities now.'

'And he discharges them, Mama. We have a fine house, and servants, and all our bills are paid.'

'That is not the only measure of reliability.' She held my hands, looked in my eyes. 'Is he – good – to you, Dodo?'

'Of course he is good to me,' I retorted. 'He is excellent to me. I am the happiest wife in the world.'

And I would have been, had not the prospect of the expected infant weighed upon my mind in the most dreadful way. I longed to share my disquiet with someone who would understand how little I wanted a second child now, and how much I wished to be able to prevent more. But I could think of no one to confide in. The only married lady of my acquaintance was Mary Evans, but I did not know her well enough to discuss such an intimate matter. Suddenly it came to me: Lottie. She seemed to know so much about the ways of the world; she would help me if it were in her power. I determined to try her out on her next visit.

When she came, however, *I* was the one to be taken by surprise. 'Well, Dodo, congratulate me! I am to be married,' she announced, embracing me warmly as soon as she entered the drawing room.

I was taken aback. I had heard nothing of a prospective lover. 'This is such a surprise!'

'Is it? Surely not! I've known Tom such a long time. And so has Fred. Since the old days in Camden, in fact. Tom does not like society, though. He is rather reserved and doesn't wish to impose on Alfred's company now that he is famous. And his parents – the dearest couple – are not in good health and he is much occupied with them.' A shade fell across her face.

'I am sorry to hear that. But tell me about Tom: is he worthy of you? Is he handsome? And tall? And clever? And rich?'

She laughed. 'Tom is good and kind and – in short – every-thing I could wish. But he only has what he can earn by the sweat of his brow, like Alfred – except Tom has less idea of money than any man alive.'

'Oh, is he a writer too?'

'Bless you, no! He teaches the flute to young ladies. And when he is not teaching he repairs every kind of musical instrument. His front parlour is so full of old fiddles and frets that there is hardly anywhere to sit. And the dear man charges next to nothing.'

'That does not sound very commercial, Lottie!' I said, wonder-ing how their romance had flourished under such ill conditions.

'That's what Fred says. He says, 'You must take him in hand, Lottie, as you did with our esteemed Papa.' I have tried, Dodo, but somehow I could not make Tom more business-like without making him less himself; and although that is very admirable, I had begun to think we would wait for ever to be able to marry. But thanks to Fred's generosity, it's now possible.'

'Alfred has given you money? Oh, I am so glad.' (I had been about to suggest he did that very thing.)

'My dear Dodo, don't tell me you didn't know? Fred is a bad boy to keep secrets from his wife. I will tell him so. Indeed I will.' She got up as if she would admonish him immediately.

I caught her arm. 'Oh, please do no such thing. Alfred is still so – delicate – since Alice passed away. I do not think he could cope with the slightest scolding. Even from his *favourite* sister.'

She laughed. 'Very well, as you ask me, Dodo, I shall simply tell him *my* news. But I think you are to be congratulated too, are you not?'

I blushed. 'What do you mean?'

She scanned my face. 'You are expecting another child; tell me I'm right.'

'Sshh. Alfred doesn't know.'

'What is it that I don't know?' Alfred emerged eagerly from his study, pen in hand. 'Hallo, Lottie dear.' He bent to kiss her. 'Well?'

She and I exchanged glances.

'That I am to be married!' cried Lottie. 'Thanks to you, Tom is able to see his way forward, and has at last been convinced that he will not be dragging me down to a life of misery by offering me his hand. He's found a shop with such a commodious set of rooms above it that his parents can move in with us straight away. I can cook and care for everyone – and we'll all be perfectly snug.'

'Capital! Capital!' Alfred beamed. He loved making people happy. 'Let's have some char! A toast to Tom and Lottie!'

I rose to pull the bell, but Alfred had already done so. He was walking around the drawing room, now, waving his quill, jotting things on his hand. 'We must have a splendid dinner to honour the occasion. Lottie will bring Tom and the aged parents, and we'll invite O'Rourke, the Evanses and Miss Brougham. A splendid eightsome! How about next week – Tuesday, say? I shall order a rib of beef from the butcher, and Dodo shall make her very finest custard tart.'

The thought of custard tart made me feel ill, but I took deep breaths, and the sensation disappeared. Alfred talked on about oysters and asparagus, parsnips, roasted potatoes, and horseradish sauce, and above all, his favourite, cheese on toast. 'We shall use our new dining-table – and the Venetian glass flower-holders I sent for only last week. It'll be capital!'

For once, I wanted him to leave the room so I could speak to Lottie in confidence. But perversely he seemed in the vein for company, complaining *I am run ragged by this Boy of mine.* (He was writing *Edward Cleverly.*) When Bessie came up with the tea, he immediately took the tray and asked her to bring Kitty to entertain the company. 'My daughter comes on in leaps and bounds, Lottie. She has four teeth now. She can take a man's finger off in one bite. Wait till you have children of your own – you'll find they are cannibals of the worst order!'

'Kitty is a delightful child. I won't hear a word against her. After all, I am her godmother-in-chief.' Lottie's dark eyes danced.

'So you give her the gift of love, do you?' He put his pen sideways in his mouth, poured three cups of tea with a flourish.

'It's all I have. But it's the best, after all.'

'And here is the Infant Phenomenon herself!' Alfred sped to the door where Bessie was holding Kitty out to him. He took her and held her aloft over his head. She screamed with excitement; that high-pitched scream that pierces the brain. 'My heart positively bursts with love for her, Lottie! I dote on her more than anyone in the world.'

'Except Dodo, of course,' added Lottie.

'Aha! Of course.' He made a comical face, as if caught out in some misdemeanour. 'Apologies, dearest wife. Have some tea. Have some cake. Have some Humble Pie.' He put Kitty down on the rug and passed me a plate with a large slice of Madeira cake. He was confident, cheery. The lost boy had vanished.

When he finally went back to his study, leaving Lottie dandling Kitty on her knees, I plucked up courage. 'Kitty likes you,' I said.

'Well, I like Kitty,' she replied.

'I suppose you'll be having some of your own before the year is out?' I ventured.

'I suppose we shall, if nature takes its course. I'd be sad if not. Children are such a blessing.'

'Yes.'

But she must have picked up some reluctance in my voice because she looked at me with that same bird-like expression Alfred had when he thought I'd said something strange. I tried to explain: 'I really *do* love Kitty. And I suppose I'll love the new one as much. But are there ways, do you know, of preventing more?'

Lottie raised her eyebrows. 'Why do you think *I* should know, Dodo dear? You are the *married* woman after all.'

'But I am ignorant, and you are worldly-wise.'

'Am I? Well, I do not have any experience, of course –' she coloured '– but I hear the tittle-tattle from the ladies' maids and I believe that there *are* such things. But why don't you ask Fred? He's the fount of all knowledge.'

'He won't talk about it – and so here I am, with child again only twelve months on!'

'Oh, Dodo, you don't need to worry! Fred adores children! You see how he loves Kitty. And he was the same with our brother.' She smiled. 'When we were children, it was always Fred who kept Sydney amused. I think he must have walked him over every inch of London, taking him to the Punch and Judy, or to watch the knife-grinders, or see the sailing ships come into the sugar wharf. He'd always contrive to find a halfpenny from somewhere to buy them some beer – and he'd wheedle stale buns from the muffin men by singing a comic song or telling them a story, right then and there on the street corner! Sydney would come home full of all their adventures. He thought Fred was the best brother anyone could have.' She gave me her bird-like look again. 'And as for money, well you and he must have the means to bring up a whole regiment. You surely don't need to be anxious about *just* one more?'

I felt ashamed. Of course I didn't need Lottie to tell me how lucky I was. I had a hard-working and home-loving husband who was amusing and affectionate and kind, and who provided me with all the money I required. I did not have to scrimp and save as she did, or share my house with aged parents and a room full of musical instruments. Yet every day I sensed that Alfred's feelings towards me were less intense than they once had been, and the more I thought, the more I felt that motherhood was the cause of it. 'Alfred may love children,' I said, with a certain asperity, 'but he doesn't have to carry them inside him for nine months and nurse them for goodness knows how long afterwards! I know it is our women's lot – but I feel so *very despondent* when I'm carrying, and no doubt I shall be looking excessively fat before the month is out. Is it so selfish to want a breathing space? A chance for Alfred and me to be sweethearts again?'

Lottie looked at me, her head still cocked to one side. 'But Dodo dearest, you and Alfred are *not* sweethearts any more. You must acknowledge the change.'

The change. It was always in my head. My increasing stoutness; Alice's slim beauty. Too much of a change, too soon. 'Yes,' I said, 'but at least I should like to keep my looks. I should like to keep something of my attractiveness.'

'Oh, Dodo,' she said, setting Kitty down and lightly brushing my curls from my cheeks. 'You are still the prettiest woman I know – if a little stouter than you used to be. I am sure Alfred loves you quite as much as when you first met. Only married people often do not say so.'

Maybe that was all it was, I told myself. Maybe I was expecting our love would go on as it had done in the heady days of our courtship. But with every day that passed, I was forced to realise that I was not the centre of his universe. He had his friends, his work, his Public. And now he had Kitty.

❦ 10 ❦

I have hardly finished dressing after my fitting when Wilson arrives at the door. 'A message for you, madam.'

I don't recognise the writing. Another well-wisher perhaps. I open it. It is folded and I see the name at the bottom first. A wide, loopy scrawl: *Alfie*. I can't believe it. I turn back to the beginning, my heart pounding. He writes in a formal way, as if I were his lawyer, not his mother; as if he is being careful with every word, in case they betray him. He expresses sorrow at Alfred's death, he proposes that now we should be reconciled; that I should meet his wife and daughter and 'mend bridges that have broken'. *I* never broke them, but it is enough that my son should want to see his mother again. I am buoyed up with joy. I make haste to the desk and sit down to pen a reply.

Dear Alfie,
What a delight to receive your letter! Of course you may come and see me. Almost any time is convenient, but please let me know so that I can prepare for you. You will have to take me as I am, very dull and quite changed from when you saw me last. As, of course, you will be too. You were still a boy when I left, and now you are a man. And Caroline, I regret, is not known to me at all. I shall be delighted to meet her, and my little granddaughter too.
Your loving Mama.

I am in a kind of delighted confusion at the thought of seeing him again. I imagine what he will be like, and what he will think of me in return.

I read the letter again and, dull though it is, I am excited to think that maybe this is but the prelude to overtures from the others. I think about them all, of course, in the long quiet hours at my disposal – wondering if Alfie's stammer is cured, if Eddie's hair still sticks up like the *Fretful Porpentine* and whether Lou is as mouse-like as ever. And I worry about Georgie on the high seas, and pray for his safe return every night. But to see them in the flesh! That is so different.

I am all too aware that I have not been the mother I should have been. It is assumed that if you've had eight children you must be full of motherly feelings, and must never for a moment have felt dismay, anger or despair at the prospect of caring for them. But when I married Alfred, all I could think of were the blissful days we would have together as husband and wife. And as time went on I would happily have settled for a small family such as my own in Chiswick.

Lottie's enquiries on my behalf had not provided a solution. There were indeed devices that could be used, she said: *douches* and *pessaries* – unfamiliar words that made us both giggle. Unfortunately she had no suggestions as to how I could obtain these items, and as I did not know either, I was obliged to do without. I despaired of talking to Alfred on the subject since he had decided, in his mercurial way, that children were, in every respect, a Good Thing. He ignored my hints as if he did not understand what I meant. So I was obliged to settle into my fate with as good a grace as I could manage. And of course I did love the babies when they came, with their plump little fists and feathery hair, and their wide-eyed way of looking at the world.

It is hard to recall now, at this remove, how each of my children looked and behaved as infants – which ones talked early and which ones walked late, and what amusing things they said and did as they struggled to make sense of everything around them. Alfred was always most delighted with them at this early stage, and had all their likenesses taken when they were still in skirts;

sketches and drawings done by London's finest artists as a favour to us both. I wanted to bring the pictures with me when I left Park House; but I dared not ask Alfred, and I doubt Sissy will part with them now he is gone.

I particularly liked the pencil studies done by our old friend, Charley Evans: Kitty and Louisa demure as anything; three of the boys reading under the robinia tree; Ada propped up with pillows on the yellow sofa; and Georgie lying in a hammock, half-asleep. My especial favourites were done when we holidayed together in Yarmouth – the girls with their skirts tucked up, the boys in their short breeches; everyone barefoot, hair blowing in the wind. It took Charley merely a few quick strokes to catch a look or gesture, and I marvelled at it. So did Alfred, though I think he was envious. *A stroke or two is worth a thousand words, eh Dodo?* he said one day as he watched me admiring Charley's quick fingers. *You clearly married the wrong man!* Of course I told him that I had not; that nothing made me so happy as being wife to the One and Only. His face broke into a smile and he gave me one of his sudden kisses, before jumping up and chivvying the children into line and marching them along the beach in search of seashells. I can see them all now, Alfred in front with his straw wide-awake hat and short linen jacket, walking at his usual cracking pace, gathering children of all ages in a long tail behind him, which strung out longer and longer until the ones at the back stopped completely and sat down and howled. And I watched Alfred turning, and running back and lifting the littlest one upon his shoulders and taking the next one by the hand, and jigging and dancing along to the edge of the waves. I couldn't hear him but I knew he was singing. I couldn't hear them, but I knew they were laughing. I watched them till they were only black shapes against the shimmering waves, as the sun grew low in the sky.

Alfred and I loved Yarmouth. We took a house there year after year, usually with the Evanses, sometimes with John and Rachel

Hemmings. Once O'Rourke and Clara came, the brief summer they had together. And dozens of people would come down to visit us for a week at a time – Lottie and Tom, Muffin, Cousin George, Lily and the twins – and any friend Alfred had recently made. Alfred himself would get up at dawn and walk along the coast for miles. He'd come back with his hair stiff with salt, and his complexion ruddy and shining. *I've had a capital idea,* he'd say. *I think this will be the best ever!* Then he'd go straight away into the room he'd put aside for writing, the room facing the sea, with a pale blind drawn half across the window to keep out the sun. He always worked every morning, strict hours, with a slice of seed cake and a glass of water at eleven o'clock and luncheon with the rest of us at two. And when he wasn't working, he was answering letters.

'You cannot propose to answer them all?' I said once, seeing the piles neatly stacked on the table he had placed by the window. Besides his correspondence with his friends and relatives, he had an ever-increasing number of letters from his readers. They wrote admiringly of his work, and he read them all with equal pleasure before sending a reply. It was as if he could not get enough praise.

'And why not? If so many good people take the trouble to write to me?'

'You are on holiday, Alfred.'

'Holiday? The One and Only is never on holiday! The One and Only is a slave to his Readers. They suck me dry. When I die, I shall be found a mere *skelington*, a bag of bones, sans *hair*, sans *teeth*, sans *eyes*, sans *everything*.' He laughed, not at all daunted at the thought.

Indeed, he loved work. Holidays were purgatory to him, unless he set himself tasks. While Charley and Mary Evans were quite content to sit with me in the garden or on the little folding stools we took down to the sea, Alfred was always on his feet, organising games – except when the children half-buried him in the sand, or when he pretended to be asleep, before leaping up to frighten them. And if he sat down, he'd be in a reverie, staring out, not listening to what we were saying. I'd watch his lips move and his face twitch, and know he was rehearsing the words for the next Number.

One year the Evanses brought their niece, Sarah. She was a pretty girl of seventeen, who spent a good part of each day arranging her frock, bonnet and parasol, and reading a small volume in a becoming position. She was a very reserved young lady and would never even raise her eyes at Alfred. If he was in the company, she was quite tongue-tied. 'She has read every one of his novels,' confided Mary. 'So I think she is in awe of him.'

Alfred seemed to wake up to this fact after a few days. He started to make jokes across the dinner-table, to draw the girl into the conversation.

'And what has Miss Evans done with herself today?' – passing the salt caster, so she had to raise her eyes.

A blush, a flutter of eyelids: 'Nothing of importance.'

'Excellent. That is what we should all do. I only wish I could learn to do that myself! But I have a growing family to keep.'

She smiled and took the salt, but dropped it, so it rolled off under the table: 'Oh dear! So clumsy!' She began to get up, flustered.

'Never fear, dear lady! The One and Only to the rescue!' Alfred dived down to get it, overturning his chair. The table rocked as he bumped about below us, grasping the ankles of everyone in the company so that the children giggled, and Miss Evans went quite pink.

'Eureka!' He emerged with the salt, his face equally pink. 'No harm done. The Spice of Life restored.' He threw a pinch over his shoulder.

'Thank you. I am so sorry.'

'Not at all. But I see you have been taking lessons from my wife. She is excellent at dropping things.'

I laughed. She laughed, too, and I hated her for it. And for a moment I hated him for saying it. Although it was true; I was very clumsy. But of course I was with child again. 'She still has a lot to learn in the art,' I said.

He stopped and looked at me, surprised. 'Dodo makes a joke!' And he came and kissed me, most heartily. Miss Evans lowered her eyes at this expression of marital ardour.

He flirted with her over supper every night after that, talking animatedly, his eyes brilliant in the lamplight. He told us of people he had encountered on his walks, sailors, fishermen, rope menders, boat builders – imitating the Yarmouth character to perfection. Miss Evans began by watching him from lowered eyelids, smiling to herself, then gradually unable to prevent herself laughing out loud. And then he'd seize napkins and silver spoons and do conjuring tricks, making the spoons disappear and reappear in a way we could not fathom. Every night she became a little more animated in response, lifting her eyes more boldly across the table, and afterwards displaying herself to best advantage on the sofa with her silk slippers tucked under her, and her ivory fan fluttering next to her cheek, as he sat in the big armchair and read out loud chapters from *Miggs* or *Little Amy*. It seemed to me that he directed his voice and expressions very much in her direction. Particularly where Miggs pays court to Prudence Eversure, when he moved in one bound from the armchair (prim Miss Eversure) to the floor (desperate, kneeling Mr. Miggs), altering his face and voice from high to low, from proud to despairing, in a *pièce de résistance* of comical acting. How we all laughed, but she more than any of us.

'A dance!' he said on our last night. 'We must have a dance! We can dance on the terrace – the weather is so warm, and there is a full moon! We might even dance on the beach!'

'Will you dance with *me*, Papa?' said Kitty. (We had allowed the older children to stay up as a special treat.)

'No, *me* first!' said Louisa, pinching her hard, while pushing towards him, and clasping at his watch chain.

'Come, come! No quarrelling! I shall dance with any young lady who asks me. And some who do not. Prepare yourselves!' He pulled up his sleeves. 'I am a demon dancer! I will not be denied!'

Then he and Charley pushed the piano through the French windows to the terrace – with a great deal of huffing and puffing and wiping of brows – and the children brought candles and a lamp, and I sat down to play. Charley asked his niece to dance, which she did, very prettily, with dancing-school airs and graces – and Alfred partnered Kitty. Alfie ran to get Bessie out of the kitchen to dance with him, and Louisa sulkily pulled little Eddie around by the arms until Alfred picked them both up, spinning them round till they screamed. I was in no state to prance about. I had only a month to go with Ada. But I played a rousing tune – 'The Borderers' – and Alfred, setting down the children, attempted a Highland Fling. I played a polka next, and Alfred asked Mary to partner him up and down the terrace. They whirled past, Mary's great hoop swinging about with the vigour of Alfred's actions and threatening to knock over the lamp we'd placed on the low wall. Then, as I was consulting my music, everyone changed partners once more, and before I could strike up, I saw Alfred waltzing Miss Sarah Evans at great speed across the terrace, down the steps and along the beach and – to our horror – into the waves. At first they danced in and out of the shallows, then they began to go deeper, and I could see she was both clinging to him and struggling to escape. But he took her further and further into the water, holding her so tight to him that she could not get away.

'He is mad!' cried Charley, loosing his wife and rushing to the wall.

'Will he drown her?' Alfie asked Bessie, staring with interest at the two figures, now quite far away and silvered in the moonlight. 'Like Jack Black drowns Poll?'

'Oh, the poor girl!' said Bessie. 'She is frightened. Mrs. Gibson, make him stop!'

Serve her right, I thought. If you play with fire you'll get burnt. But all the same I called to him to stop, and Charley echoed my call with his booming voice, and the children added their high-pitched shouts. Alfred looked up and saw us all arranged along the wall watching him, and stopped. He bowed, as if acknowledging a fine performance. As he loosed her, Miss Evans made her escape up the beach, dragging her soaking skirts over the sand to the flagstones. She was crying. 'My frock!' she sobbed. 'My frock is ruined!'

Be thankful it is only your *frock*, I thought. And was ashamed of myself.

When we closed the door of our bedroom and Alfred started to take off his soaked trousers, I asked, 'Why did you do that?'

'*Why?*' He seemed surprised at the question. He was not in the habit of querying his actions. 'No reason. It was a lark.'

'I'm not sure Miss Evans would agree. Couldn't you hear her screams?'

'Oh, yes. They were very thrilling. She was quite exhilarated. Not every young lady gets to dance in the sea with the One and Only!'

'*You* were the one who was exhilarated, Alfred. *She* was frightened. She was struggling and you wouldn't let her go!'

'I had to keep her from falling, Dodo. She'd have gone down like a ninepin in those waves.'

'You were behaving like Jack Black, weren't you?'

'Jack Black?' He laughed. 'Do you compare your benevolent spouse to that low-life villain?'

'Yes. You can be a villain too, you know. After all, you write them so well.'

He laughed again, a shade uncomfortably. 'Then must one *be* a murderer to *write* one? That's nonsense, Dodo.'

'Maybe. But one must know how it might feel. One must get some – satisfaction – from it. I've heard you in your study, ranting aloud. One day Bessie thought you were being attacked by a burglar and came upstairs with a rolling pin.'

'*Did she?*' He chuckled. 'Did she, though? I shall have to increase her wages on account of the extra services she offers.'

'Be serious.'

'I am always serious.'

'Yes, I know that, Alfred. Which is why I know this *lark* is more than it seems. You cannot laugh it off.'

'I'm not. I kept the young lady away from the cruel sea. It is only her gown that's suffered.'

'It is more than that. You took advantage of her.'

He frowned. 'On the contrary, she is such a stiff and formal young lady, I merely tried to shake her up a bit.'

'You know she is in love with you, don't you?' I did not mean to say this but it was out of my mouth before I knew.

He looked away, started taking off his coat and waistcoat, putting them in the press. 'I know no such thing. She's merely a silly girl with a head full of vanity.'

'You don't really think that.'

'Don't I? What *do* I think then?' He turned to me, his eyes dangerously bright.

'I don't know – but I do know you needed to have her in your power.'

He hesitated a second, then laughed. 'But Dodo dear, I have the whole *nation* in my power. Why should I concern myself with one young lady of seventeen?'

'Because you find her attractive, of course. Anyone can see that.'

'Ah, Dodo, don't you know that I find *all* young ladies attractive? Even if they are foolish enough to wear their best silk dresses to the seaside and display themselves on sofas as though butter wouldn't melt in their mouths.'

I took him by the arm. His shirt-cuffs were wet and he smelt of the sea. 'But matters are not simply one-sided, Alfred. A young lady's feelings are important too. Don't you remember how I wore my best silk dress to watch a certain play in Stepney so you would look at me? And *she* wore her best dress tonight so you would look at *her*. And now you have humiliated her.'

'Good Grief, it was simply a lark. And I wager she'll make a good story of it when she gets back to town and takes tea with her school-friends. She will be proud of herself then. She will exaggerate the size of the waves, and the depth of the sea, and the tremendous vigour of the One and Only in defying it all.' He chuckled.

'I doubt it. She is not you, all drama and excitement. She is an impressionable girl, and you terrified her. You cannot do as you like with women merely because you have a stronger will. It's not respectful to them – or to me either.'

I could hardly believe I was saying these things, straying again to the dangerous territory I had vowed so many times to avoid. He did not get angry, however. 'You place too much importance on a piece of innocent fun,' he said, fussing a little with his lapels and cuffs as they lay in the press. But he was uneasy; after a moment he turned and said: 'Do you really imagine she thought the worse of me?'

'Of course she did, Alfred. As I would have done, had it been me. Her evening is ruined, her dress is ruined, and her opinion of you is ruined. If she says anything at all to her school-friends it will be that Alfred Gibson is either mad or bad.'

He looked shocked, perplexed, alarmed. I knew he never could abide anyone thinking ill of him, even when he was clearly at fault. 'Well, we can't have that. The One and Only will make amends immediately!' He threw on his dressing gown and stalked out. I heard him knocking on Miss Evans' door. By the time I was on the landing, he was prostrate on the floorboards outside. 'Oh, dear Miss Evans! I am a wretch who does not deserve your good opinion. Say you forgive me! I shall buy a new frock, a better one, one decked with diamonds and pearls – but say you will forgive me!'

The door opened and Miss Evans peeked around the crack. She was in her nightgown, with a shawl hastily thrown over it. Her hair was down, and framed her face in a fine, dark cloud. Her eyes and cheeks were still red from crying.

Alfred put out his hand and touched her bare foot. Lifted it gently. Held it in his hand, the hand where Alice's little ring still circled his finger. Then he kissed it. She let him do so, letting her toes linger in his palm, smiling forgiveness; and I thought how easily she was won over, how easily we *all* were.

11

I am sure that I am not jealous by nature. From my earliest years I was always happy to share in the joy of others. I never minded in the least when my sisters received an extra kiss from my mother or a special present from Papa — or if my school-friends had finer frocks or possessed daintier hands, or were quicker at arithmetic or more graceful at their dancing steps. Indeed I was generally reckoned to have an amiable and obliging nature. Had I been wife to Cousin George, I cannot imagine resenting his atten-tions to other ladies or time spent away from me on his business affairs.

But loving Alfred was unlike anything I had ever known. From the moment I met him, I should have liked everyone else in the world to disappear and the two of us to lie in each other's arms for ever. I was young, of course, and romantic. No doubt in time, and had our lives followed a normal course, I would have devel-oped a more prosaic attitude. But our life was far from normal: not only was Alfred exceptionally attracted to company of every kind, but almost everyone he met — man, woman or child — was exceptionally drawn to *him* in return, so my possessive nature was being perpetually put to the test. In New York, when we were but newly-married, I was forced to sit aside, neglected, while he allowed young women to bear him off to the dance floor and then to the refreshment rooms, so that I hardly saw him at all. In London, he seemed to make new friends every week, and imme-diately they were part of his circle, he'd be off on some jaunt with them, walking, riding and dining in an ecstasy of *enthoosymoosy.*

From very early in our marriage it seemed as though I could possess only what the world had left behind – the cuffs and coat-tails of his existence.

And I was not good at hiding my feelings. When we were first married, Alfred would instinctively sense when I was pettish or displeased. *I see Princess Pug is growling again*, he'd say. *What has put her out? Come, let me see!* And he'd take my hands and affect to read my palm, tracing the lines with his ink-stained forefinger: *Ah! The flat-iron's too hot and the dinner's too cold and Yours Truly has been out all afternoon when he should have been here kissing his wife and devouring pork chops and gravy. Am I right?*

Indeed, it was a matter of pride with him that he could divine the thoughts of others; even feel their pain and pleasure. He had been profoundly shaken by his premonition of Alice's death that awful night and was convinced some sort of magnetic power had been unleashed between them, transmitting her agony directly to him. He became even more convinced when, on a visit to Mr. Faraday's laboratory, he watched iron filings cluster around a magnet in wonderful patterned lines. He could hardly take his eyes off them: *All that invisible energy floating around in the ether, unharnessed! If only one could make good use of it, Dodo!*

It was no surprise, therefore, that when the great French hypnotist came to London only a year or so later, Alfred could not wait to be present. The hall was crowded with people of all kinds and qualities, and I felt almost faint at the heat and the press of the throng. From the advertisements, I'd expected it to be a rather sensational thing, but to my astonishment, perfectly respectable members of the audience ascended to the stage and subjected themselves to the mesmeric influence, and afterwards many testified to its healing powers. Alfred watched everything intently, his eyes fixed on the hypnotist, watching his every move and listening to his words. 'This is a tremendous power for good,' he'd whispered to me excitedly. 'Don't you think so?'

I wasn't at all sure; in fact I thought it rather alarming. And when we got home, I sank upon the bed complaining that the whole proceeding had left me with a headache. Alfred immediately pulled up a chair: 'Let me cure it – I'm sure I can.' I wouldn't agree at first – after all it was disturbing to see people fall asleep to order, and not knowing anything that had happened while they were in that state. And Alfred had no expertise in the matter. 'Suppose I stayed asleep for ever?' I said. 'Suppose I never came back to the world of the living?' 'Come on, Dodo,' he said. 'You trust me, don't you? Just look at my eyes.' So in the end I looked. And went on looking. And waited for something to happen. And the next thing I remember was Alfred laughing at me: 'By George, you went under quickly. Now, tell me, is your headache any better?' And indeed, as if by magic, it was quite gone. But I could scarcely believe he had done anything at all, as I had no memory of it. He assured me that he'd only had to whisper a suggestion in my ear for my brow to clear immediately.

He was cock-a-hoop at his success and over the next few days he tried it on me several more times – and each time I was subdued in seconds. He told me that on one occasion Kitty (who was not yet three) had tried to wake me, shaking me and crying, but I did not hear the child or respond to her until Alfred gave me the command.

It seemed such a simple process that I asked if our positions could be reversed. He acceded readily enough and sat in the basket chair which had become our customary 'patient's seat', but he would not stay still and made so many faces, produced so many comical ailments, and inhabited so many different characters all at once, that I could do nothing for laughing. 'I doubt you could mesmerise him anyway,' remarked O'Rourke, who was watching the proceedings. 'You have no wish to impose your will on anyone else.' But Alfred was ready – indeed eager – to try his powers on everybody we knew: Charley and Mary Evans, Bessie, Lottie and

Tom, O'Rourke, and even Miss Brougham all put themselves in his hands. Moreover, in the years that followed, he extended his skills beyond our circle so that even casual acquaintances came under his spell. And thus it was that we became involved in what O'Rourke jokingly called 'The Mysterious Affair of Madame Brandt'; although there was no mystery, and certainly no joke.

We'd met the Brandts in Paris, where we had spent a pleasant few days *en route* for Switzerland. I had persuaded Alfred that he needed a rest after producing four novels in three years; he had persuaded me in turn that we needed to save money by taking a house abroad. The Brandts were also bound from Paris to Lausanne, and Alfred proposed taking the couple as travelling companions in our carriage. I thought we should be seriously crowded, with the four children, Bessie, a hired man, and all the luggage, but Alfred declared the men could ride outside and 'endure wind and weather and have, moreover, the chance to smoke a number of excellent cigars'. So it was done his way, as always.

They were a strange couple. Monsieur Brandt was short and plump, with a deal of gold about his person by way of numerous rings, watch chains and cravat pins, as if he was determined to display upon his person every item of adornment that he owned. Madame Brandt was, by contrast, thin and pale, with beautiful aristocratic features, and a nervous, strained look. Her dark hair was very thick and lustrous and worn in ostentatious piles, not at all the fashion. I could not help but notice that she held a cambric cloth to her face a good deal of the time, a cloth steeped in clove oil, that made a pungent smell in the carriage. She admitted that she suffered from a kind of neuralgia, and that when attacked by the pain, she could hardly speak or eat, and sleeping at such times was impossible.

'She is a martyr to her condition,' said Monsieur Brandt at our first stop. 'I have never known a woman suffer so much. You are a martyr, are you not, *ma choux*?'

Madame Brandt nodded. Alfred stared at her until she became aware of his gaze and lowered her eyes in becoming modesty. He continued staring and eventually said, 'Would you allow me to try something? I think I may be able to help.' He leaned forward, his eyes still on her, and I knew what he was going to do.

'Alfred really has remarkable powers,' I said to her, by way of encouragement.

'Do you really think you can aid me, Mr. Gibson?' she said, sighing like a tree in the wind and turning her sad eyes at him.

'Oh, please let him try!' I said.

'I suppose it can do no harm.'

'Oh, no, Madame Brandt,' I urged her. 'No harm at all. It is akin to sleeping. One knows nothing.'

So that evening, in the dining room of the *Relais des Bois*, on the road between Troyes and Dijon, Alfred attempted to mesmerise her, using only the repetitive movement of his hands and the intense gaze of his eyes. Madame Brandt immediately fell into a trance, and seemed to lose her rigid posture, almost lolling over the edge of the chair. He lifted her gently and spoke quietly to her, telling her repeatedly that the pain was fading and would go away. And when he told her to wake up, she sat up straight and said she felt very much relieved. But at ten o'clock that night Monsieur Brandt knocked on our bedroom door for Alfred to attend her again. And Alfred, who was already in his nightshirt, put on his silk dressing gown, combed his hair, dabbed lavender water on his wrists, and went to do her bidding.

I was still nursing Eddie. He was always hungry, and a difficult child to settle, so I stayed in our room, singing him nursery rhymes and rocking him to sleep. After an hour, when Alfred did not return, I began to wonder if there was something amiss, so I slipped on my dressing gown, gave the child to Bessie, and knocked on the adjoining room. Monsieur Brandt opened it quickly: 'Sshh!' he said, as he ushered me in. 'This is quite remarkable!'

Madame Brandt was sitting in an armchair in the centre of the room. She was wearing only her nightgown, and the outlines of her uncorseted body were visible for all to see. Her mass of dark hair was unpinned and falling loosely over her face. Her eyes were closed as if asleep, but she was moaning and muttering disjointedly. Alfred was sitting opposite her, holding her hands and murmuring in a low voice.

'She has constant nervous spasms,' confided Monsieur Brandt. 'But she responds well to your husband, I think.'

I watched as Alfred bent forward and whispered to her. 'She can hear him?' I asked.

'Oh, yes. She hears him. And she answers. She is telling him all her fears.'

I could see then that she was muttering in response to Alfred's questions, but I could not hear what she was saying, she was speaking so low. And Alfred had to bend even closer to hear her. 'What fears?' I asked Monsieur Brandt.

'All the fears of her soul. The fears that creep into her and cause her pain.'

'But it is nearly midnight. We are to depart at six o'clock tomorrow.'

Alfred, hearing me, turned impatiently. 'Then go to bed, Dodo. It is important that I stay with Madame Brandt. We are at a vital stage. I cannot stop now.'

So I went to bed. But I did not sleep. Occasionally from next door I heard a moan and stifled murmurings. Alfred did not return to my bed until half past one. He was exhausted, but also excited and tense. He pulled me to him urgently.

'It's late,' I said, pulling away.

'We have time.'

'No.' I wrestled his hand away.

'What's the matter?'

'How dare you come straight from her to me!'

'From her to you?' He let me go, sharply. 'What *can* you mean? Are you suggesting improper behaviour?'

'You have been with her for over *three hours.*'

'And so? I can assure you that Monsieur Brandt was with us the entire time.'

'What can you find to say to her for *three hours?*'

He lay back on the bolster. 'I really cannot believe this. I cannot believe you are jealous of a poor invalid.'

'It only took you *minutes* to cure my headache. Why were you so long with *her?*'

'Because, my dear wife, her symptoms are more complicated. Her pain is not a simple defect of the nerves. It stems from a kind of hysteria deep within.'

'How do you know? You are not a doctor.'

'I can sense it. I know these things.'

'Why did she need to be so – dishevelled? So immodest?'

'She was not aware of how she looked.'

'Well, have you *cured* her, at least? That would be something.'

'It is a deep-seated malady. But I honestly think I can do it in time.'

'In *time?*'

'We shall be in their company for five more days. I shall mesmerise her each morning and again at night, when the pain is at its worst. I am determined to do my best for her. She has fearful memories. Her childhood was wretched. As bad as – well, as bad can be.'

So as we travelled through France and on to the Alps, as we bowled through majestic mountains and picturesque valleys, we were forever preoccupied with Madame Brandt's condition. And Madame Brandt *was* wretched and fearful. Especially when Alfred was present. Especially at night. It seemed to me that she babbled and moaned more and more each time he tried his powers on her. And that he became more and more exhausted as he tried to will her into some semblance of serenity. Some days she improved; then she swiftly succumbed again. But he would not give up. He tried all manner of things, sometimes holding her hands, sometimes holding her head, sometimes passing his hands down the side of her face, sometimes supporting her neck. Monsieur Brandt stood by, fingering his gold jewellery, seemingly unconcerned at the way my husband was paying such intimate attention to his wife.

When we arrived at Lausanne, the Brandts travelled on to their house on the outskirts of the town, and I was relieved that at last our household could get back to normal. But Alfred paced about our apartment, expressing anxiety about his patient's condition, and seeming obsessed with her situation. He even failed to make his usual tour of the accommodation, and made no comment about the broken door on the broom cupboard and the dusty condition of the kitchen shelves.

'I must go to her!' he said, after only half an hour.

'But we have only just arrived!'

'Nevertheless, I must go!' And he set off – even though Kitty was crying for him to read her a story and Bessie was asking for his help in lighting the kitchen boiler, Alfie and Louisa were quarrelling, and little Eddie was so over-tired he wouldn't suckle but clung to me and screamed.

He returned after midnight, elated. 'I think I may have done it! I have never seen her so at peace.' And he took up his quill and some paper and went away to write. The next day, at nine in the evening, there was another call from the Brandts. He was absent until two. The next night, the same.

'I absolutely forbid you to see her again!' I said when the servant came on the fourth night.

'*Forbid* me!' He looked shocked. And for my own part, I could hardly believe I had uttered such a word. But I carried on: 'You have a duty to your wife and children. They have a prior claim on your emotions, and your company.' Then, somewhat frightened at the look on his face, I went up and kissed him on the cheek. I strove to be calm, so as not to ignite his passion further. 'We are all wretched without you, Alfred,' I said. 'Kitty, Alfie, Louisa and the baby – we all miss you so much.'

He looked at the children, then at me, silent for once. So I went on: 'We know you are the One and Only; that you can do things others cannot. But please leave this woman alone. If you go on paying her such attention, you will make us all miserable.'

He went on staring at me. Then he turned away. 'You make too much of this, as usual, Dodo. I am simply trying to help another human being in distress. This seems to me to an act of kindness. But you choose to see it differently, and I should not want you or the children unhappy. I shall write to Monsieur Brandt and tell him I shall come no more.'

'Will you say *why*?' I suddenly felt foolish. I felt sorry for Madame Brandt too; I did not wish her to be in pain.

'What should I say? That my wife does not trust me?'

'I *do* trust you, but –'

'Do you? Yet you are jealous – and jealousy and mistrust go together. It is mean-spirited. I am disappointed in you.'

'But if you say I am jealous, you will make me seem foolish.'

'Well, indeed, Dodo, you *are* foolish. But how else can I extricate myself?'

'I am sure you will think of something if you try. You are so clever with words.'

'Maybe. But I try not to tell untruths.' And he went to the writing-desk and scribbled a few lines which he gave to the boy. I never saw what he wrote, but I suspect he must have held me to blame, as over the summer I kept hearing rumours that I had stopped Alfred visiting Madame Brandt because I was jealous of her beauty; or that I had threatened to end my life (or his) unless he kept away from her.

It was difficult to face the ladies of the Lausanne drawing rooms after that. They all looked at me curiously – and many sidled away from Alfred if they saw me glance in his direction, as if they thought I might have a dagger concealed about my person, ready to do mischief to them. I hoped Alfred would say something – defend me, perhaps – but when I complained to him, he laughed, and said that trying to interfere in the affairs of women was too much even for the One and Only. He was amused, moreover, by my modest notoriety. Sometimes he would jokingly refer to *my wife the murderess*, and would inspect my hands for bloodstains, and affect to be struck with dread every time I picked up a knife at table. Although we continued to receive invitations to every social gathering, I often let him go alone so that he could be fêted and lionised as much as he desired, while I sat at home quietly with Bessie and the children. I read a great deal in those evenings, taking courage to begin Mrs. Shelley's *Frankenstein*. O'Rourke had sent me a copy, explaining it had been written at a villa not far away across the lake, and had a 'note of philosophical horror'. I found the story at once bizarre and unsettling, and I couldn't help wondering which particular dead person Alfred would have brought to life, if he had had the chance.

12

It's the day I am to go to the Palace. O'Rourke calls when I have hardly finished dressing. He stares at my black gown and at Wilson hovering around with my best shawl and bonnet. 'What is this, Dodo? An *outing*? Where are you off to?'

I blush with annoyance that he has caught me in this way. 'To Buckingham Palace, as a matter of fact, Michael. And don't delay me with questions and queries. I must *not* be late.'

'The *Palace*?' As if I had said the Moon.

'Yes, to see the Queen.' The words reminds me of the nursery rhyme. I can't help smiling to myself.

'The Queen has *invited* you?' He looks nonplussed.

'Well, Michael, do you think I would be calling on her unannounced?'

He puts down the wide-brimmed hat he has been wearing. It's rather racy. And he has a smart cravat and a buttonhole. 'Of course not. But when did this happen? Why did you not tell me? How are you getting there?'

'I didn't tell you, Michael, because I did not know. You remember the letters you brought? Well, the invitation was among them, and already delayed by half a week. So there's hardly been time to do more than get these blessed mourning clothes made up. And in answer to your other question, I am proposing to go there by cab.'

'Cab? No, Dodo. I have the gig outside. Let me drive you.' An eager smile spreads over his face.

It is a long time since I rode in a gig. It's not the most comfortable of vehicles, but the idea of having company for my new foray into the world is attractive. 'Oh, Michael, I'd be delighted. It will lessen my anxiety greatly.'

He looks pleased. 'That's settled then. But why are you making this visit if you are so anxious?'

'She wrote so beautifully to me, I hadn't the heart to decline. But I know that she is a demanding conversationalist.'

'And you are still going? *Well, you're a game 'un, and no mistake!*' He imitates Alfred imitating Boodles. We both laugh.

'Your gloves, madam.' Wilson hands me a pair from the table. 'And you'll need your umbrella, in case it rains.' She draws my old green one from the elephant-foot, and gives it a shake. I can't think when I last used it, although Kitty has borrowed it many a time.

I take it, and we go downstairs. The steps are steeper than I remember and the passageway darker and more constricted, so that O'Rourke and I bumble against each other as we descend. Then Wilson opens the front door, and for the first time in ten years I feel the smack of fresh air on my face. I catch my breath with the surprise of it. I blink, too, half-blinded by the sudden brilliance of the unfiltered sun after the soft gloom of lace curtains and half-drawn blinds. I stagger a little and Michael steadies me with his arm – how thin it seems! – as I step forward as gingerly as if I had just learnt to walk. It is good to embrace the world again, to feel part of the wider concerns of humanity. But as O'Rourke climbs up on the gig, I hesitate, suddenly afraid. It's ridiculous that my first foray is not to some familiar location where I can lurk among the shadows unrecognised – but to Buckingham Palace, amid courtiers and ladies-in-waiting and goodness knows whom! I have taken leave of my senses; I half-turn, back to the safety of home, but O'Rourke is extending his hand and smiling encouragingly at me, and before I know it, I'm climbing up beside him, Wilson assisting me from below, guiding my skirts away from the mud-caked wheels. Now I am up and exposed, the sharpness of the air is even more marked; and I am further struck by the hot odour of the horse and beyond that, the acrid smell of a thousand chimneys. In my ears I hear the hum of the giant bee-hive that is London by day; I had forgotten the sound of it. I sit and look around at all the new things, feeling for a brief moment like a young girl. O'Rourke spreads a rug over my legs and clicks the filly into a trot. As we set off, I look back and see Wilson watching us from the pavement. She turns away quickly as I catch her eye.

'It's a very long time since we rode together,' I remark, as we thread our way through carriages and cabs, avoiding darting pedestrians and slinking dogs. The weather is dry but extremely cold, and people are well-muffled. I watch them all going about their business, and wonder about their lives; what stories Alfred could make of them.

'How does it feel, Dodo? To be out in the air again?'

'Quite stimulating,' I say. I can't stop smiling.

'You've been a hard person to prise from that blessed house. In fact I can see it takes a *Queen* to dislodge you.'

'You know why I wouldn't go out, Michael.'

'Do I?'

'Of course you do! I've explained often enough. How could I meet people? How could I look at their faces, imagining what they were thinking of me? *Poor woman,* or *How did he stand it for so long?* And I certainly didn't want my dear friends to have to take sides. It was better to become invisible.'

'All the same, I hope you plan to become visible soon. It would make a big difference to my lonely old life.' He shakes the reins.

'Lonely? Don't say that.' But I know he must be. No wife, no children, and now Alfred gone.

'Well, my acquaintance has dwindled to a whisker, and a very thin whisker at that. Now, hold tight, there's a good woman!' He executes a fancy manoeuvre between a rag-and-bone cart and a little girl with a basket of laundry. She looks up and for a moment

I think it's Emmie, until I realise that she would be a woman of forty by now.

Forty! It makes me feel even older. Michael is old too. And he fares badly as a widower. 'You should have married again, you know,' I tell him. 'You'd have had children and grandchildren to keep you company now.'

'Yes. *Marry again*: everyone told me that. Everyone except Alfred. He said some losses can never be replaced.'

We jog along in silence. I hear *My darling girl! I can't do without you,* and think how that dreadful loss was always with us, forever rubbed and made raw by constant repetition. O'Rourke, by contrast, speaks little of Clara, and I cannot gauge his feelings on the matter. It was a long time ago, certainly, but I doubt Michael can forget his young Irish bride with her fresh cheeks and dark curling hair, and the soft manner that made her a favourite with us all that brief summer in Yarmouth. I can see her sitting in the wicker chair, watching the waves day after day, her outline gently swelling with child. And I recall Alfred writing the scene where Edith Markham is washed up on the shore, her dead child still within her, and I wonder, not for the first time, whether Alfred really had the gift of premonition.

We are turning into the Mall. The autumn leaves are falling, and they brush the uniforms of the horse guards as they clatter past in red, white and gold. Now the Palace is so close, I feel my nervousness return. Will I trip over my gown or fall down in a faint through standing up too long? What shall I say to Her Majesty? How much does she know of what passed between Alfred and me? I feel as if it is my first ball, and I have no faith in my social graces.

We stop at the gates and they let us through at the side entrance. A grey-haired gentleman in court dress escorts me into the building; O'Rourke says he will wait for me in the stable yard.

'Please follow me.' The courtier takes me to an ante-room — very bare, no fire in the grate. He addresses me in confidential tones: 'I take it you have not so far had the pleasure of an audience with Her Majesty? No? It is therefore important to impress upon you that Her Majesty is ever vigilant that protocol is maintained. When you are bidden to enter, take three steps into the room and curtsy to Her Majesty. Do not under any circumstances speak to Her Majesty unless Her Majesty addresses you first, and address her at all times as 'Your Majesty' or 'ma'am'. Do not sit unless Her Majesty requests it, and *never* sit while Her Majesty remains standing. If Her Majesty graciously offers you tea, please be so good as to accept. And do not, on any account, stare at Her Majesty.'

I wish Alfred were here to hear him; to catch his rhythms, to delight in his pomposity. But the man turns abruptly and we are on our way to the Presence. The corridors are, for the most part, surprisingly narrow and poky, and my crinoline is too wide for us to walk abreast, so I follow the man as he guides me through. Maids carrying trays and footmen with coals stop and flatten themselves against the walls as we progress. Then we pass through a heavy door and the décor is suddenly grand – gilt, ormolu, plush. Greyhead eventually comes to a stop, and passes me over to a younger man in morning suit, very superior in manner. He hardly lets his eyes rest on me, but knocks on a large mahogany door: 'Mrs. Gibson, ma'am.' And I am in.

She is shorter than I am, and about as stout. Although her face is so very familiar, at the same time it is different. I am conscious that I am committing the crime of staring, and that I have not yet curtsied. I contrive the three steps and execute a kind of bob. I cannot trust myself to go low.

'Ah, Mrs. Gibson! We both find bending the knee trouble-some. The penalties of increasing age!'

I look up. She is smiling. I smile back – then quickly avert my eyes.

'Please sit down.' She is still standing. I hesitate.

She seats herself. 'Dear Mrs. Gibson, we cannot say how sorry we are that such a sad event has brought us together.'

'Yes indeed, Your Majesty.'

'We saw the crowds. Such a spectacle. Such a loss.'

'Indeed, ma'am.'

'He was much loved.'

'Yes, ma'am.'

'Like the Prince Consort — although we do not think the nation fully understood his particular genius. But *your* husband spoke to them direct. To the heart.'

'Indeed he did, ma'am. Oh, indeed he did!' I feel my eyes moisten. I hope I shan't disgrace myself by weeping.

'You were so very fortunate to be his wife.'

'I believe that I am, ma'am. Very fortunate.'

I dread what she may ask on this subject, but she fingers her wedding ring, seems to drift into a reverie, then turns to me suddenly. ' — But one feels *angry* as well, does one not?'

I don't know her meaning. I make a demurring sound, eyes down, tracing the pattern on the carpet, noting it is rather worn in places.

She senses my uncertainty. 'I mean, of course, angry that men of worth are taken from our midst, whilst fools and knaves continue to thrive. What is God up to in those cases, do you think?' She looks at me very directly, as if I should have my answer piping hot on a plate.

'He works in mysterious ways, Ma'am. At least so we are told.'

'Indeed. Most mysterious. What was He about in Mr. Gibson's case, do you think? With a novel only half-way through? Could He not have spared him another year?' She trains her eyes on me again.

To my surprise, I manage a sensible answer. 'My husband was ill, Ma'am. It is a wonder he lived as long as he did. Perhaps God was sparing him more pain.'

'Hmm.' She taps her fingers against the chair. 'We admit he seemed a little frail when we saw him last – but very bright. Sparkling, in fact. Just as when he played the father for us in *Lord Royston's Daughter*. He was excellent in that; so natural, yet so thrilling. We were very impressed.'

Lord Royston again. Always that wretched play. I want to shout *Bah, humbug!* and give it a good drubbing. But I must speak well of it, as everyone does. 'Oh, yes. My husband never did things by halves, ma'am. He felt he owed it to his Public – and his Sovereign – to give of his best. Even when he was ill and could hardly walk, he still went on performing.'

She nods. 'Admirable, admirable.'

'And he wrote right up to the last, ma'am. He died with the pen in his hand, desperately trying to finish *Ambrose Boniface*.'

'But it was not to be.' She sighs, and shakes her head.

'Sadly, no.'

'Do you know how he meant to end it? Did he discuss his works with you?'

'Oh, indeed, Ma'am, he did!' But I realise as I speak that this is not quite true. When we were newly-weds, sitting in front of the fire in Mrs. Quinn's upstairs rooms with our arms around each other, he never seemed to tire of telling me about what he had seen and done, and his new ideas for *Miggs' Tales*. But those intimate times did not last for long. I look down, unable to meet the Queen's piercing blue gaze. I cannot deceive her, or myself. I give a wry smile: 'But after the children came, it was difficult to find the time to talk. Alfred was so busy. Either in his study, or at the office editing his magazine. Or with Miss Brougham on some committee or other. Or rehearsing plays. Or out walking all over London till the early hours. And I was – well, I was with the children.'

'Ah, children. The cross we women have to bear.'

I look up, somewhat surprised, and she raises her hand sharply: 'Please do not misunderstand me, Mrs. Gibson. Children are a precious gift. But childbirth itself!' She shudders. 'Again we ask, what is God thinking of? Can it all be the fault of that one silly female led astray by a reptile? Why do we, all these years later, have to go on suffering for *her* sins?'

'Indeed.Ma'am.' I am taken aback by her candour, and indeed at her turn of phrase. But I do not feel intimidated. There is a warmth beneath her severity, and in some ways I can see she is as emotional as I.

'One hopes you made use of the chloroform, at least?'

I know she is a great champion of the chloroform. As was Alfred. *Come on, Dodo,* he said. *Do you want to suffer when you need not? The Queen herself recommends it.* 'Oh, yes. Alfred insisted,' I tell her. 'And it was most efficacious.'

'Exactly. It is a boon to all women.' She looks closely at me. 'You have had eight children, I think, Mrs. Gibson?'

'Yes. But sadly, we lost our youngest shortly after birth, and our daughter Ada –' my chest tightens, and I have to pause '– passed away, aged seven.' Every time I think my grief for Ada is conquered, I find it is not.

'I am sorry, Mrs. Gibson. It is difficult to understand why these things are sent. Two children lost. Most distressing.'

I want to tell her about it all, about Ada and Florence May – and the other babes that never even had a chance to breathe, infants too small and unformed even to be buried. But I fear I shall weep aloud if I speak of it.

The Queen glances at a photograph on the table next to her. 'No doubt we should count ourself fortunate that our battalion of children remains brutally healthy in limb – if not always in character.' She laughs a little bitterly.

'Your Majesty's family life is much admired by all.'

'Yes. The Prince set much store by a happy family.'

'Oh, my husband felt the same, ma'am!'

She smiles. 'Indeed. He spoke warmly of your children; of

your eldest daughter in particular. He told me she had *his* spirit and talents. I was forced to wonder if she would have done better as a boy.'

I am so astonished that I cannot help blurting out: 'It is probably better that she was not. Alfred would never have brooked a rival.'

'A rival? No, of course not. He was after all, *the One and Only.*' She laughs delightedly at her stroke of wit.

I smile too, and am emboldened to ask a question. 'But does it not strike you as unfair, ma'am, that a simple question of one's sex should condemn one for ever to a particular sphere? Your Majesty, so active and busy, with so much responsibility for matters of state, must understand that. You do not have to be satisfied with domestic matters alone.'

'Oh, we would willingly cede all matters of state to be a simple housewife in a crofter's cottage!' She smiles in a far-off manner. 'But when we are called to high office, it is our duty, and we cannot refuse. But we struggle, Mrs. Gibson. We struggle! Even more when we are forced, as now, to shoulder the burden alone. But we do the best we can, using what meagre skills we possess.'

'I am sure Your Majesty has many skills.'

'We have developed a certain facility. But women's true nature is not suited to high office. We are too much at the mercy of our feelings. Men, we find, have more concentration and are better able to think without the constraints of emotion. We have always agreed with the Prince that the highest rôle a woman can aspire to, whether she be Queen or commoner, is that of wife and mother.'

I am silent. That she – the most powerful woman in England – should hanker after nothing but domestic life seems almost absurd.

'You do not agree?' She gives me a narrow look.

'I find at this time in my life that I do not know.'

'You surprise us, Mrs. Gibson.' She looks disapproving.

I surprise myself. After all, her sentiments are Alfred's too, and for much of my life they have been mine. But it is as if a door has been unlocked in my mind. I feel a rush of courage: 'It is simply, Ma'am, that I see my daughter longing in vain for something more in life. I see her baulking at the smallness of our womanly concerns. I see her as a wild horse champing at the bit.'

The Queen draws back. I see she does not like the picture of a young woman champing at the bit. She shakes her head. 'She is a little spoilt, perhaps. Young women these days seem to think they can have what they want without making any effort. She should have been with Miss Nightingale at Scutari! That would have tamed her wildness.'

I try to envisage Kitty ministering to the rows of sick and wounded, walking the wards, raising her lamp in encouragement and benediction. I cannot conjure the image. 'I fear Kitty is too impatient for nursing.'

'Well,' she says, 'we are all called in different ways. She has no children?' The sharp look again.

'Alas, no.'

'Well then, she should make a *serious* effort at Good Works. There is much to be done by those who have energy to spare.'

'Oh, she has tried, ma'am. But she was always convinced she knew what was best. She would not compromise and quarrelled with everyone who tried to tell her different. Very like her father, I'm afraid.'

The Queen frowns. 'Surely not! I myself observed his character: he was the kindest and most genial of men.'

'That was his general temperament, ma'am. But –' I stop, afraid I shall commit a *faux pas*.

'But?' The piercing look again. I realise I cannot retreat now.

'But where he felt wronged, he could be implacable. Even to those closest to him.'

She looks at me more gently now. 'Great men are not always kind to those who serve them at close quarters. But we have to excuse them because they embrace the Greater Good. One has only to look at those affecting scenes on Monday to know in what esteem Mr. Gibson was held by one and all! I read in *The Times* that women fainted, men were openly weeping – in effect, it said, the whole country was in despair at his loss. That, Mrs. Gibson, is the true measure of your husband!'

'Oh, I know the Public adored him. But their very adoration made it harder for me!' The sob that I have attempted to suppress all this time bursts forth and I try to stifle it with my handkerchief.

'Dear Mrs. Gibson!' She leans forward and extends her hand. 'Do not distress yourself. Your sacrifice has been vindicated. The whole world has cause to be grateful to you. All the causes he has espoused, all the *passionate* words he has written against injustice and cruelty! No doubt he met with opposition – as do all who try to break old ways of thinking. The Prince Consort met with the very same when he proposed the Great Exhibition. But, like your husband, the Prince would not be dissuaded. He was deter-mined. And what a success that proved to be!'

'Indeed. A great success.' I went with Alfred and Sissy, but the crowds and the heat under the glass made me so faint that hardly had we seen the great statues from Egypt than Alfred had had to put me into a Hackney carriage and send me home. How-ever, I do not want the Queen to know that. She, I know, has a great deal of stamina, and expects others to be the same.

But she does not question me further. She draws back, flushed with pleasure: 'Such dear people from all over the Empire! So many of our loyal subjects bringing so many wonderful artefacts! And the Crystal Palace itself! Was there ever such a structure?' Her voice breaks. She has tears in her eyes, and I realise she does not want to hear about Alfred any more. She wants to talk about her own husband. I understand her feelings. I nod while she expounds

on the Prince's achievements, his patience under travail, his devotion to his family. She continues at some length, and I am finding
standing up very uncomfortable. I lean gently against a small
satin chair at my side.

Eventually the Queen comes to a peroration: 'And you wonder
that the Queen is angry? That she does not question her Maker
every day? We have to submit to our loved ones' death, Mrs
Gibson. We *have* to submit. But we do not do it willingly!'

I see that she is very angry at her loss. Perhaps I should be angry
too? With God, as she is? Or with Sissy? Or with that faint figure
in grey with a seductive smile on her face?

The Queen clears her throat and wipes a surreptitious tear
from her eye, becoming business-like in an instant. 'Mrs. Gibson,
we are remiss. Please sit down. Will you take tea?'

I remember my instructions. 'Thank you, Your Majesty.' I
squeeze into the nearby chair.

She rings a small bell on the table next to her. The superior
gentleman appears at the door, and seconds later a liveried footman
and an elderly maid bring in a silver tray and a small cake-stand. I
wonder how they could have known when to have it ready. It's as
neat a trick as one of Alfred's. They dispense tea and cake with
practised efficiency, and depart in the same manner. No word has
been spoken. The superior gentleman closes the door and we are
alone again.

The Queen smiles. 'You must be used to a great variety of
hospitality, Mrs. Gibson. Your husband was lionised everywhere
he went, we believe?'

'Yes.' I nod, contriving not to shower myself with crumbs. 'I
think he must have eaten more banquets and been the subject of
more toasts than any person living.'

'We had that experience ourselves, of course.' She looks rather
icy, and I hasten to recover myself.

'I exclude Your Majesty, of course. Your Majesty is used to

acclaim. You were born to it. But we were not, and it was a hard thing to manage.'

She seems mollified. 'But you *did* adapt yourselves?'

'To some extent. At first it was not so difficult, when we were here in London, where fame crept on us by degrees. But when we went to America —'

'America! Ah, yes. An interesting country.' She drinks her tea, moves her cake around on its plate. 'Mr. Gibson's books are as popular over there as they are here, we think?'

'Yes, indeed, ma'am. If not more so. During our great tour, we could hardly set foot outside our hotels without being mobbed. On one occasion, the people set up chants under our bedroom window, refusing to let us sleep until my husband had gone out to the balcony to give them a few words. And in the morning when we went out, they simply swooped around us, so I was forced against the doorpost, and Alfred had to call out to let them allow me through: *Do not suffocate my wife, dear sirs! I should be obliged to think badly of this great country if you do!* They were quite wild, those American crowds. Reporters asked his opinion on everything: *Do you like America? Do you think it is the best country in the world? Will you set your next novel in the United States? What do you think of our womenfolk?*'

'How very disconcerting.'

'Yes. But it was also quite thrilling. I suppose that was when I first realised what a Great Man he had become. It seemed as if everybody in the world wanted to shake his hand! And if they couldn't shake his, they'd shake mine, as a kind of proxy. *Mrs. Gibson,* they'd say, *I am De-lighted!*'

I stop. I fear I have spoken too much. I see Greyhead ticking me off for not keeping to protocol. The Queen nibbles daintily at her cake, thinking the while. 'Mr. Gibson went there a second time, did he not?'

'He was ill, by then, though. He should not have travelled.'

'Men do these things in spite of anything we poor women say. They are driven by such impulses, such need to master challenges. Even the dear Prince Consort worked himself to death.' She pauses. 'The Prince of Wales, we must admit, is not in the same mould. But now he is married, we hope he will settle down.'

I nod, but think how vain a hope it is that marriage will change people. It did not change Alfred, and it did not change me. It has not changed Kitty or Augustus either. In marriage, we may learn to check our words, and to submerge those feelings and actions which will inevitably lead to strife, but we remain essentially the same.

The Queen breaks into my thoughts. 'We are so sorry,' she is saying. 'It is only a week or so since the sad event, and we have kept you talking. You must be tired.'

'I am a little.' (Has it really been hours?)

'It has been so good to meet you; to talk to you. We have so much in common. Perhaps you will spare us a little of your time in the future?'

I nod, and she rings the bell again, and the superior gentleman enters as if he has had his ear pressed to the door expressly for the purpose of responding. 'Ma'am?'

'Mrs. Gibson is leaving.'

I haul myself out of the satin chair. I am aware that the superior gentleman is eyeing my inadequate mourning with a critical eye, and I am glad that at least I gave in about the edging and the frogging. I contrive a half-bow, half-curtsy which he clearly thinks entirely unsatisfactory, but he ushers me out of the room as if every second I am there beyond my allotted time would provoke a constitutional crisis. I am then handed back to Greyhead, who is waiting a few yards off, and I leave the Palace in exactly the reverse way from which I entered it.

~ 13 ~

As we walk back along the passageways, I feel I have acquitted myself well. But I can't help reflecting on the Queen's situation; and how even *she* was under the thumb of her prince. And I see as if for the first time how we put aside all that is strong within us, all that is particular about us, and bend to the will of our husbands. The famous opening of *Richard Masterman* echoes in my head and I think how Alfred, with the deep and better part of himself, seemed to understand that even before I did:

After Richard Masterman had brought his young wife home, he set about murdering her. Everything he had loved about her during their courtship — her silvery, inconsequential laugh, her girlish habit of rushing into rooms as though a fire were about to consume her, her charming tendency to enthuse about any novelty that came her way, her innocent manner of taking his arm and kissing him boldly on the lips whether anyone was looking or no — he systematically set about destroying. He did not think he was destroying her. By no means. He thought he was improving her. As a husband has a right to do. Nay, as he has a duty to do. The house in Berkeley Square which was to have been their abode of bliss became the battleground for his justified campaign. 'She is all very well as she is,' he reasoned, 'but she could be better.' It would be more becoming in a wife of Mrs. Masterman's status, he thought, if she were a little more sober in her manner, a little more restrained in her exhibitions of affection, a little more discriminating in her tastes. Instead of clinging to his arm in her artless way and breaking off to chatter to her canary or her lap dog or her old dear nursemaid, he would have her comport herself in a dignified way, give graceful bows, and speak only when spoken to. So he set about correcting her. Day by day he corrected her. He corrected her speech, her manners, her voice, her conversation, her affections. And in her efforts to please him, she became more sober, more considered. She no longer jumped up to greet him when he entered a room. She left the canary to its own devices so it trilled away unheard and then grew silent for want of attention. The girlish roses in her cheeks faded and she became fashionably (some would say dangerously) pale. She no longer sang as she went about her duties and was reserved and stately in her conversation. She disregarded the old nursemaid, whom she banished to an attic room. In short, she was no longer Celia Masterman. Richard Masterman was pleased at what he had wrought. And rubbed his hands together with a sense of profound righteousness and went about his daily doings with his head held high.

But Alfred never acknowledged such perceptions in real life. Only once – when he'd been complaining about Mary-Ellen's inefficiency in cleaning the grate, and by implication, my inefficiency in supervising her – did I speak up. 'You know, you're rather like Richard Masterman,' I said (lightly, of course, so as not to offend him).

He looked startled: 'Good Lord! Because the maid doesn't clean the fender properly?'

'No, because you are always finding fault with your wife.'

He considered for a brief moment. 'Well, I may put you right when you make an error, Dodo dear. But have I ever made you give up any person you loved, any thing you cared for? Have I gradually squeezed the life out of you until you are reduced to a faded wraith? Have I caused your demise in a silk plush bedroom hung with portraits of my disapproving ancestors, and laid you in the earth with much weeping and all too tardy promises to make amends?'

I couldn't help laughing. 'Of course not, Alfred. But –'

'It seems to me that, far from fading away, you are positively *bursting* with health, positively *thriving* on the company of Yours Truly and his not inconsiderable fortune.' He laughed and caught me round the waist and pretended not to be able to get his arms to meet on the other side.

I persisted, even while I dreaded his response. 'But you would like me to be different. Own it.'

He laughed. 'Different? Well, only in that we can all be *better*, Dodo. We are all imperfect. It is the human condition. But marriage is for better or for worse. And you and I have not done too badly, have we? And as for the aforesaid Mary-Ellen, surely it is possible for her to clean one small grate without depositing black-lead on the hearth-tiles, the fender, the tongs, the poker, and sometimes even the mantelpiece? One cannot approach within two feet of the fire without becoming a veritable Blackamoor. Perceive!' And he held up his palm and smeared it over his face till he looked like a surprised recipient of Mrs. Betterby's Foreign and Native Child Catechism Corporation. And of course I laughed, as he knew I would. And it stopped me in my comparisons, as he also knew it would. And in that moment I realised how evasive he was about anything that touched on his own character. It seemed an odd thing for a writer. But when I'd remarked on it to O'Rourke, he'd laughed and said, 'Oh, Alfred does things by instinct. It wells up from the depths of his heart and passes by his head entirely, so although he writes what he knows, he doesn't always know what he writes.'

I suddenly remember – O'Rourke! Poor fellow, what will he be thinking? I hurry my steps along and as soon as we arrive at the ante-room I ask Greyhead what has happened to my companion. 'You mean the gentleman in the gig?' he says, somewhat disdainfully.

'I do,' I answer, with equal disdain.

'I believe he is still waiting. In the stable yard.' He waves his hand grandly, and I step outside and see O'Rourke sitting in the gig, the horse fretting a little. O'Rourke is blue with cold.

'Have you been sitting here all this time?'

'All two hours and twenty minutes.' He consults his pocket-watch with a wry smile. 'You and Her Majesty are obviously the best of pals.'

'Did they not take the horse away? Or offer you any refreshment?'

'They were distinctly frosty. When they heard my Irish brogue I think they expected me to start demanding Home Rule and making a dash at the Queen's Person. And then they were confused as to what to make of me; in attendance but not invited, neither servant nor gentleman. In short, I think I embarrassed them.'

'I am sure the Queen would have wanted you to be looked after.'

'Oh, you know her mind, now, do you?' He raises his eyebrows.

'Yes, Michael, I think I do. She is much misunderstood.'

'Well, well. You surprise me. But come on up, Dodo, or I shall be turned into stone, and incapable of so much as holding the reins to drive you back.'

I get up with some considerable effort on both our parts, and we set off back through the gates. He turns to me: 'Do you fancy a little trot around Hyde Park? The horse would appreciate the exercise.'

I should like to oblige him, but I am unsure. 'I don't know, Michael. Only four days after the funeral, to be riding with another man in a gig!'

'You were happy enough to ride with me here. And who's to notice, anyhow?'

I cannot explain it. It's irrational, I know, but riding round the park seems different – too pleasurable, somehow. 'In any case, it's getting dark.'

'I see.' He is silent for a moment, then clicks the horse into a trot. After a while he looks sideways at me. 'I take it Her Majesty did not allude to anything too unanswerable?'

'No. Her Majesty has a proper sense of decorum. But I had a feeling she knew of the estrangement, and that it was not of my choosing.'

'Well, I daresay she reads the papers.'

'Yes.'

I am not a friend of newspapers. Even now, when I read them, I fear to come across some disparagement of him: accusations that he was venal, greedy, vulgar or hypocritical. If only he had not encouraged such speculation by making our differences so public! Lord knows, I tried to dissuade him from announcing our domestic situation to the world, pleading that such matters were no concern of anyone but ourselves. But he would not have it. *The Readers have a right to know,* he insisted, in that dogmatic way of his, as he secretly composed the list of all my failings as a wife and mother. But I cannot feel that the Readers' rights were as paramount as he claimed. Afer all, they were as nothing when it came to Miss Ricketts. He clearly never felt the obligation to tell them about *her* in several paragraphs of black ink.

Miss Ricketts. Bewitching Miss Ricketts. Ever since Kitty spoke of her light grey mourning and her hat with the 'very smallest of veils', I have been prey to that view of her, as over and over again she turns and looks at me with a mocking countenance. I always try to put the picture from me, but this time a sudden curiosity comes upon me and I decide to ask O'Rourke what I have always vowed I would never do. 'How well did you know Miss Ricketts, Michael?'

O'Rourke coughs prodigiously and suddenly begins to pay a great deal of attention to the conduct of the filly, who is trotting along perfectly nicely as it is. 'Miss *Ricketts*?' he says rather vaguely, frowning as if at a distant memory, a name that is hard to place.

'Yes,' I say, somewhat sharply. 'Wilhelmina Ricketts. I think there is only one.'

'Not well at all.' He flicks the whip. 'In fact I met her on a few occasions only.'

'And what opinion did you form on these few occasions?'

He sighs. 'Dodo, why are you dragging this all up now?'

'Why are you reluctant to tell me?'

'What good will it do? Are you determined to add to your pain? Is Alfred's passing not enough for you?'

'I've never pressed you before, have I? I've never asked you to be disloyal. But Kitty says I must admit the truth.'

'I've told you the truth. She was simply a nice-looking young woman. No prettier, certainly, than many others. Not very well-educated, as far as I could ascertain. But with a certain appeal in the way she held her head. And with a certain charm in the way she talked. I could see from the start that Alfred was taken with her.'

A cold feeling runs through me. 'You didn't tell me that at the time.'

'But you know how Alfred was taken with many young ladies, and never any harm in it. To be honest, he was something of a father to her.'

'He was old enough to be one, certainly. Kitty was the exact same age.'

'Well, that's what he said, Dodo: "Imagine if she were Kitty or Louisa. Without a father, and fallen on hard times? Would not I – would not you, Michael – wish there were a well-disposed person to come to their aid?"'

'Hard times? Well, she was hardly a Dick Crawley or a Little Amy, was she?'

O'Rourke scratches his nose. 'Maybe not. But all the same, she and her mother lived pretty much on the edge – that's what he told me, at least. Always on the edge of destitution and debt, trying hard to remain respectable.'

'Ah. That would have struck a chord.'

'Well, you know how generous he was when his heart was touched. I can never forget that he gave me thirty guineas so I could set myself up to marry Clara. How was I to criticise him for helping someone else?'

'So, are you saying that it was merely a matter of *money* between them?'

'Yes – I mean, no. Well, not in that way. Or not very much. Oh, Heavens, Dodo, you're confusing me!' He flicks the whip again. We travel on in silence. Then he murmurs in a low voice: 'If you want the complete, utter, unvarnished, out-and-out truth, Dodo, I suppose I suspected something. There now! But I told myself I was wrong, that I was imagining things. And it was easy to do that, wasn't it? Because Alfred always made sure you saw things exactly as *he* saw them. If he said it was an innocent friendship, another of his charity cases, then it *was*. It was so much simpler to agree than to challenge him. I was a coward not to do it, though. I let you down.' He's becoming agitated and breathless.

He *was* a coward; I cannot deny that. Yet I cannot blame him wholeheartedly. I, of all people, know how hard it always was to make a stand against Alfred's certainties. In fact I cannot think of a single person who did. 'You didn't let me down, Michael. No more than I let *myself* down, at any rate.'

He shakes his head. 'I should have had the courage to speak when things were in the bud, before he'd let himself get drawn in beyond recall. Although I don't imagine my feeble powers of persuasion would have accomplished much.' He smiles wryly. 'He'd have sent me away with that iron-hard look of disapproval and the conviction that somehow *I* was the one in the wrong.'

I knew that iron-hard look only too well. I remember first seeing it when he spoke of his parents, his jaw tight, his eyes flinty: *They will do as I say from now on.* I'd been taken aback then; the expression had seemed so out of character. But, as time went on, I became more familiar with it, usually in response to some action – or inaction – of mine. Many an evening I would quake in antici-pation as I heard his foot on the stair, or saw his reflection in the mantel glass as he came into the room. Would he take me in his arms and give me a resounding kiss? Or would he see only my untidy dress and the pins falling out of my hair? *Please, Alfred,* I would beg him beneath my breath, *please be pleased with me.* It was not his wrath I feared; I knew he would never be so low as to strike me. It was his coldness, the withdrawal of his love that made me hold my tongue when I would rather have spoken, and submit when I would rather have resisted. Like Celia Masterman, I would have done anything to keep him happy. And no doubt it was the same for O'Rourke and all the others who lived in the fitful light of his eye.

We continue around the park. The street lamps are already lit and they give the trees ghostly auras. The sound of our wheels gets louder in the cooling air. O'Rourke finally turns into the thoroughfare that will take us home. There is an elegant house on the corner where the lights are already blazing. A cluster of people is coming out. A woman in a stylish green hat looks up at me, and a man laughs.

I imagine they know me; that they are talking about me, sitting up in a gig with a man who is not my husband. I feel my cheeks burn. I turn to O'Rourke: 'Tell me, the truth; was it common gossip? At the beginning, I mean – when I was so conveniently away in Leamington. Did everyone speak of him and Miss Ricketts?'

He answers quickly now: 'Well now, people will say all sorts of things when an older man takes an interest in a younger woman. Montague made his usual jokes about the 'Great Hypocritical'. And Thackeray couldn't resist referring to 'people living in Gibson-houses'. But truthfully, Dodo, it was idle talk. There was nothing to gossip *about*.'

'Would you have told me if there were?'

He pauses a long time. 'Would it have made you any happier?'

'It might have prepared me. You can't imagine the shock I felt when it all came at me so suddenly – like a locomotive. For all our disagreements, I never thought he would put me out of my own house.'

'We were *all* shocked at that, Dodo.' He looks glum. 'To be honest, I felt he was not the man I'd known all those years – and loved more than any man I have ever met. What he did then was shabby.' I catch the glimmer of a tear on his cheek. He has both hands on the reins, and cannot wipe it away.

'Did he speak about her?' I am determined to press him now I have begun.

'Only as I have already said – to sing her praises as an actress; to tell me what a difficult time she and her Mama were having; to remark on her prettiness and grace and his determination to do something to help her in her profession. But once *Lord Royston* was over, she and her Mama both seemed to disappear as if they were living in Timbuktu – although I gather it was only Peckham or somewhere. He never mentioned her to me again.'

He is tantalisingly vague. 'But before that – you saw them together?'

'Not exactly *together*. I sat in on rehearsals a few times and he'd be his usual self, jumping up and down, telling everyone what to do, like J. Samuel Soapstone. She'd stand there next to her Mama – meek, and a bit awestruck. But she knew how to make an entrance all right. Once she came downstage, slowly and gracefully, then stopped, lifting her head and asking him in a very coy manner whether that was 'as he wanted her'. And he said, "Perfect, exactly right." He whispered to me: "That girl will have 'em all in tears, mark my words."'

My mouth is dry: 'And did she?'

'Yes, I confess. She was totally heartbreaking. And *he* was heartbreaking, too. They were heartbreaking together.' He shakes his head. 'Good God, now I look back, it should have been obvious . . . but for some reason it was not.'

We have arrived back home. Wilson must have been looking out for us, because she is at the door immediately: 'Come in quick, madam. You must be perished.' She helps me down.

'It's Mr. O'Rourke who's frozen. He had to wait two hours and twenty minutes while I was inside!'

'Well, he *would* take you in the gig.' She looks at his pinched face and relents. 'But if he'd care to come in, I've got a good fire going.'

'Not today.' He looks relieved that he will not be forced to answer any more questions. But he seems rather sad, too. 'I shall call tomorrow, if I may. And you can tell me all about your new friend, the Queen.' He clicks the horse into a trot and drives off.

'I don't think *his* day turned out how he imagined,' says Wilson.

～ 14 ～

'*Mr. Norris* called while you was out,' Wilson says casually, when I have taken off my bonnet and cape and am back in front of the fire.

'Augustus?' I am astounded. 'What did *he* want?'

'Oh, he wouldn't tell me; I'm only a servant.' Wilson pulls a table close to my chair, puts the lamp on it. 'But he left you this. "Be sure to see she gets it," he says. As if I'm in the habit of forgetting my duties.'

It's a note, on my own notepaper, in Augustus's cramped hand. I take it. I'm not sure I want to read it. 'Thank you,' I say. I don't open it. Wilson hovers around me expectantly.

'Well?' I say. 'Is there something else?' I know perfectly well what.

'The Queen, madam. What was she like?'

'Much as in her pictures. Shorter than I expected, though. And a bit stouter, perhaps.'

'I meant, in character. Was she very severe?'

'No, not at all. Very kind, in fact, very agreeable. We got on excellently. I find we have much in common. A surprising amount.'

'You see?' She looks triumphant, although I can't imagine why she is taking the credit. For getting me into mourning, perhaps. For not showing myself up. 'And is she as sad as they all say?'

'She is *very* sad, certainly. She cannot stop talking of her dead husband, poor woman.'

'Poor woman.' She looks at me meaningfully.

'I have more excuse. Alfred is hardly in his grave.'

'That's as may be. But you've been thinking of him every minute these last ten years. Don't think I haven't seen you sitting and reading his books and letters over and over. I don't need to be one of them clairvoyants to know what's been going on in your mind.'

'Well, he was my life, I suppose . . .'

'And Mr. Wilson was mine – after Davie was took. And then he was took in his turn. But there's no point in grieving over what can't be changed.'

'No point? Oh, Wilson, were you not *angry*?'

'Angry?'

'Have you never raged against the unfairness of it all?'

She looks uncomfortable. 'A bit, maybe. When I was at my lowest. But I picked myself up and took myself in hand. It's all for a purpose, I said.'

'It's hard to see the purpose, though, isn't it?'

She is silent. Then she clears her throat: 'I'd better go and see to your supper. And you'd better open that letter of Mr. Norris's. He was most particular you read it.'

'Yes. Thank you, Wilson.' She goes. I open the letter.

Dear Ma,

Forgive ths scrawl but I did not expect to find you out. Kitty says yr always at home. I am in consultation wth my solicitors and thr is something I need to ask on Kitty's behalf. I wd appreciate an appointment at yr earliest convenience.

Augustus.

He's up to no good, I'll be bound. Why else is he seeking a confidential appointment? I sense desperation; I suspect he cannot wait to get his hands on Alfred's hard-earned cash. If only the law permitted Kitty to have control over her own money! It's monstrous that it will all go to Augustus. Perhaps if they were separated, maybe the lawyers could set something up to her advantage. (*As they did for you?* I hear Kitty ask, sardonically.) And then again, I don't know her mind. Maybe she loves Augustus, after all. She is loyal to him, certainly. Right from the time they first met.

I suppose that meeting marked the beginning of the end, although I had no idea of it at the time. We were living at Park House and Sissy had been our 'little housekeeper' barely six months. Kitty, I suppose, was about fourteen, and I was expecting Fanny. On the surface, our life was enviable. Alfred was more successful than any writer had ever been before, and our new house was very grand, with steps and porticos, and velvet curtains and tasselled blinds and acres of crimson carpets. Yet, under the surface, matters were rather less agreeable. I had been sick every morning for months and Alfred himself was not in good spirits. He complained of feeling claustrophobic, had headaches to shame the sorest of bears, and insisted his seasonal colic was due for a rampant return. I suspected that the real problem was his new book. 'The English scenes are boiling up nicely,' he said to O'Rourke over supper one night, 'but the French scenes drag; there is no life in them. I need to hear the language around me, see the faces of the people, walk the city streets. In short, Yours Truly needs a trip to Paris!' And the next day, he suited action to word and began to make plans for an early departure.

He asked me (in a rather luke-warm way) if I wanted to accompany him; but although I loved Paris, I felt disinclined to be crushed for hours in a railway carriage and then the steam-packet – and I certainly had no wish to languish alone in the salon of a French hotel while he tramped about in narrow alleys for hours on end. So I declined – and he immediately set about persuading O'Rourke and Charley to go instead: 'It'll be a lark, you'll see; three poor English innocents set loose among the enchanting *demoiselles de Paris*. The *monde* awaits – and the *demi-monde*, too!' I confess I felt a little uneasy then, knowing his jokes were never without a measure of truth. Indeed, he seemed so conspicuously glad to be deserting the domestic hearth that I wondered if it were politic to leave him so entirely to himself. Even in my condition, I was capable of strolling gently along the banks of the Seine, admiring the fashions of the ladies in the Tuileries or the *rue de Rivoli*. But then I realised that my need for copious amounts of luggage, extra stops along the way and the services of a hired maid would render him even more irritable. So I let him go without me, hoping that a change of air and companionship would revive his spirits and make him glad to see me when he returned. With such solid and trustworthy souls as O'Rourke and Charley at his side, I thought he could not go far astray.

While Alfred was in Paris, the children were not idle. I could hear their voices as they rushed excitedly about the house trying to solve a series of riddles that Alfred had left them, and following a treasure-trail in order to earn the half-crowns he had promised. Too old for such diversions, Kitty was devising a musical entertainment for his return. It had only two parts, and she'd made Alfie take the rôle of the wandering knight (which he did not relish) on the grounds that 'Papa will be so pleased with us for using our time to useful purpose' – a prospect she knew Alfie would not be able to resist. She'd found an old-fashioned silk dress from somewhere, and had made a costume for Alfie out of some workbox pieces and a pair of my old stockings. They often woke me up with their arguments as they rehearsed in the empty schoolroom above me.

On the day of his return, Alfred telegraphed us from Calais to say the company was taking the express train to London and should be arriving about four – 'So prepare the fatted cup of tea!' I was on tenterhooks all afternoon, Kitty at my feet, singing the words from her song so repeatedly that I soon knew them all by heart myself. The moment we heard the wheels of the carriage stop outside, Kitty rushed from the drawing room and bounded down the stairs to greet him. I eased myself forward to peer from the window, and there he was, bandbox-fresh, leaping down to the pavement, and executing a little dance there, his hat at a rakish angle, looking as though he could accomplish a ten-mile walk without breaking sweat. I had almost forgotten why I loved him so much, but the sight of him doing that dance warmed my heart. Charley and O'Rourke seemed to be moving at half his speed as they bumbled around in the carriage, impeding the descent of a fourth figure. Someone much younger. Someone tall, and slim, dressed in a fashionable jacket with a large soft hat. Someone with the certain knowledge that he was handsome, and taking pleasure in it.

I watched the three alight, stretching and brushing down their clothes as John unloaded the luggage and was almost knocked over as Kitty came galloping down the steps. I saw her stop short. She had noticed the stranger, who gave her a brief and languid bow. Alfred laughed and made a pantomime of introducing her. And Kitty curtsied. And the stranger bowed, in the cool manner of a man-about-town when faced with a pretty child.

My spirits rose immediately to see Alfred looking so cheerful. But I wished that he'd come alone. I knew that Kitty wanted him to herself too. She had devised her entertainment for *his* eyes and, much as she loved an audience, I knew she would be nervous of going wrong in front of strangers. But being Kitty, she couldn't bide her time. As they came up the stairs, I could hear her talking about it in her loud and excited way: 'It's called *Isabella and her Lover.*'

'Her lover, eh? *Un Vrai Amant?*' Alfred's voice, laughing. 'It all sounds far too grown-up for my dearest Kittiwake.'

'I'm not a child, Papa. I may write a love story if I choose.'

Alfred laughed. 'Incontrovertibly! Everyone loves a love story! And you, my dear, especially, being *a young wooman with her eyes and ears in all the right places – and an art to match to 'em*. But come, child, don't keep your Papa and his guests on the landing. Having spent a Sultan's fortune on the gilt and splendour of my drawing room, I am under an obligation to sit in it from time to time, and gloat extravagantly. No doubt your Mama is already ensconced; I think I glimpsed her at the window looking agreeably ecstatic at the return of the One and Only. Shall we go in?'

And then there was the bang of an upstairs door, and a sudden noise and rush of feet, and I could hear the other children come flooding down the stairs: *Papa! Papa!* Seconds later, they all erupted into the drawing room, Alfred still in his coat with the children hanging on his arms, demanding their half-crowns for solving the riddles. He shook them off good-humouredly, saying he would deal with them all in good time when he'd had a moment to change his boots and comb his hair and go upstairs to Ada – for whom he had a doll such as had not been seen in the streets of Paris since the time of Charlemagne. But he hoped in the meantime that they had been good for their Aunt Sissy. 'Like little cherubim?' he asked. 'Like little seraphim!' they shouted in unison. And he turned and kissed Sissy on her smooth, unblemished cheek – and she blushed, as usual. Then he came and kissed me, too.

'Dodo dear, this is my new friend, Augustus Norris. Augustus, may I introduce Dorothea, my wife?'

The stranger came up, and I saw his eyes flicker across my body, noting my thick girth, my unmistakable condition. I saw a ghost of surprise on his handsome features. Alfred saw it too, and said sheepishly: 'As you see, Dodo is doing her best to populate the world, regardless of expense. Charming though my children are –' he waved his hand at the maelstrom surging about in the middle of the room '– I could wish there were not quite so many of 'em. No doubt you will come to feel the same once you are a family man. There's nothing to compare with it for taking the wind out of one's sails!'

'I daresay. But I have no plans in that direction.' Augustus Norris smiled. 'There are too many lovely women in the world to restrict myself to one.'

I smiled too. 'All in good time, Mr. Norris. Wait until you fall in love.'

Alfred laughed, looking uneasy. 'Ah, yes. Love. Ha, ha! Is that the cause of it all? If only I'd known.' Then he turned suddenly, taking out his pocket-watch: 'Fifteen minutes after four, I wager! Let the trays be brought forth! Let us slake ourselves with the lambent liquid!'

Sissy, of course, had it ready. In came the trays and cake-stands, the teapots and hot-water pots, the milk jugs and sugar basins – all gleaming and neatly arranged. Alfred darted about, passing bread-and-butter and fruit cake to his guests and sometimes to me. He fidgeted a good deal, poking the fire, straightening pictures, talking about his meeting with Victor Hugo and other French writers whom he admired, peppering his conversation with French phrases. (He spoke French well by then, with a good accent, and it seemed odd to remember that once he had known hardly a word, and it was I who had had to instruct him in the use of verbs and nouns, testing him from *Wentworth's Primer* until far into the night. But he had made himself more than proficient now, having taken pains over the years to fall into conversation with every French peasant, shopkeeper and passer-by he ever met.)

Kitty could not keep still either, but followed him around, full of the entertainment to come. 'It's quite short, Papa. I've only got two actors – Alfie and myself – so I've had to cut it down.'

'Very sensible,' said Alfred. 'If you can't write to your audience, write to your cast! I take it you will be the eponymous Isabella?'

'Of course!'

'And what is she, this delightful creature of your imagination?'

'You should really wait and see, Papa.' Kitty smiled, and put her arm through his. 'But to whet your appetite, I can tell you that she's a lonely maiden who dwells in the very heart of the forest –'

He laughed. 'Deuced inconvenient place to dwell. No wonder she's lonely!'

'But she's enchanted, Papa. That's the tragedy. She's there against her will. And every day she sings from her high window, longing for a lover.'

'A lover? The devil she does!' He eyed Charley, and laughed more heartily.

Kitty reached up and put her fingers playfully over his mouth, now covered with a fashionable growth of beard and whiskers. 'Papa, stop laughing or I won't tell you at all!'

He made a grave face. 'I beg pardon. I shall be mute.'

'I hope so. You are so *very* distracting! Where was I? Oh, yes – night after night Isabella sings to the night air in her distress, but of course there is no one to hear her. However, Rodrigo –'

'Ah, now we come to it! The Romance.'

'You said you would be mute, Papa!'

'I am. I shall be. Perceive.' He took out his handkerchief and tied it across his mouth.

She laughed. 'At last! The One and Only is silent. Now, I can continue.'

Alfred made some muffled expostulation, looking as if he were about to choke, and we all laughed.

'I shall ignore you, Papa. I shall tell the story in spite of you. Now – Rodrigo is a knight *sans peur et sans reproche.* By magic, he hears her song from afar, and he falls in love with the sound of her voice –'

'Merely her voice! A disinterested man, then!' Charley piped up.

The men all laughed and Kitty's voice rose above them all: 'If you're all going to laugh I shan't play it for you! It's very – discouraging – after all the trouble I have taken!'

'It is, y'know. We should be applauding the efforts of such a fine young author – and actress.' I noted Augustus Norris had the sort of flat, languid voice that was becoming fashionable.

'Ah, you have a champion, Kitty!' said Alfred, putting his arm on the shoulder of his new friend. 'But be aware, dear sir. I will kill any man who comes between me and my daughter.'

'I will risk all to have the chance of seeing *Isabella and her Lover*,' Augustus replied, with a sardonic laugh.

So after tea, we repaired to the schoolroom, Kitty having relented once the men had promised faithfully not to laugh; and Alfred saying he would personally horsewhip any who did. The men sat clustered together, hands in pockets, leaning against the wall or rocking back on their chairs and eyeing each other jovially. When Kitty came on in a trailing dress and with rouged cheeks, Augustus muttered something in a tone I did not care for. And when she addressed the night from the high elevation of a broken chair, Charley became very red in the face with suppressed amusement. Even O'Rourke chuckled when Alfie came out from behind the book-cupboard astride a hobby-horse, holding a riding crop in his hand, and feigning ignorance of the fair maiden only a foot away. But all laughter suddenly ceased when she lifted her head and sang. She had such a sweet voice, such excellent phrasing. Everyone clapped tremendously when she had finished, Alfred most of all.

'There's more to come,' I called out, trying to quiet them so Alfie could make his speech.

'More?' murmured Augustus. 'Even more? Can a man bear it?'

Poor Alfie, overcome by the noisiness of the audience and a sense of his own ridiculousness, forgot his lines almost straight away. I tried to prompt him from the scribbled copy Kitty had given me to hold, but he wouldn't listen and strode off towards the door saying he wouldn't be laughed at – especially for such a *stupid* play.

'Come and finish it!' Kitty hissed. 'Rodrigo must declare his love! It's the essential part.'

'*I'll* be Rodrigo!' Augustus was on his feet. 'If Mrs. Gibson will be so good as to give me the script.'

So I gave it to him, and he immediately began to speak. They were foolish, hackneyed words, but he looked very fine, and knelt and bowed and walked about in a very elegant way, and Kitty was so glad to have a real man – a handsome man, moreover – making his declaration of love, that she forgot to be angry, and accepted his vows with relish. They took a bow together at the end and Kitty was pink with delight.

'Charmed,' he said, as the applause subsided. 'Now I'm afraid I must bid you delightful people goodnight.' And he shook hands with Alfred and sauntered away, taking out a small cheroot which I saw him light before he left the room.

⚘

'Where did you meet him?' I asked Alfred that night. He was busy in his dressing room, re-brushing the clothes Mary-Ellen had already brushed, and setting his boots straighter than she had left them.

'In Paris, *naturellement*. He is something of an *habitué*.'

'Do you like him?'

He stopped what he was doing. 'Of course I like him! Why else would I be inviting him to my house?'

'He seems different from your other friends.'

'Well, he's more adventurous, by a long chalk. Michael can be a stick-in-the-mud at times, you know. And Charley the same. All they wanted to do was look at paintings all day and tuck great napkins under their chins at night. I mean, pictures and statues are all very fine, *homard à la normande* is all very fine – but a man wants a little gaiety: theatre, opera, ballet-dancing. Augustus was ready for that.'

I felt myself grow hot. 'I thought your intention was to see the people, the streets, ordinary life.'

[189]

'And I did! I have a whole bookful of notes!' He held up one of his little notepads. 'But do I sense a tone of reproof? Is my lady wife afraid I would be tempted to run off with a pink-and-white ballet girl with roses in her hair and an ability to spin round on one toe like a veritable Dervish?'

'And *were* you tempted, Alfred?' I smiled, to make the question seem of no importance.

He laughed. 'All those silk stockings and white bosoms! Oh, a man was certainly *tempted*.'

I could see him – backstage, perhaps – or in a private supper room. Laughing. Flirting. Turning his luminous eyes on every woman there. But I knew better than to dwell on foolish (he would say *fevered*) imaginings. What mattered was that he was back with me, and seemingly in so much better spirits. I was even so bold as to think that perhaps he would take me into his confidence once more. 'And so your *petit congé* has helped you with your book, Alfred?'

'Inestimably.' He pulled off his tie. 'Augustus is more intimate with the streets of Paris – and places under the streets, for that matter – than *un vrai Parisien*. We left the other two gorging in the rue Saint Martin and took off into the night like black bats. One moment, we're in a gloomy old cemetery with graves sinking as if they were ships at sea; next we're in a curious courtyard where our two sets of footsteps seem to echo around as if we were a whole regiment. In the corner, there's an ill-looking tavern with an even worse-looking landlord, who I swear gave us the Evil Eye. And then, when we were least expecting it, we come upon the most delightful little theatre, crammed between an ironmonger's and a tobacco-shop, offering seating for at least twenty under-employed gentlemen and one or two ladies who have seen better days!' He laughed. 'And, dear Dodo, having seen them all, I have – hey presto! – transferred them into my notepad and thence into my head.'

He seemed so much his old self that I dared to reach up and kiss him on the lips. I knew then how my whole happiness depended on his presence; and once more I made the resolution that I would stop thinking of myself and my little jealousies and annoyances. Everything I did from then on would be done with Alfred's pleasure in mind. 'I am so very glad you are home, Alfred!' I said. 'I have missed you so very, very much.'

He patted my arm and smiled.

I look at Augustus's note again, and then put it aside. I need be in no hurry to reply. There is nothing Augustus can possibly want to say to me that cannot wait. I do not have to accede to every request that is made of me. I am, after all, an independent woman. Then Wilson comes in to tell me supper is ready. 'It's brown soup first,' she says. 'Then boiled ham and cabbage. Then a nice rice pudding. I reckon that should warm up an elderly party as has been gallivanting in a gig.'

15

Wilson is taking down my hair and brushing it carefully. She always says my hair is quite the finest she has ever known. Fine as thistledown. Although when it is let out, the grey strands show themselves thick and wiry, reminding me that their glory days are done. 'Will we be seeing Mr. Norris again soon?' she says, plaiting it into a long braid. 'He was most insistent about speaking to you.'

'I daresay,' I murmur. 'I shall write to him tomorrow.'

I should so much rather I had nothing to do with the man – but we are inextricably connected and I have a feeling that if I do not see him, he will force my hand with some unpleasantness.

That first night I hadn't been blind to his effect on Kitty and I'd had to listen with indulgence as she rattled on about him for days afterwards. *He is very handsome and tall, isn't he? And very mysterious and romantic.* But Kitty was always prone to sudden attachments and I'd taken her words as no more than hero-worship. She and I had never been in the habit of sharing confidences; and at the time I was too distracted to pay her my full attention. Dr. Phelps was in almost daily attendance on me, but nothing he could do seemed to lift my heavy spirits or make me more alert. I dozed wherever I could and on more than one occasion fell asleep at the supper-table, sliding sideways and dropping my knife and fork with a crash. Alfred would give me an impatient look, as if I were doing it on purpose. Indeed, he could not forbear to joke about it whenever we had company: *Dodo, as you see, is a veritable Sleeping Princess – albeit of a slightly more mature and substantial appearance than is normally associated with that personage. I fancy any regular Prince would have a job to wake her — kiss or no kiss — let alone raise her from her bed and carry her off in his arms. Yours Truly himself — for all his superior powers — is hardly up to the task!*

Through all this, Augustus was much in evidence. He would turn up in the late afternoon — usually yawning and asking for coffee — and proceed to lounge about, trying to amuse himself while Alfred was occupied in writing. He'd bring sweetmeats for the children, and sometimes he'd help Georgie sail his boat in a tin bath on the kitchen table, or build a house of cards with Louisa, or make a little sketch of Kitty. Sometimes he even spoke to *me*. But more usually he draped himself elegantly in some corner and read the newspaper. After which he'd stay for supper, where he'd rarely address a remark to anyone except Alfred, and then it would be about some subject to which the rest of us were not party. It was odd to see him there in his loose, fashionable clothes, and I was never comfortable with his sardonic observation of us all. Supper-times were noisy events (Alfred always insisted the children should dine *en famille*), but Augustus remained detached from it all, idly examining his (rather long) fingernails or staring at the contents of his glass as if there was something more amusing to be seen there. Alfred would preside at the head of the table and, when I was able, I'd take the foot. Sissy would sit at Alfred's right hand, helping Georgie with his fork and spoon and ensuring that the servants cleared away promptly between each course. Kitty would habitually hold forth, trying to capture all the attention for herself, attempting to better her father's stories or criticise his jokes until he'd eventually lose patience and tell her to hold her tongue. Lou would smirk to herself, and Eddie would pipe up, *Shall we cut her tongue off, Papa?* And Alfred would reply, *Yes indeed! Cut it off and fry it in butter so that it is of at least some use in this world!* Augustus would laugh in his staccato, hollow way; and Kitty would blush.

After supper, Alfred would tell the children stories; and the men would then smoke for an hour or so before setting off into the night. Alfred had always enjoyed nocturnal jaunts, and I was used to him putting on his greatcoat and muffler at some ungodly hour, saying he needed an *infusion of London streets* – and then creeping back into my bed at five in the morning, cold as ice. But he'd always gone alone, like a dreamer or sleepwalker, drawn into the life of the city. These excursions with Augustus were different. He didn't tell me where they went.

'Alfred seems much taken with young Mr. Norris,' said O'Rourke one evening when he called only to find him absent yet again. 'I've not had a proper conversation with him for weeks. In fact, I've no idea how *The Weaver of Silver Street* is going – if at all!'

'He spends all his spare time with that young man,' I said. 'If Augustus were a woman, I'd be quite jealous of all the attention he enjoys.' In fact, I resented *anyone* who took up Alfred's time; who took him away at the only part of the day when I had him all to myself.

O'Rourke fiddled with his cravat pin. 'You know, I'm surprised at Alfred. He's normally such a good judge of character.'

I looked at him quickly. 'Do you know something untoward about Augustus, then?'

O'Rourke sucked his teeth. 'Nothing *untoward*, exactly. Only that he has a poor reputation with money. You know the type of thing – gambling; horse racing; lavish expenditure in all directions. They say he's run through half his father's fortune already, and is set fair to finish the process by the end of the year.'

I was relieved; it was only money – and in money matters, Alfred was sharp as a needle. 'But if Augustus chooses to ruin himself, that's not Alfred's fault. In fact,' I said, pondering it further, 'I expect Alfred is doing his best to guide him towards the straight and narrow path.'

'Do you *really* think that, Dodo?' O'Rourke looked disbelieving.

I wasn't sure; I suspected Augustus was not a man who could be guided much on anything. But that would not stop Alfred trying. Alfred always believed every life could be reclaimed. 'Why not?' I said. 'Just think of Utopia House.'

'Ah, dear old Utopia House.' O'Rourke sucked his teeth again.

'What do you mean?'

'Oh, nothing, Dodo. Nothing at all.'

But I knew why he'd said it that way. After all, I too, had questioned the intensity of my husband's interest in that particular scheme. It was one thing to campaign for women of a certain sort to be brought from their ways, but I did not see why Alfred had to be involved in such detail with their daily lives. However, I'd taken comfort that Miss Brougham was always at his side; and that she never failed to find him helpful and ingenious: *Your husband is a marvel,* she wrote. *He has drawn up plans for every room, and every item needed in the room: a picture of Our Saviour with the Children; a vase where each inmate can put wild flowers to cheer herself; a table with a New Testament which she can learn to read and study; a simple coverlet on each bed. And he has sketched out all the plots in the garden where each woman may work and raise her produce; and the kitchen where others may make the meals. He has drawn up a weekly bill of fare – and directed how the women should have their dress – plain, clean cotton in a modest style; nothing reminiscent of their former ways. And he has addressed the women so beautifully, and read the Bible to them so movingly! I swear they were all in tears.*

I could imagine it. Although I didn't *have* to imagine it, because he talked about it himself. He'd come home and stand by the fender and poke the fire, and tell me how he'd encountered some new young inmate called Sal or Annie, as beautiful as though the very Sun of Heaven shone from her eyes. 'But she knew nothing of right or wrong, Dodo. She'd never heard the words of the

Bible, never known indeed that there *was* a Bible to have words in it to guide her path and redeem her spirit. Never known anything but brutality and vice. Never known there was anything but coarseness and deceit. You can't blame such girls for the lives they've led, can you, Dodo? You can't despise them. You should rather despise the men who have made them that way, the country that allows such things to flourish!' And he'd pace around, his face flushed, shaking with anger.

So why should I not believe he might have a mission to save even a dissolute man such as Augustus? 'You do not have much faith in your best friend,' I told O'Rourke, 'if you imagine such a callow young man could turn him to evil ways.'

'Oh, Dodo!' O'Rourke seized my hand. 'You are always so ready to believe the best in Alfred – and I love you for it. But even the One and Only can make mistakes. This so-called friendship with Norris will come to a bad end, mark my words.'

Sadly, that proved to be the case. And I was blamed for not seeing the harm; for not preventing it.

The discovery happened suddenly. It was a Sunday evening; the household was quiet, and I'd been half-listening to a duet Kitty and Augustus had been playing, a favourite sentimental song of Alfred's that made them stop and whisper and start again. The halting rhythms had lulled me into a dream in which numerous and very handsome young ladies were competing for the honour of singing before the Queen. Kitty was due to step forward in all her finery, but had forgotten her music, and the Lord Chamberlain, got up in a very large powdered wig, began to berate her: *What are you doing?* he kept asking. *What are you doing?* His voice became louder and louder and I woke up to find Alfred standing white-faced at the open drawing-room door, his hand still on the doorknob: 'What are you doing?' he cried. 'What is the meaning of this?' I turned and saw Kitty and Augustus standing bolt upright – Kitty by the piano, Augustus by the sofa next to the stuffed owl; and looking equally startled. Kitty was pink; Augustus paper-white. Kitty spoke up defiantly, saying there was no need to 'go on so'. After all, Augustus had only given her a kiss: 'That's allowed, isn't it? Uncle Charley and Uncle Muffin kiss me all the time!'

Alfred seemed to leap the whole length of the room. I thought he was going to attack Augustus with his bare hands, but he stopped two feet short of him: 'How dare you kiss her! How dare you put your hands on her! It's unspeakable!' I had often seen him angry, but only once – on the night of Alice's death – had I seen him lose his self-possession so completely. His eyes were danger lamps, his whole body rigid, as if it were costing him everything he had to keep control. He gestured at Kitty: 'Go upstairs, child – now, I tell you – *now!*' But Kitty did not move, and it seemed as though he had no strength to force her, but turned back to Augustus: 'As for *you*, Norris – after all I have done for you; after all we have shared! Get out of my house – and don't come back!'

Augustus lifted his graceful hand and made a sound as if to interrupt, but Alfred raged on: 'Don't say a word; it is futile. Go – and keep away. I never want to hear from you again. And, by God, don't even *dream* of communicating with Kitty!'

I stared at them. It all seemed unreal, like a melodrama, and I half-expected them to stop and consult their scripts and start again. Augustus opened his mouth to speak, but seeing Alfred's furious expression, shrugged his shoulders and walked past him through the open door, trying to look insouciant, and muttering something about 'not being in the theatre now'. But Kitty ran at Alfred and pummelled him with her fists: 'You can't send him away. I love him!'

Alfred held her off by the wrists, glaring at me the while: 'Love, you say? *Love?* What's been going on? What horrors have been taking place under my own roof? Have you condoned this behaviour, Dodo?'

[197]

I shook my head dumbly. My mind was whirling. It seemed only yesterday that Augustus had been bringing Kitty presents of sugar mice and kaleidoscopes — and now it appeared he'd been sitting on the piano stool, kissing her on the lips and touching her bosom. I looked at her pink face and mutinous expression. Why should Augustus be making love to a mere child? Yet when I looked again, I could see that Kitty had grown fuller in her figure, and that she had put her dark hair up in a very grown-up manner — in short, that she was no longer a child. And I was shocked and ashamed to think she had come to womanhood without my realising.

Alfred pulled her across the carpet with a face like thunder-clouds: 'But it was going on *under your nose*, Dodo! Under your very nose! Here in your own drawing room! What kind of mother allows that? How can I ever trust you with our children again?'

I could think of nothing except how much at fault I was, how narrowly Kitty had escaped disgrace. Alfred was right: what kind of mother fails to notice her child being seduced by a grown man, and a man of ill reputation at that? What kind of mother misses the vital looks, the stolen caresses, the significant phrases that should have put her on her mettle? I begged Alfred's pardon, begged Kitty's pardon, begged God's pardon. I blamed my tired-ness and the medicine. I raved hysterically: *Forgive me, forgive me!* I fell to my knees in a heavy heap, and had to be taken upstairs by a consortium of three or four servants. As I lay on the pillows with a cold compress on my head and the taste of laudanum on my lips, I could hear Kitty making a terrible wailing sound in a far-off room, being comforted by the steady voice of Bessie — and I blamed myself more than ever, because I knew I should have had my daughter's confidence, and that it is a mother's rôle to protect her children, no matter what. I was too absorbed in my own error to consider that it was Alfred who had first brought Augustus among us.

Alfred's threat was, needless to say, carried out to the letter. We never saw Augustus again – and Alfred made sure Kitty was always chaperoned by Sissy or one of the servants when she went out. He never once mentioned Augustus's name; and it seemed that the man who had recently been almost a member of our family was, at a stroke, deprived of his whole existence. I suppose I should have been forewarned by such implacability on Alfred's part; such an ability to excise a once-loved person from his life like a malignant chancre. I should have known that with Alfred there were no half-measures. But at the time, I was so glad to be rid of Augustus that I failed to question Alfred's capacity to act in such a thoroughly cold-hearted way.

As it happened, Augustus had not quite vanished from our lives. He made a final appearance in an unexpected way: when *James Bartram* came out the following winter, there he was again in the person of Miles Danvers, with his flat drawling voice, sardonic character and easy grace. A villain, of course – but a charming villain; a man of promise who yet had chosen to go to the dogs; a man who seemed to be humorous and clever, but who had no moral heart. The virtuous James Bartram weds the faithful Madeleine, and Miles Danvers ends as a broken wreck, floating in the Thames with no one to attend his funeral except the crossing boy to whom he has given his last sixpence. Yet when James Bartram looks at his friend's dead body, he puts his hand over his face and weeps: *And I could see him again, not pale and expressionless, but handsome and free, his long curls blowing back in the wind as we took the steamship across Lake Geneva on the last leg of our last journey together. I see him now, staring into the distance, his cheek flushed, his face so handsome and full of hope, his body so graceful and young. God knows I should prefer that he had died then, when he was still dear to me, than come to this dreadful end.*

I couldn't help wondering what Augustus made of this literary valediction, and whether he had suffered half as much in paying court to Kitty as I did for not noticing it. And suffer I did. Alfred made sure of that, believing that I was no longer capable of caring for my own children and that they were better off entirely under my sister's control.

᳅

It grieves me even now to think it was *I* more than anyone who was warm for bringing Sissy among us; that it was *I* who not only set the seed of the enterprise, but who cultivated and brought it to fruition. How deeply I rue that day! Yet how could I have known? There had been nothing to suggest that the arrangement would not be to mutual advantage. Sissy had grown up to be amusing company (albeit with an inclination to be sharp at others' expense). She was a great admirer of Alfred's work and could mimic his characters almost as well as he. Every time I'd visited Chiswick, I kept thinking how delightful it would be if she could join us in London; and with the birth of each of my children, the prospect seemed more and more attractive.

By the time Georgie was born, the matter had become pressing: I was failing in my health and, although Bessie did most of the hard work, she had only one pair of hands, and Alfred said that it was wrong to expect a half-educated girl to instil our children with all the proper thoughts and feelings, to instruct them in their manners and hear their prayers. He always ran up to the children himself as soon as he came home, and played with them and read to them in his inimitable way – but he could not always be there. Sissy, by contrast, had an excess of time on her hands and fretted at her secluded life in a place where there was 'nothing to do except grow older'.

For a while I did not dare to broach the subject for fear of upsetting Mama. The old wounds had not healed and Alfred was still largely *persona non grata* in the Chiswick household. However, once Ada took to her couch, and with a baby and toddler to keep an eye on as well, I decided to sound out Sissy's views.

'I fear Mama will never agree to let you go,' I'd said, as we strolled along the laburnum walk, baby Georgie in my arms, and little Eddie toddling and tumbling by my side as he searched for pebbles in the path.

'I am twenty-four, Dodo. I can do as I please. Mama cannot bear a grudge against Alfred for ever – and if she does, well, she will have to do so and there is no help for it. She cannot stand in my way.'

'But I fear it is selfish of me, Sissy dear. You should be marrying and having children of your own.'

'Oh, *that!*' she'd declared, picking Eddie up from a fall, and dusting him down and hushing him as if she had been a nursemaid all her life. 'I've yet to find a man I would remotely consider worth sacrificing myself for. Mama and Papa do their best, of course, and we have an endless procession of tight-collared young men coming to hold teacups in the drawing room every Sunday. Even Cousin George has been talked of again since poor Lily passed away. But why should I hide myself in *Coventry* of all places when I could be at the heart of London society! Indeed, the more I think of it, the more certain I am!'

Needless to say, Alfred was delighted at the prospect of my clever – and undoubtedly handsome – sister joining the family. He himself fetched her from Chiswick in the carriage, and carried her (she was very slim and light) all the way up to the drawing room, while the children lined up with Union Jacks. Alfie blew a fanfare on his tin trumpet, and even Ada made an appearance in Bessie's arms, clapping her hands in welcome like the cherub she was.

'What a grand house you have, Dodo!' Sissy had said, twirling around, admiring the crystal chandeliers and the vast mirrors that Alfred had had installed. 'All this glass must take a great deal of keeping clean!'

'Oh, yes,' I said eagerly. 'Alfred is most particular. Everything is cleaned with vinegar and newspaper. He has it all laid down. The servants report to him every morning for their list of duties.'

She looked surprised: 'Good Heavens, Dodo! Surely Alfred has enough to do without bothering himself with domestic matters?'

'I don't think it *bothers* him, Sissy,' I said, glancing quickly at Alfred, and feeling for the first time that there might be something wrong with the way we managed our household. 'In fact, it pleases him to see to such matters himself. I've no wish to interfere as he is *so very particular* and liable to be *such a bad-tempered bear* if things go wrong!' I laughed, and to my relief Alfred laughed too.

Sissy did not laugh. 'Well, now I am here, I can take it all in hand. Simply tell me what needs doing, Alfred. Poor Dodo need never be disturbed.'

Poor Dodo – how quickly I came to live up to that description! As soon as she learnt that Fanny was expected, Sissy began to treat me as an invalid, advising me on my diet and need for regular rest; admonishing me if I did anything so foolish as opening a window or trying to take a book down from a high shelf: *Do try and be sensible, Dodo.* She made me loosen my stays and put back my hair, and would not let me drink more than a glass of wine each night. Instead she brought me *tisanes* and dried biscuits by the score. I have to confess to a certain mute rebellion as I poured half the tea away in the potted ferns, and gave the biscuits to the dog or, when the dog refused, threw them on the fire, where they burned with a resentful glow.

I felt I should be glad that she was relieving me of all the chores that I found tedious or simply did not have time – or strength – to do. But I was envious of her ability to elicit praise from Alfred and, instead of being grateful, I was inclined to be cold to her. Maybe if I had made more effort to be sisterly, the course of my life from then on might have been different. But in all honesty, she didn't seem to care about what *I* said at all. For her, the important thing was Alfred – and second to Alfred, the children. She made some sort of pretence at consulting me, standing in the doorway with a pencil and notepad: *Shall we have rabbit pie or a mutton joint?*

Is it time the chimneys were cleaned? Do you think Georgie should be in breeches by now? But it was clear that she had her own methods, and no real intention of allowing me to disrupt them with my vagueness and indecision. She was up early every morning — before even Alfred was up — and she'd make sure his breakfast was to his liking, his shoes properly polished, his newspaper folded, and that his study was clean, the fire banked, and his writing implements arranged as he liked.

So Alfred saw no fault in her, and the children (as children will) cared only for the moment, responding with gusto to her enthusiasm for outings, games and competitions, activities I could no longer attempt. It was 'Aunt Sissy says' and 'Aunt Sissy thinks' from morning to night, especially from Lou. Only Kitty held out against her charms, spurning the list of duties Sissy had drawn up for her. *I hate her!* she'd say, glowering in at me from the doorway. *She thinks she is my Mama — and she's not!*

For a long time I swallowed my resentment, feeling some rapprochement would surely take place; but instead she began to encroach more and more on my wifely duties. One day I could bear it no longer. I went looking for Alfred and found him in the library. 'I am no longer Mistress in my own home,' I complained, barely managing to keep back the tears in my voice. 'Sissy keeps all the keys in her possession, and today I can't even arrange the flowers in the drawing room because she has done them already.'

He looked up from his book. 'Ah, yes, she has quite a talent for it, don't you think? Such cheerful colours! But if you wish to arrange the flowers yourself, I have no real objection. It's hardly a hanging matter.'

'It's not only the flowers, Alfred. It's everything.' I felt like a little girl, pouting over some imagined slight, and his surprised look made me even more conscious of it.

'But surely that is why Sissy is here, Dodo! You should be glad she is so willing to take on the work, and that she is so efficient at it. I think she would be worth two hundred pounds a year if we had to pay her a salary. And you have to admit, dearest, that the household now runs much more to time.'

'Oh, *time!*' I said, with a great rush of annoyance. 'You and your time! Tick-tock, click-clock! Pick-pock!'

'Dodo, you are being childish. And ungrateful. I'll hear no more of it. I have serious matters to attend to.' And he went back to *Health and Sanitation Amongst the Labouring Classes.* And I left the library, feeling a terrible inner rage I could direct at no one.

The worst thing was that she kept me from my children. I tried to tell myself she was only concerned for my welfare as she dutifully brought them in to kiss me good morning and goodnight with every expression of loving concern. But she forbade them to bother me at any other times, saying *Your Mama needs her rest.* I felt I did not need quite so much rest as was being prescribed, and I would have welcomed the comical liveliness of the children's conversations to break up my lethargy. I longed for the chance to set little Georgie on my lap, kiss the top of his head and feel the chubbiness of his arms and legs as he wriggled about. But Georgie was under a precise regime of naps and walks, and the other children had tasks to do with which I dared not interfere. Even my visits to Ada were rationed, for fear she would become more excited than was good for her health. 'We have to be sensible,' Sissy said, somewhat sanctimoniously. 'I know you like to see the child, but we cannot always do as we should like in this world.' I knew Ada was always eager for my visits, though, and her eyes seemed brighter when I was there to talk to her. So whenever Sissy was out walking I crept to Ada's couch and read to her, stroking her silky hair as the clouds raced past the window outside. *Don't tell Aunt Sissy,* I'd say. *This has to be our secret.*

I did my best to not to be jealous of Sissy. I tried to smile as I saw her with Alfred, their heads together over some bill or letter, or as she sat copying out his manuscripts. I tried to persuade myself that such things were a tedious part of my life I could happily be without. *She is not his wife*, I said to myself; *and she never will be. She will never share his bed or know his loving embrace. I need have no fear.* So whenever Alfred slipped in beside me and said, 'Are you well enough tonight, Dodo?' I'd always say yes, even though I dreaded the idea of another confinement – not only for my own health but because Alfred himself had distinctly fallen out with the joys of fatherhood, complaining continually about the excessive number of children I had already provided him with, how costly and troublesome they all were, and how he had a mind to become a hermit to escape it all. Sometimes I would catch him looking at one of the children with such a dead eye of disapproval that my heart would sink within me. In those moments I wondered if he really cared for children at all.

But the children kept coming. After Fanny was born I'd hoped that nursing her would spare me for a while but, barely six months later, I woke with the old, familiar feeling of nausea and knew that I would have to face Alfred once more. When I screwed up the courage to tell him, I only got as far as 'Alfred dear, I have some news . . .' before he closed his eyes in despair and silently lowered his head upon the final chapter of *James Bartram*. I could not help but rejoin, a little testily: 'You must own *your* part in it, Alfred. Lord knows I cannot beget children entirely on my own!' – but he did not reply, or even look at me, merely groaned in a theatrical manner.

And the poor babe-to-be seemed to sense she was not welcome: she gave me continuous pain, so that I could hardly walk a few yards without having to stop and stretch out my leg with the cramps. Alfred fretted and fumed and paced about, angry at my awkwardness and his impotence in the matter: 'This is too bad, Dodo. Phelps will have to find something stronger for you.' Something stronger was duly found, and had the effect of making me lose what sense of time still remained to me. Some days I was too distracted even to venture downstairs. And in spite of spending so much of my time asleep, I seemed to have an unerring ability to act foolishly when awake. I had sudden unaccountable bouts of hiccoughs. I forgot things. I lost things. I blundered about half-dressed, surprising the servants and alarming the children with my unkempt appearance and continual queries about Alfred's whereabouts. I felt agitated and restless and somehow lacking in air, as if I were choking from some invisible dust.

And then Ada passed away. She had been growing thinner all through the summer, and Dr Phelps was always going from my room to hers and back again, looking grave and sighing a little more than usual. But in my distraction with my own condition, I had not seen that the end was so near for my darling child, and it came upon me with all the force of a steam hammer. I was given so much laudanum I can remember only blackness. Blackness and more blackness, and a permanent ache in my throat. Alfred standing like stone at the bedside, and Bessie's mouth open in a silent scream; and somewhere in the distance, the sounds of the children crying. And the black coats and tall hats of the undertakers as they massed in the hallway, and the empty coffin being carried up the stairs. And the floor coming towards me and some unknown person holding me up and someone carrying me away. And my head and limbs and stomach and back feeling one great conglomeration of pain as I was put in my bed with the blinds drawn and the lamp draped with a dark cloth.

Barely six weeks later, Florence May was born. I was not ready for her, and she was not ready for the world. The poor thing could hardly open her eyes, and her breath was so thin and fluttery it barely made a movement in her chest. I held her poor wizened body against me, trying to make her suck, trying to will her into life. But even as I looked at her, her mouth turned blue and her body grew limp; and I knew it was useless. I wept then; I crushed her hard to my bosom and refused to let her go. 'I must see Alfred,'

I kept repeating. 'He will know what to do.' But they said that there was nothing he could do; even Alfred was not a miracle-worker, they said; even *he* could not bring her back from the dead. The midwife tried to release the child from me by force, but I held on to her. Then Sissy leant over me, smelling of carbolic soap, saying I was tiring myself with all this screaming and must let the child go for my own health and sanity. But I still held on, as if Florence May contained in her tiny body some part of my own real life. 'Get away from me!' I cried out to Sissy. 'You devil, get away!'

Finally, Alfred was summoned. He came into the sickroom like sunshine. He came to the bedside and touched me on the hand: 'Let me hold the poor child, Dodo.' And he took her from me gently, and wrapped her in the tiny shawl I had embroidered for Kitty so many years before. As he stood there cradling her, tears started from his eyes and he shook his head: 'There must be no more babies, Dodo. I cannot bear to stand over another little grave – I think it will quite unman me! And you, poor dear girl – you must have complete rest. As soon as all this is over, I shall see to it.' I grasped his hand, and we wept together over our child as we had once wept over Alice.

16

I can see Alfred so clearly. He is lying on a strange kind of dais, draped with velvet. He is young, his skin is smooth, and his lips are full. He is dressed as Abanazar. Sissy and Alice are standing beside me, holding huge bunches of flowers. My own hands are empty. I know that I meant to bring forget-me-nots – the flower that matches my eyes; the flower he'd put in his buttonhole the day of Alice's funeral.

But that cannot be right. Alice is here beside me. She is looking at Alfred and smiling. 'I love you so much,' she says. 'You are my Good Angel.' Sissy says: 'I love you too.' She looks as young as Alice, and even prettier. They are almost twins; dressed in the same blue gowns with white veils tumbling down their backs like brides. They look desirable, whereas I am dismayed to find that I am wearing an old black dress, musty and rusty and stained down the front with Dr. Phelps's mixture. I am mortified; I cannot be seen in this. I must go back home and find my *own* blue gown.

'It will hardly fit you now!' says Sissy, laughing unkindly. 'You are far too stout.'

'Yes,' says Alice, more judiciously. 'I am afraid you have broadened a good deal since I saw you last.'

'But I was fitted for a new one!' I wail. 'Miss Walters came. I was promised it for today!'

'Too late, as usual, Dodo!' says Sissy, shaking her head. 'Shame on you! It was his last request that we should all dress in blue. He was quite specific on that. And, as you know, he is always right.'

'Yes, Dodo. You of all people should know that.' Alice is

gliding towards him. She stoops over him and it seems as though she is about to kiss him. But she is only pulling away the Arabian drapery and, as it falls to the ground, I see that Alfred is wearing a sailor's outfit.

'He may wish to dance the hornpipe later on,' Alice explains gravely.

'Dance? So he is alive?' My heart lifts in a great explosion of happiness, but before I can speak, Sissy shakes her head.

'He is dead to *you*, Dodo, because you are such an earthly creature. But he is immortal to us because we are creatures of the spirit. We will always be by his side for ever and ever.'

'But he is *my* husband! *I* love him the best! *I* should be by his side!' I move forward and start to beat them away, but their bodies strangely have no resistance. I wake up gasping.

I can still feel that flaming of hope. I try to hold on to it, to embrace and conserve it within me. If only he were still alive! If only he were here in this room dressed in a sailor-suit ready to prance about the furniture and hold me tight to his bosom – nothing he has ever said or done in these last ten years would matter. I would forgive him everything. I would let him have as many women as he liked – even my sisters, if that made him happy. He could sit in state with adoring women all round him, like an Arabian prince in a harem.

I am aware that Wilson is by the bed. She is looking agitated. 'Beg pardon, madam. I wouldn't have disturbed you – but Mr. Norris is here, very insistent. I told him to come back, but he says he'll wait on the stairs till Kingdom Come. I didn't know what to do.'

'Mr. Norris?' I am confused. 'What time is it?'

'A little after eight, madam.'

I am astonished. I see he can rise early when the mood takes him. 'I can't possibly see him now.'

'He says it's very urgent.'

'Indeed?' He can go months without seeing me. Now he calls

on me every day. 'Well, he'll have to wait *on my earliest convenience,* like Boodles.'

'He won't like it.'

'I daresay. But he'll have to put up with it. I'll have my break-fast here, then. I'll let him know when I have time to see him.'

Wilson goes out. I hear a commotion at a distance. Augustus is not taking my refusal well. 'I'll wait,' I hear him mutter. 'I'll wait all day if I've a mind to!'

The voices are coming closer. I cannot believe it – Augustus is almost at my door. I shall clearly have no peace while he is under my roof.

Wilson edges in with my breakfast tray. 'Mr. Norris says he intends to wait until you are in a fit state to see him. Which he begs to request will be sooner rather than later.'

Wilson is ruffled. It is not fair to let her bear the brunt of Augustus's anoyance. 'Oh, very well,' I say. 'You may tell him I shall see him at half past nine.'

'Yes, madam.' She goes out. I hear words exchanged, then silence. I sigh with relief. Then attempt my porridge and poached eggs. It's not often I have my breakfast in bed; I don't like to, as it reminds me of all the time when I was 'indisposed'; when Sissy contrived to keep me away from the rest of the family as much as possible. But once in a while it is an agreeable indulgence.

At half past nine, I am ready. Augustus is sitting moodily watching the street from my window, sketching the scene. 'You've a fine view of the world,' he concedes. 'I'll wager you know more of what happens than you let on.'

'Maybe; maybe not. But that is not the reason you are here. Please state your business – this business that is so pressing that you disturb my whole household.'

'One bad-tempered servant, you mean.'

'No, not only Wilson. *I* have a routine too. This is the second morning you have intruded upon it.'

'What routine? Reading old letters and such, you mean?' Kitty has clearly told him things. I am cross with her. But Augustus suddenly seems to realise that if he is asking a favour, he is not going the right way about it, and his manner softens.

'Look here, Ma. To be frank, I've come to ask you to intercede with Sissy.'

'With *Sissy*?' Even *I* have not expected that. I look at him, astonished. He must know that Sissy and I have never spoken – never corresponded even – since I left Alfred's house and she stayed on. Kitty hates her too, but even *she* is on better terms with her than I. 'What on earth can *I* do to help you? And what help do you want?' As if I didn't know. He wants her to release the money. And for some reason he thinks I can persuade her.

'You're her sister, aren't you? And Kitty is your child. Surely that counts for something.'

'Sisterhood has never counted in the past. She has abused the very meaning of that name. If you are so anxious to influence her, why don't you see her yourself?'

'I've tried. She's been 'not at home' these four days.'

'Perhaps she is busy. I imagine there is a lot to do.'

'Oh, she was there all right. I saw her at the window, lurking behind the curtain.'

'Why don't you write to her, then?'

'I *have* written.'

'Well, give her time to reply. Why are you in such terrible haste, Augustus?'

He swings his long legs down from the window-seat. 'Well, Ma, to be frank, I'm in dire trouble. Kitty knows nothing of this and I ask you to keep it a secret, but I owe a deal of money and if I don't pay it next week I'll lose my house and everything in it. Kitty and I (not to put too fine a point on it) will be paupers.'

I am horrified. 'How have you managed to get in this state?'

'You know me, Ma. I'm a man who takes chances. Some I win,

some I lose. Generally it evens out. Don't look at me in that way! Have I ever come to you for money? No, and you know it damned well. But I had a bad loss recently. I've bills out all over town and the Jews are at me. We need Kitty's legacy to sort things out. And the quickest way to get it is by Sissy handing it over. As he intended.'

'I think Alfred intended the *opposite*. He could see the way you lived – and he didn't approve.'

'High-minded as always! Yet Yours Truly enjoyed it enough when we were out together. He'd back some old nag without any form and it would always come in. He was lucky at the tables, too – said he could see the wheel in his mind's eye and willed the ball to fall in place.' He laughs and strokes his moustache. 'I never lost a farthing when I followed his lead. By God, if he hadn't gone cool on the whole thing, perhaps I wouldn't be here now, grovelling to you for a favour. A favour that's in Kitty's interest, too, I might add.'

'You know I would do anything for Kitty. But this is preposterous.'

'You stuck up for her against *him*. Can't you do the same against Sissy? Are you more afraid of your little sister than of Alfred?'

'I was *never* afraid of Alfred.'

Augustus smiles, that inward, sneering smile: 'Is that so?'

I colour. 'How dare you sneer! You know nothing!'

'Oh, come off your high horse! You let him do as he liked with you. Even let him turn you out of your own house and said thank you for the privilege! Kitty says as much.'

'Kitty talks wildly. She doesn't understand. And yet she *should* know how it feels to be an abandoned wife. She loves *you* in spite of everything.'

He glares. 'Has she ever complained about me?'

'No. She knows she has made her bed and she is too proud to do other than lie in it. Even if she has to lie there alone.'

He laughs. 'You can hold your corner when you want to, I see. Well, if you won't see Sissy, you won't. But I hope you'll remem/ber that bold defiance of yours when Kitty hears the bailiffs at the door and sees the summonses put through the letter/box.'

My blood runs cold. Bailiffs! Summonses! Everything Alfred worked to avoid all his life. He would truly hate me if he thought I would let Kitty suffer such indignities within days of his pass/ing. 'Very well,' I say hastily. 'I shall try. I can do no more. But I doubt I'll have any more success than you.'

He gets up and extends his hand. 'Thank you, Ma. You won't regret it. But will you be sure to go today? Time is precious.'

'Yes, today,' I say. Anything to make him go away.

'Then I'll await *your earliest convenience*.' He grins, picks up his hat, and goes out, whistling.

I am in a complete state of nerves. My breakfast is digesting badly and I can taste the eggs in my mouth. I hold on to the table edge and try to breathe slowly. How can I have agreed to see her? How can I face her condescension and triumph? I, who was so wronged, and she the perpetrator! What on earth will I say? But there is no time to compose a careful letter or to observe the niceties if I am to prevent the bailiffs banging on Kitty's door. I shall have to take a chance that Sissy will be in; and that she will see the sister she so despises.

'Wilson, bring my cape and bonnet. I am going out!'

She appears at the door. 'Out? Are you riding with Mr. O'Rourke again, in that there gig?'

'No.' My agitation makes me turn on the poor woman. 'But if I were, I'm entitled to do so. If I wish to ride in gig – or on an elephant, come to that – I think I have the right.'

She flushes. 'Beg pardon, madam. After all these, well, quiet times, I can't get used to the commotion.'

I smile at her. She is a good soul. 'I know you are only con/cerned for my welfare. But I need to go and see my sister.'

'Miss Millar? I thought —' She stops, not sure of what she is supposed to know.

'That we are not on speaking terms? Yes, you are right. But I have to see her all the same. It concerns Mrs. Norris.'

'*Mr.* Norris, you mean. It's him as has put you up to it, I'll be bound.'

'Never mind who's put me up to it. I need a Hansom cab as soon as you can get one. And a little something to settle my stomach.'

She gets me a glass of Dr. Phelps's tonic and I find my bonnet and shawl, and my purse with a few shillings in it, and by the time Wilson is back with the cab, I am ready.

'Park Lane,' I tell the cabman. And we clatter off.

As we drive, my stomach churns to think of meeting my sister again. My mind keeps going back to the time when I so unwisely left the whole household to her care. After my poor dear Ada's death and the brief agony of Florence May, Dr. Phelps was of the opinion that Leamington Spa was the best place for me to recuperate. I didn't want to go; I felt I should remain in London, and that Alfred was the best doctor I could ever have. He came and sat with me every morning and every night. He held my cold hands in his warm ones; he put his arm around me and read the comforting words of Our Lord. And when I was a little stronger, he read my favourite chapters from *Miggs,* which made me laugh so much that for a shameful moment or two I almost forgot our dear dead children's faces.

But he could not spend all his time with me. He was struggling with the early numbers of *The Red House* and editing *Our Daily Lives,* and due to start the casting of another play. His grief seemed to have been transmuted into a kind of frenetic activity, and I knew how it would drive him till he dropped with exhaustion. I tried to persuade him to come with me; to rest himself, but he would not: *You know how I am, Dodo. God knows I wish it otherwise; that I could rest my mind and sail along in calm and healing seas. But I have to work; it is all I can do. Until the day I drop.*

So, in a matter of weeks I found myself bundled off to the Midlands with my trunk in the luggage van, a hired nurse by my side, and a copy of *James Bartram* under my arm. 'Captain Sissy will take command of the family ship,' Alfred said, as he handed me into a First Class carriage. 'You need have no concerns.'

If I had been unhappy living under the same roof as my sister, the prospect of leaving her behind was infinitely worse. As I'd headed north through the flat Midlands landscape, blinds drawn against the flickering sunshine, Alfred's last jocular words echoed in my mind: *Cap'n Sissy will take command.* Of course she would; it would be easy now I was not there.

I was in half a mind to get out at the next station and return to London, but I had only a single ticket and a half-crown in my purse, and my little nurse had nothing, so I let myself be carried on. Once at my lodgings, I wrote immediately saying I would only stay a week. *A week will be ample,* I wrote. But Alfred telegraphed DO NOT RETURN – ALL WELL. EXPECTING PRETTY WIFE AT END THREE MONTHS. YOURS TRULY.

In a strange way, I began to find the change soothing; and as the days went on and I grew stronger, there were many new things to engage my attention and fill the dreadful void in my heart. I tentatively began to go into society. I took the waters each day, rested or wrote letters in the afternoons, and in the evenings I attended soirées where I played cards with a wide variety of pleasant people who showed a considerable degree of interest towards the wife of Alfred Gibson. In return I was happy to furnish my audience with many an anecdote about our lives together. As the days went by, they began to ask me my opinion of matters, and were interested in what I had to say. Indeed for the first time I began to

[215]

feel a person in my own right. The shock of Ada's passing and the death of Florence May began, at last, to recede. My body felt renewed, and I began to feel my heavy spirits lift. Before I realised it, I had been away for four and a half months.

Alfred had had no time to come and see me, but he'd written to me every day, short, cheerful notes. In one he told me that he was *steaming ahead* with rehearsals for the new play, and that he had assembled *a wonderful company with excellent actors and actresses, down to the smallest servant with half a line. Yours Truly is in splendid form (as always!) as the eponymous Lord Royston, and I have the best of daughters – a charming young person of the name of Ricketts – who comes in a bargain package with her equally Thespian Mama, who is playing my unfortunate shrew of a wife!! I am cheered to hear my actual wife is recovering well – but I entreat you to stay in Leamington as long as you need to do so. Your sister is managing marvellously, as always. What would we do without her?*

The name of Ricketts was of little interest to me: it was Sissy's doings that absorbed my attention. Every letter contained further encomiums about her indispensability. As I had feared, she was using my absence to increase her sphere of influence, gaining Alfred's admiration and affection more with every day, whereas I was like poor Isabella in her enchanted forest; no one could hear my voice.

And indeed, when I returned to Park House, it was Sissy who greeted me at the front door like a *châtelaine*, keys dangling from her waist, while John, more grim-faced than usual, humped my luggage up the stairs without a word. 'Welcome back, dear Dodo!' she'd cooed. 'You must be tired after your journey. Do you want to go straight to your room? I can have tea and sandwiches brought to you there.' She was over-sweet with me, as if I had become a harmless person.

'Where are the children?' The house was strangely silent.

'Out walking with Bessie.'

'All of them?'

'Well, the little ones. And Lou is helping, as she always does. Such a dear, sweet girl!' She started to help me off with my pelisse. 'Alfie's still at Rugby, of course.'

'And Kitty?'

'She is about the place somewhere. It is impossible to keep an eye on her; she is as wrigglesome as an eel.'

'But why are they not here to greet me? Didn't they know their Mama was coming home?' I thought of how they all rushed to greet Alfred when he came back from every one of his travels.

'Well, Dodo, the truth is they are nicely settled these days, and Alfred agreed I shouldn't tell them in case – well, in case arrange ments had to change. It will be a nice surprise for them when we all sit down to supper together.'

I swallowed my disappointment, and followed her up the stairs. 'And where's Alfred?'

She put her finger to her lips. 'He mustn't be interrupted.'

'He's in the *house*?' I couldn't believe he had not come to meet me.

'Sshh. He's working.'

'I must see him.' I began to descend the stairs again.

She stepped in front of me. 'No,' she said.

'What do you mean – no? He is my husband. Let me pass.'

She faltered. 'Please, Dodo. He's been having such difficulty with *The Red House*. He so hates to be disturbed. Please.' She gave me her sweetest smile, and I thought she looked even prettier than Alice. I thought of how Alfred had always written amid the hurly burly of children and visitors, not locked away in silence. But in his letter, he'd admitted that *The Red House* was being drawn from him *slowly and agonisingly, like a bad tooth*. So I con ceded. 'Very well.'

I went with her to unpack my things. She'd put a vase of flowers on the bedside table and she was very amiable as she laid out my gowns and placed my undergarments in the drawers. But a cold feeling was spreading through my veins. Something was wrong.

When Alfred came out of his study at five o'clock, he looked at me rather distantly. Then he smiled and said he hoped I was quite recovered from the daily exertions of playing cards and drinking my own weight in water, and he put out his hand, as if to shake mine. For my part, I almost knocked him over with my embrace. 'I have missed you so much!' I said joyfully. 'Have you not missed me too?'

He started slightly, before laughing and adding airily: 'Oh, the old place has not been the same without you. We've been under iron discipline. Cap'n Sissy has seen to that. But we've got along by dint of *taking in breaths and letting 'em out again and walking with one foot in front of the other like we was reg'lar soljers!*'

For a moment he seemed exactly his old self, and my heart was so full of love for him I could hardly let go of his hand, but kissed it over and over again. And when the children came home, he leapt up and lined them all up by age so they could come and greet me – which they duly did, saying politely that they hoped I was 'feeling better'. Except for Kitty, who appeared from nowhere and was loud and sulky by turns, they seemed almost shy of me. As we sat around the supper-table, even Alfred's insistence that they 'tell Mama' this or that largely went unheeded. Lou and Eddie seemed to ignore me as if I were a deaf or elderly aunt; and Georgie and Fanny stared at me with a kind of terrified curiosity as if I were some sort of infernal mechanism that might suddenly explode in their faces.

It was only when I retired that night that I realised what, in the confusion of unpacking, I had half-sensed but not fully observed: that Alfred's lamp and books and favourite armchair had disappeared from our bedroom. And when I tried his dressing-room door, it was not only shut – which was unusual – but fast locked.

I felt a dreadful sense of foreboding and dismay but I continued to rattle the doorknob, thinking that sooner or later it *must* open. Then I pushed against the door with my whole weight, but it seemed to stare back at me with an awful sense of brown-varnished triumph, as if I should have known better. I hastened out of the room in a state of agitation. Perhaps Alfred had been sleeping in the dressing room while I was away and Mrs. Brooks had neglected to return things to their normal state. It made no sense, but it was the only answer I could think of. As I began to descend the staircase, stepping on my hem in my haste, and almost stumbling headlong down the stairs, I met Alfred coming quietly up.

'Oh, Alfred!' I said, grasping his arm. 'The door to the dressing room is locked! And your belongings are gone! What has been happening?'

'Calm yourself!' he said. 'Everything is in order. *My* orders in fact. You need peace and quiet, and I'm a restless sleeper.' He smiled and patted my arm, as if the matter were of no great importance; as if it were no hardship to him to sleep apart from me after so many months. And when I saw his face so unperturbed and dispassionate, all the doubts that had been chafing at me since I first climbed those wretched steep steps to the front door began to burst in my head like an explosion of skyrockets.

'I don't mind if you are the worst sleeper in the world!' I said, grasping his coat as he made as if to pass on. 'I don't need peace and quiet; not now! I need you with me; I need your arms around me!'

'Now, Dodo,' he said, removing my hands from his coat, 'we both know what that can lead to. The last thing we want now is another infant. Be a good girl and do what I say.'

'We can be as brother and sister. There need be nothing further . . .' I grasped his coat again, aware that my voice was rising in my desperation.

'For Heaven's sake, Dodo!' He looked around, embarrassed, as he tried to extricate himself from my grip. 'You are making a ridiculous fuss. You will have the whole house wondering what is the matter with you.'

'I don't care!' I fell to my knees, grasping first at his waist and then at his legs, and finally his ankles. 'I don't care if I disturb the whole house!' I clung at his trousers and wept on to his beautifully shiny boots.

I must have made a dreadful commotion because Sissy and Mrs. Brooks came running up the stairs in consternation. And he told them not to blame me; that I was over-tired: *She needs some rest.* So they prised me away from him, and I felt the sharp tang of smelling salts as I was bundled back into my room. When I came to myself, Mrs. Brooks' brisk hands were washing my face and undressing me for bed.

'Come along, Mrs. Gibson,' she said as she helped me climb in. 'You're overwrought. It's understandable – first night back home. Things will look better in the morning.' She tucked in the sheets, dimmed the lamp and, after watching me for some time, went out.

I lay there alone in the cold, waiting for him – for the sound of the door opening, the weight and warmth of him as he slipped in beside me. That night and every other, I waited for him. But he never slept with me again.

Many women complain of the demands of the bedchamber, but bedtime was for me the only part of the day when I felt my husband was truly mine; when he did not belong to his friends, his readers or the entire population of England. And although I had to admit he became less ardent as our marriage progressed, he was always as kind to me as on our wedding night – the night when I'd truly felt myself to be the happiest woman on earth.

On that first night, I'd been as ignorant as it was possible to be. Mama had told me to expect blood and pain, but had told me little else to the purpose, and as I waited for Alfred under the sheets, I tried to reconcile the anticipated ordeal with the pleasurable sensations of our courtship. Alfred could never hurt me, I told myself. Yet I could not altogether put from my mind the disconcerting stories of erstwhile model suitors who on the instant of bedding their brides had become transformed into veritable Bluebeards. So I'd looked at Alfred with apprehension as he drew back the bed-curtains, his eyes sparkling and his colour high. But, as so often, he seemed to know what I was thinking. 'Now, Dodo dear, I do not mean to hurt you, and I shall try my very best not to. But I am a man, and we men are wretched clumsy creatures. So you must forgive me, or I shall never forgive myself.' But I had no need to forgive him. Indeed I may have cried out at the surprise and delight of it all. And afterwards, when he lay back on the bolster with his hair more tangled than I had ever seen it, he laughed and said: 'Well, Dodo! I confess I did not realise that young fillies were apt to show such enthusiasm at a first outing. I fear that you have not been lady-like. Not lady-like at all. And as a result we might have to do it all over again!' And all I could do was lie back against the pillows and smile, thinking that married life consisted only of such bliss.

~~ *17* ~~

The cab is stopping.

The first thing I notice about the house is that the tree has grown. It was a sapling when we moved in and not much bigger three years later when I left. Now it towers over the house, bare branches almost touching the third-floor windows. The front steps are the same, though – steep and awkward for a woman in skirts, and especially one not in the first flush of youth. I toil up them slowly. I ring the important-looking bell and hear the jangle that I used to hate so much. It meant visitors; it meant having to rouse myself, to make conversation. Even now, my stomach turns over.

An unfamiliar servant answers the door: 'Ma'am?'

'Is Miss Millar at home?'

'Who should I say it is?'

'Mrs. Gibson. Mrs. Dorothea Gibson.'

The man blenches slightly. He hesitates, and then ushers me in. The big hallway is exactly the same. I catch my breath – Alfred's cane is still in its place on the hallstand, and so is the spare hairbrush he liked to keep by the looking-glass.

'This way, if you please.' The man leads me into the morning room. It has been repainted a dull green, but is otherwise unaltered. A fire roars in the grate. Alfred always liked to keep a good fire. I can see him now, calling out to the servants to bring more coal, more logs: *Bank it up high. Let's have a blaze!* And he'd stare into the flames for hours sometimes: *Do you see pictures there, Dodo? Pictures of Times Past, or Times that are Yet to Be?* And all I'd see was red coals and grey ash.

I look into the garden. It has an abandoned air. The tree-house and the swing are still there, but there are no children playing. There are no children in the house now, of course, and in any case it is a cold October. I wander around the room, fingering the ornaments. Things that I had forgotten about: still here. The ship-in-a-bottle that Sydney gave us, a painted plate Lottie and Tom brought back from their honeymoon in Portsmouth, the leather collar from our old dog Master, who was buried in the back yard at Channon Street to the accompaniment of all our sobs. Poor creature, he had to endure having his tail pulled and being dressed up in petticoats and taken for daily rides in Alfie's little chariot, with Kitty and Louisa pulling the reins; but he was always good-tempered and docile. *I never knew a dog more ill-named,* said Alfred. *He'd lick the hand of the most villainous burglar that ever lived, and by way of friendship, would no doubt lead him most directly to the silver knives and forks.*

There is a footstep at the door. It is the manservant again. 'Beg pardon, Mrs. Gibson. My mistake, but I'm afraid Miss Millar is not at home after all.'

I look at him as I imagine Augustus looked at poor Wilson. 'Then I'll wait.' I sit down on the brocade chair that was always Louisa's favourite. It is rather low, and having put myself there, I wonder if I shall be able to get up without help. But I look around airily, pretending I am entirely at my ease.

The man hesitates. 'I think Miss Millar may be some time.'

'I'll still wait. Thank you.'

'Perhaps I can take a message.' Poor man, he is trying hard.

'No, thank you.'

He withdraws.

I glance round again at all the objects that once constituted my home. Not much is new. It is as if the household had petrified ten years ago and I am back again to that dreadful time when my life moved from dream to nightmare, when I came back from Leamington and found my whole life had changed.

It may be my imagination, but I think I hear whispering in the hallway outside. The door opens. A face I recognise. 'Mrs. Brooks!' I try to get up.

'Oh, dear Mrs. Gibson!' Tears start to well in her eyes, course down her cheeks. 'Mercer said it was you, but I couldn't hardly believe it.' We embrace, awkwardly, neither sure of our positions after the passage of years. I have always liked her, but have forgotten how much until now.

'It's a great loss, the Master. I feel for you, I do.'

'Thank you. It was a shock. Even after all these years, you know, I am still his wife.'

'Don't speak of it! He should never have done it to you. It was cruel – cruel beyond anything. Bessie and I talked it over many a time, begging your pardon. And we felt Mr. Gibson was not quite in his right mind when he done it. And Bessie said she'd never known him in such a state, and she'd known him ever so much longer – known you both, in fact, and she said –'

'Oh, you still see Bessie! How is she?' My heart lifts just to think of her.

'She does very well, thanks to her pension from the Master. She comes to see me sometimes. She has a nice little cottage in Putney, and it's handy for the omnibus. Drops her right at the corner of Park Lane. She misses her old life, though. Especially the children.'

'Poor Bessie. She gave her *whole life* to us.'

'She was glad to, ma'am. She always says she couldn't have had a better master and mistress if she'd paid good money for them. She said she had a better life in your service than anywhere else you could mention.'

'I am glad to think so – truly. Putney is not so far. I must go and see her. We can talk about old times.'

'I'm sure she'd be delighted. She's always telling me such stories – the Master dancing in the sea or doing his magic tricks or appearing at windows with a false nose and wig, or singing comical songs as he ran up and down stairs with Kitty under one arm and Alfie in the other . . .' Her eyes moisten. 'I can't hardly believe I'll never see him again.'

'No. Nor I.' We lapse into silence, our hands clasped.

She rouses herself. 'Have you come to see Miss Millar?'

'I understand she is not at home.'

Mrs. Brooks hesitates. 'She has a good deal to do with the sale of the house and all the furniture . . .'

I look round. 'What is happening to the furniture?'

'I think Miss Millar is taking the best pieces for when she moves to a new property. The rest will go to auction, I suppose.'

Auction! How dare she? 'But so many of these things are *mine*! She cannot auction *my* belongings! Not Master's collar, Lottie's vase, the pictures of the children – they must be mine by right! And all the gifts that were inscribed to us both – they have nothing to do with Sissy! I have half a mind to go round the house and simply *take* things!' I pull myself up from the chair and start to examine all the items. 'This!' I say, pointing to the dog collar. 'And this, and this!' I see things I know in every nook and cranny.

'Now, Mrs. Gibson, don't get excited. I am sure she'll keep back anything you want. She's already put aside all his notebooks and manuscripts. They are important for posterity, she says.'

'But I want what's important to *me*! I don't care about his blessed manuscripts, and Kitty's getting all his books anyhow –' I suddenly remember why I am here. Kitty, of course. And Augustus. I calm myself. 'I shall wait until she comes back. I am not leaving until I have seen her!'

Mrs. Brooks looks as uncomfortable as the manservant did. Clearly Sissy is somewhere in the house, ear to the door, waiting for me to go. 'Would you like some tea?' asks Mrs. Brooks, and I think of Kitty, drinking cup after cup in this very room, then hearing his dying groan through the wall.

'No,' I say. 'I'll take the opportunity to look around.' I realise she cannot stop me. No one can. They cannot lay hands on me and evict me; I can do what I like. 'Will you get me a box, Mrs. Brooks?'

'A box?'

'Yes. I'll need somewhere to put things. My *particular* things. Sissy clearly has so much to do. It will be a kindness to take some of the work off her hands.'

I make my way out into the hall. Mercer is loitering awkwardly near the hall table, on which there is a silver salver. That's typical of Sissy's refinements; we never had a salver all the days we were married. Alfred despised calling cards, wouldn't have them: *Either I know you, and you don't need to be introduced – or I don't know you, in which case you can go to the devil!* Those who did leave cards would have been mortified to see them gathering dust in an old rose bowl. One American visitor, chagrined at not being allowed immediate entry to the house when he paid his respects, remarked that up until then he had taken Alfred for one of the century's Great Men, and that he was disappointed to find that he was 'pretty darn unfriendly in person and noticeably lacking in the hospitality he so much celebrated in his books'. Alfred at that point had appeared from his study and announced in a loud voice to no one in particular: 'I think there are some travellers to London who are persuaded – by virtue of parting with a dollar or two at some unspecified bookshop at some unspecified date in the past – that they are now entitled to come and stare at me as if I were Windsor Castle or the Houses of Parliament!'

But as I said to him afterwards, he *was* a kind of monument. His image was on all his books. Everybody knew his plaid coats, his velvet collars, his bowler hats worn at a jaunty angle. Even costers and street boys would call out 'Hallo, Mr. Gibson! Make way for Mr. Gibson!' as he appeared among them. And for those who couldn't see him in person – readers as far afield as Edinburgh or Penzance – he was there with them on the page. Every month he wrote to them; his Dear Public. He shared with them the thoughts of his heart, the workings of his mind. He delighted them, he thrilled them, he educated them. It was as if an umbilical cord ran between them.

⁂

'Would you obtain a box for Mrs. Gibson?' Mrs. Brooks says to Mercer.

'A box?'

'Yes. To put things in. A large one.'

He departs in a stately way, as if merely to acknowledge the existence of 'a box' is to demean himself.

'Where's the portrait of us?' I ask Mrs. Brooks. 'The one by Mr. Evans.'

She demurs. 'Which one is that? This house is so full of pictures. The Master had a new one of himself every year.'

'There's only one of us both together, Mrs. Brooks. Surely you know it. It used to hang in the dining room.' I open the door to the dining room. It's not there. Over the mantel, there is a landscape by Landseer instead, and next to it an oil portrait of Alfred and another of Louisa and Kitty when they were young. I glance at the great mahogany table, set with silver candlesticks – the scene of so many of my failures as a hostess; my failures of wit and grace and beauty; my failures of organisation; my failure to keep awake – Dodo Dumpling doing her best to embarrass her husband. I don't want anything to remind me of that time. I don't want the silver or the glass. I don't want the candelabra. I don't want the landscape with its dull-looking cattle on a purple mountain against a muddy sky. I don't even want the portrait of Alfred. He looks strange, worn, old; he is not as I remember him. 'Maybe the study?' I suggest.

Mrs. Brooks hesitates. 'We mustn't go in *there*. Miss Millar says –'

'Well, she's Not At Home, is she? Where's the harm?'

I open the door. A faint smell of tobacco greets me and I can see him again in his green buttoned armchair, reading the newspaper, legs crossed, cigar in hand. He never smoked while he worked, he didn't like the way the smoke *got into his brain*, but he liked to have a cigar with his brandy after supper. His black velvet smoking jacket, with its satin collar and cuffs, is still hanging on its hook.

The room is immaculate. The blind is half-raised. The desk is dusted, his pens and quills neatly aligned along the top. His ink-well full. The blotter new. A sheaf of clean paper stacked on the left-hand side, a pile of finished pages on the other. All as if he is about to come in and write. I feel a lump in my throat so painful that my whole face aches. I go to the desk; I caress the polished rosewood of the chair, and the worn leather surface of the desk, stained with patterns of ink. My fingers brush the edges of the manuscript. It seems to be a chapter from *The Death of Ambrose Boniface* and is much crossed out and written over. I turn to the last page. It is creased and covered in blots; but it's in his charac-teristic hand:

'Your Honour won't mind me saying as it's more than a little uncommon for a fine genleman such as yourself to express an interest in the melancholy details of a calling such as mine. Was there anything Your Honour was pertickly wanting to know?'

Ambrose places his hand upon the coffin Mr. Slattery is currently engaged upon. 'How heavy, would you say?'

'Now, that's a question not often asked. May I be so bold as to enquire whether Your Honour is referring to this pertickler harticle?'

'Are they much of a muchness?'

'That would depend. Empty, do you mean? Or with the party concerned?'

'Let us say, with the party concerned.'

Mr. Slattery puts down his plane. 'Well now, that would depend on the size of said party, and whether said party is a man or a woman. Or again, a child.'

Ambrose shudders. 'Not a child. A woman, say?'

'And again, before I gives you your answer, I should have to enquire as to the general construction of the aforesaid party – whether it would be a delicate young indiwidual with bones as light as a songbird, or a more buxom personage who has enjoyed the benefits of good living, if you takes my drift.'

'Say a young woman,' Ambrose replies quietly. 'Say of a delicate construction.'

Mr. Slattery nods, and begins to make a reckoning in his head, and taking an extremely short stub of a pencil from behind his ear, jots down some figures on his apron, upon which there are already written so many other calculations, that it resembles the arithmetic book of a particularly untidy child. 'Brass handles, I'm assuming?'

Ambrose nods.

'And memorial plate, ditto?'

Nods again.

'And I'm a-reckoning on elm. Your oak would be heavier, of course. A deal heavier. Not more of a weight than four men could easily carry, though; one at each corner as per the usual arrangement. Is that what Your Honour was thinking?' Mr. Slattery has a strange wrinkled face, like a knowing old baby. And when he looks at Ambrose, it's as if he reads his thoughts.

The young man looks away. 'Yes, indeed. The exact arrangement. Four men. One at each corner.' Ambrose pauses. 'Or maybe – could two men lift it?'

'Two would do it, sir. Although popular prejudice is against two, on account of how the carrying is hawkward – if you sees my meaning.' Mr. Slattery holds up his apron to show the results of his reckonings, then after five seconds lets it drop.

'Much obliged. Much obliged. It's an idle interest of mine.'

'No pertickler person in mind, then? No deceased young party of a delicate construction already a-lying on the cold sheets?' Mr. Slattery is drearily waggish.

Ambrose smiles. 'No such person in the world.'

'What a singular young genleman Your Honour is! I'd say Your Honour has the temperament to be in the funerary line yourself.'

'And what temperament is that, if I may ask?'

'Cool, sir. Werry cool.'

And Mr. Slattery takes up his plane once more and the fresh white shavings fall to the floor at his feet, as if it is snowing. Layer on layer. Snow on snow. Mr. Slattery does not succumb to the prevailing wintriness, however. He works until beads of sweat cling to his forehead. He whistles as he works, but sotto voce, out of respect for the anticipated occupying parties.

Ambrose watches him. Watches the working of the wood, the smoothing of the pieces, the dovetailing of the joints, the tapping in of the nails, the fitting of the lid. He can see her in his mind's eye, being lifted, being laid down. White. White as ice. White as the silken dress around her. His in death, if not in life . . .

A wild line trails off the paper.

I can hardly bear it. I look at it for a long time, then put it down. My fingers encounter a little notebook. I pick it up. It is in his own peculiar shorthand. I turn the pages at random, hardly seeing them.

'What on earth are you doing here, Dodo?' Her voice makes my stomach turn over. I whip round hastily, pocketing the note-book. She is standing in the doorway, the man Mercer behind her. She looks remarkably the same, her figure still neat, her face still clear and pretty. She is wearing a dark frock with a white collar and long paper cuffs. She has a workman-like apron on.

'Oh, Sissy!' I say, affecting surprise. 'They told me you were not at home.'

'I am not seeing callers.' She wrings her hands, but her look is defiant.

'I am hardly a caller.'

'Indeed! You might well say that! But why *are* you here? And in this room?' She looks around distractedly. 'The servants have strict instructions —'

I feel my anger rising. 'But *I* am not a servant, Sissy. I was once mistress of this house —'

'That was ten years ago, Dodo – and *I* am in charge now. You cannot simply walk in as if nothing has happened.' She hurries to the desk and neatens the already neat pile of paper, her eyes checking over all the items in her sharp-eyed way – but failing to notice the missing notebook. She turns to me and speaks in a low voice: 'What is this visit all about? Why have you asked for a box? You cannot take any of his writing things, you know – they must stay exactly as they are.'

'I don't want his writing things, Sissy! I want *my* property! I won't let you put them up for auction, for the world and his wife to pick over.'

She flushes. 'Who is talking of auctions? Have you seen an advertisement of such an event? No, you haven't, because there will be no such thing. We'll find a home for everything between us. The girls and I shall need to furnish a new house, Alfie and Caroline have asked for Alfred's wardrobe and some looking-glasses, and Eddie wants to keep his own dressing-table and bed, so I doubt there will be anything to spare –'

'I hardly need *furniture*, Sissy. Not in a small apartment with three rooms and a basement kitchen. But I have a right to the smaller objects – the pictures of the children, the gifts we were given in America, the presentations that were made to us in towns all over England. And where is Charley's portrait of us both?'

She gives me a look of deep disdain: 'Do you really expect it to be still up on the wall?'

How foolish. Of course, he would hardly have wanted me staring down at him these last ten years. 'But where is it now?'

'I don't know. I daresay we could find it for you, given time. You don't need to come like a thief in the night.'

I am aware of Mrs. Brooks and Mercer hovering awkwardly in the background, Mercer with a tea-chest in his arms. I take her arm, and feel how much she quivers and tenses at my touch. 'Sissy,' I whisper. 'I need to speak in private.'

She glances at the servants. 'Put the box down, Mercer. You and Mrs. Brooks may leave us now.'

They go, and shut the green baize door behind them.

She stands facing me. 'Well? What is this all about? I hardly expected to see *you* again in this house. You are bold-faced, I must say.' She speaks as though *she* is the injured party.

'Am I? Well, to tell the truth, I never expected to come. I hate this house. And to be honest, Sissy, I can hardly summon much affection for *you*.'

'The sentiment is mutual, I assure you. After all those rumours you spread.'

I stare at her. 'What do you mean?'

'Don't pretend to be innocent!' She has gone quite crimson.

'I'm not pretending! Surely you can't believe it was *I* who started those rumours? For Heaven's sake, they injured *me* as much as you!'

She makes a gesture of disbelief, as if my protests are of no account. So I take her by her paper cuff. 'I am speaking the truth, Sissy!'

She gives a short laugh. 'The truth? Is that so? You hated me, Dodo. I could see it every day in your face, even when you sat in your quiet corner and looked as if butter wouldn't melt in your mouth.'

'What did you expect? You came to our house on false pretences. You said it was for my sake, but it wasn't. You always had your eye on other things: power, influence – and Alfred, of course. *I* was of no account. Once you had stepped over the threshold, you changed. You never talked to me as a sister, or stood up for me in any way. You usurped me, Sissy! Of course I hated you and wanted to see you humiliated. But never – never – at the price of Alfred's reputation!'

She seems hardly to hear. 'I had to be *examined*, you know. I had to be subjected to prying fingers!' She breathes heavily. 'You cannot imagine the humiliation, the shame!'

She forgets that I've had eight children, and Dr. Phelps's clumsy hands upon me every time. 'Yes,' I say. 'But surely you can't believe it was *I* who made it necessary?'

She shrugs again. She won't look me in the eye. And it occurs to me with absolute certainty that she has indeed believed all these years that I was the one who made those vile accusations against them both, and that I have spent the interim gloating about it. 'Well,' she says peevishly, '*someone* wanted to ruin us. And you were always so spiteful to me, so underhand in complaining to Alfred – of course I thought it was *you*.'

Spiteful! Underhand! Is that how it appeared? I stare at her reddened complexion, her angry tears. She is undoubtedly in earnest. 'But do you think I would have chosen to start a rumour that would ruin Alfred too? Incest, Sissy! Incest! He could never have held up his head again.'

'Don't you think I know that? That was what was so unforgivable. That was what made him so beside himself; so determined to prove our innocence.' She pauses. 'I didn't see why we needed to prove it. I said that if he and I both knew we were without blame, what did it matter what the Public thought?'

'How little you knew him, Sissy, if you can say that!'

She holds her head in her hands; she knows it, of course; but she can't abide to admit that she was bullied. He bullied everybody he was fond of in the end. I can see that now. 'Don't you see?' I say. 'Don't you see that you and I have both suffered to preserve Alfred's unsullied reputation? Except *I* have suffered rather more than you, I think! One humiliating examination for you; but for me, public shame, loss of everything I loved, my whole world reduced to a few cramped rooms – and no chance to bury my husband, and mourn him as I should wish!'

She looks up. 'You want me to be sorry for you? Well, I can't be. Because you brought it all on yourself. You had everything, Dodo! His name, his children – and his affection. And you squandered it all! You gave the poor man nothing back! How else could he respond?'

That was Alfred's much-rehearsed complaint: that I received without giving; that I broke his love with my indolence and indifference. And that I made his life a misery with my jealousy. And she – along with half the world – has chosen to believe that is the truth. Sometimes, turning it over and over in my mind, I've been foolish enough to believe it myself. But it's not true, and I won't let her say it. 'I may have had faults, Sissy. I may have been far from the woman of his dreams, but Alfred was always at the forefront of my thoughts and I always – *always* – loved him.'

She colours. 'You say that, Dodo. You speak up for yourself now, with high words. But while he lived, I never saw you make the slightest effort to please him.' She crosses her arms truculently.

I am incensed. 'And how long did you live with us? Five years? Six? When I was at my most worn-down, certainly. You weren't there when I stayed up with him when he couldn't sleep for the amount of work he had taken on and was at his wits' end with fatigue. You weren't there when I left my infant children so I could go with him on his travels. You weren't there when I attended the most tedious of engagements week after week, where everyone wanted to talk to the Great Original, and no one wanted to talk to his wife. Don't dare – *don't dare* – say that I never tried to please him!'

She looks chastened for a moment. 'Well, maybe you did at first. But you gave up, Dodo. It was crystal clear from the moment I stepped over the threshold that Alfred was bitterly unhappy. He covered it up, of course. He was jovial and kind and everything I had always known him to be. Yet I could see, under it all, how desperately lonely he was.'

I start to laugh, but she silences me with her look. 'Yes,' she says levelly. 'I never saw a man so lonely. If that surprises you, Dodo, consider why. Could it be that you were too preoccupied with yourself to notice? But *I* saw it straight away, and it wrung my heart. Yet for all your indifference, how wonderfully he cared for you – always trying to find remedies to improve your health, and outings that would interest you. But would you go? No. You seemed almost contrary in your determination to thwart him. Night after night I saw him come stumbling over the threshold, ravaged with exhaustion, to find – what? That you had already retired to bed or that you were dozing in the parlour over your sewing with a half-drunk cup of coffee at your side and the fire practically gone out. You know how much he loved a blaze with everyone gathered around. If *I* hadn't been here, Dodo –' her voice falters, and I see she is near to tears '– If I hadn't been here, the poor man would have been obliged to eat his toasted cheese alone in the kitchen, with no one to cheer him up when he was feeling all the terrible weight of his responsibilities.'

She is distorting the facts. My conduct, disheartening though it undoubtedly was, had never stopped Alfred enjoying himself. Indeed, I had often felt distressed by his undoubted ability to be happy without me. 'When was he ever obliged to eat alone except by choice?' I counter. 'The house was forever full of people – all his cronies making free with his generosity, new acquaintances dropping in every night, supper parties, games, charades . . .'

'Not *every* night, Dodo; we didn't live in a circus. And anyway, has it occurred to you to ask why he felt the need to surround himself so comprehensively with other people? Has it never occurred to you that he was making up for a lack elsewhere? A lack at the very heart of his life?'

I feel the blood stinging my cheeks. I know Alfred always compensated for every lack in his life by an overabundance in another direction. If he couldn't write, he'd walk till he was exhausted; if he couldn't sleep, he'd get up and write for hours. When he was his most unhappy, he'd be at his busiest. Maybe in grasping at every friendship that presented itself, at every pretty face that smiled at him, he was indeed making up for my failures as a wife. Maybe I am wrong and Sissy is right. Maybe Alfred was unhappy and I didn't see it. But I cannot believe it was entirely my fault. 'I did my best,' I say. 'But even Alfred knew that child-bearing made me ill.'

'Not so ill that you couldn't entertain O'Rourke in the afternoons,' she says tartly. 'You seemed to wake up then.'

The insinuation makes me gasp. I turn on her: 'If I did 'wake up' then, as you put it, it was because Michael O'Rourke was the only person who seemed to care for my company in those days. He never minded if I was vague or forgetful, and he never made me feel that he'd prefer it if I was somebody entirely different. He was my true friend. More than you were, Sissy, with your busy ways. And more than Alfred was, much of the time.'

She snorts. 'Are you saying *Michael* cared for you more than Alfred did?'

'You were the one who implied that, Sissy. But you know that Alfred could never forbear to make sarcastic remarks at my expense. He may have been full of the milk of human kindness when writing his novels, but he could be very hard in reality.'

'Well, he was embarrassed by you, Dodo. Good Heavens, we were all embarrassed by you – the children, who had no mother to rely on, the servants who never knew what you would take it into your head to do, and worst of all, our guests. You behaved as a madwoman, Dodo. Alfred was a Great Man. He needed a wife who could add honour to his name, who could understand his heart and mind.'

'One like you, you mean?'

She blushes brick-red. 'That is not the point. But since you ask, why not? In all our years under the same roof, I never quarrelled with him.'

It is true. They never had disagreements. She was clever; she weighed and measured Alfred, and fitted herself to his desires in a way I never did. I never set out to quarrel with him, of course, and cannot count the occasions on which I bit back words of complaint or censure even as they rose to my lips. But it is not always possible to hide one's feelings, and my very love for him seemed to draw me into querulous demands that were out of my mouth before I knew, and jealous tempers that I despised even as I was in the midst of them. He accused me of having a limited mind; and wanting to limit him too: *You would quench my light. You would silence my voice. You would claw me down to the commonplace.* But to be commonplace is not a fault. The world needs commonplace people as much as it needs original people, and it is the worship of the commonplace people that made Alfred who he was. Sissy standing there so holier-than-thou has no right to set herself in judgement on me.

I turn: 'Who is to say he would not have quarrelled with *you*, Sissy, if you had been in my place? If you had given birth to eight children, and put two of them in their graves, you might not have found it so easy to stay trim and pretty, to wait up for him until two o'clock and wake again at six. To be always there at his beck and call with a ready smile and perfect obedience.'

There is silence. 'Well,' she says slowly, 'I am not you, and you are not me, and we shall never know how we would have fared in each other's shoes. But I envy you for the chance you had. And I despise you for failing at it.'

'Despise me by all means. But don't envy me. To know his love and then lose it is a terrible thing: total darkness when one has been used to the brightest of light.'

She is silent again. All I can hear is the sound of the brittle leaves skittering drily against the window pane. And it seems as if all our wretched disagreements are swirling around too – anger, jealousy, pain, sorrow – even though the great centre and cause of them is no more. We stare at each other; I see a tear seep slowly from beneath her eyelid and my own eyes moisten in response.

I see her as the child I loved, the sister I once admired. 'We should not have let our wish to serve Alfred drive such a wedge between us,' I say, seizing her reluctant hand and clasping it to my bosom. 'We should have remembered all our happy hours in Chiswick; we should have bound ourselves together as true sisters. But I was jealous and you were proud. We hurt each other, and diminished each other with our differences. But we should not compound the loss. With Papa and Alice gone from us, and Mama hardly acknowledging us, let's not waste time in regret.' I look at her most earnestly: 'Will you be a true and loving sister to me once again?'

She is torn, I see. In spite of her pride, she is not an evil woman. Maybe the remembrance of the three of us playing in our Chiswick garden moves her at last. Maybe she even acknowledges the harm that has been done to me in which she has been complicit. But I do not ask her to apologise; I am conscious that I am here on sufferance, and have a favour to ask. I cannot let Kitty down; it is my chance to redeem myself and I must not make a mistake.

She shrugs her shoulders and I can hardly hear the words as she murmurs: 'Let it rest, then, Dodo. I am content.'

I smile at her and nod. I am not sure how to go on. My hand drifts down distractedly and touches the surface of his desk, and I see her glance at it, as if she fears that I shall disturb the arrangement of papers and pens. I see that everything is as he liked it – neat, orderly, ready to hand. I slide my hand along the curving back of the chair and imagine his high-cut collar, his vivid necktie, and the springing mass of wavy hair as he bends his head over his work. 'You've changed nothing,' I say.

'I couldn't bear to.' She pauses, draws breath briskly. 'And besides, Frank Lucas is coming to paint it. He said it was the kind of thing the public will clamour for: the desk, the chair, everything as it was. Everything but . . .' Her voice dies away. I can see her chin trembling. Then she turns and gives a desperate little laugh.

'You know, sometimes I think I hear him at the door, that quick step of his coming across the floor, that voice calling out: *I've a capital idea! The best ever!*' Her voice trembles and, before I can think whether it is a good or bad thing, I put my arms round her. To my surprise, she lets me. I don't think I have held her in this way since she was twelve and we mourned Alice together. She leans her head against me and groans: 'Oh, how can I live, Dodo? However hard I work, however hard I scrub or polish or sweep or tidy, I can't forget him. He seems to be in the very walls of this place. Every time the clock chimes two I look up, expecting him to appear for lunch, or again at five, to see him put on his coat to take a walk to town. But he's not here and he doesn't come and the whole place is so *dead*!'

'I know.' I have known that desolation only too well. I've been ten years without the touch of daylight, like mad Miss Winterman. Yet for Sissy it is all so fresh and raw.

She shakes her head: 'I feel exactly like a widow.'

'Yes,' I say. 'You have shared his life for a long time. But you must acknowledge that I *was* his wife by law and by promise, and *I* am his widow now.'

'But you have not seen him for ten years, Dodo; it cannot be the same.' She shakes her head wildly.

'No, it's not the same. The difference between us is only that I am a good deal more used to it.'

She looks up at me and sets her chin firmly: 'I shall *never* get used to it.'

'You will, Sissy. Or you will go mad. And I think you have too much sense for that.'

She shakes her head. 'You think I am all good sense, do you? Oh, Dodo, how well do you really know me?'

I am taken aback by the pathos of her voice. 'Well,' I say gently, 'I knew the best of you once. And you knew the best of me. I taught you to sew and knit and read, remember?'

Her dull eyes brighten. 'Oh, yes! That Alphabet book! And that dreadful old S for snake, curled round the Tree of Knowledge with his tongue hanging out in a most lascivious manner!' She laughs.

'Oh, Sissy, how good it is to hear you laugh! I thought that all those long-ago days meant nothing to you.'

She reddens. 'On the contrary, they meant a great deal. You were my favourite sister, Dodo. I thought you'd be with us for ever. You have no idea how much I suffered when you took yourself off to be married. And I was quite beside myself with jealousy when you called Alice to be your best companion – to be there with you and Alfred, playing (as I imagined) charades and games the live-long day! I begged Mama to let me go too. Once I said I would lock myself in my room and eat nothing but bread and water until she changed her mind. But she said, "One has to be asked, Sissy. And you are in any case too young for such a harum-scarum household." That made me all the keener to be with you. Then Alice died and Mama and Papa were so grief-stricken that I knew I could not leave them. But every time you and Alfred visited it seemed you brought with you such a wonderful sense of the greater world – of Art and Literature and Society – that my one hope was to be part of that world. I never came with the idea of ousting you, Dodo – how could you think that? But once I was with you, I could hardly sit on my hands and do nothing while all around me perished. There was so much to do. You were exhausted, Alfred was as busy as sin, and Bessie was all very well, but she had no authority. I did what I did because I *had* to, Dodo – and I did it in my own way. I knew it was not your way, and I do not expect gratitude – but my intention was always for the best.'

She looks at me sincerely. She believes it, I'm sure. But she was, and is, mistaken. 'You did your best for Alfred and the children, perhaps. But not for me, Sissy; never for me.'

She shifts uneasily, and I release her from my embrace.

'And the children – why didn't they write?'

She colours. 'I never stopped them.'

She didn't *encourage* them, though, I imagine. 'How is Louisa, for example? Is she at home now?'

She avoids my look. 'She is lying down. I've tried to send her away to the seaside – Sydney would have her at Dover – but the foolish girl won't leave my side.'

'Would she see me now, do you think?'

She hesitates, wipes her eyes, then pulls the bell. Mrs. Brooks comes in.

'Ask Miss Lou if she is well enough to see her Mama.'

Mrs. Brooks smiles. 'Certainly, Miss Millar.' She goes out.

'And the others?' I ask tentatively. 'How are they?'

'Alfie and Carrie have a house out at Hampstead. The child, bless her, is a delight.' Her face breaks into a reflective smile, and I realise in this moment that she would have dearly loved to have infants of her own.

'Alfie has written to me,' I say cautiously.

She looks surprised.

'Yes. He is to bring Caroline to see me soon. And Lucy, too.'

'Ah, yes.' Clearly she did not know this. 'Well, Alfie's a dutiful boy. Not like Eddie. He's out in town as usual, talking of setting up an outfitter's shop or some such ridiculous nonsense. Can you imagine the son of Alfred Gibson – in trade?' I don't think that's so outlandish, but she rushes on: 'Georgie, of course, is still bound for the Far East; we've informed the Admiralty, but there's no word of him yet.'

I wonder what Georgie is like now. I remember only a mild, moon-faced, silent child whose shirt was always outside his trousers, and who drew ships with full rigging on every piece of paper he could find, his tongue following the line of the pencil. And who loved to lie in the hammock and stare at the sky as if already navigating by the stars.

'Fanny's back at school. She objected – as she objects to every-thing – but we thought it best to keep her mind occupied. Kitty you've seen, naturally.'

I cannot postpone it any longer. 'It's about Kitty that I've called.'

She looks at me warily. 'Oh, I see. I've had Augustus's letters, scrounging as I'd expect. But he can't have any money. The will has not been proved. There is much to do before any disburse-ments can be made. It will all take time.'

'You don't understand. It is *urgent*, Sissy. Augustus is about to have the bailiffs in. He has lost *everything*.'

'Is that so? Have you seen any evidence of this state of affairs?' Now money is mentioned, she is becoming the sharp, organised Sissy once more.

'Evidence?'

'Yes. Bills, receipts, contracts, notes of hand . . .'

I redden. 'Of course not. I accepted his word.'

'My dear Dodo, don't you think it is too convenient for him to have such a crisis at the precise time when Alfred's money becomes available?'

It occurs to me for the first time that I may have been duped. 'In that case, why could he not *wait*? Why would he be standing on my doorstep every day in the hope I can do something for him? I don't care a fig for *him*, but I care for Kitty. I don't want to see her humiliated.'

'She should never have married that man.' (I am struck, not for the first time, how unmarried people are so prolific with marital advice.)

'Maybe not. But there is no changing it. And her fortunes go with his.'

The door clicks open, and the person who must be Louisa creeps in. I am shocked. She is well-grown and buxom, but her eyes are dreadfully red, her hair is awry, and she has an expression of complete misery. 'Hallo, Mama.' Her voice is as small and quiet as ever. *Miss Mouse,* he used to call her. *Mademoiselle Mousepatch.*

'Hallo, Lou. *What changes, eh?! I see you're a young woman grow'd.*'

'Yes.' She looks at me listlessly. 'Well, I suppose it's been a long time.'

Yes. Too long. I don't know her, and she doesn't know me. I take courage: 'I hope you're not too grown-up to give your Mama a kiss?'

She glances at Sissy, then presents her cheek at me. I kiss its smooth surface. She makes no attempt to return the compliment. Instead she draws back: 'What brings you *here?*'

I daren't mention Kitty, so I speak half the truth. 'I need a little money, Lou. I am hoping Sissy will help. I've not been left as wealthy as the rest of you.'

She says nothing. Then, 'Why are you in the study? I thought no one was supposed to come in here.'

'We were looking for something. A picture. But it's not here.'

'Why don't we all have some tea?' Sissy is suddenly as brisk as she used to be. 'Let's go in the morning room; it has a good blaze.'

And so we sit down, all three of us, in the little green room with all the mementos of our early days. Louisa is silent and lumpish and fiddles with the button on her dress for minutes at a time. I'm irritated by the way she doesn't join in the conversation, the way she sits apart as if sunk in her own concerns. I wonder if that is how *I* appeared to our guests in the past. If so, I wouldn't blame them forming a poor opinion of me.

'If you select the things you want, I shall ask Mercer to pack them in the box,' says Sissy, magnanimously. 'On the *other matter,*' she says, meaningfully, 'I shall consider it, but I need bills or letters to give to Mr. Golding. I cannot ask him to do anything without them.'

'I have thirty pounds, Mama. If you are short of money.' Louisa speaks from her corner near the fire.

A gush of warmth envelops me. She is not cold and indifferent after all. 'What a kind offer!' I say. 'But it is not necessary at present.'

'Very well.' She goes on staring at the fire. But she becomes more animated when I go around picking up ornaments and mementos for the box. She gets up and fingers them herself, recalling the anecdotes attached to each one, and laughs as she does so. 'What fun we used to have when we were all together! Do you remember, Mama?'

'Yes,' I say, 'I remember it clearly.'

I see on Sissy's face a mixture of love and anxiety as she watches us together, and I realise that she fears she will lose her hold over the children now Alfred is not here to champion her, and that she will end a lonely spinster, all her work for nought. I have thought so badly of her over the years, but in truth, where would my children have been without her? Left to the less than tender mercies of some governess, or to the hands of some Colonel's lady paid by the calendar month to prime and polish? Poor Kitty would have died a thousand deaths rather than submit, and Lou would have withered to nothing. Sissy has kept my family together.

I should be grateful.

18

Of course, it was not gratitude that I felt when I first returned from Leamington. Finding Sissy governing the house with a new authority while, at the same time, Alfred absented himself from my bed made me fear what I could hardly bring myself to acknowledge: something that was against the laws of both Man and God. When I first faced that dreadful locked door, it entered my mind unbidden. As I sank to my knees in front of Alfred, my whole body shuddered at the possibility. In the cold light of day, it was too horrible to contemplate. I told myself over and over again that I was wrong, and wicked, and that Alfred's coolness to me was nothing to do with Sissy; it was simply connected to his travails with *The Red House* and, as soon as it was finished, he would regain his old spirits. I took comfort in that Alfred was by no means unkind; indeed, he would come into my bedroom and sit on the bed and make suggestions as to how I might employ my time, *because we all need to keep busy, don't we?*

But he consulted me about nothing and slowly I realised that there was no duty that would be missed if I did not do it, no person who would be in distress if I were not there to comfort them. Sometimes I would be so much left to my own devices that I would even wonder if everyone else had mysteriously disappeared and I were the sole occupant of an empty house. Sometimes there'd be a burst of laughter and Alfred would come out of the smoking room or the dining room: *What, you here, Dodo?* as if I were the last person he expected to see. But more often his coat and his cane would be gone from the hall after breakfast, and would be still gone by the time I took myself to bed.

Left to myself for so much of the day, and wondering what had happened to all the people who had once thronged my life, I quickly realised that almost all my acquaintances were in fact *Alfred's* acquaintances, and that my access to them was largely through him. Our old friends the Evanses were now living in Florence, and although Mary wrote encouragingly, her letters were infrequent. Lottie was too busy nursing Tom to make visits and Tom himself was too ill to receive visitors, becoming alarmed if Lottie left him even for a minute, so I could not call on her without causing disquiet. And of course I could not go to Chiswick. My mother, now a widow, despairing that *both* her daughters were now living with the man she reviled as a 'vulgar showman', had shut up the house and gone to reside in Coventry with Cousin George, whence she made it clear that any communication with her daughters should be of the briefest sort. Only O'Rourke came to see me for my own sake – but even he could not take up all the slack on my seemingly endless leisure.

'Why don't you help Sissy?' Alfred said one day. 'Bessie is taking a holiday; I am sure there will be things to do.' I agreed readily, hoping to please him and delighted at the prospect of making myself useful, but I found myself thwarted in subtle ways. When the children were not in the schoolroom, they were engaged in dancing lessons or fencing lessons – or were out on the lengthy walks essential to Sissy's military regime. I had to make a particular arrangement with her if I were even to *see* Eddie or Georgie, and unless I patrolled the nursery passageway at six o'clock sharp, Fanny would be whisked off to bed before I could even kiss her goodnight. There was, alas, no dear Ada to sit with in the afternoons; Alfie was at Rugby and might as well have been on the Moon; and Kitty seemed to be forever doing her best not to be found. So I developed habits which Alfred later referred to as 'eccentric' when he brandished them in front of the whole world to show how idle and purposeless I had become. I generally got up late, often lunched alone, spent the afternoon dozing and reading on the chaise longue, and retired to bed after supper for want of company. *The Vanishing Lady* he called me – or, less charitably, *Dame Dawdle in a Dressing Gown.*

I could no longer keep telling myself it was merely *The Red House* that was keeping Alfred away from me, although I knew the writing of it was giving him unusual anguish. He never ceased to complain that it was *the damnedest, hardest, pickiest work I have ever done* – and indeed it was as sad and melancholy as any-thing he had written. I'd read the monthly numbers as they came out, and had been moved and stricken by poor Arthur Grayling's hopeless love for a woman of stone. Inevitably it crossed my mind that there might be some real-life counterpart to that woman; someone who occupied Alfred's thoughts and feelings far more than I did. I noticed he worked less regularly now, taking to his desk in fits and starts, and sometimes getting up in the middle of writing, putting on his coat and going out with an excited and determined air, a fresh flower in his buttonhole.

'Is Papa in love again?' said Eddie one day, watching his father sunk in thought at the dinner-table, his head in his hands. Alfred raised his head and looked at the boy with a strange expression, half-comical, half-despairing: 'When was I not in love? I am always in love. The mildest of women can make mincemeat of me.' In that second I knew that something was afoot, and that, unlike his usual flirtations – which he enjoyed inflicting on us *ad nauseam* – he was being secretive about it. For the first time, I noticed that he wrote letters which he did not leave in the post-box by the front door, but put carefully into his pocket. However, look as I might among his papers and drawers, I never found a reply. Letters there were in abundance, but they were all from his admirers or his publishers. Once I came across a crumpled bill for a Spanish shawl that had certainly never graced my wardrobe, and another time I found an invoice for hot-house flowers that had never adorned any dining-table at which I'd been present, but I told myself there was an innocent explanation; some theatrical requirement, some gallant gesture to a leading lady. But then came the delivery of a crate of pink champagne addressed to *Miss Jenny Wren*, which Alfred ordered hastily to be sent back, declaring that Granby and Porter were becoming careless and there was 'no one of that name' in our house. I knew no one of that name either – if indeed it was a real name – and when I questioned Mrs. Brooks and John, they could not enlighten me. But it was so unusual for me to enquire about any domestic matter that it came to Alfred's attention: 'I hear that you have been making enquiries into the delivery of household items, Dodo. Is it not a little late to be starting down that road? Twenty years ago I should have welcomed such an interest, but now you are merely upsetting the very nicely arranged apple-cart.'

I said nothing. But when his friends grew loud over the port, I kept my ears open. It was not an easy task: so many ladies' names were bandied about – so many correspondents, acquaintances and contributors. But in among the anecdotes, the laughs and jokes, and the accounts of who had said what, there was one name he could not seem to keep from his lips: Wilhelmina Ricketts – the *Thespian daughter* he had written about so amusingly while I was at Leamington, but for whom he now appeared to harbour a considerable admiration. *For one so young, she is exceptionally talented. And her Mama, too – an excellent creature.*

I doubted the Mama was the source of his interest. But if it *were* Miss Ricketts whom he had fastened on to, I was, in a curious way, relieved. Actresses had always been Alfred's weakness. They shot across his horizon as brightly as comets, and as surely disappeared. Nevertheless, I took to reading the notices of the latest plays and discovered that, like my husband, the critics seemed to be lavish in their praise of the young lady's talents. She was 'transcendent', 'strong' and 'moving' in one play. And she was 'charming', 'tantalising' and 'seductive' in another. I should have liked to go to Drury Lane and see how she managed this singular feat, but Alfred no longer invited me to the theatre, and there was no one else to take me.

I felt that letters were my only chance of finding out the truth. He kept his dressing room locked, but it was cleaned between nine and ten every day, and I knew that Mary-Ellen – amiable but still inclined to be sloppy – would one day leave it unsecured. Which in due course she did. And as soon as she had gone, singing fitfully about 'Poor Molly Ryan' and catching her broom handle in the banister rails, I slipped in and closed the door, my heart palpitating. It looked strange then – the room that had once opened into mine, and through which I used to hear the low sound of his whistling as he shaved or dressed. It smelt of lavender, and the pungency of it almost stopped me in my tracks. But I had to be quick. I opened each drawer and took out all the contents, putting them back as carefully as I could, knowing the displace-ment of half an inch would be noticed. Nothing. Then I opened the hanging wardrobe and went through his pockets. Again nothing. Red-faced, and fearing at any moment to be discovered, I dragged a small cane chair over to the wardrobe to reach the hol-low space above, but as I mounted, the chair skidded under me, flinging my head sharply against the corner of the marble wash-stand as I toppled to the floor. The pain was agonising. I lay there, unable to move; my vision blurred, my eyes blinded with flashes of light. Then I heard a sound – and suddenly there was Alfred's angry face looking down on me. He was in his outdoor clothes and he made no attempt to help me up: 'What do you think you are doing, Dorothea? Why are you in my bedroom, climbing on chairs?'

'Looking for something,' I said, lamely.

'What could you possibly be looking for in my room?' An iron voice.

'Forgotten now – my head hurts – I feel sick.' As I raised myself, I retched. He jumped back smartly, and suddenly there were more people – I saw their shoes and the sweep of skirts – and I was lifted up to a sitting position. Someone put a bowl in front of me, and someone else put vinegar-paper on my temple. Then I was taken to my own room and put to bed. Alfred had disappeared without a further word.

I was in bed for two days. Dr. Phelps said I was severely concussed and prescribed bed-rest and soothing medicine three times a day. If Alfred came to see me, I do not remember, but on the third day, Mrs. Brooks brought up a letter from him. His handwriting was very clear and bold, as if the very look of the words were impressing on me the hardness and seriousness of the contents. *I shall not stoop to enquire as to the reason for your intrusion into my privacy; it is clear to me that you are suffering from delusions, and have been for some time. Your imagination is fevered; you nurture unreasonable fears, and fritter away your energies on fantasies and matters of no importance. I am sad to say, Dorothea, that you are – and always have been – prey to an excessive jealousy. And if that were not in itself a difficult enough burden to endure in the place of the mutual love and trust which a husband looks for in marriage, I have to watch while you make yourself miserable on account of it. We cannot go on in this fashion; we shall kill each other in spirit, if not in fact. We are no longer compatible. I venture to suggest that we would be happier apart.*

I stared at those so unforgiving words. The black letters seemed to spring out at me like words on a newly-cut gravestone. I could not believe he was in earnest. To indulge himself with an actress was one thing; separation was another. It was unthinkable. Impossible. I had to stop such absurd ideas. I pushed away the quilt, and struggled to get up. Mrs. Brooks tried to urge me to remain horizontal, to rest my head. And indeed I had to gulp a glass of medicine to steady myself. 'I must see my husband,' I kept repeating as I fumbled myself into my clothes. 'I must speak to him. Is he in the house? I must send him a message. It's urgent, urgent. Oh, dear Mrs. Brooks, I don't know what to do! Help me dress! Help me dress!' I was beside myself. I admit it, and I think she was too overawed to do other than assist me.

I almost fell downstairs, and finding Alfred in his study, burst through the door. 'Who is she?' I demanded.

He spoke without turning. 'I see you are better, Dorothea, and back to your usual good spirits. Excellent! Now, may I ask, who is *whom*?'

'The woman you write to. The woman you give presents to. The woman you prefer to me. The woman who has made you wish to end our marriage.'

'There is only one woman who has made me wish to end our marriage – and she is in this room. I think I explained that in my letter.'

'There is truly no one else?'

He turned to me. 'Dorothea, you do not look well. You still have a dreadful bruise. Please sit down and rest yourself.'

I sat down and waited while he carefully wiped his pen and put it down. 'I chose to write to you in order that we should not quarrel further, that you could have some time to reflect on your position without becoming heated. I see by your – vehemence – that I did not succeed.'

'*Vehemence!* What did you expect? You write that you wish to live apart from me! What wife would find that sentiment consoling – let alone one who loves her husband as much as I love you! And you know I love you, Alfred! I do so very, very much!' I rushed to him and put my arms around his neck. 'I'll do anything – anything – to make things right.'

He ignored my caress. 'I fear, Dodo, that it is too late. We were never made for each other from the beginning, and with each year we become more unsuited. Can't you see that?'

'No! That's not right. We've been happy. We've had eight children. I know I haven't been the wife I should have been, the wife you deserved – but I'll be different, I promise.'

He took up his pen again. 'Well, Dodo, we shall have to see. In the meantime I have a Number to finish. If you will permit me. Whatever the state of our relations, I still have money to earn.' He started to write and I knew he would be deaf from then on to anything I said.

What was I to do? As I looked at him, bent over his desk with such an adamant, grim expression, I remembered all the times when, tired of waiting for him to finish his day's writing, I'd creep up and kiss him on the back of his neck. And he'd look up and smile, reaching out his quill to tickle me on the nose: *What a delicious little nose! And what a very naughty Princess Pug it is to have such a nose on its face!* And he'd take me on his lap and kiss me so ardently that I could barely contain my desire for him. To see him now, turned away, so composed, so indifferent to my feelings, made me almost insane. And sometimes over the following weeks, in my own room, in the dark hours of the night, I swear I *was* insane. Several times on waking, I found the bed-sheets torn from my bed, pillows emptied of their feathers, clothes thrown from their drawers. And, once, I know, I raised my fist to shatter a looking-glass that showed me all too clearly my fat and ugly face. At some juncture, in my most desperate straits, I attempted terrible bargains with the Almighty. I asked myself what – or whom – I would sacrifice to keep my husband's love. I would bend over Fanny as she slept, and think I could bear her loss if Alfred would only stand beside me at her grave, and weep once more on my bosom. And when Fanny prospered and was spared and I thought a greater sacrifice was needed, I mentally delivered up, one by one, Louisa, Alfie, Eddie, Georgie and Kitty. I would have sacrificed any of them to have Alfred love me again.

These were dreadful, wicked, murderous thoughts, and now

I am utterly ashamed of myself for having them. I can only plead that I was so disturbed in my reasoning that I truly did not know what I was doing. And my confusion was not confined to my private actions: I made a public spectacle of myself, too. I made remarks at the supper-table; I indicated that I was a Wronged Woman and he a Beast, and ran out more than once in tears.

In desperation, I tried to revive our secret habit of correspondence by hiding affectionate notes in his waistcoat pocket, using our old pet names of *Princess Pug* and *Mr. Merrylegs* – but he pulled the papers out with a frown and, after a brief glance, threw them in the fire. I realised then that it was no use attempting to charm him; I no longer had the grace or beauty to play the coquette. So I appealed in more sober vein, promising in future never to question anything more that he said or did. I would curb my unnatural jealousy, I said. I would get up early and put on sensible gowns; I would dress my hair neatly in the old way he always liked; and make sure my hairpins did not fall into my soup. I would host dinners every night and learn all about the Irish Question and Cemetery Reform. In fact, I'd do anything he wished as long as we could stay together. 'What I wish is for you to sign the agreement,' he replied. 'That is the best thing you can do for me and for our children. We must separate, Dorothea, and that is that.'

In the end, what else could I do? Staying as we were – under the same roof, but so far apart in every other way – was an agony. In the end, I persuaded myself that if by signing I could please him and see that wonderful smile light up his face, then I would do it. Of course, I did not know what the separation would mean. I was an innocent in the matter; and had no inkling that I would be packed off in disgrace to lodgings while my husband and children continued to live so snugly in our matrimonial home with my sister. O'Rourke was against my putting my name to anything (*You will lose by it, Dodo, sure as eggs is eggs!*) but the lawyers assured me I would be well provided for, and Sissy urged me on. 'You will be very comfortable,' she said. 'You will be able to do entirely as you please. The children will be able to visit you. Your life will be hardly different from what it is now – except that you will be your own mistress. Surely, Dodo, you must see this is the best way. This continual bickering is not good for Alfred, nor for you, and certainly not for the children.'

So I gave in. I suppose I hoped against hope that it would be a thing of short duration; that his amorous obsession with Miss Ricketts would be over in time, and he would come back to me as he always had. In the interim I thought things would go on much as before. Even at that late stage, I didn't realise how very much my life would change, how much public humiliation I would have to endure, how Sissy's words of reassurance were empty and untrue.

But I had not expected the public announcement. Alfred had come to me in an off-hand fashion asking if I would agree to a 'statement of our positions', saying it would save us both embarrassment if the situation were clear and we did not have to explain ourselves over and over again. I did not like his penchant for living our lives in public, and had hoped we could do the thing quietly – but he said misleading rumours were already abroad and they would damage his reputation unless scotched. So I'd agreed. Two days later, the statement appeared. It was very prominent, bordered in black. It said that Mr. Alfred Gibson was obliged to announce that, after many years of unhappiness due to incompatibility of temperament, he and Mrs. Gibson had decided to live apart. It went on: *The children will remain with their father as, owing to incapacity, Mrs. Gibson has become increasingly unable to carry out her maternal responsibilities, which have largely fallen upon the shoulders of her husband and sister. Because of failures in her health and disposition, Mrs. Gibson is unable to meet her children's needs. She has thus given up the right to be called Mother, and regretfully – but Mr. Gibson is obliged to say it – to be called Wife.*

I always say my feelings for Alfred have never changed, but I think they hardened more than a little when I read that. 'Why has he said those terrible things?' I asked O'Rourke. 'I am going, am I not? I am doing what he wanted. I am leaving my home and my children. Why does he need to take my reputation too?'

'I am afraid, Dodo,' said O'Rourke sadly, 'that it is in order to preserve his own.'

'But is that not cowardly?' I could hardly believe Alfred could behave this way.

O'Rourke shrugged his shoulders. 'Poor Alfred is like a cuttlefish. When in danger, he attempts to disappear into his own ink.'

Two days later I left my house for the last time. I went out by the side door while it was still dark. My belongings – such as they were – were already in the carriage. No servants were yet up except Bessie (who stood in her nightgown at the doorway, a handkerchief pressed to her face) and John the coachman, who was silent as usual. No other member of the household was awake. Alfred was not at home.

Thus I began my long period of virtual widowhood. Once settled in my apartment with Wilson, I had no wish to go out into society, or even into the streets. I feared being recognised and having to endure either pity or blame. And I wished to do nothing that would further incur Alfred's wrath. I thought the world would come to me, but it did not. I half-expected Alfred every day, but he never came. Neither did Sissy. And although it was written down by the lawyers that the children could visit me at any time, I was grieved to find that they did not do so. There were a few forced letters in the early days and a picture of a battleship from Georgie – then nothing. I had to resign myself to it. Children cannot be forced to love their parents, and if they did not wish to communicate with me, I would have to bear it. After all, I had already let them down in so many ways. Maybe in some inner recess of their hearts they knew I had been ready to barter their lives away.

But one damp summer's day, three years after my departure, Kitty came knocking at my door, all wide-eyed and trembling – and so grown-up and elegant that I would hardly have recognised her, had she not resembled Alfred so strongly. She put her arms around my neck and kissed me so hard I almost lost my breath. 'Mama, dear Mama, I need your help!' I could hardly believe it – Kitty asking for help, and from me!

'It has been dreadful!' she cried, casting herself down in a dramatic way and letting her very beautiful green silk dress spread over the entire sofa. '*He* has been dreadful! He won't let me do *anything* I want!'

'And what *is* it you want, Kitty dear?'

'Nothing he couldn't help me with if he chose! Simply to be a *real* actress. Not a mere amateur in family plays.' She tossed her head about so that her dark ringlets fell prettily around her face and neck.

'An actress! Oh, Kitty –' But her words made me cry out, aghast.

'Now, Mama, don't start! What could be easier than for the Great Actor-Manager to secure me a part? Remember *Two Gentlemen*? Remember my Sylvia and how proud he was of me then? For years I've longed to do something I could throw my whole soul into.' She breathed heavily, as if her whole soul were actually straining against her bosom. 'But will he help me? No!'

'I expect you went about it in your usual headlong way.'

'No, Mama. I know his temperament by now. I waited until he was in a mellow mood. He'd just made up with Michael and the two of them were talking about old times with a bottle of port. When they got round to the plays Papa had acted in, I said, 'Why don't you do *Lord Royston's Daughter* again? You could be the father, but this time I could be the daughter! That would be novel, wouldn't it?' And he refused point blank, saying he didn't want to see any child of his "with rouge on her face, pouting and preening on a public stage." And I said, "So what does your friend Miss Ricketts do, except wear rouge, and pout and preen – and you think she's admirable and lovely, don't you? What's the difference?" – and he made almost to strike me!'

'Strike you? Kitty, surely not!' I am horrified. He had never lifted a hand against any of our children and thought any man beastly and cowardly who did so. But clearly she had hit home.

'Well, he didn't do it.' She sat up and straightened her gown. 'But you don't know how he's been behaving since you've been gone. For months he raged about like a bear, daring any of us to say anything about 'any young lady' who might be mentioned in connection with him. Then he was all noble and full of praise for Sissy and everything to do with her. Now he's in the very worst of humours and finding fault all the time. He can't write that's the problem. He can't write – and we all have to suffer for it. I can't wait to get away. And with your help, dear, dear Mama, I can. You see –' she hesitated, colouring to her hairline '– I intend to marry Augustus.'

My heart sank. 'Augustus *Norris*?' I had thought that dreadful business was at an end. 'But he is so much older than you. And quite the wrong sort. And moreover he is in disgrace with your father.'

'Oh, please listen before you judge him – before you judge us both! Please, Mama! You are my only hope!'

So I listened, and she told me how she had always cared for Augustus since that first night, and how, shortly after the fateful kiss at the piano, he had contrived to have a note delivered to her in which he'd vowed that 'Rodrigo would wait for Isabella for ever'. And how, after that, they'd managed a clandestine correspondence through the carpenters who built the stage for our summer play – which had kept Kitty buoyed up and cheerful. But after a time, no further notes had come, and Kitty had construed that her childish romance had come to an end. 'I supposed I was too young. I was sure he must have found a proper grown-up woman to love. I could bear it, you know, because I had his letters and knew he had cared for me once.'

It made my heart stop to hear her say that, as I thought of Alfred's letters and how they kept my hopes fresh in spite of everything. 'Oh, Kitty!' I said. 'My poor dear Kitty.'

'No, Mama.' She jumped up and came to kneel by my chair. 'Not poor at all. Because about a year ago I met him by chance in the Bayswater Road, and – well, he only had to bow in that wonderful way of his and all my love for him came back instantly! I told him how grateful I'd been for his intervention in the play: "I fell in love with you straight away, I think." And he laughed and said he'd admired me from the moment I'd galloped down the front steps with my hair flying in the wind. "You were a spark of light in the gloom I was feeling in those days. I'm inclined to be bored, you see, but you got me out of it. I've always remembered your wonderful liveliness. If I went too far in my affection for you, I'm sorry for it. And I've paid the penalty. I thought that you had forgotten me – and to tell you the truth, I thought you were better to have done so. Your father was right, you know. You were far too young, far too innocent; left to my own devices, I'd have ruined you."' Kitty had begged to disagree, and told him how desperately she had wanted to grow up, in order to be his equal. And he had said he was sure she was now *more* than his equal. At which point she had reached up and kissed him to prove it. And he'd said she was a saucy minx who was far too wicked to be Mr. Popular Morality's daughter – and they had laughed and found themselves walking together towards Hyde Park. They'd gone in, and strolled around and listened to the band, and had talked together as if they had never been parted.

'I feel I can say what I like with him without having to mind my tongue, or apologise for daring to be alive,' she went on. 'And when I told him I wanted to be an actress, he said, "Why not? It's a profession I admire." '

And so they had continued to meet every time she went for her singing lesson, and been drawn to each other more with each meeting. And finally he had asked her to marry him, 'although I am a *roué* who doesn't deserve such a fresh young thing as you'. But as Kitty was not yet twenty-one, she needed Alfred's permission. 'Please say you'll speak to him! Please say you'll be on my side.'

'But why should anything I say carry weight with your father? And on the topic of Augustus, moreover? You can't have forgotten how furious he was?' I couldn't help thinking that in 'taking her side', she was asking me to go deliberately against Alfred's wishes – a thing I had not done since the matter of the sovereign given to his mother that day on the Dover cliffs. But I was fearful that if I did not agree to intervene, I might never see my daughter again. And if I am honest, I welcomed an opportunity to write to my husband. Somewhere in my mind was a faint hope that if Alfred and I could resume our correspondence, we might perhaps contrive a reconciliation of our own. Maybe I could *see* him at least; maybe we could speak and remember how much we'd once loved each other. So, with this hope, and with a good deal more apprehension, I wrote to him, begging his pardon and asking if a compromise could be reached. I reminded him of the long engagement my parents had proposed, and how desperate we ourselves had been, and how we had not waited, but followed our hearts. I thought he would remember our own history, and be softened. But his reply was implacable:

Dorothea – I am disappointed that you see fit to encourage Kitty in this tainted and unstable relationship. I think you know only too well – or if you do not, then you have been blind this many a year – how Kitty is both extreme in her attachments and headstrong in pursuing them. You and I both know Kitty to be innocent and romantic, unskilled in charting the deeper and more troubled waters of this existence. You and I both know Augustus to be worldly and dissipated — if not a good deal worse. A very good deal worse. Have you forgotten the man we are talking about? Has the passage of years dulled your faculties? Has he flattered and charmed you into complacency, as he has done so many others?

I cannot believe that you are unable to see that any liaison between them would be entirely to her detriment — and doomed to disappointment and failure; if not a lifetime of regret. Therefore, in attempting to take his part, I can only assume you are affected by the basest of motives: a wish to elevate yourself in your daughter's affections by setting her against the Father whose only desire is to protect and nurture his most beloved child.

I cannot — and I will not — be Kitty's gaoler. I cannot — and I will not — clip the wings of her freedom. She knows my views, and the extent of my disapproval of this proposed match, and I hope her affection for me will guide her actions. I would see an equal disapproval on your behalf, Dorothea, as a disinterested and motherly act; any encouragement, on the contrary, as a measured act of opposition to me.

I hope you will see fit to agree with me in this matter. You and I, of all people, should know the agonies of an ill-matched union.

Alfred.

It was hopeless. Hopeless for me and hopeless for Kitty. 'He always has to be right!' said Kitty with a passion. But implacable as his words were on our own account, they aroused many doubts within me regarding Augustus. I suspected Alfred was right. But I couldn't forget my own history, my own love for a man who was far from my parents' choice. I could not regret one whit of my life with Alfred, in spite of all the pain it had brought me. In my choice of husband, I had followed my heart; and I had to let Kitty do the same. So I suppressed my fears and let Augustus make himself pleasant to me — more pleasant than he had ever been in those interminable afternoons when he had been a guest in our house. He called upon me several times a week, spoke amusingly – if in rather a louche way – on a variety of topics, and brought me gifts of cake, biscuits or port wine. And I let myself be convinced that he had changed; that Kitty's transparent love for him had done what Madeleine Fairbright's affection had singularly failed to do for Miles Danvers. They would sit together on my old sofa and Augustus would put his arm around her, and Kitty would look at him with such adoration as he talked of their future life together, a life where she would be free to sing and play and do whatever she chose – 'especially if it is calculated to annoy the One and Only'.

The day after she was twenty-one, they married. I did not attend the ceremony, but Wilson made them a wedding cake, and on their return we drank a toast. It resembled a funeral more than a wedding, though. The weather was icy, and the champagne seemed to freeze my lips as I raised the glass to drink. Poor Kitty, I thought. She'd lived all her life as the daughter of a great man and might have looked forward to a grand reception at Park House – silver, mirrors, candles, flowers, and a dining-table stretching to infinity. Instead she had to make do toasting her future in front of a fat old woman and a grim-faced servant, with Gyp barking at Augustus's heels.

'Well, Kitty,' said Augustus. 'You've done it! You've defied the Great Man.'

'Serve him right!' She laughed, although I sensed panic under her laughter. 'It's time someone stood up to him. Beg pardon, dear Mama, but you never did, did you? So he expects everybody to cave in sooner or later. But Augustus and I are made of sterner stuff.'

'Yes indeed!' Augustus kissed her ardently, and I wanted to cry, because I knew no one would ever kiss me in that way again.

'God Bless you both!' I said, with tears in my eyes. 'Look after her, Augustus, won't you?'

'I can look after *myself*!' said Kitty.

I only wish she had been able to.

~ 19 ~

When we have finished our tea, Sissy suggests, to my surprise, that we should tour round the whole house and see what things I might like to take away with me.

Louisa looks suddenly wan. 'Would you mind if I don't come with you? My head is so bad, I need to lie down.'

I look at the poor thing, such a lump of misery in her plain black gown, her hair scraped back so unbecomingly. I take her hand: 'I hope you've chosen something for yourself, Lou? I shouldn't wish to deprive you of any keepsakes from your father.'

She looks awkward, flushes – and I see in a flash that they have already picked over his belongings. 'I've already got his travelling pencil case,' she says. 'And the little mirror he used to carry in his pocket so he could make sure his hair was tidy!'

'Not that it ever was,' I add.

She looks at me with the sudden recognition of a shared memory. 'No, it would spring up like a jack-in-the-box, wouldn't it?' She laughs, a lovely free, open laugh, and I see the child she used to be.

'Oh, Louisa, my dear Mouse!' I go to her; hold her in my arms. She is soft and cushioned, not brittle as Kitty is. We resemble two cottage loaves .

She lays her face against my bodice. 'Oh, Mama! What shall I do? What shall I do? I miss him *so* much!'

'We all do, Lou. But it has to be borne.'

She lets herself be embraced, then pulls away suddenly, as if stung. 'I'm sorry, Mama, I must go upstairs. I must lie down again.'

'You are *always* lying down, Mousey,' Sissy says gently, but with submerged exasperation. 'It's a little morbid to be moping around all the time doing nothing. If you don't want to help *me*, why don't you go to the seaside for a week or two? Muffin's offered to have you at any time. You can amuse young John and Leticia. It may help you forget.'

She glares at Sissy. 'You don't understand. I don't want to *forget*. I want to *remember* – and he's already starting to fade!' She makes blindly for the door and blunders through, her handkerchief at her face.

Sissy shakes her head at me. 'I can do nothing with her.'

I remember Lottie's words when Alfred was similarly steeped in grief. 'Allow her some time,' I say.

We get up and walk slowly around the ground floor. Sissy flings open doors and ushers me into rooms like a major-domo, and I try not to be annoyed by her patronage. The house is familiar yet strange. Colours have been changed, some new furniture bought, but the rooms are much the same. We progress up the red-carpeted stairs to the drawing room with its long windows overlooking the garden; then to the library, still with its complement of books; and then up a half-landing to our bedroom – *my* bedroom, as it became for that unhappy year, and then his again. Sissy hesitates, then opens the door. The light floods in as it always did, but now the tree has grown up outside, and the autumn sun flickers through its branches, making patterns on the walls. Our big brass bed is still there, but with a more sombre quilt. The marble washstand is the same, with its nice blue jug and bowl – and the hanging wardrobe with the oval looking-glass in the middle. But there is a new round table by the bed, with a new lamp on it; and my dressing-table has gone, and his chest of drawers has been moved in from the dressing room next door. On top of it are a small looking-glass, his dressing-case, and his tortoiseshell brush and comb. Over the mantel is an etching of a view of the Alps, and on the shelf a pair of candlesticks and a clock. Otherwise no ornaments. The room seems so plain, so sad. I want to embrace and love it.

Sissy stands in the middle of the room. 'There's not much here, as you see, except his clothes.'

My heart jumps. 'Clothes? Oh, may I see?'

She opens the wardrobe, and there they are: his favourite checked travelling coat, his silk-braided evening coat, a red-quilted smoking jacket, and others I do not know – all brushed and immaculate. On the shelf, a pile of trousers folded neatly. And above them, dozens of waistcoats in a blaze of pattern. Along the bottom, his boots – six pairs, shiny as the day they were bought, but worn down in the heels from his endless walking. I see the shape of his feet in them, see his quick walk and the way he stood as if ready to spring forward on the instant.

She crosses the room and opens the drawers. Shirts – dozens of them. I walk over and bury my head in them: lavender; 'O Mistress Mine'; that first night; the hornpipe; dancing till our feet ached. 'I'd like to have one.'

She shrugs. 'Well, there are plenty.'

I look around for the sight of any intimate object. But it is as if he has removed everything of himself from the room, except for his clothes. My eye lights on a small inlaid chest in the corner. It has a curved top and a small ivory escutcheon. 'What is in *there*?'

She shrugs. 'It's locked, and I can't find any key that will open it. I need to get Mercer with some sort of tool. But it's a pretty thing. I don't want to break it.'

I have a moment of blinding enlightenment: a key that opens nothing in the house; a little intricate key that I have seen him with a million times, taking it out of his coat at night, placing it carefully with his watch and chain, and putting it back again next day. I had always assumed it was a key to a cash-box at his office. But this little chest looks made for it.

'Which coat was he wearing that day?'

She looks at me, startled. But she goes to the wardrobe and pulls out an alpaca jacket. I put my hand inside and feel for the slim opening within the pocket which he had made in all his clothes. *For my most pertinent pencil,* he said. At the bottom there is metal. I draw it out. We look at each other. My heart is racing.

'Try it.'

I bend with difficulty and put the key in the lock. It fits perfectly, turns easily; it has been kept oiled. Sissy and I open the lid. We stare down at something white.

It is a woman's frock. I know it; I know it very well. I lift it gently from its folds, the smell of camphor rising up around me.

Sissy is puzzled. 'Whose is it? Yours, Dodo?' Although she would have been hard-pressed to imagine when I would last have fitted into something so small.

'No,' I say, pulling it up to its full height. 'It belonged to Alice.' I recognise it as one of the five new gowns she had made before she came to live with us. It is almost thirty years old.

We look at it in silence. Sissy turns to me: 'Did you know?'

I shake my head.

In the bottom folds of the frock is a little calf-bound book. I pick it up. It is *The Lyric Poems of John Keats*, her own copy, given by him. I remember her taking it with her everywhere, tucking herself into corners, reading till her eyes gave out. There is a single sheet of notepaper acting as a marker, and the volume falls open at 'Ode on a Grecian Urn'. The third stanza is underscored in pencil. The writing on the marker is in his hand: *This book belonged to my darling Alice, who adored to read about love, and who awakened love in all who knew her. Especially me. Especially me. Especially me.*

Sissy takes the book from me, reads the words on the paper. Her face flushes.

'He wrote that? Is that why Mama – ?'

'No, she never saw it, I'm sure. Nor did I. Alfred took the book away from her bedside the night she died.'

My heart is thumping. I know what Sissy is thinking. It does seem a lover-like thing to have written. But for Alfred, love was such a radiant feeling that he never stopped to divide it into what was suitable for a wife, or for a sister, or for a friend. All the same, I am struck at the depth of his feelings. He must have taken the frock from her closet during one of those vigils he used to keep after she died, sitting alone in her room, sometimes with a candle, sometimes in the dark. I imagine him burying his face in her frock as I have buried mine in his shirt. I imagine him taking the delicate white muslin, folding it very carefully, and putting it in the little chest. And taking her favourite book, and reading where she had marked. Adding his own words; tucking the book into the deepest creases of the gown; closing the lid; and locking it. I realise that all the time we were married he must have kept the chest in his dressing room and the key next to his heart. He must have looked at its contents in private, enjoyed endless moments of grief: *Forever wilt thou love, and she be fair.*

'Anyway,' Sissy says stoutly, 'Mama was wrong about Alfred. He was a man of morals.' Then she colours. I know what she is thinking: Wilhelmina Ricketts.

We have not spoken of Miss Ricketts, and I can see that Sissy does not acknowledge Miss Ricketts' existence. And Miss Ricketts, in her wisdom, has clearly kept out of Sissy's sphere. But as I stare down at this little chest, I wonder what other intimate objects he left behind, and what else that loathsome woman has managed to lay her hands on. A thought occurs to me: 'Where is his watch?'

'Alfie has it.'

Thank God. I shouldn't want Miss Ricketts to have the thing that was always with him, that was literally closest to his heart. I can see Alfred now, drawing it out by the chain with his usual flourish, opening the case swiftly, checking the time, and then spinning it back neatly into his pocket in a way that never failed to amuse the children.

'And Alice's ring?' I ask her. 'What became of that?'

'He wanted it buried with him. I made sure it was.' Sissy strokes the fabric of the gown as if it is a sleeping child. 'It was her dying wish, wasn't it? That he should wear it for ever?'

'Did he tell you that?' He told the story so often I wonder if he'd come to believe it in the end. 'It wasn't strictly true, you know; she was insensible when we found her. But he was so devastated with grief, I don't think he remembered it rightly.' Or, rather, he changed it to what he wanted it to be; but I don't tell Sissy that.

Sissy shakes her head. 'He was quite distracted, wasn't he? I remember you arguing with Mama. And I remember Alfred coming into the room with tears streaming down his face and his hair all awry – telling you both to be quiet. Young as I was, that impressed itself on me. The way he was so wild and yet so severe, and moreover dressed in a bright blue waistcoat with the buttons done up the wrong way.'

'Yes, he was quite beside himself in those first few days. He said that when he died he wanted to be buried in the same grave with her. Mama said the idea was indecent; a married man and a single girl. But he was so deranged with grief, Papa said it was better not to argue.'

'Well, he's buried in the Abbey, now. Mother need have no fears; Alice can rest unmolested.'

'Oh, Sissy, that Abbey business! You know how he hated all that *stuff and nonsense*! Why did you let it happen?'

She shrugs. 'The Public. There were demands.'

I nod. Of course. The Public.

We sit together for a while, lost in our own thoughts. Then we close the chest and lock it. I take his shirt in my arms and we leave the room. We continue round the whole house, collecting items on the way, and when we have finished, Sissy insists that I go home in the carriage. She says it is ridiculous to attempt to take a

[267]

huge tea-chest in a Hansom cab, and that I shall need the services of Robert to take it up the stairs – so I accept. I have forgotten that the old brougham is such a comfortable vehicle, and I ride home in style.

✦

When I get back, I find O'Rourke and Kitty are in attendance. They are surprised to see the carriage, and intrigued by the box Robert lugs up the stairs together with the carpet-bag of letters.

'Mama!' says Kitty, jumping up the moment I come in. 'Wilson says you've been to see Aunt Sissy! Is that true?'

'I have indeed.'

'Why didn't you tell me?' She pouts, like a child.

'Because I wasn't aware that I needed your permission, Kitty.'

She flushes. 'Not permission, Mama. Only – why did you go? What did you say to her? Did you see Mousepatch or Eddie?'

'I saw Sissy. And Louisa. And Mrs. Brooks. And that strange man, Mercer.'

'The one who lurks in the hall, holding a silver salver, looking disapproving?'

'The same.' We laugh. Kitty and I always *did* find the same things funny.

'But what did she say?'

'Many, many things.' Kitty is crowding me as usual. I shoo her off. 'Give me some space, child. Let me take off my bonnet and shawl!' I turn to O'Rourke, who is keeping out of the way on the window-seat. 'Michael, I hope you've not been waiting long.' I notice he has a pink carnation in his lapel today.

'Not at all! And I've been royally entertained by Kitty. She can make a story out of anything, exactly as her father could. And Wilson has provided us with many excellent cups of tea.'

Oh dear – more tea! I ease myself down by the fire. 'Well, I can hardly believe that I've seen not only Sissy, but Lou as well.'

'I'm surprised they let you past the front door. They guard that place like a prison!' Kitty looks cross, as though she wished they had *not* let me in.

'Well, admittedly, she hid away at first. Hoped I would give up and go away, no doubt. But when I started to help myself to the ornaments –'

'Mama, you *didn't*!' Kitty looks up with a pleased expression quite at variance with her words.

'Well, not quite, but I ordered a box from that Mercer man, and when she thought I was about to take things away unobserved, she had to face me *faute de mieux*. And I'm glad. She is my sister, after all – and I believe we have come to something of an under standing. Most excitingly, I've brought back some wonderful mementos.'

'More things to dust, I'll be bound,' Wilson remarks, coming back into the room. 'This place is enough of a museum already.'

'It's a very *nice* place,' says O'Rourke. 'I won't have anything said against it. I am always most comfortable here.'

'Well, *gentlemen callers* don't have to keep it all clean. And *gentlemen callers* can sit and drink tea all day with no thought to the cost involved.'

'Wilson!' She may take liberties with me, but I cannot allow her to bully my guests.

'Oh! Master's collar!' Kitty has fished it out from the top of the box and is holding it up like a diadem.

'Good Heavens,' says O'Rourke. 'I'd forgotten all about that poor hound – how you'd call to him, and he'd run the opposite way! Alfred loved to demonstrate that singular prowess of his. He'd cry, "Here, Master!" – and the dog would set off like a rocket straight to the coal hole. It never failed.'

'Now, don't meddle with things!' I pull the collar from Kitty's hand and put it back. 'Time enough for that, later.'

'Talking of which, madam,' says Wilson more loudly. 'Are

Mrs. Norris and Mr. O'Rourke staying for luncheon? I'll have to go to the pastry-cook's for a meat pie this very minute, if so.'

'Why not?' I'm feeling buoyant. 'Let us have *two* meat pies — veal *and* fowl! Let us have oysters too, and a bottle of wine! Let us lunch in style. I am sure the housekeeping will stretch.' For a moment I feel like Alfred, who adored impromptu feasts.

Wilson goes out with a certain Look on her face, and I know the man at the pastry-cook's will be in for some hard dealing. But I feel very blithe somehow, so I ask Kitty to bank up the fire, and while we are waiting, I tell them what has happened — some of it, at any rate. Kitty clearly knows nothing of what Augustus has told me, so I can't explain the reason for my adventure. But she is pleased that I have stood up to Sissy, and have had some of my own things returned.

'You have more correspondence, I see.' O'Rourke indicates the carpet-bag full of black-edged letters.

'More people I don't know, I expect. But it's good of them to write.'

'Sissy has been inundated with correspondence!' remarks Kitty. 'I've seen them in her sitting room, all neatly stacked. And I've had dozens myself, and so has Alfie. In fact, Mama, I can hardly believe there was enough paper and ink in the world to accommodate them all.'

I laugh. 'How can you say that, when you know the amount of paper and ink expended by your own father! He almost never sat down unless he had a pen in his hand.'

Kitty smiles. 'Sometimes I thought he preferred writing to speaking. Do you remember how he'd write notes to us every day, and leave them in the nursery or on the dining-table, or tucked into our apron pockets or Bessie's gloves? Silly things, you know, riddles and poems. And then he'd pretend he had nothing at all to do with them. *What, write you a poem about Miss Penelope Prattle who couldn't hold her tongue even if her life depended on it? I have better things to do! But read it to me, pray, as I have pretensions to being a writer, and am not too proud to pick up a point or two from one who has clearly got to the heart of the matter!* And he'd make me read it to him, and he'd listen and laugh as heartily as if he'd never heard it before, so that sometimes I wondered if he had *really* not written it, after all – even though the evidence of his handwriting was there in front of me.'

'He could always keep a good straight face,' O'Rourke adds with a laugh.

'And every other kind of face,' Kitty retorts, remembering suddenly that she is supposed to hate her father. 'Especially the one that has two sides.'

She won't let go. Nor will I. 'You know I won't have that, Kitty. Your father was not a hypocrite.'

'So what are we to make of his relationship with a certain person in the theatrical profession – if not the oldest one?'

'Kitty!' Her language betrays Augustus's influence, as ever.

She ignores me. '*You* are hypocrites, too, if you cannot admit that my father – my wonderful father, the great family man – kept a mistress half his age for more than ten years. And that he went into paroxysms of rage if you so much as referred to her!'

We are silent. Kitty has gone red. O'Rourke looks uncomfortable. His wheezing is obvious when he speaks: 'I think, Kitty, you should have more respect for your mother than to say such things.'

'My mother is not a fool. She knows the truth.'

'Oh, my dear little Kittiwake!' He shakes his head at her again. 'You have always been a stickler for 'the truth'. But the Truth has many shades, you know. You'll learn that as you progress through life.'

The colour is high on her cheeks. 'So it was right for him to do that, was it? It was right for him to cast out Mama and never speak to her again? It was right for him to take up with an actress, and yet forbid me to practise the profession myself?'

'No, it was far from right. But we don't know all the facts, do we?'

'We know *enough*!' She gets up and starts to march around the room, as is her wont. As I watch her quick, nervous pacing, I cannot help thinking of Alfred, his energetic step, and the way he acted out the story of *Death's Dancing Boots*, throwing himself about the house like a madman with such a look of mortal dread on his face that it was hard to believe he was not in earnest. He'd rush out of the house and accost complete strangers, beseeching them to *take off the boots, for mercy's sake,* while keeping up the manic jig. One day, in his enthusiasm, he almost fell down the area steps, which brought the notion of death too close for comfort. But I remember that Kitty was the one who was always the most horri-fied and absorbed of the children, the one who would try to follow and hold his coat-tails: *Let me help you, Papa. Let me help!*

'On the contrary, Kitty,' I say, 'None of us really knows the Truth.'

'*He* knows.' She flashes her eyes at O'Rourke. 'Don't tell me my father never confided in his best friend? Men talk to men, don't they? About their conquests? About their *whores*?'

O'Rourke blenches at the word, but answers her manfully. 'Not in this case, I assure you. You use that word of her, but all I know is that she was a young actress. And that she had a mother who was also an actress –'

'I know all *that*! And I know about the house he gave them, and the presents. And the money he has left in his will. And I know that she simpered about the room with Mr. Golding all agog, while her mother had the gall to call me *Miss Kitty*!' She stares at us angrily.

'If you know all that, what exactly is it that you wish to know further?' O'Rourke is very busy with the fire-tongs now, covering his agitation.

'I don't wish to *know* anything; I'm disgusted with the whole

[272]

thing! But she exists, doesn't she? He made Mama leave our home because of her! He embroiled us all in dreadful scandal to protect her! But however badly he behaved, he managed to end up as the virtuous one. That is why he was two-faced! Why am I the only one to acknowledge that?'

O'Rourke and I are silent, but at that moment Wilson comes in to say that lunch is all laid up, and that she supposes we'll be wanting the oysters first. So we leave the vexed topic of Miss Ricketts and adjourn to the dining room, where an opened bottle of Hockheim sits proudly in the middle of the table, and two dozen oysters lie opened on a platter.

'This is *capital*,' says O'Rourke, with emphasis. He pours wine into our glasses. 'I have not lunched with you for *such* a long time, Dodo – and I have not had oysters for a good while either!'

'I'm not surprised,' I say, 'after that time at Wellard Street.'

'To be sure!' We both start to laugh at the recollection.

'What's so funny?' Kitty slides an oyster down her throat and munches on some bread as if she is famished.

I laugh again. 'Well, when your father and I were first married, Michael decided to give us a present –'

'In recompense for all the hospitality I'd had at your parents' hands –'

'So he bought several quarts of oysters –'

'All very alive and best quality, I was assured –'

'And brought them back and presented them to us still in their box.'

'And were they not good?' Kitty looks up from her own oyster.

O'Rourke and I laugh again: 'We shall never know!'

Kitty looks perplexed.

'They had not been opened,' I tell her. 'And between the three of us and the people upstairs and the people downstairs, and even our landlady herself, there was no such thing as an oyster-knife to be had late on a Tuesday night.'

'Alfred would not be defeated, of course,' says O'Rourke. 'He attacked the shells with a kitchen⁄knife, then a bread⁄knife and then a pocket⁄knife –'

'And then the fruit⁄knives!'

'And the teaspoons! And then, in desperation, he set about them with the poker and the fire⁄tongs. I never saw anything so funny – until the poor fellow's hands were so gashed he had to retire from the fray.'

'So we had to sit and eat our bread⁄and⁄butter while looking at the oysters and using our imagination, which, as Alfred said, was *the best sauce in the world*.'

'He used that scene in *Edward Cleverly*.' Kitty pours herself more wine.

'Well, why shouldn't he? It was very comical.'

'Everything was grist to his mill, wasn't it? Even us – his children. Even his wife.'

'I am tired of your complaining, Kitty. This was meant to be a congenial luncheon. I insist we only talk of pleasant things.'

'As usual,' I hear Kitty mutter under her breath. She looks so mutinous that I wonder why I have gone to so much trouble on her behalf. But after lunch I tell her I have a note for her to take back to her husband.

She eyes me sharply. 'For Augustus? Is it about the will?'

'In a way,' I say, sitting down at the little writing⁄desk.

'He hasn't asked you for money, Mama?'

'No, he has not.' That is true at any rate. I write briefly; I am a slow writer, although very neat.

Dear Augustus, Sissy needs some proof of the situation. Please furnish documents to Mr. Golding as soon as you can and there may be hope. I can do no more, Dorothea Gibson.

I fold and seal it, then hand it to her. Kitty looks at it as if it's about to burst into flame. 'What's this all about? Is that why you went to see Sissy?'

'I can't say.'

'I shall speak to Augustus directly I get home.' She crams her hat on and fixes it with a vicious pin. 'You mistake my nature if you wish to conceal things from me.'

'Yes, do speak to him, dearest. That is by far the best thing.' It's not Augustus's usual practice to be at home in the afternoons, but I imagine with no credit at the tables, and no welcome at his club, he may well be there. Kitty will get 'the truth' out of him, I'm sure. And I shall be relieved of this awkward third-party position.

20

When Kitty has gone, in a whirl of beads and trailing pieces, and with her characteristic look of determination, O'Rourke and I sit down by the fire once more.

'So what made you call on Sissy?' He looks at me with eyebrows raised. 'I suppose it was Augustus.'

'Yes. He needs money. Did you know?'

'It's common knowledge, I'm afraid. The man's been living on air for months. Everyone's after his blood: Jews, bailiffs, everyone.'

'Why did you not tell me?'

'What could you have done?'

'What I *have* done – spoken to Sissy.'

'I hardly thought you would do that. You once said, if I recall, that you'd like to put her in a barrel of tar and pitch her out in the China Sea.' He smiles. 'I was quite entertained at the thought.'

I am surprised I put voice to such a desire, even though I thought such things all the time. 'Sissy wasn't to blame for everything,' I say.

'Maybe not. But she had a choice, and she chose to humiliate you – staying on with Alfred while you were sent packing like an unsatisfactory servant!'

That was how I had felt, certainly; there was no ceremony at all about my departure. But if Sissy had not stayed – what then? 'It wasn't easy for her to brave it out,' I say grudgingly, 'when all the so-called friends who had once been so glad to drink his wine and eat his food now seemed only too eager to believe the worst of him – including, it would seem, my own mother.' I take a deep breath. 'It is a terrible thing to admit, Michael, but the more I think of it, the more I believe Mama may have been at the bottom of those dreadful rumours.'

'Surely not. Not about her own daughter.' O'Rourke frowns in disbelief.

'But you see, she hardly regarded Sissy or me as her daughters by then. We'd both followed the primrose path to perdition as far as she was concerned. I honestly don't think she minded if our names were dragged through the mud, as long as some of it stuck to Alfred.'

'But what would she have gained from such slander?'

'Gained? I don't know. Maybe she thought she was avenging Alice – though God knows Alice never needed to be avenged. Maybe she simply hated Alfred for being there at the end; the last person to look at her; the last person to hold her in his arms.'

'But why should she hate him so badly for that?'

'I don't know. She felt deceived, I think. Alfred had always been a great favourite with her. She'd even forgiven him for marrying me before our engagement was out. But the moment Alice died, it seemed as though everything she had once liked about him, she now deplored. The day of Alice's funeral, when he was beside himself with grief, she looked at him as if she would have struck him dead upon the spot. And after that she took every opportunity to imply that he was some kind of Bluebeard. It would have been laughable had it not caused such constraint between us. Every visit I made to Chiswick was purgatorial; and if Alfred were ever in my company she would refer to him in the third person: *Would your husband like tea? Will your husband kindly pass the cake?*'

'Oh dear, I never knew it was so bad.' O'Rourke purses his lips. 'So when Sissy defected to the other side –'

'– she wouldn't speak to either of us. But Papa died barely a year afterwards, and she was left alone. I did try to repair matters then. I asked Alfred if she could come to live with us, and he said she could if she were so minded – *after all, my house is known as the General Infirmary.* But she didn't seem to want reconciliation. She spurned Alfred's olive branch and wrote saying that she had heard that he was gambling and drinking, and – well, making all sorts of accusations that were not true. I wrote quite sharply to her. I told her that some of his *friends* were disreputable, but that Alfred had no time to indulge himself in vices, even if he had wanted to. I told her his nose was forever to the grindstone, and what leisure he had was always put at other people's disposal. I said it was disgraceful of her to impute otherwise.'

'And did she admit she was wrong?'

'Not at all. She said she had her information from "the most reliable sources". She said it was *I* who was blind to Alfred's real character, and I would come to rue the day I'd married him. Of course, when our separation occurred, she thought herself vindicated. "I suppose it is some young actress," she wrote. "And he with his high-and-mighty attitude about self-sacrifice and family love."'

He looks surprised. 'Did she know, then? About Miss Ricketts, I mean?'

'She can't have done; after all, you know how little I knew myself. But I'd once foolishly confessed my jealousy of his theatrical ladies. And as he'd been performing *Lord Royston* while I'd been conveniently away in Leamington, she was putting two and two together. And was not so wrong, as it turned out.'

'But to spread rumours about him and *Sissy*! Surely that is spiteful beyond belief.' O'Rourke takes out his handkerchief and wipes his forehead in an agitated fashion. 'Did she care nothing for *your* feelings?'

'On the contrary, she revelled in the way fate had proved her point, called me her 'poor dear girl' and invited me to live with her and Cousin George. But I had to be her ally, and plot against Alfred; telling the world how he had neglected me and favoured other women. "You could write a piece for the *Lounger*," she said. "You could tell your own side of the story. That would teach him!" But I knew enough about Montague Miles to warn me of the dangers of engaging with the gossip-writers. I didn't want that. Nor did I want to live in Coventry, seeing George's children day after day and knowing I could never see mine. So I said no – and she seemed to wash her hands of me from that moment.' I shrug. 'So there I was, with an implacable husband and an implacable mother, too. And a sister who took my husband's part, and lawyers who were pressing me every minute of the day. And friends who seemed to have melted away like dew. Except you, of course, Michael! You kept me sane, I think – if I ever was.'

'You were as sane as anyone could have been. And I cannot take any credit for it. I should have been more alert to the Ricketts business.' He turns to me, and grasps me with both of his cold, dry hands. 'You know, don't you, that I fought for you afterwards? I did everything I could. I begged, I implored – I practically lay down on the floor in front of him. But he gave me that iron look and asked me how I, a single man, could presume to lecture him, a man of twenty years' experience? In spite of the fact that *his* wife was alive and mine was long dead and our child within her, he still maintained that I was in some ways the happier man because the "gilt of romance" had never been rubbed off my particular piece of gingerbread by the "slow attrition of dispute and disagreement". "How can you know the anguish of those locked for years in a loveless union?" he asked me.'

'He can't have believed that, though, can he? Not *loveless*. Not *for years*.'

He looks sadly at me: 'On the contrary, Dodo, I am sure he was utterly convinced of it. He'd worked himself up to a perfect passion on the subject, and nothing I could say, nothing I could remind him of, would make him think otherwise. Instead he paced up and down the carpet, accusing me of adding to his woes. And when I wouldn't speak ill of you, he ordered me out of the house, and went in search of people whose views would be more congenial – sycophants, hangers-on, lawyers. People who didn't really understand him; who didn't know what such a public scandal would do to him – or you.' O'Rourke takes my hand again. His grasp is weak, his fingers almost bloodless. 'Dodo, believe me, you were only a little cog in the great machine of unhappiness that he was caught up in. As far as he was concerned, it was the Whole World that was against him and he – poor little eight-year-old Edward Cleverly – was fighting the Whole World.'

'But why say we had a *loveless union*?' I feel the tears prick at my eyelids. 'I know we were the most wretched of couples at the end. But to say that we'd *never* been happy after all the loving things he said to me; after all the letters he wrote – that was a simple lie.'

O'Rourke makes a wry mouth. 'Oh, have you forgotten that Alfred never told a lie? If facts didn't suit him, he simply brought his mind to bear upon them, and they miraculously took on different form – so different that he could raise his hand and swear black was white in utmost sincerity.'

O'Rourke is right; once an opinion formed in Alfred's mind, it became to him as inviolable as Scripture. I think of Alice and the ring she never gave him. And I see his busy pen striking swiftly through all the pages of our past, crossing out *affection* and *happiness,* and writing in *misery, incompatibility, disharmony* instead. 'He reinvented our lives, didn't he?'

He laughs dispiritedly. 'You could say it was his most accomplished piece of fiction.'

'But why did he have to go to such lengths?' I burst out. 'Couldn't he be like other men and admit that he'd got tired of his old wife and wanted somebody younger, fresher, more to his taste?'

'My dear woman, can you see him admitting that – even to himself? Alfred, the exemplary father? Alfred, the great advocate of family life? No, it had to be *you*, Dodo. It had to be *your* character that was at fault. *You* had to be sullied and vilified so *he* could be excused – and not only excused but positively praised for his forbearance.' He bangs his fist on his knee, and starts to wheeze. 'By God, my blood boils when I think of it. I wonder I was ever able to speak to him again.'

I rise, and put my arm around him. 'Oh, take care, Michael. Don't get so agitated. It's not good for your health.'

But Michael is in full flow. 'Sometimes, I swear, he behaved as if he was above the laws of nature! But Nature overtook him in the end, Dodo. He was forced to realise that life is not a novel, that those around him were not his characters, and that in spite of all his fame and success, he couldn't will himself a happy ending.' He coughs and takes out his handkerchief to wipe his whiskers.

'What about Miss Ricketts?' I say cuttingly. 'Wasn't *she* supposed to be the happy ending?'

He shrugs. 'I doubt it – or he would have looked more content. The last time I saw him, he was so old and ill-looking, I was appalled.'

'Don't say that.' I cannot bear to think of that. I want to remember him at his best – young, quick, vigorous, *sharp as a Sheffield knife.*

He sighs. 'But it's true, Dodo. He'd lost all that wonderful exuberance. When I last saw him he was walking along the Strand, limping and looking as miserable as it is possible to look. We talked for a little and he said he wished we could all go back to the good old days in Wellard Street: "I was a better man, then. A far, far better man."'

Wellard Street. When we were so happy. 'Did he speak of me?'

O'Rourke shakes his head. 'I wish I could say yes. But you were too much of a reminder to him; a reminder of the wrong thing he had done. The only way he could manage you was to flatten you out of existence, as he'd flattened Jack Black under the wheels of the Dover coach. But he could not quite suppress his guilt. He told me that he was continually laid low with stomach cramps or monstrous headaches.'

'I'm not surprised. Kitty said he never ate a proper meal.'

'Only bits here and there. And he smoked like a chimney and downed more champagne than was good for him. The doctors kept warning him; Jenkins even said there could be a brain seizure, but it seemed as though he didn't care – started on new reading tours as if he were still young and fit. Put himself through months of travel, all over England, all over America. Trains, boats, cabs and carriages. Snow, ice, rain and sleet. Strange hotels and hot concert halls night after night. New audiences clamouring for his every word and gesture, new critics ready for the kill. The wretched Miles wrote an article saying that he wasn't satisfied with being the richest writer in England but had to hawk himself around like a cheapjack, piling up more and more booty. But you and I both know that it wasn't the receipts that drove him on. He needed to know his Public still loved him, that they still communed with him on this great shared stage that is Life.'

'And they did, didn't they? I heard they came from everywhere to see him.'

'Oh, yes. Lamming told me he'd seen men actually plying their fists outside the box office. Alfred dared not cancel a single performance for fear of riots breaking out.' He shakes his head. 'The halls would be filled to capacity, people packed as close as it was possible to be, the temperature near to boiling. He should have seen what he was doing to himself. He was sometimes almost dead with exhaustion, had almost to be carried into the building, saying: *I can't disappoint My Public.*'

I'd have loved, if only once, to have slipped in at the back of the hall, *incognito*, to watch him as Miggs and Edward Cleverly and James Bartram. But in truth it would have been too much for me. 'I try to picture it, you know,' I tell O'Rourke. 'I imagine him like Abanazar at Christmas.'

'Not so different, in fact. The same red curtain; the light arranged to fall exactly on his face. But now it was a finely-tuned performance and he'd wait, watch in hand, for the exact second to show himself. And when he did, the cheers would be deafening. But he'd put up his hand, just so, to request silence, as if our adulation was absolutely nothing to him. And when there was silence – and only when – he would open the book, and begin. No introduction, no address to the audience – straight in. Something from *Miggs,* usually, to make us laugh. Then *Little Amy*, or the death of Tom Welby, to make us cry. Or the ghost chapter from *The Red House* to make our hairs stand on end, or the drowning of Poll Lowton to horrify us all and make the ladies swoon.'

'Kitty hated it when he did Jack Black.'

'I'm not surprised. He became a different person.'

I have often wondered why Alfred was apparently so compelled to re-enact that particular scene, and whom it was he wished he were throttling so comprehensively in the *black, black water* of Hungerford bridge. Maybe I am glad, after all, that I did not see this scene played out, that I was spared the violence that so distressed Kitty. She was always sensitive to that streak of cruelty in him – the jokes that went too far, the frightening bedtime stories, the sudden changes of mood – and mystified as to how it ran alongside his tremendous compassion, tenderness and affection.

The violence is in her too, I think, in her restlessness and passion and sudden displays of rage. I think of her at lunch, flitting between anger and guilt, and I feel ashamed that I have not spoken to her more kindly; that my preoccupations have overshadowed hers. She needs me more than ever now that Alfred is gone and Augustus in such a wretched state. I turn to Michael: 'Do you think Augustus will tell Kitty frankly of his troubles? It isn't right for a man to keep his wife so much in the dark.'

He coughs. 'I've no idea what that man is likely to do. He's a mystery to me. And it's a mystery what Kitty sees in him.'

I suppose, as ever, it all comes back to her father. I think that in cleaving to Augustus, she was attempting to be free of Alfred. 'Poor girl, she took his indifference for tolerance and his idleness for good nature – and will never admit she is mistaken.'

'Like him, then.' He sighs as he rises to go: 'You know, Dodo, before you came back today, she was recounting some incident she had seen in the street, some altercation between a Hansom cab driver and a dogs-meat man, and I could see him right before me: the red curtain, the light, the compelling gestures, the vivid eyes. It was eerie. His ghost come to life.'

⁂

Many ghosts are coming to life. No sooner has O'Rourke gone than Wilson comes in with a note. It's from Alfie again. He wants to bring Caroline and the baby to see me tomorrow after-noon. *Around tea-time, if that is convenient for you, Mama.*

I write excitedly to tell him that it is. I inform Wilson, who compresses her lips at the thought of more refreshments. She is already in bad humour about the cost of the impromptu lunch, and the positioning of the Box (which is impeding her accus-tomed path between the door and the fireplace) but I will not be deterred from arrangements to see my own son and very first grandchild. 'See that we have plenty of cake, and make sure the tea caddy is replenished with some decent Darjeeling. Oh, and some China tea too; I don't know my daughter-in-law's tastes.' I fish from my purse the coins I did not spend on the Hansom cab. 'I'm sure Mr. Collins will be grateful for a little cash in advance, and you may need to encourage the baker too. Seed cake isn't suitable for a child. Perhaps a Dundee. Or a good Madeira.'

'Madam.' She takes the money, bobs very slightly, and goes out, heavy with disapproval. Sometimes she's worse than Kitty.

[284]

21

It's late afternoon, and I start to look through the box. Wilson is right; I don't have space in this apartment for anything new. I'll have to sit down and make a proper list, set aside time to sort through it all at my leisure. I can now hardly believe what a dread word *leisure* used to be; how I had to parcel out my time, make every small activity – breakfast, luncheon, supper, reading the newspaper, combing Gyp's coat – last as long as possible. Now, no ingenuity at all is required to keep myself amused; events occur of their own accord.

Gyp fusses around my skirts as I kneel on the floor by the box. He's out of humour with me lately; he's not used to his mistress being absent from her favourite chair, nor to the strange scents of tobacco-smoke and camphor that Augustus and O'Rourke have been bringing with them every day. He has found another new scent now – he is wagging his tail, sniffing at something in my pocket. I remember suddenly the little notebook I filched from Alfred's desk, and pull it out.

It's the kind of notebook Alfred always favoured – small enough to slip into his pocket, large enough to carry all the information he needed. He must have gone through dozens of them in his lifetime – but at the end he always tore them up, putting them on the fire for good measure. So I suppose this book must be the last of its kind, the final notes for *Boniface*. I don't know why I stole it; if Sissy finds out – as no doubt she will – there will be repercussions for our new-found amity. But for the moment I am infused with a new spirit of insouciance.

I am excited as I open the first page. It is jammed with his own peculiar shorthand, but I can see straight away the word 'Boni-face' written in full among the crabbed symbols. Even as I look at it, though, I realise that it resembles none of his other notebooks. It's too neat. There are no random jottings, no ideas for titles, no lists of wild and wonderful names. The writing is minute, but consecutive. It is, I am sure, a narrative. Can he actually have started to write a chapter in this book? I strain to make out the words, astonished to find I can still remember how to decipher his strange abbreviations.

As soon as I piece together the first sentence, it is clear that this is not a novel. Indeed, it is not even fiction. I stop short, guilty, wondering whether it is allowable for me to go on. He didn't mean this to be read, that is certain. But my curiosity is more intense than I can say. If I *do* read it, who is to know? *He* is not here to reprove me. All the same I can't help looking up, afraid for a moment that I shall find him standing in the doorway, with damp yellow earth on his clothes like the spirit of Jonas Buckle-berry. But there is no one there; the door is closed, the chenille curtain is drawn tight against the draughts and the whole room is cosy and warm. Anyway, I don't believe in ghosts – and never did, even when Alfred read the *Haunting of All Hallows' Eve* so thrillingly that every hair on my head stood up in horror.

I draw my shawl close and start to read:

I have always been blessed (or maybe cursed) with the gift of premonition. And as this year draws to a close, I feel that my life, too, is near its end. I am ill with the colic, I can hardly walk, and my sight in one eye is so poor that the page in front of me retreats and blurs and sometimes disappears altogether. I hope only to stay alive long enough to complete Boniface. I should not want to leave it a mystery to my readers – although at this moment I have to admit it is something of a mystery to myself. Every time I pick up my pen I am filled with a strange sense of unease and I have an almost superstitious dread as I see the last chapters come towards me, as if they are some kind of Nemesis; and I shy away from them. Perhaps my powers of invention are failing. I am very tired, certainly.

Jenny Wren says I should 'write down my life'. I tell her that is precisely what I've been doing since I was twenty. But I need a relief from Boniface — he drives me hard to no good purpose at present. So I shall humour her.

They say I am a Great Man. I suppose that's true. I have certainly accomplished a good deal in my fifty-eight years, more than I could have thought I was capable of when, as a small boy of no very good education and indifferent health, I first conceived the notion of becoming a writer. I was a reader first, of course, as most writers are. I was enthralled by the worlds of fantasy the books of my childhood opened up to me; how in reading them, I could escape completely the dullness of my life, or its sufferings. I read and re-read the same favourites, and it did not seem to matter that I knew not only the endings of my heroes' adventures, but could almost recite each narrative word for word, and engage with them as if with my friends.

Of course, I was not encouraged in this life of the imagination by my early circumstances. I have written of them in many guises, but they still demand to be described over and over again. Even now, as a man, I can feel all the anguish of my childhood as fresh as if it were a new wound. I can hear again the sound of threats from butchers' boys and bailiffs, as unpaid bills mount, creditors clamour at the door, and we are turned out of rooms for which the rent has not been paid in the past and is unlikely ever to be paid in the future. Once more I bundle up my pathetic belongings in the flight from bad lodgings to worse; once more I endure the shame of hiding behind curtains in a back room, holding the dog's muzzle so he does not bark; once more I stammer out a false name to the court constable in a vain attempt to evade recognition. And finally, when there is nowhere else to flee to, I follow my father to a dingy room in the Fleet Prison. Even now as I think of it — even as I write of it all this time later — I am in tears.

Yet while I regret those wretched times as much as I have regretted anything in my life — I know they have made me what I am, given me the determination to struggle against all odds. My daughter has called me 'implacable'. Well may she do so. She has — thank God — never had to suffer the privations I knew or had to steel herself against daily disappointment and despair. She does not know what it is at the tender age of eight to be put to work; to any work that was available; to any work that would bring in a few shillings; to any common work where a tender newcomer might rub shoulders with boys whose only object in life was to give a good drubbing to their fellow labourers; in short, to any work where the life of the imagination was as nothing.

And I was a sensitive little fellow. I don't think I belie myself to say so. If I had been less aware of the existence of finer feelings, perhaps I would have been content to subside into the general life of drudgery that my parents were satisfied to see me in; happy to do nothing more than work like a donkey during my allotted hours, and eat, drink and sleep when the work was finished. What more, after all, do poor working boys do? What energy do they have, after hours of toil, to indulge in fantasy and speculation? What money to pay for books or entertainment? A song in an ale-house perhaps? A Punch and Judy show got up in haste down some back alley? A dance with a ready girl who takes pity on a small boy and kisses him on the lips while she waits for a paying customer? Had I not determined otherwise, with the most solemn of promises to myself, those miserable entertainments would have been the sum total of my enjoyment.

But even at my most despairing, I could not settle for this. From my earliest remembrance, I determined to do well. I even had ambitions to be famous. I have always felt this need to be active in the matter of my own fate; never to rely on others. But I have to own that I had the narrowest of escapes. An unexpected legacy caused my father to be released, and I was put back into a respectable school with a suddenness that surprised me. How delightful it was to wear new clothes and boots; to have clean hands, clean linen, and friends of whom I was not ashamed! And to reside for whole periods at the same address, eating off china that would have once only graced the interior of the pawnbroker's, and willing for the servants to open the door to the tradesmen when they called!

My chief comfort throughout my whole childhood was my sister, Lottie. I do not know what I would have done without her. Indeed, I hardly know *how I manage now. She was a steady rock in my life; the only person who never failed me.*

Although she was exactly one year younger than me, she had an understanding well beyond her years, and was possessed of such a wonderful, joyous spirit that I would have defied anyone to be sad in her company. We were close companions as children; night after night we invented wild stories or played out charades, pulling from the old attic basket a variety of ancient clothes which my mother was always going to mend but never did. I sported many a brocade waistcoat and dun-coloured frock-coat as worn (said my mother) by her own Papa when times had been 'more favourable'. Lottie would seek out threadbare shawls and prance about fluttering feathery fans that were so full of dust that we would sneeze as profusely as if we had been taking a juvenile form of snuff. And when Sydney was left in our charge (as he increasingly was) we would assign him the rôles of pet dog or monkey and let him crawl about on the floorboards until he was a veritable porcupine of splinters. I see them both now, Sydney grimy from the floor-dirt, his mouth sticky with bread and jam; Lottie neat and bright, her hair in braids around her head, making him a paper boat or cradling him against her childish frame. Sometimes she cradled me too, and I remember the sense of comfort that came from being in her arms, as we lay like Hansel and Gretel in the midst of the wild wood of our parents' chaotic affairs. But I could not indulge these moments too often; I knew that someone in our family had to be grown-up, and it was clear our parents were to be despaired of in that direction. So it fell to me to be the strong and self-reliant one. I had to whistle and stride about like the hero of my own story, and forgo the delights of Lottie's firm little arms.

Did my mother not embrace me herself? I think back as hard as I can, and have no remembrance of it. Her hands, as I recall, were usually busy wringing themselves into a genteel state of anxiety, and her contact with my person was usually confined to a curious attempt to 'smarten me up' by ruffling my hair sideways, or giving me a sharp poke in the region of my ribs when she wished to emphasise how fortunate I'd been to benefit from the generosity of her deceased relative: 'I hope you will always be a credit to us,

Fred. Goodness knows your father and I have suffered enough for you.' But anything nearer an embrace I do not recall. As for a kiss — no more than the habitual proffering of a hard cheek even while she was in the midst of talking to someone else.

And my father? I once had hopes of my father's affection. He was an affable man and took a more sanguine attitude to existence than my Mama. He saw there were matters beyond the mundane, and aspired to them. It was his library of books that I had devoured from childhood, and I believe his love of words must have affected my own enjoyment of the same. My father, I recall, would not use one word where four or five would do — and this impressive characteristic was, I am sure, significant in his ability to borrow money in circumstances in which a more taciturn man would have failed; he wound words around people until they did not know what they were at. Perhaps I have inherited that ability — but I have put it to better purpose, I believe. My father was proud of me, but proud only insofar as he could make use of me. He would show off my facility for remembering whole swathes of poetry by standing me on the table at the ale-house or coffee-shop and letting me spout Shakespeare by the yard. It must have been quaint to see me there, barely four foot high and dressed as a diminutive gentleman, lamenting my fate as Cleopatra or defying the world as Lear. People would put money in my hands, or in my pocket, and chuck me under the chin, saying, 'Well done! You're better than Kean!' And after the performance, my father would solemnly relieve me of the coinage I had amassed, patting me on the head and offering to buy me a half-pint of porter as a treat.

So it was Lottie I turned to; Lottie who seemed to combine a pure and loving heart with such easy ways, such liveliness, such ability to create a comfortable atmosphere everywhere around her. As she grew up she made even our parents' home a pleasant place to be. She cooked and cleaned and sewed for us all, and cared for my brother in a way that almost made my heart break. I see her now, holding him between her knees to comb his hair, or taking his feet upon her lap to lace his boots, or turning him round like a spinning top while she brushed his clothes. She looked after everybody. She mended my old shirts and made new ones frilled in the latest style, and cut up

[290]

the old dressing-up clothes in order to render them into spectacular waistcoats for me. And she rationed out father's money in the most delicate way possible, kissing him and making him promise to be 'a good papa' as she handed over a florin or two, and thus prevented the worst excesses of his spendthrift temperament. She managed to stay on good terms with every servant we ever had — which was more than poor Mama had ever done — and toiled alongside them in perfect amity. Shrieks and vilifications and the giving of notice were things of the past. And she read — how she read! All my own childhood favourites, then all my schoolbooks. I passed my exercises on to her each day, and helped her to understand the lessons I had so recently learned. And she learned them all — history, geography, arithmetic — quite as quickly as I, but without benefit of teacher, writing everything in the neatest of scripts, sitting by the window with the smoothest of brown hair. I could say that she was remarkably pretty — in fact I would assert it most fervently, except that she was commonly held to resemble Yours Truly. She was certainly well-dressed, making her own gowns and bonnets in a fashion that would not have disgraced a duchess. Above all, she had a natural gift for music. She had the sweetest voice I have ever heard — bar perhaps my own daughter — and the most natural ability to follow a tune. I remember her voice even now, and her bright, bright smile as she lifted her eyes from her sewing to look at me.

To do myself justice, I always contrived to be a dutiful son. But I found it easier to manage my parents from a distance. As I grew up, I could not anticipate quickly enough my severance from them. My mother was forever bewailing the fact that if only she could get away from the dismal demands of London Town, all her problems would be solved. So, once I was set up at Webster and Potts, earning my own wage and feeling my way as a young man about town, I became determined to bring about her heart's desire. My father's widowed sister had for a long time inhabited a small cottage in Dover, and when another became untenanted in the vicinity, I encouraged them to take it, with the agreement that I would underwrite part of the rent myself. Sydney was off to join the Navy, and Lottie (who would not be parted from me) was to stay in London and take in sewing. 'You cannot support all of us, Fred,' said Lottie. 'I will work as hard as I can, so that I can be independent and not ashamed of myself.' And she did — topping and tailing sheets and shirts, turning cuffs, tacking and hemming every garment imaginable. She cleaned our modest little rooms above the corn chandler's so that everything seemed to wink at us with cleanliness. And she cooked such capital meals! At the end of my day's labours, I could walk along the dusty streets knowing I'd climb the stairs to find delicious smells wafting down, and a splendid suet pudding all done up in muslin waiting on the table, or lamb cutlets grilling in the little Dutch oven in the corner of our parlour . . .

I think that Lottie, being the dear girl that she was, thought me unduly severe in my attitude to our parents. My wife was the same when I first introduced them to her. Dorothea could not understand why I had not brought them up to London to meet her as soon as we were engaged, and I am sure she must have imagined that I came from a den of barbarians, so silent was I on the topic of parental affection. Although in the general way I was not ashamed of my parents (who were genteel enough as these matters go), I could never trust them as wholeheartedly as I should have liked — as a son should be able to trust his parents. However much money I placed at their disposal, they contrived to use it up. Although I had given tradesmen an absolute veto in allowing them credit, somehow there were always further demands — a bookbinder, a grinder of inks, a haberdasher — that I had not foreseen. I was under continual hope that my father would find employment, and he always wrote to me in a state of optimism, saying that he was on the point of securing a post to which his capabilities were 'ideally suited'. But at some point between the arrival of his letter and the commencement of the employment, something would inevitably Go Wrong, and once again my parents would be relying on my small means to make ends meet.

My aunt at Dover wrote to me frequently, admonishing me for having conceived such extravagant parents. 'I am advised, dear Fred, that your allowances to them are regrettably meagre, and the extent of their debt is beginning to cast a shadow over Innocent Members of the family — members such as Myself, to whom shopkeepers' eyebrows are now raised at the prospect of even a yard of ribbon or the smallest of lace collars being purchased

[292]

without the immediate exchange of — how shall I put it? — cash. For the honour of the Gibson Name, and the sanity of your Ever-loving Aunt, please endeavour to ensure my Brother and his Wife are, in future, properly provided for.'

At this time, my father was forty-four years of age. I was nineteen.

I close the notebook. I cannot face reading on. I am dismayed that he kept all this from me. In spite of all his intimate knowledge of the very poorest of the poor, I had never thought that *Edward Cleverly* and *James Bartram* were based on his own experiences. Rather I'd thought that such knowledge had come from the conversations he struck up with beggars and crossing-boys on his night-time walks, and his tireless work with Miss Brougham in the slums. I was aware, of course, that he had known a measure of hardship and debt in his earlier life — he had talked obliquely of such things before we were married — but I confess that I never understood, in those days, what 'hardship' and 'debt' really meant. I imagined some sort of momentary discomfort, like having a little less cake or sugar, or not lighting the fire until the evening, or making do with one candle to read by. I'd think of Lottie in her little garret room, with its plain and simple air, and later, of our own humble days with Mrs. Quinn. I could not begin to conceive that Alfred, with his cheerful spirits and fine clothes and manners, had suffered more than a temporary embarrassment. I thought him, as my Mama would have said, a member of the 'genteel poor', a little *stretched* — no more. I could not conceive that he had once lived inside a prison or had been set to rough work at the tender age of *eight*. I can hardly endure to think of such a thing. Eight! I imagine my own self at that age: dressed in white muslin with a taffeta sash around my waist, playing in the garden in Chiswick: Alice still in small clothes, Sissy a babe in arms, Papa pushing me in the air on a swing, Mama supervising my amateur stitches on a sampler; the servants always in order, food always provided. My mind would have been easy, unquestioning; the world would have finished at the garden's end, and there would never be any reason to know what lay beyond. The only ragamuffins I ever saw were the gypsies passing by in the road outside, jangling their tins, or the chimney-sweep's boy with his scabbed feet and elbows as he sat in the kitchen with a tankard of beer and a sour smell that made me wrinkle my nose.

I suppose Alfred would have given off a sour smell too if I had met him while out walking as a child. But I hope I would not have spoken to him as Arabella Chalmers did to poor Ned Chester, casting proud eyes on him and asking, *Must I be forced to consort with a boy who has broken fingernails and drops his aitches as if they were live coals?* Someone said it to him, though. And Alfred remembered the slight. Yet all our married life he kept these wounds from me, showing the scars only in his books. Did he not trust me, I wonder? Did he think I would love him less? That I would be ashamed of him? Sometimes I think he knew me so little.

By the same token, I never knew that his feelings for Lottie ran so deep. He always liked to joke about his 'favourite sister' when she was indeed his *only* one, but I did not realise what a true favourite she really was. I'd always thought it uncanny to see them together, so alike with their bright dark eyes, glossy hair and natty clothes, so in tune with each other's humour and imaginings that they would sometimes finish each other's sentences – but where he was full of high spirits, she was calm. She too was clever and had read hundreds of books – but she wore her cleverness lightly, whereas Alfred, I must admit, liked to show his off. I often used to think she might have made a writer too, had she had time to pursue the art. She wrote such wonderful letters, so observant, so funny – almost as if it were Alfred speaking. And I remember how she would sing simple carols and ballads to us at Christmas – and her voice was so haunting that we would all be in tears, and Alfred would rush to her and take her in his arms, saying she was *the very best sister in the world.*

But poor Lottie had little enough time in her life for writing or singing. She was always busy caring for others. I'd marvelled at her energy and cheerfulness as Tom became such a dreadful shadow of himself. Lottie was forever running upstairs attending to him and then running downstairs again, seeing to the fat boy and shock-headed girl who were supposed to be minding the shop, but were always to be found in the back yard chasing each other around the pump or frightening the pigeons, and never noticing when the bell rang. And then, when anyone else might think of resting, Lottie would be ministering to Tom's aged parents who, in spite of their frailty, seemed set fair to outlive their son. If all that was not enough, between times she would travel down to Dover in the coach to carry out Alfred's requests concerning their *own* parents. Alfred himself visited them as little as he could: 'If I go, there will be quarrels, I know it! Please take fifty guineas and do what you can to restrain them. They love to see you, Lottie dear – whereas I – well, in their eyes I am an ogre, an ingrate, the worst son in the world, a Croesus who keeps his own parents in penury! And for my part, I am beyond speaking to them without wild words forming in my throat. You, by comparison, are a Dove of Peace!' And Lottie would smile and say: 'All it needs is a little patience, Fred.' And he'd reply, 'That is a commodity I am always short of when it comes to Mr. and Mrs. G.! Merely to see them, to hear their voices, makes me feel as if I am in the grasp of an Indian python and it is squeezing the life out of me! After such a squeezing I swear I return to London as flat as a shirt from a mangle – and am no good for anything!'

In spite of Alfred's penchant for letter-writing, it was Lottie, I remember, who wrote regularly to Sydney, who followed his career in the Navy, who sent him presents of new linen and bottles of lavender hair oil, and who went down to Chatham or Portsmouth whenever his ship was in dock. In many ways I felt Sydney was *her* child, and nothing seemed to delight her more than receiving a letter from him, unless it were the chance to enjoy his company for a few days while he was on leave. I remember the first time she brought him to our house, resplendent in his uniform and blushing pink as a girl. 'This is your Uncle Sydney,' she'd said to Kitty, and Kitty had stared at Sydney's legs in their white breeches, before moving her eyes up to the brass buttons on his coat, and holding out her little fists and shrieking with glee as he picked her up.

Alfred was fond of Sydney too, of course. He'd call him the Muffin Man (shortened to *Muffin* or even *Muff*) and delighted in telling how, as a child, he'd had a propensity to eat anything he could manage to cram in his mouth, including an entire copy of *The Times* and two pairs of pigskin gloves; and how he had enjoyed sitting in the dark for hours on end with a mad old recluse of a woman who'd once lived next door, holding her skein of wool while she knitted a long scarf that was never finished; and how his face was forever dirty, however often you mopped it with a dishcloth. Sydney was discomforted at such stories, and always tried to change the subject, to praise our house, or our children, or even myself. 'Well, you've done well for yourself, Fred! This is a far cry from Brigg Lane. I'm tempted to leave the Navy and try my hand at writing too, if this is the result!' And Alfred had laughed and said, 'It's damned hard work, Muffin, I'd have you know! You try writing three thousand words before breakfast! It's worse than climbing the rigging in a storm!'

'And what would you know about that?'

'Oh, nothing at all! But I can *imagine* it – and that, my dear Sydney, is why I am the One and Only and you are All at Sea.'

Yes, I make sense of it now, his curious distaste for his parents, his enduring love for his sister, the vital energy, born of those early deprivations, that propelled him forward. But I wonder why he chose to tell his secret now, and in this way. I riffle through the notebook again. I can see that the narrative goes on for only another half-dozen pages, as if he lost heart and gave up. 'Writing

his life' was someone else's idea, of course; someone whose suggestions he was at pains to indulge: his *Jenny Wren*. It's a sweet,
inconsequential name, and I can't help thinking of her flitting
about the room, chirping away — then coming and sitting at his
feet, laying her head in his lap, perhaps; stroking his beard; playing with his watch chain; feeding him little bits of seed cake and
sips of Madeira wine; kissing his cheek, his lips —

No, this is madness. I must not think of this. What good does
it do me to torture myself with these scenes? For the last ten years I
have done my best to ignore her existence, and I have largely succeeded — in spite of Kitty's insistence on mentioning her.

I put the book back into my pocket. The dark has come
suddenly and it's impossible to read by the firelight alone. But the
wretched Miss Ricketts is not so easily set aside, and I can't help
wishing that *Lord Royston's Daughter* had never been written; and
that he and she had never met in the playing of it. I regret even
more idling my time away in Leamington, playing cards with
Colonel Jibbins and Mrs. Badger while, night after night, the
foundations of my marriage were being carefully undermined.
What an innocent I was! With what amusement I read Alfred's
accounts of his rehearsals — the Thespian young ladies, the Thespian Mama, the crises with the scenery which *fell down and nearly
carried off our juvenile lead*; the inefficiency of the property manager
who *has a propensity for losing every prop he is responsible for — so that we
are forever reading from ghostly scrolls in place of real letters, and I am
obliged to shoot the villain Murdock using only the first two fingers of my
right hand.* How little did I suspect any subterfuge as I laughed so
heartily at his words! Nor did I suspect Alfred's fond feelings for
one particular Thespian young lady whose courage and tenacity
he praised to the skies. She had recently lost her own father, he
wrote, yet trod the boards 'like a veritable trouper'. I suspected
nothing. She was only seventeen, after all, and in spite of Alfred's
romantic susceptibility to very young ladies, I could not imagine

he would have chosen to fasten on a newly-orphaned child, however much of a trouper. I had been jealous without cause on so many other occasions, and had been chided by him so often for 'seeing things where there was nothing to see', that my guard was down the one time I needed it.

Of course, I cannot help but wonder what there was about Miss Ricketts that made him willing to risk everything to pursue her. It seems she was (and is) neither wonderfully clever, nor wonderfully beautiful – although I can't judge, for I have never seen her. But she must have had some remarkable virtues to have tempted him away from everything that touched him most deeply – wife, children, the sanctity of home and hearth, and the admiration of the Public to whom he was almost a god. Of course I can hear Kitty's sarcastic voice admonishing me. *Are you green, Mama? She was young and pretty; he was middle-aged and wealthy. What more do you need to know?* Sometimes, I confess, it is easier to think it was her slender body that delighted him – and her unlined face. After all, what treasures of mind or spirit would a young woman of that age have been able to offer a man so famous, so talented, so widely read? Yet I know it would not have stood easily with him to take advantage of *any* woman, however low in society; to have blighted her life and then passed carelessly on. Alfred did not pass on, moreover. That was Miss Ricketts' good fortune. And my tragedy.

Wilson has decided it is tea-time. She bustles in with the tray and lights the lamp, then pokes the dying fire so that the yellow flames break through the ashes. 'I've made some of That There Darjeeling for you to taste,' she says. 'It looked a bit of a funny colour to me – but I expect you know more than me about such niceties. And I've been and got you a nice Chelsea bun. They was selling at two a penny –'

'Not stale buns again!' Wilson can't resist a bargain.

'They're hardly stale at all. And I've took the stones out of the damson jam so you don't go breaking your teeth.'

She cajoles me as one would a child. But there is something comforting in it and I don't object. There is something in me that likes to be told what to do. It must be all those years of practice with Alfred. I let her pour me a cup of tea.

'What are you going to do with That Box?' She nods at the tea-chest.

'I'll sort it out as soon as I have time.'

'A body can't hardly get through with the tray. It's right in the way.'

'Well, *we* can't move it, Wilson. It's too heavy.'

She stares at it as if to make it get up and move of its own accord. 'You'd have thought That There Robert would have chosen a better place to put the thing,' she grumbles. 'Not stick it down right inside the door.'

'I'll have it moved, I promise. After Alfie has been tomorrow, we'll take out some of the items, then we might be able to carry it. Or Kitty can help.' Kitty! I wonder how she has got on with Augustus. I had quite forgotten her in my perusal of the note-book. There is too much excitement for me to carry everything in my head.

Wilson hands me the cup. She stands, arms folded. 'Well?'

I take a sip. 'Very good.' The delicate taste reminds me of home. 'My mother always had Darjeeling tea.'

'Very nice, I'm sure – when you don't have to worry about the cost. But Mr. Collins' own blend comes out more economical.'

Mr. Collins' own blend sometimes seems fortified with coal-dust. I hate cheap tea and I see Alfred in the upstairs room at Mrs. Quinn's, peering into the tea caddy, spoon in hand: *Ah, what have we here? 'Selected Sweepings', I see. The very thing! Don't ever palm me off with Darjeeling, my dear, when there is such an excellent dusty blend to be had!*

'For tomorrow I thought I'd do some nice thin bread-and-butter and a few sandwiches to go with the cakes. There's some potted meat at the back of the pantry that could do with being used up.'

'I'm sure that will be fine. They're not coming for the food, after all.'

'Just as well.' She nods, and goes out, giving the Box a look of profoundest disdain. I need to sort it out quickly. And I need to be thinking of what I say to Alfie and Caroline – and to Kitty. But more than that I need to finish this narrative of Alfred's. I gulp down my tea in a most unladylike fashion and open up the notebook again.

I felt it necessary to keep my parents and the family of my future wife as separate as possible. I feared that if they met, the distressing topic of debt would be raised, and would contrive to embarrass me with those who would have no understanding of the subject. But I was glad to see my new wife take so well to her sister-in-law. They were two birds together – Lottie a bright robin, Dorothea a gentle turtle-dove. The differences between them at first seemed immaterial, if not delightful; but later, when household chaos threatened to overwhelm us, I found myself wishing that the robin would deign to scuttle about and guide the turtle-dove a little in some active management of her duties. But Lottie was adamant that such interference would be the end of all friendship between them. She took me by the arms and looked in my eyes: 'Dear Fred, you love your wife, do you not? I hope so, for you have chosen her, and any faults that she has will have been part of her character when you courted her. She has never been a practical woman, that much was clear from the outset. But when you courted her, you did not care about that. Indeed, I think her innocence of practical matters was part of her charm. Dorothea loves you, Fred, and you must love her back. She looks to you, not to me for help, and you must be the one to give it. You have always been the strong one. You must be so again. And if I am to be practical, I would suggest a nursemaid for the child. Poor Dorothea is run ragged.'

Oh, dear Lottie! Always so wise and kind. I never knew it was she whom I had to thank for the arrival of Bessie — Bessie who saved my life, and without whom I don't think I would ever have survived. But I sense already from his words that there are bad things to come. Perhaps better not to read. It's similar to eaves-dropping; one never hears well of oneself. But I can't help it; I must know.

I have pondered Lottie's words often — at the time she spoke them and many times since — and wondered what impulses had been at work in my heart when I chose — so mistakenly — my life's partner. Without doubt, I chose Dorothea freely and with no other thought than that of mutual happiness. I never sought her — or married her — for financial gain. Indeed, I gave up her settlement by marrying her before our agreed time. It meant hardship, but I was used to that — and Dorothea, I have to admit, did not baulk either.

My only excuse for such headlong and impatient behaviour must be that I was very young, and that I had already endured a number of painful attachments to young ladies, the dissolution of which had driven me near distraction. How thrown about I was, even at the age of twenty, by the ways of women! How cast down by the indifference of the dark-eyed Rosa as I waited outside the stage door night after night with lines I had penned on her talents and beauty, only to see her walk away with some coarse clod in an ill-fitting top-coat! How hopeless I felt when Miss Georgiana Mills declined three times in a row to dance with me at the Christmas party at Lincoln's Inn Fields, although I had bought her two glasses of champagne at one-and-sixpence a time and endured for her sake the tightest boots it was possible for a man to put his foot in. But my worst chagrin by far came at the hands of Miss Catherine Bond, who sent me pretty notes and pressed her deliciously tiny hand up against mine, admiring my new lavender gloves with the pearl buttons; and who, time after time, made me sit at the piano next to her in preference to any other young man in the room. But who laughed in my face when I suggested we might become engaged. 'Alfredo dear, what an idea! Now, don't be cross — you are very, very charming and quite the most delightful companion — but you could hardly keep me in silk stockings, let alone maintain a house and servants and Sally's livery costs.' (Sally was her little Welsh cob.) 'You must see how ridiculous it is! You do, don't you?' And she looked up at me in that way that always made my heart turn over, and I wanted to tell her that we could do without servants and stockings and Welsh cobs if we loved one another — but I saw she was bright and laughing and not at all cast down, and the words died on my lips. That night I think I came the closest I have ever come to putting an end to myself. I roamed up and down beside the Thames and thought dark thoughts and even — I do believe — climbed up upon the parapet and looked down into the water below. Why I did not take the plunge — whether from cowardice or good sense — I do not know, but as I walked back to my lodgings in the early dawn, I truly felt that if I did not find someone to love and marry soon, I would go mad.

I was therefore fortunate (or unfortunate, if one takes the long view) to be introduced to my future father-in-law within weeks of this romantic disappointment. I had taken to scribbling all sorts of things — dramatic monologues, comical poems — and had been encouraged by the fellows at Webster's to consider a full-length play. I had, for some time, been a member of a company of amateur actors who staged entertainments in any hall we could lay our hands on — provided we had the means of hiring it and also of paying for the costumes, wigs, musicians, ushers and all the other incidentals. I had read bits of my play to Tom Treadwell and Jeremiah Links as we sat in the chop-house after work, and they nearly choked on their meat pies for laughing. 'Which part will you act, Alfred?' they said. And I remember saying that I wished I could act them all. And Jerry laughed and said, 'You could, Alfred. I truly believe you could.'

I was told that Mr. Millar was the man to see; that he took many a young hopeful under his wing as a financial benefactor. I was told he was especially a man of the theatre, a veritable éminence grise behind the scenes. And so it proved. I remember with what trepidation I took my play to his offices in High Holborn and sent in my name and business. His ancient, creaking, articulated clerk came back, and begged me to wait while Mr. Millar 'cast a look at it', and I sat on an old Windsor chair in the ante-room, hoping he would not be too long about his casting as I had to get back to Webster and Potts for one o'clock. After a while I heard guffaws from the next room, which made me a little uncertain as to whether Mr. Millar was finding the play funny or merely ridiculous. Then he appeared in the doorway in person, saying he 'liked it enormously' and was prepared to advance the sum of thirty pounds in order to have it put on. He knew a theatre in Stepney that would be ideal. All I had to do was to get my actors and company together. I verily believe I could have kissed him, such was my joy. Instead I wrung his hand, rather too hard I believe, as he kept saying: 'Yes, yes, my dear sir, that is sufficient. That is sufficient, I beg you, sir!'

It seemed rather grand to have a Benefactor, and I was determined to justify his faith in my writing. I got together my Thespian friends and doled out the parts with a flourish, reserving the major rôle for myself — which I rather self-righteously felt I was entitled to — and began rehearsals immediately. A pale young man called Tom Titmuss emerged from somewhere in Clerkenwell and wrote some capital music for the songs, and accompanied them solemnly on the tuba. I tried to persuade Lottie to sing too, but she would not appear on the stage. 'I shall stitch the costumes if you wish,' she said. 'I'll leave the public glory to you, Fred. You suit it so much better.' However, I noted that she often liked to sit and watch the rehearsals, and I further noticed that she and Tom Titmuss often fell into each others' company, and that if we had to walk from our place of rehearsal, he would offer her his arm — even though I was there to take it myself. 'You may take Nellie's arm, Alfred,' he'd say with a twinkle in his eye. 'She's looking lone and lorn tonight; perhaps she's looking for a beau.' And Nellie would give me one of the droll, sideways looks which made her such a comical performer, and say if she hadn't been spoken for already, she'd have been happy to give a chance to a young fellow so full of fine words and weskits.

So there I am, balanced on the brink of Fame and Fortune. Longing for happiness. Longing to be loved. And then, as if by magic, here I am in this delightful garden with this delightful family and here comes the most enticing young girl with laughing blue eyes, who seems to be encouraging my every

look and gesture; who seems, as she dances in my arms, to be made of the
substance of pure heaven. Dear God, I couldn't wait to kiss her on the lips.
My nights were feverish with imagining it. And then when I had kissed her,
I couldn't wait for the ecstasy of taking her to bed. My blood ran wild;
I worked like a fiend to be worthy of her, to shorten the time when we could
be truly together. Had she rejected me, I think that the waters of the Thames
would indeed have closed over me in my wretchedness. But she did not, and
my determination to work for her enabled me to start on the course that has
brought me to where I am now. However, the passion I felt for her during
our courtship blinded me to what was, even then, a deep disparity of mind
and purpose; a disparity that showed itself more clearly with every year –
nay every day – that we were married. Too late I learnt that my wife was
weak, and that she would never be any different. Our marriage would never
be one of true minds. She would never be the helpmeet I craved. But I had
courted her and won her, and I was determined to do my duty.

So that was how he chose to see it: I was too young and too silly
for him. I had no education, no knowledge, no wit – all I had was
a blue dress which showed off my bosom to advantage. I had
come upon him when he was desperate, and I had entrapped
him, if not against his will, against his better judgement. And he
had been thus condemned to a life of duty and regret.

He writes convincingly – but how could Alfred, whose powers
of observation were second to none, have been so easily taken in
by an inexperienced girl with the most transparent of intentions?
He may have been crossed in love before, but he had not lost his
senses. Whatever Alfred did, he always did with determination
and a clear sense of purpose – and his courtship of me was, I
believe, no exception. He knew what I was; I had never hidden
my ignorance from him. On the contrary, it was *he* who was set
on marriage, and who wrote and spoke as if his heart were on fire;
who never stopped looking forward to the time when we could be
together; when we would have a dear little home all neat and

bright, and rosy-cheeked children to tumble about in it. In the early years of our marriage, even if I disappointed him in many small ways (as is natural in all marriages), he never complained of unhappiness. After all, no one made him write so extravagantly to me; no one forced him to refer to me among his friends as *the best wife that ever was*.

No, as Michael says, he is convincing *himself*; justifying why he did not love me at the end by saying he never loved me at the beginning and that the marital mistake was not his. He was a mere victim of circumstance: his wretched childhood; the rejections of his youth; and his fatal susceptibility to a girl in a blue dress. He is not Alfred the adulterer, the caster-off of wives, but Alfred the gentleman-hero — standing up nobly against the trials of life, bearing sadness with a smile, sacrificing himself for the sake of those weaker than himself, spreading goodness around like Abanazar spreading golden tinsel in the air: Yours Truly. The One and Only. The Great Man.

22

I am in a state of dreadful excitement. I'm expecting Alfie and Caroline for tea at any moment and, as usual when one wants things to go well, they have a habit of doing the opposite. The chimney has been smoking all morning and Gyp has eaten something disagreeable and has vomited all over the hearthrug, which now smells of carbolic. My hair will not plait properly, and I have got very hot and red trying to pin it up. Wilson has burnt her finger on the range and can't cut the bread thin enough for the sandwiches, so I've had to do it; and have got crumbs and butter all over the front of my gown.

I am especially anxious about meeting Caroline. I wonder what tales she has heard of me; what a wreck of a woman she expects to see. And here I am, living up to my own reputation by being so flustered and unprepared. I keep poking the fire, and plumping up the cushions, and ejecting Gyp from his favourite chair, then poking the fire again, so I get even hotter and redder.

I hear the sound of a Hansom cab; the knock on the door; then the cry and high-pitched chatter of a child. They are early. I drop the poker and shove Gyp hastily into my bedroom. Wilson opens the door and announces them very formally, before disappearing sharply to attend to the making of two kinds of tea, a feat that has been preying on her mind all morning. A clutch of people comes into the room: two black figures and a child in white. The man comes towards me with an uncertain smile. It must be Alfie but I hardly know him, and I feel shy as we stare at each other. I am no doubt stouter and greyer than he imagined. He is taller, of course, but not *very* tall. Still pale in the face, though, with light brown hair receding a little from his forehead. And still the slight stammer as he utters my name – 'M-mama!'

I say his name in return, and he almost leaps into my arms. He is thin, like Kitty, and I feel his bones through his coat – his ribs, and the ripples along his spine. He hugs me as if he never wants to let me go, as if he will smother me. And I am happy to be smothered. I hold him tighter and tighter, making up for all the embraces we have missed over the years. I haven't realised until now how much I have missed him, how terrible it is that I have been cheated of all his growing up. He speaks into my ear, his voice muffled by my hair, but his voice is music all the same. 'I'm so sorry, dear Mama. So very, very sorry.'

I can hardly speak. 'Yes,' I whisper with a little rueful squeeze to his arm. 'So you should be. You absolutely should be!'

He lets me go. There are tears in his eyes. 'Oh, I promise on my life that I'll make amends. Carrie and I both will. See, here she is –'

The young woman comes forward. She is small and dark and bright-eyed. Her mourning clothes are neat and unshowy. She holds the child in her arms, a golden-haired child who wriggles and squirms and cries out to be set down on the floor. As soon as she is, she stops grizzling and gazes solidly at me, and I see a look of Kitty in her. Carrie shakes my hand firmly, the modern fashion. 'I'm so pleased to meet you. And this is Lucy. She's just started to walk, so I'm afraid nothing is safe.' She has a quiet, low voice, full of humour. I like her immediately.

'Goodness, I remember that time so well! My husband always used to say, "Two-legged chaos is come again – pawn all the waliables!" But I don't think there is anything very "waliable" here, so Lucy may wander around to her heart's content. Wilson's put the fireguard in place, and I've locked Gyp in my bedroom.'

'Is Gyp your dog?' Carrie puts the child down, but holds on to her petticoats with a firm grip.

'Yes, he's rather crotchety these days; I'm not sure how he'd take to children. He's only used to me and Wilson – and Kitty, of course. Not like our family dogs in the old days. They were used to no end of bad treatment.'

'Like poor old M-master,' laughs Alfie.

'Would you believe I have his collar in that very box? Sissy was going to throw it out.'

'Sissy? Throw it out?' A shade comes over his face and I realise I need to be careful of disparaging her in front of Alfie. She is a favourite with him, according to Kitty.

'Oh, I'm not blaming her!' I add quickly. 'Master was dead long before she came to us, so she doesn't have all the happy memories. But – Alfie, Carrie – please sit down and let's talk of more important things than a wretched dog-collar.'

Alfie grimaces. 'More *important* things? I hope you're not going to take me to task after all.'

I look at his anxious expression, the nervous way he twists his watch chain. From earliest boyhood, he's always expected the worst. But I cannot be angry with him; I feel full of amazing love, like an opening flower. 'I *should* take you to task, you know. There are many things that I could say in reproach.' I look up and see his anxious eyes and cannot help forgiving him. 'But as you said in your letter, water has flowed beneath the bridge. It's time for a new start.'

'There! I told you your mother would not be angry with you; that her joy in seeing you would overcome any other feelings.' Carrie smiles and puts her hand gently on his knee.

He puts his own on top and smiles back. 'You put me right, as always, dearest.' He turns to me. 'For my part, I should have remembered how kind and forgiving my mother always was. Even when provoked most severely by others.'

'Well, *you* never provoked me, Alfie.' Indeed, he was always the most obedient of my children.

'Didn't I? I'm sure I was always at you to m⁄mediate between me and Kitty. She always seemed to get her way in the end, though, so I went about in a perpetual state of resentment, m⁄moaning how everything always went against me. Don't you remember how Papa called me the Perpetual M⁄moaner?'

'Oh, yes.' Alfred loved nicknames. We all had several.

'He shortened it to the P.M., of course. And he'd run up the stairs and rush in through the schoolroom door, calling out, *Is the P.M. ready to answer questions in the House?* And I'd try to hide so he wouldn't make fun of me again. But he always knew where I was, and he'd find me and make me stand on a chair and ask me questions about *per capita* income and annual expenditure and whether we should send an expeditionary force up the Zambezi River to Darkest Africa. And everybody else would laugh their silly heads off and I'd want to kill him.'

'I don't remember that.'

'No.' He thinks carefully. 'I expect it was one of those times when you weren't – well, up to the hugger⁄mugger of family life. Papa was always at his worst when you weren't there to keep him calm.'

'Was he?' I'm taken aback. 'Was he really?'

'Well, you know how he was – one minute we'd be having the time of our lives, larking about and dressing up – or listening to him read to us, doing all the voices and faces – but the next minute one of us would do something to displease him and he'd pull up short and get that distant, disappointed look on his face. And I used to feel quite sick with wanting to please him, but not knowing how to. I'd have to come upstairs and lie on the couch with you and let you stroke my eyelids –' He stops, a catch in his throat.

Carrie gives him a quick look. 'We had resolved not to talk about Mr. Gibson today,' she says to me, gently. 'But I see that is too much to ask.'

At this point, Wilson comes in bearing a tray so loaded that I wonder how she has got it up the stairs. She stands still in the doorway: 'I'll need That There Box moved before I can get in with This Here Crockery.'

Alfie jumps up to push the box nearer to the wall so that Wilson can pass through and put her burden on the table. He staggers a little: 'Good Grief, what's in here, Mother? It weighs a ton!'

'Mementos, I told you. Sissy and I picked them out.'

'Ah, yes. Oh, M-master's collar!' He picks it up and admires it. 'That poor dog! What fun we had with him! You know, I think our happiest times were in Channon Street.'

'Yes.' I think of that tall house; all those flights of stairs, Alice lying in that third-floor bedroom, the Scotch doctor, Alfred on his knees. 'But it was sad, too. Your Aunt Alice died there hardly a year after we moved in.'

'But that was before I was born, Mama!'

'Yes, of course it was. It's so easy to forget that. But your father and I could never forget. We always felt her spirit about the place.'

'And yet no one really talks about her.'

'Well, as you say, it was a long time ago.' I think of the dress and the book and the secret key – and think that to Alfred it might have been only the day before. 'She had a sweet and lovely nature,' I say.

'Like *you*, then.'

'Oh, Alfie! I only wish that were true.' If I had been 'sweet' as Alice was instead of 'weak' as I appeared to him, perhaps Alfred would have indeed loved me better.

'It *is* true. You see, you are not even cross with me after all I have done – or not done.' Alfie starts to hand around the sand-wiches while Wilson stands with a teapot in each hand. Carrie pours a little milk into a cup for Lucy and I notice how lovingly she helps her drink it. I see Wilson watching, too, although she affects to be absorbed with the double teapots. In the end, no one has China tea, and Wilson has a look that means 'I told you so.' She cuts the cakes into grudging slices, and retires.

'Wilson's very fond of you,' observes Carrie, dipping small pieces of Madeira cake into her tea and giving them to Lucy, one at a time. 'Has she been with you long?'

'Oh, yes. She came with the apartment, so to speak. She was here on the doorstep the day I arrived. So that's ten years, and she has always been most satisfactory – except for a tendency to order me about!' I laugh, and Carrie and Alfie laugh too.

'Yes, Kitty told us.' Alfie moves Lucy to his own knee. A lump rises in my throat as I see how gently he speaks to her. I can see he loves the look and feel and scent of Lucy, exactly as Alfred loved the look and feel and scent of our own little girls – and how, when the others grew pettish and contradictory, Ada remained his special angel. He never seemed to tire of being with her, even when her breath came so harsh and slow it was hard to hear what she said. He'd tell her the story of the princess and the pea, and pretend to put a pea beneath her mattress and ask her if she could feel it. *I think I can, Papa*, she'd say. And he'd say: *That shows you are a real princess, my love. Although I never had any doubt.*

But Lucy is made of sterner stuff; she wriggles and pokes her finger at her father's face, and he sets her down again, holding her by the hem of her dress.

'You see Kitty often?' I have heard nothing from her today and I fear Augustus's troubles have come to a head.

'Not exactly *often*, but that we see her *at all* is largely due to the efforts of my remarkable wife!' Alfie puts his hand on her knee again, and Carrie smiles. The smile lights up her face and makes her plain features quite pretty.

'I have done very little – and nothing at all *remarkable*. Alfie always exaggerates my skills.'

'M-my love, if you knew what internecine strife there has been

[311]

in this family, you would not say such things so lightly! It's *your* efforts alone that have brought Kitty back into the fold!'

'Well, a stranger can sometimes see what others cannot. It was obvious as soon as I met her that Kitty longed to be reconciled to her father — and that he equally longed to see *her*. That I was able to bring them together — however briefly and belatedly — was a joy to me.' Carrie jumps up and rescues Lucy, who has jammed herself behind the sofa and is writhing like a conger eel.

'She speaks as if it were a simple matter of brokerage!' exclaims Alfie, admiringly. 'But you know the personalities involved, don't you, Mama? You know what a super-human effort it must have taken to make those two agree even to *meet*!'

'Yes, indeed. Indeed.' I think of Alfred's furious letter about Kitty's engagement; I think of Kitty's delight in inflaming him further by her marriage. The brokerage required would indeed not have been simple. I cannot help wondering if Carrie's skills could ever have extended to our own estrangement, but I put the thought away. Instead, I wonder who she reminds me of as she walks about the room, neat, bright and dark-eyed, leading her child by the hand, showing her the clock in its glass dome, the stuffed owl, the old dog-collar from the box. And then it comes to me: Lottie, of course, Lottie the peace-maker. I look again at Carrie's open face, her cordial air, and how the very space around her seems to give off peace and good nature. And wisdom too, I think. I have noted how my son has looked for her opinion so often throughout our conversation; and how readily she smiles to encourage him, and nods to confirm her agreement with what he has said. It occurs to me that Alfred never once looked to me for confirmation of anything. If we were in company he would refer to me often — sometimes affectionately, more often jokingly — but he never sought my views. I don't know what I'd have said if he had — been flustered, no doubt, at the unexpectedness of it all, thus confirming his opinion on my so-called weakness of mind.

Alfie bites into a potted-meat sandwich. 'It was *Sissy* who was the sticking point, you know. Kitty was always uncivil to her – well, downright rude in fact. It was most unfair considering all she had done. And Papa wouldn't stand for it.' Alfie starts agitating his watch chain again and I recognise with a start that it is Alfred's watch. I can't help wondering with a pang if the curl of chestnut hair is still there inside the case.

Carrie adds, 'But it wasn't *Sissy* who was to blame for the divisions, Mrs. Gibson. I regret to say that it was Alfie's father who was most at fault. He'd made the children choose their allegiance as if they were troops drawn up for battle. There was no room for compromise.'

'Oh, that is no surprise,' I say. 'Alfred never compromised. He drove the hardest bargains in the world. Indeed, his publisher once told me that if my husband had not been such a towering genius, he would have told him to take his books to the Devil and see if he could get as good terms there.'

Carrie continues: 'Oh, I knew how adamant he was; and I knew how disagreeable he became if criticised. But he was making everyone wretched and I really could *not* be silent. I told him that his children needed *both* parents; that the unnatural divisions had already caused too much guilt and unhappiness.' She has taken Lucy upon her lap and is rocking her quietly. I am taken aback by her words. I think that Carrie has been braver than many a man in speaking so to Alfred.

'What did he say to that?'

'He seemed perturbed. He said he had never intended there to be any such divisions; that he had never set them up; that he had merely hoped his children would be grateful for all the care they had been given, and that he would never be the one to stand in their way if they wished to seek succour with their mother.'

'That's what he told you then, my love.' Alfie smiles ruefully. 'He didn't want to appear an out-and-out villain to you. But when we were younger he'd made it clear there was a price to pay. He said that any of us could go with Mama if we wished. "Step forward," he said, "and your bags will be packed. But do not expect to enter this house again while I live."'

Did he really say that? How cruel he could be at times! But I feel a little tug of jealousy that they all fell so easily to his side of the line. 'And none of you stepped forward? None of you wanted to join me?'

Alfie shifts in his chair. 'It was not so simple, you know. With him and Sissy there in the house, and you gone and –'

'I understand, Alfie. You were young. You deserved the sort of life that you'd always had; that your father – and Sissy – could give you. Right at the centre of things, with all the pleasures and excitements of a great man's house.'

Alfie reddens. 'You make us sound so selfish. But Sissy took us aside and explained that you and he had come to a good arrange ment. And to be honest, Mama, I wondered whether you would really have wanted us with you.' He catches my astonished eye and adds quickly, 'Well, you seemed to find us children so exhausting. You went off to Leamington for all those months as if you didn't care about us at all!'

I stare at him. 'It was not a seaside holiday, Alfie; I was ill. And as for not caring about you – I wrote to you all. I wrote every week.' Surely that is right. I cannot have imagined that. I can see myself sitting in my little cell of a room, tears trickling down my face as I pushed the pen across the paper.

'Oh, yes! Little notes about people you'd met and played cards with, and at the end a glib little sentence telling me to "be good and work hard". I was all on my own, Mama. Many a night in the dorm I'd sob myself to sleep, thinking you didn't care.'

I feel as though a lead weight has smashed right into my heart. 'Oh, Alfie! If only you knew how much I thought about you all! But I tried not to let you know how wretched I was feeling. I tried to be cheerful. Your father would always urge me to be cheerful. *Try to look on the bright side*, he'd say. So I'd think of amusing things that had happened – Colonel Jibbins losing the wheel off his Bath chair – or the way Mrs. Badger's front curls were a different colour from her back hair.'

'That's the sort of thing *he* would have written, blast him! But I didn't want entertaining; I wanted you to say you were coming back. And when you didn't come – well, it truly seemed as though what Papa was saying was true.'

'What was he saying?'

The watch chain is twisting again: 'Oh, you know – that you were more comfortable away from us all, enjoying yourself play-ing cards with half-pay officers and genteel widow-women.'

How subtle Alfred was! Taking the truth and making it a lie. Yet how true it must have seemed to my children at the time, as I connived so innocently in my own banishment. No wonder they seemed indifferent when I returned. 'Oh, Alfie,' I burst out. 'I was *never* comfortable away from you. Some nights I couldn't sleep for thinking about you all. Now you are a father, Alfie, you will know what it is to love your children, to have them always in your thoughts, to expect them to be always there somewhere behind you or in the next room, connected by a silken cord, so that one tug brings you running. I decided several times that I must go home so I could see your dear faces and hold you in my arms. But your father insisted it was my duty to make myself completely well; and that I must stay at the Spa until my lassitude had quite gone and I had roses in my cheeks again. So I stayed. And gradually I began to feel different. Not only less tired, although the air and the waters seemed to agree with me, but more – how can I say it? – more *myself*, somehow. More the person I might have been if I had simply followed my own inclinations every day. Of course, I had no responsibilities, and could read silly novels, play cards, or tell an anecdote without fearing I would make a hash of it because your father was standing over me eager to tell it better. In fact – this may surprise you, Alfie – I discovered I had quite a skill as a *raconteuse*. I found myself fêted, just as Papa and I had been in America all that time ago. People crowded around me, and even quite young gentlemen were eager to offer me their arm. I confess it was a pleasant sensation, to be regarded as inter-esting company. Perhaps that is why I wrote about it so much in my letters, and why, for a moment, I forgot what it was to be a mother. Which was wrong, of course.'

'It is not wrong to wish to be yourself.' Carrie is looking at me with such an understanding smile. 'I confess that even with *this* little one, I feel not quite the person I once was. If I'd had *eight* Lucies I would appreciate even *more* the chance to have a little time to myself. After all, *men* have such time. They do not become *dissolved* into parenthood the way we do.'

I cannot help laughing. What a good expression! 'All the same,' I tell Alfie, 'I would never have willingly given you up. You believe that, don't you?'

'Then why *did* you? Was it to please Papa? Regardless of our feelings?'

There is such pain behind his eyes that I am devastated all over again. He thinks I am to blame. Yet how can everything be *my* fault? 'Don't you remember?' I burst out. 'Do you really not remember all that happened?'

'I had it all at second-hand. He wrote, of course. He said that your presence was causing so many quarrels in the house that it was impeding his work –'

'Yes, he always said that. Although you of all people should know that no living person could ever come between him and his work, let alone a poor ill wretch of a wife!'

'Well, your state of health was the other thing. He said all the noise and confusion of our house was delaying your recovery. He said it was better for you to go and be cared for elsewhere.'

'Be cared for! He makes me sound feeble-minded.'

Alfie shifts a little more. 'Yes, Mama. I do believe he implied your m-mind was not quite right. And to tell you the truth, it seemed possible.' He looks at Carrie as if for help, and she nods encouragingly. 'Lou said you'd been quite – strange – sometimes, like Old Mrs. Pottomy, talking to the ghost of the Lord Chancellor on the stairs. I thought you'd get over it, though. You'd got over it when Georgie and Fanny were born. I thought you'd write, or come to see me at school. I imagined you stepping down from the carriage with a plum cake and a kiss. But the weeks and months passed, and you never did.'

'I'd agreed not to see you. He said I would be too "excessive", too "uncontrolled". But he said *you* could write to me if you wished.'

'I *did* write.' Alfie puts his hand to his eyes. 'I wrote hundreds of times.'

I look at him, aghast. 'I never got a single one!'

'No,' he says quickly. 'I never posted them. I told myself that if you'd cared about me, you'd come, no matter what. And I didn't want to go on crying night after night. Fellows rag you for it. So I let you go, Mama; I put you away in a nice neat drawer and turned the key. I stopped thinking about you. It was only when I met Carrie, and even more when we had this little one, that I knew what a dreadful thing I'd done.'

'So why has it taken you until now to come and see me?'

'I was too ashamed. All those years . . .' The watch chain is twitching madly. 'But I should have known your nature better than to think you would hold a grudge.'

Alfie remembers me kindly. And I note that he has not spoken of Miss Ricketts. No one speaks directly of Miss Ricketts, except Kitty. 'Well,' I say, 'all that is past now. But you must take care that Carrie does not become so *dissolved* in motherhood that she becomes unfit to do anything else.'

Alfie puts his arm around her. 'Indeed not! We have already hit on a splendid plan. Dear old Bessie has come to the rescue; she comes each week to perambulate Lucy, so that Carrie can take up her pen. She wheels her around for fierce rides whatever the weather, "to get rid of them cobwebs". And when she gets back she unwraps her like a parcel, puts her next to a roaring fire as if she needs browning, and feeds her warm milk and bread-and-butter so she falls asleep in an instant, like Mrs. P.'s Last!'

We all laugh.

'And you know, Mama, she's full of tales of the old times. I caught her telling Lucy all about Papa — "the cleverest man that ever was!" — and about the *slap-up* Christmas party, when the children from the Foundling Hospital came and had tea with us, and how their little eyes widened when they saw all the food. And how they all clustered round Papa with their mouths open while he read aloud that bit where Edward Cleverly meets Will Tanner on the Old Kent Road and gives him his lovely moist pudding done up in a clean white cloth in exchange for his *mouldy pie with its hard-to-bite outside and hard-to-see inside.* And how they laughed and clapped when he dressed up as Abanazar and did his magic, with smoke and glitter everywhere. Of course,' he says, 'Lucy is too young to understand —'

'But I am so glad that Bessie remembers it all! She really was the dearest girl in the world, and the greatest help to me.' However, I am struck at the revelation that this is all in order that Carrie may 'take up her pen'. The words burst from me: 'But Carrie, are you a writer?'

'Oh, yes,' says Alfie proudly. 'Indeed, that is how we first became acquainted. She came by the office with a manuscript and asked for 'Mr. Gibson'. Father was out and I was in, so Noakes naturally brought her to *me*.'

'Yes.' She laughs. 'For a moment I was surprised to find him such a young man, and not at all resembling his portraits in the books. But then I realised my mistake – and the little speech I had prepared vanished from my mind, and all the courage I'd screwed up seemed to seep out of me –'

'It didn't appear to! She simply put down her manuscript and said: "Well, Mr. Gibson, it's a ghost story, three thousand words, and I am looking for five guineas."'

'And what did you do?'

'I said I would have to consult with my father but asked her to write down her name and address so I could communicate with her in due course. And she blushed so prettily that I almost fell in love with her on the spot! In fact I think I did!'

'What nonsense!' Carrie smiles fondly at him all the same.

'Then I read it and thought it was very good. Very good. And I passed it on to Papa with a note saying the contributor had called in person. And the next day he came out of his office asking, "Who is this C. Andrews? One of Wilkie's *protégés*? He writes a pretty fair hand – and a pretty fair story for that matter. Give him his five guineas and let him come and see me on Tuesday!"'

'He thought you were a man?'

'Yes,' she chuckles. 'In spite of his much-vaunted ability to tell the difference!'

'And I was damned if I was going to put him right. So when she came, I put my head around the door and said, "C. Andrews to see you, Father," and he grunted in that way he had, without looking up. And then when he *did* look up, he was most taken aback to be caught in his shirt-sleeves and eye-shade, with his hair wild, and a torrent of paper all over his desk.'

She laughs. 'He flung away the eye-shade as if it were on fire, and positively *rushed* into his coat, trying to comb his hair with his fingers and straighten his waistcoat at the same time. And I realised then that the great Alfred Gibson was just a man. And a vain one at that. And I stopped being afraid of him.'

Ah, yes. Alfred very much disliked being taken unawares. For

[319]

all his fooling, he hated to be made a fool *of*. And he was always anxious to make a good impression with a young lady. I can imagine how for a moment this bright-eyed girl might have shaken his composure. 'But, tell me, have you written many stories? Might I have read them? I take all his periodicals.' I am delighted to think there is another writer in the family. Alfred had always hoped one of our children would follow in his footsteps.

'Mr. Gibson was kind enough to publish three of my stories in the *Miscellany*. They were intended for children, but he said that what pleases children pleases the general public. "Children are our most discerning readers," he said. "You cannot fool them." '

'I shall look through my back numbers and find your stories. But was he kind to you? Kitty said that Alfred was very demanding of his lady contributors and that Hetty Casby walked out in high dudgeon –'

Alfie sighs. 'She did. And he was quite dumbfounded – for about ten seconds. Then he made a face, said, "Ho-hum! Spilt milk, spilt milk!" and went on writing. But he was demanding of *everybody*, you know. Not shouting or raging, but – oh, I don't know – he wouldn't let you do what you wanted, or get your hands on anything important. I mean, I was his Assistant Editor, but he didn't allow me to do much assisting *or* editing. To be honest, Mama, it was difficult to find things to fill my day. He had his own m-methods all worked out, and he really didn't like me to interfere. Sometimes he'd throw me a bundle of articles to look at, saying he had a space for twelve hundred words – and to pick something that would fit the bill. But when I did, he wouldn't be satisfied, and would look over all of them again, and choose something different. And if I told him I'd rejected it because it was too long, he'd say, "That's what the blue pencil is for," and start cutting out whole sentences, quick as anything. So one day, I decided to show him I could edit with the best. I picked up a story that looked a bit long-winded, and started on it with a will. I was quite pleased with myself. "There was a lot of superfluous stuff here," I said, "although the writing itself is quite funny." And then he looked at it and said, "*Quite funny? Only quite?*" – and I realised to my chagrin that it was his.'

We all laugh – Lucy too. In fact, she is the most delighted.

'To do him justice, he kept the changes, but he never let me edit anything else. He put me in charge of the regular contributors. You know – Wilkie, Mrs. Lynne, Erskine Dolls. Trouble was, they all wanted to change their deadlines or change their pieces, and they insisted on writing to Father about it, or calling to see him in person. Then he'd get irate, tell me that keeping them in order was m-my job – and didn't he have enough to do, with the editing and writing the current number of whatever it was, without doing other people's jobs as well? I once asked to do the Letters page instead, but he wouldn't let me touch that. He wouldn't let anyone touch the Letters. *The Public writes to Alfred Gibson. They want it to be Alfred Gibson who replies.* So you see, Mama, after five years in that blessed office, I'm as green as the day I started.'

'I'm sure that's not true, dearest.'

'Well, we'll soon see. I'm going to keep the mag on. Get Wilkie to edit it with me, perhaps. Carrie will help, she says – but I don't know if people will buy it if Papa's not in it. A bit like *Hamlet* with no prince. But I must have a livelihood. I'm a family man, after all, and have absolutely no other talents to call on.'

'I'm sure that's not true, either.'

'Oh? Go on then, M-mother, tell me what else I can do.'

I try to think of what to say. Alfie has never been the most talented of our children. Sensitive, yes. I think of Alfred's account of himself: *a sensitive little fellow.* But Alfie has not had the hard knocks his father endured. In experience of life he is still green. I flounder.

'Now, that's a little unfair of you, Alfie,' Carrie interrupts. 'Don't ask your mother such things. If she can't tell the truth, she'll be obliged to flatter, and what's the point of that?'

[321]

At this juncture, the doorbell rings. 'This must be Kitty,' I say, relieved.

But it's not Kitty. The footfalls are heavy on the stairs and a tall young man with startling blue eyes and thick blond hair and whiskers erupts into the room. He bounds over to me and takes me in his arms: 'Mama!'

23

'*Eddie?*'

I do not recognise him at all, but think it can be no other. Very handsome, positively shining with vigour. He is wearing a very elegant black suit and puce waistcoat with a clove carnation in his buttonhole; and smelling headily of lavender.

'Indeed, the very same. Sorry I missed you yesterday.' He speaks as if we last saw each other a few days ago, rather then ten years. 'But I heard via Sis that P.M. and Carrie were coming today, so I thought I'd make up the party! And what a party it is!' He turns to embrace the room. 'Why, here is the Infant Phenomenon herself!' He stoops and makes a face at Lucy, who emits an ear-splitting shriek of delight.

I see Wilson in the doorway. She has come upstairs in more laboured fashion, and stands with her hands on her hips. 'Shall I get another cup and plate for Mr. Edward, then?'

Eddie turns to her. 'You're an angel, Mrs. Wilson; I'm spitting feathers here.' He grabs one of the teapots. 'Oh, this one's full. I'll put it to warm.' And he puts it on the hob. Then he picks up a slice of Dundee cake, despatches it in three bites and takes a second one, walking around, spilling crumbs. 'No seed cake, Mama? What were you thinking of?'

'I fancied a change.'

'Indeed. We've had seed cake for nigh on twenty years. I think we've given it a fair trial.' He looks up at the ceiling, examines the gas lamps, peers out at the street from behind the curtains. 'Well, this isn't a bad place. Not bad at all. Kittiwake's always going on about it being so poky. But there's only one of you, so it's not so bad.'

'I'm glad you approve.'

He gives me a quick look. 'Now don't go all prim and proper on me, Mama. I know I've done wrong. We all have. But I'm ready to make amends, *mea culpa* and all that.'

Wilson returns with the crockery and Eddie takes it off her with a flourish. 'Thank you, fair Ganymede.'

She gives him a sideways look. 'Fair or no fair, the pot you're warming on the hob is that there China tea.'

'Oh, lapsang?'

'You'll have to ask Mr. Collins if you wants to know its name. All I know is that it comes out pale, which to my mind is not how a good cup of tea should be. If you'd be so good as to lift it up for me, though, I'll do the pouring.'

'No indeed! Astounding though it is, I can pour for myself. And I see that you have a wounded finger which I should not wish to endanger!'

She blushes: 'Sauce!' But goes off smiling.

So Eddie is a charmer.

He takes out his handkerchief, doubles it neatly and bends over the fireguard to retrieve the pot. 'Who's for Mr. Collins' finest? Mama? Carrie? P.M.?'

'We're having the Darjeeling,' I say.

He pours and sniffs the brew. 'Very wise. Tea-blending is, I think, not Mr. Collins' strong suit. You should change your supplier, Mama.'

'Mr. Collins does me well. And he gives good credit.'

I did not mean for that to slip out. Carrie and Alfie exchange glances. Eddie seems not to notice, then says, 'Papa kept you short, then?'

'No, not at all. I have been very comfortable. My wants are few.'

Eddie puts another coal on the fire: 'This stuff's a bit steamy.'

'It's perfectly fine. And Eddie, please mind your manners. It is most unpleasant to have every bit of my housekeeping criticised.'

'Not meant as criticism, although clearly taken that way. Apologies once more.'

It is all very strange. Not how I thought a reconciliation would be. All this talk of tea and cake and coals. 'But how are you, my dear Eddie?'

'Pretty fine. Pretty fine.'

I hesitate, but I must ask: 'Have you thought of me at all?'

He gives a wide grin. 'Of course. Hundreds of times. Whenever Sissy did something I didn't like, I'd say, "*You're* not my mother!" and form a plan to run away across the rooftops. Except I didn't have the slightest idea where you were living, so usually I'd hide in a cupboard until the Old Man came looking for me like Florence Nightingale with the lamp, only not so forgiving. He made me sit for three hours in the schoolroom once; until I said I was sorry. I'd rather have had a thrashing.'

'He didn't believe in thrashings.'

'Noble of him. But there are worse punishments – I nearly died of hunger.'

I can't help laughing. Eddie always had a good appetite. Even as a baby at the breast, he could never have enough. He grins widely, takes another slice of cake; 'Compliments to Mr. Collins. Excellent cake. Be it not said that I criticise blindly.'

'Be serious.'

'Ah, serious. No, I don't think I can. I daresay the P.M. has been serious enough for us both, though. Laid himself bare at the altar of regrets.'

'Well, there is much to *be* regretted,' I say reprovingly. 'Ten years without a word from either of you.'

He wanders about, taps the barometer. 'But to put the shoe on the other foot, didn't you care about us being left with our wicked stepmother?'

[325]

'Hardly wicked, Eddie.'

'Oh, *wonderful* stepmother, then. Miss Honey Bun with Sugar Sauce, yum-yum! No need to worry about us, then. Oh, no!'

I cannot make him out. But I see that I cannot question him on any serious matter while he is in this mood. I think of Sissy's grimace, her lip jutting as she said the word 'trade'. 'Sissy says you are thinking of starting in business.'

'I'm looking about me, yes. Fellow I know is looking too.'

'What kind of thing?'

'Oh, you know. This and that.' He brushes the crumbs off his trousers and sits down.

'Give me a little clue,' I say. '*This* can be so different from *that*.'

He laughs. 'Ah, Mama. You always liked your little joke.'

Yes, I remember now, Eddie liked to tell me jokes. He'd write them down on a scrap of paper and come to my room and read them out, sitting on the end of my bed. And we'd laugh until Sissy came to shoo him out: 'Come on, Porkie, Your mother needs her rest!' Porkie – I'd forgotten that name until now! It was short for porcupine – because Eddie's hair always stuck up in spikes. I look at it now. It's immaculate.

'Well, I am glad at least that you are thinking of doing *something*.'

'Well, now the Great Man has gone, we'll all need to find a way of keeping ourselves in the manner to which we have become accustomed.'

'You could always help Alfie at the *Miscellany*.' There is silence, a frisson between my two sons. I have, as so often, said the wrong thing.

Carrie steps in. 'Of course, we'd love to have you if you wish. But there won't be much money, for a while, at any rate –'

'My dear Sister-in-Law, don't distress yourself! I've had enough of the *Miscellany* and the *Monthly Mirror*, and *Our Daily Lives* and every form and version of God's Own Little Periodicals. I want a quiet life. Away from the Public in any form. The Public has had its pound of flesh from the Gibson family. Now the Public can go hang itself. I shall be happy running a discreet little outfitters in Piccadilly – finest linen shirts, moleskin waistcoats, silk cravats and white kid gloves. I shall stock what I like. I shall sit high on my perch and watch the profits roll in. No one will know me. And I shall have peace of mind.'

'Are you serious?'

'Why not?'

Why not indeed? Why should that kind of life not be happy and useful? We all need clothes after all. Although perhaps not always silk and linen. But Eddie, I see, is a connoisseur.

The doorbell rings again. Perhaps *this* is Kitty. Everyone turns to look, as footsteps come up the stairs and the door opens. Kitty rushes in: 'Mama, such good news!'

Eddie is embracing her before any of us can move: 'Hallo, Kittiwake. Join the party.'

'Eddie! Why are you here? And Alfie too! And Carrie!' She stares round at us all. She is still wearing her mourning, although she's given up the veils and streamers, and looks softer and more human. I also see that there is a light in her eye that I haven't seen for years.

'Well, dearest, I told you Alfie and Carrie were coming. And Eddie has surprised us all by –'

'– turning up. *Sans* manners, as usual!' Eddie smiles his brilliant smile.

'I'd forgotten. I've been rather distracted. So much has happened since I saw you last.' She pauses, reddens slightly, and turns to address them all. 'I don't know if Mama has told you – but Augustus and I have found ourselves in a somewhat – uncomfortable – situation this last day or so.'

Eddie starts to whistle slightly under his breath. I recognise the tune: 'I'll Give Sixpence for a Kiss'. Kitty affects not to notice. 'Well, I don't need to go into detail, but we are looking for more modest accommodation. It is really ridiculous keeping up that big house merely for the two of us.'

'Money troubles, Kit?' Eddie pours a cup of tea, takes the last slice of Dundee cake and puts it on a plate for her.

She takes the plate and cup and sits down. 'Tradesmen can be so *unreasonable*!'

'Well,' says Eddie, '*If you wants the waliables, you must possess the wherewithall! That's been the case since Time Hin Memoriam.*'

Carrie and Alfie laugh, and so does Lucy, although she has never heard of Boodles' philosophy. Kitty carries on: 'Augustus will pay, of course. He has always paid. He simply needed his creditors to give him time. There was no need to make threats.'

'Threats?' Carrie widens her eyes. 'Surely not?'

'Oh, indeed! They threaten to take the roof from over your head and the rugs from under your feet!'

'And why shouldn't they?' says Eddie. 'I speak as one who is about to embark in commerce myself. It is not for us humble shopkeepers to maintain the style of the genteel classes by giving infinite credit. We have families to keep and bills of our own to pay. Papa would have been shocked to hear you talk so, Kit. He was always prompt in his dealings.'

'Oh, yes! He hated owing a penny – even a farthing! Augustus said it was not gentlemanly to have such a book-keeping kind of mind.' She stirs her tea, vehemently.

'Oh, no doubt – not gentlemanly. But a damn sight more considerate.'

'Considerate!' She snorts. 'How can you use that word about him?'

Eddie flicks a crumb of cake off his waistcoat. 'Merely because he did some disagreeable things –'

'*Some* disagreeable things? The way he treated Mama? And me? All of us, in fact?'

'Yes, we all know the history; you don't need to knock us

around the heads with it again! But have you forgotten everything else? How hard he worked for us? How he dragged himself around doing the Readings, even though he was hardly able to stand sometimes?'

'I never asked him to! He did it because he wanted to. To get oodles of money. And to speak to his precious Public at first hand.'

'They wanted him, Kit. And he wouldn't let them down, although you know he was little more than a *skelington in a suit* at the end, and had to be laid out flat with a dark bandage over his eyes as soon as he came off stage.'

'He still enjoyed it,' she says, sulkily.

'Is enjoyment to be despised, then?' Carrie looks levelly at her. Kitty looks discomforted and doesn't answer.

All of a sudden Alfie chimes in: 'Talking of money, Sissy and I have been going through his correspondence, and I think he must have got more begging letters than anyone in history. He seems to have answered them within the week, giving advice and encouragement. And from the sound of the replies, money too, sometimes. I never knew that. He always kept it quiet.'

'Oh, he always cared for the poor more than for us! Show him a beggar and his heart would leap.' Kitty puts down her cup with emphasis.

Eddie looks nettled. 'Well at least he made sure his family was provided for.'

'Are you making reference to Augustus?' She looks sharply at him.

He shrugs. 'Well, Kittiwake, I'm sorry to say that the whole of London knows about your husband's debts. It's common talk in the clubs. Fellows clam up when they see me because he's my brother-in-law, but I know how much is involved because he tried to cadge from me himself.'

'And you refused? Another Holier-Than-Thou?' She glowers at him.

'I don't have a bean, Kit. Or at least not in *that* league. Hund⁄ reds of pounds, you know. Moneylenders and God knows what. One thing Papa taught me was never to sign bills you know you couldn't redeem.' He strokes his neat golden beard. 'But from your excitement when you came in, I take it that you've persuaded the creditors to wait a bit now your fortune's coming through.'

Kitty's face changes. 'Oh, yes! We ran around half London last night. Such strange people in such outlandish places! Dark, dank alleys and poky upstairs rooms! And a Jew in robes and a little cap – like something from Papa's novels! But Mr. Golding's letters did the trick. And when they knew who *I* was, of course – that made a difference! They were so courteous, you'd hardly have thought they were trying to screw money out of me. It was sud⁄ denly all "dear Mithis Norrith", as if they hadn't been threatening to have Augustus dragged from under our very roof ten minutes before.'

'So it's been agreed?' I am so glad my mission to Sissy has not been in vain.

'We have a time to breathe at least. They've renewed the bills.'

'Well, I'm glad of that.' Alfie stands up, agitating his watch. 'But take care, Kits. If this goes on, Augustus could run through your inheritance as quickly as his own – and before you even get it, at that!'

She rounds on him, and he quails, as he always used to, but half⁄humorously, now. 'You want to think badly of him, don't you? This whole family's always been against him! But you should see him! He couldn't be more sorry for having landed us in this shameful situation. He even went down on his knees and begged me to forgive him.'

'Said he wasn't worthy of you, no doubt?' Eddie chimes in from his place by the mantelpiece.

'Why is that amusing? A man can change his ways, can't he? Without becoming a laughing⁄stock?'

'Oh, to be sure.' And Eddie starts to sing quietly: *I'd give you sixpence, sweetheart dear, But I hain't got a penny, that much is clear . . .*

Kitty ignores him. 'I can honestly say that Augustus and I are more at one now than ever. We are embarking on a different mode of life. Once the debts are paid, there will be enough left over to set Augustus up in business. There is an opening he knows of in the wine-shipping trade —'

Eddie raises his eyebrows.

'— and I am to be active, too. I am to take my share. I shall give piano and singing lessons. And, if opportunity arises, and Lamming can arrange it, I may give dramatic recitals.' She looks round with a smile. 'I think we shall do very well between us.'

Carrie rises and takes her hand. 'I'm so glad, Kitty. I'm sure you will have great success. I shall tell everyone I know, and I promise to send Lucy along for lessons as soon as she utters her first note.'

Kitty glows with pleasure, and ruffles Lucy's curls. 'I'll make you sing like an angel, Lucy. Doh-re-me-fah-soh-la-ti-doh!' She trills up the scale and the beauty of her voice fills the room like velvet.

'You'll have to curb that temper of yours, first, or you'll find you have a school with no pupils,' laughs Alfie.

'I am very patient with children, P. It's adults who annoy me. Adults who talk humbug.'

I don't know whom she means by this. Me, I suppose. And Eddie and Sissy. And Alfred, naturally. But I'm pleased that she has some occupation in mind and I would not be surprised if she attempts the theatrical life. I wish I were as sure about Augustus in the wine-shipping trade. Wine is not the area I would have chosen for a man of his disposition. More and more I see that Alfred was right. But unlike him, I do not see that these matters are within my control.

Kitty gives Alfie a playful push, and he half-heartedly pushes her back. They both laugh. 'Pipsqueak!' she cries, and he responds:

'Know-all!' Eddie has put on Master's collar and is crawling around on his hands and knees, putting his beautiful clothes at risk, but not seeming to mind as he entertains young Lucy. I can see Alfred that first night: *Over-excitement – a fault of mine when in the company of Young Persons*. It's as if the old days have returned, and I find my eyes moist at the sight of them all.

'It's so lovely to have you all here. If only Lou and Fanny will join us next time. Then we'll all be a family again. Only Georgie will be missing.'

'He'll be back before Christmas,' says Eddie. 'And you'll never recognise him; he's taller than any of us. He looks very fine in his uniform, but he still has no conversation worth speaking of.'

Yes, I remember, a boy of few words. When Alfred once taxed him about it at the dinner-table, Ada piped up, saying, 'Don't blame him, Papa. I think you have used up all his share and there is nothing left for him to say.' Which made us all laugh, and got Ada an extra kiss from Alfred for being so clever. 'Never mind,' I say. 'Seeing him will be enough.'

After a while, Carrie intervenes in the romps, saying she will soon have to put Lucy to bed. Alfie takes out his father's watch to check the time. 'By the way, whose hair is this, M-mama? It cannot be Ada's, surely? It seems the wrong colour.'

I shake my head. 'No. It's Alice's.' I answer his unspoken question: 'Papa was very fond of her.'

'Oh.' He stares at the watch case. 'I see. But *I* didn't know her; it seems odd to carry her hair around with me. Would *you* like it, Mama?'

'Yes, I should.' The watch is Alfie's now; and will hold his own memories – Carrie and Lucy and maybe others yet to come. As he picks out the curling strand, not very reverently, I realise that it has no significance for him at all. I hold out my hand and he drops it into my palm. I fold it into my handkerchief, and Alfie returns the watch to his pocket with an air of satisfaction.

I feel a pang to think of Alice's hair separated from its shrine of so many years, so lovingly looked at every day. But its devotee has gone, and it is no longer sacred.

Alfie says they must depart immediately, before Lucy becomes overwrought. Lucy, however, thinks differently. She doesn't want to leave her uncle and aunt – who have both been jumping around the floor as if they were organ-grinders' monkeys – and protests loudly. We hear her wails all down the stairs and into the cab. Kitty dusts herself down and announces she has to speed off to meet Augustus who, she says, is measuring up a very pretty house in Fulham with a front parlour that will be ideal for giving lessons.

'Goodbye, Mama,' she sings out. Her face is flushed and prettier than I have seen it for some time. I wonder if she is merely excited by the rough-and-tumble or if she is wearing rouge.

I decide it doesn't matter.

24

It's strange to be alone with Eddie, and *he* seems somewhat uncomfortable too, poking the fire for rather a long time before sitting back in the armchair. He eyes my out-of-fashion plaid gown and my even more out-of-fashion figure in it. I, in turn, admire his handsome features, and find it difficult to believe that he is the same Eddie who used to climb on my bed with his porcupine hair and rumpled clothes and tell me jokes from bits of paper he'd pull out of his pockets. He seems to read my mind. 'No jokes today, I'm afraid.'

'I'll expect an especially good one next time.'

He smiles. He doesn't look like Alfred, but he smiles like him. 'I'll bring the Mouse too,' he says. 'It'll be good for her to get some fresh air. And I might prevail upon Fan as well.'

I try to picture Fanny, but I can't. Of all of them, she will have changed the most. And she won't remember me at all. 'Don't force her,' I say. 'I'd hate that.'

He chuckles. 'I couldn't force her however hard I tried. She doesn't take the slightest notice of anybody – even Papa. When she came up to see me at Oxford last year, she got poor Dodsworth to punt us up and down the river the whole afternoon while she recited all the verses of *The Lady of Shalott* draped in an Indian shawl. I had to tell him she was only fifteen and still at school, but he was so smitten he insisted we took her out to dinner at the Randolph. If Papa had got wind of it, she'd have been in hot water, but she's too damned clever to be found out. In fact, she's too damned clever – full stop.'

'She does well at school, then?'

He pulls a face. 'Yes and no. Too contrary. Only last month Miss B. wrote to Papa asking him to bring her to a 'better under-standing of her responsibilities'. Of course, Papa had her on the carpet, going on about the money he was paying for her education while the children of the poor were starving in gutters, and how she should be ashamed of herself; and how work was something we all had to do, and how he himself would have had no success without hard work, and so forth. But she smiled sweetly at him and said that she didn't see why she should pretend to be inter-ested in Euclid and Latin when there were so many more intrigu-ing things in the world; and that she'd prefer to educate herself along her own lines, if he didn't mind, and let him give the money he saved to the said starving children. "I believe some of the best people are self-educated," she said. And he started to laugh. That's the thing about her. You can't be cross with her for long.'

'Oh, do bring her, if you can.'

'I promise.' He hesitates. 'But *you* must promise something, too.'

'Oh? What's that?' I feel uneasy. I dislike making promises. Kitty is always trying to bully me into them, whether it's going back to Chiswick or admitting the fabled Truth. I hope Eddie is not going to do the same.

He takes out two ten-pound notes: 'For Mr. Collins' account.'

I colour. 'There's no need. I manage very well. And anyway, twenty pounds is ridiculous.'

'*Reason not the need.* Take it, please. I'll only spend it on kid gloves and satin weskits. I'm ashamed the Old Man left you so short, and it'll make me feel better if I know you're a shade more comfortable. You want me to feel better, don't you?' He smiles that golden smile. He is impossible to resist.

'Very well.' I tuck the money into my sleeve. 'I believe you could disarm anybody with that smile, Eddie. I doubt any young lady is safe.'

'Oh, they're pretty safe. Alfie's the romantic one. The way he went on about Carrie, day and night! A fellow could hardly stand it.'

'Oh, yes! It's been wonderful to see them so happy together. But I can't believe you're indifferent to the fair sex, Eddie. Your father was *very* romantic at your age.'

Eddie gives me a droll look.

'I see you find that amusing, but Papa was almost *exactly* your age when we met. He used to walk miles to see me. And he wrote such wonderful letters!'

'Ah, no doubt. But letters are the easy part. Especially when you are as steeped in ink as the One and Only. It's easy to imagine love; not quite so easy to live it, I think.'

I look at his neat head, his fine, intelligent face. 'How wise you have grown, Eddie! Quite the philosopher.'

He shakes his head. 'A mere observation. As far as I can see, marriage is a deuced difficult proposition. Two people too young to know their own minds agreeing to live together for the rest of their lives. Perfect madness!'

'How would you have it then, Eddie? What would you put in its place?'

He shrugs. 'Oh, I don't have the answer. My philosophy doesn't extend that far. I suppose I'll bow to the inevitable one day. But I'm in no hurry.'

I watch his face. 'You're thinking that Papa and I hardly set a good example.'

He smiles wryly. 'Well, the Idyll Shattered, and all that. Happy Times Vanished. Children Forlorn.'

'Not too forlorn, I hope. You children have much to be grateful for. A doting father, a loving aunt, a good education, travels abroad . . .'

He says nothing.

'And the *Idyll*, as you call it, is still there; the happy times are still in our memories.'

'Ah, the Good Old Memories,' he says sarcastically. 'The bright, magic-lantern shows of the never-to-be-forgotten past. Holidays and Christmases such as no one ever had since *Time Hin Memoriam*.'

'But they *were* wonderful, Eddie! Remember Abanazar?'

'Who could forget?'

'And in the summer — all those impromptu excursions!'

'*Get your bathing drawers. We're off to Margate!*' Eddie does Alfred's cockney voice to perfection.

'And how we'd all have to shout together when we saw the sea? *The sea, the sea! The salty sea! The slithery-slippery-shimmery sea!*'

'Oh, yes,' he says, 'the shouting was obligatory.'

'Don't pretend you didn't enjoy it, Eddie. I remember your face. You and Georgie riding two-at-a-time on the donkeys, and sailing your boats in the little pools until the tide rushed up and nearly washed them away! And Papa running into the waves to rescue them, and the wind whipping his sailor hat off so he had to go after that, too! Oh, Eddie, *what larks, eh?*'

'Oh, Papa was full of beans then! But a deal of the time he was almost invisible. I swear I had visions of his coat-tails perpetually vanishing round corners. And I'd run after him only to find a trail of cigar smoke by the front door and the sound of carriage wheels as he drove away.' He shakes his head. 'You know, Mama, every night after Bessie had got us ready for bed, I used to press my face against the nursery window, straining to see him turn the corner with that jaunty step of his, hoping against hope that he'd come back with a new trick or a new story — and that this time *I'd* be the one to sit on his lap to hear it. Sometimes I would be so sick with longing for him, I'd almost ache in my bones —'

'Oh, Eddie! You never once showed it.' He was the child who always seemed contented, absorbed in himself, resilient to the vicissitudes of family life.

'Good Lor', no!' He ruffles his hair, and a spike or two appears. 'I saw the way Kit went on, as if she were the only one who loved him. And Lou was almost as bad. I was damned if I'd do the same. I always made sure I hid in a cupboard to shed *my* tears. Even Georgie didn't know.'

I am dumbfounded. I'd never realised that Eddie had suffered so. It was always poor Alfie I'd felt the need to comfort. I take Eddie's hand. 'But, you know, don't you, that your father loved you all equally? And that he missed you more than anything when he was away?'

Eddie shakes his head. 'I doubt that, to be honest. I think we went out of his mind like that –' he snaps his fingers '– as soon as he turned the corner; as soon as he was *into the book*, living every-thing in his head. We didn't matter twopence then.'

'No, Eddie, you're wrong. He used to take your pictures with him. And he'd write so longingly about seeing you all again, about being *back in the family bosom*.'

Eddie raises his eyebrows, gives me that droll look again.

'Don't you remember how he once travelled all through the night from Exeter to London outside the mail coach, to be with us by morning? He came home a veritable mud-man, with his hat in shreds. *You will not believe how I have rattled and racketed and knocked myself about! How I have held on, when there was nothing to hold on to but an equally knocked-about lawyer in a Welsh wig. How the wind howled around us! How the lightning flashed! I tell you, I almost lost hope of ever see-ing my dear family again, convinced that the coachman was the Devil himself and we were being driven on a particularly ill-maintained road to Hell!*'

Eddie laughs in spite of himself. 'That happened before I was born, you know – although he told us about it on innumerable occasions, so we could all understand what a regular out-and-out family man he was. But it was only a coach journey, after all.'

'But it was no mean feat in those days, Eddie – all draughts and jolts and wet straw and more than a chance that you'd overturn and end up in a ditch. He could have stayed in a comfortable inn. Most men would have. But your father loved his family.'

'His idea of it, you mean: that collective hullabaloo with him at the centre.'

'Eddie!'

'That's harsh, I know! But I hated the way everybody scrummaged for his attention; and how he seemed to thrive on it all, as if the family were a miniature version of his damned Public. He had no real idea of me – what I liked or didn't like. I was only a boy with porcupine hair. And who did he say was his favourite child? Kitty? Alfie? Ada, even? No. Edward Cleverly, of course!'

I feel my colour rising. 'Oh, I see you are of Kitty's mind after all. You think your father could do nothing right!'

He looks at me directly. 'No, Mama, I've always given the Old Man his due. We got on pretty well at the end, you know – played billiards, went riding, smoked the odd cigar. I didn't try to beat him at his own game, you see. I realised a long time ago that no one could win a battle with Pa – not his publishers, not his friends, and certainly not his family. You could make yourself miserable fighting him, or you could accept his will and make the best of it. *You* realised that in the end, didn't you? That's why you went so quietly.'

Not all that quietly, I think.

He examines his fingernails. 'Unfortunately, you left the rest of us high and dry.'

'High and dry? You children had everything you could possibly want.'

'Except our Mama.'

He looks at me so pitifully that I cry out: 'Don't say that! Don't *blame* me, Eddie. For Heaven's sake don't do that!'

'I've tried not to – believe me, I've tried – but all my life I keep remembering that you didn't even say goodbye.'

I feel hot with guilt. 'I wanted to, Eddie, believe me. I begged your father to let me have a few last moments with you all, but he was adamant: *I won't have wailing or gnashing of teeth,* he said. So I had to creep round the bedrooms after you were all asleep and say goodbye to each of you in the silence of my heart.'

'Did you do that?' His face breaks into that beautiful smile.

'Of course. You and Georgie had that corner room. The one with three stairs up to it and the big wardrobe in the corner.'

He nods. 'It was always a capital place to hide. Except Georgie had a tendency to sneeze because of the dust – and I had a tendency to pummel him for it. And those wretched stairs always creaked.'

'They creaked that night, too. I was afraid I'd wake you – but you were both dead to the world.'

'If I'd have known it was my last chance to see you, I'd have stayed up all night, pinching myself.'

'Would you?' I am touched. 'I pictured you both for years afterwards – sleeping sweetly on your pillows with the moonshine on your faces. Georgie cradling that little wooden boat of his, you with your hair on end, wearing gloves for some reason.'

'They were new gloves. I was so proud of them I didn't want to take them off.'

We laugh, then fall into silence. Suddenly Eddie leans forward and grasps my hands tightly. 'How could the Old Man have allowed all that to happen? For some young girl! When he could have stopped it with a single word and saved us all that misery?'

'How do you know that, Eddie?' I look him in the eye. 'Could *you* have stopped if you'd been in his place and there was some-thing – someone – you wanted more than anything in the world?'

He springs up. 'You still make excuses, Mama! But we both know what extraordinary will-power Papa had. To do and think only what he wanted to do and think. To the exclusion of all else.'

I look at him, so clear, so definite, so very young. 'Oh, my dear, have you never been in love yourself?'

He drops his eyes for a second. 'Well, if I have, I've never lost my senses. I mean, she was the same age as Kitty! And there's no doubt he was guilty about it – he got to be so touchy at the mere mention of the words 'theatre' or 'actress' that we hardly dared speak on the subject. O'Rourke will bear that out; *I'm treading on eggs, Ned,* he'd say. Honestly, Mama, you've no idea how he carried on when you first left.'

'Kitty said he was 'mad'. Although she exaggerates, I daresay.'

He leans against the mantelpiece. 'For once, I think not. The only way *I* survived was to pretend it was all happening to somebody else, some other Eddie whom I knew slightly but didn't care much for. They all thought I was content, because I went about with a smile on my face, but deep down I hated everybody – including you, Mama, I'm sorry to say.'

'Me?' I look at him with shock. It has never occurred to me that my children would hate me. Ignore me perhaps, despise me even; but not *hate.*

He turns and looks me in the eye. 'Oh, Mama, did you never ask yourself why I didn't write or come to see you until this very afternoon? Why do you think I waited until I knew the others would be here? I was afraid of what I might say to you if we were alone!'

'But what could you have said? I acted for the best – what I thought was best for you all.'

'Really? Did you *ask* us what we wanted, what *we* thought was best?'

'Well, of course not. You were far too young!'

'Mama! Kitty was seventeen, Alfie fifteen, and I was eleven. And may I remind you that the sainted Edward Cleverly was only eight when he left the workhouse with a loaf of bread and two pennies, and went to London to look for his grandfather? Papa didn't think *he* was too young to know his own mind. The difference is that Papa sympathised with the poor, sensitive boy with the fine feelings – whereas he didn't sympathise with a bunch of pampered silver-spooners such as us.'

Eddie speaks so harshly, he frightens me a little. 'It's silly to compare yourself with Edward Cleverly,' I say. 'He wasn't real.'

Eddie snorts. 'You tell that to Papa. You ask him what was most real to him.'

'Nonsense. You and Kitty both talk nonsense at times.'

'Have it your own way, Mother.'

There is silence. Eddie taps his boot against the fireguard. They all feel so aggrieved, my children. Alfred gave them so much, but they always wanted more. And apparently I have contrived to make Kitty rebellious and Alfie miserable, and Eddie fearful of addressing me. I look at him: 'And do you still hate me?'

He smiles. 'Isn't it obvious? The moment I saw you with your teapots and cake-stands and your lovely gentle smile, I realised I'd always loved you. And I remembered how much you loved me.'

'Oh, Eddie!' I open my arms, but he remains leaning against the mantelpiece.

'It doesn't excuse *him*,' he says, pushing a coal fiercely with the poker. 'Or her – Wilhelmina Ricketts, I mean.'

Her name comes as a shock from Eddie's lips. 'Ah, yes, Miss Ricketts,' I say, feigning calmness. 'What is your opinion of her?'

He shrugs: 'Hard to say. I met her only twice. Unless you count the stage at the Haymarket when I was ten.'

That wretched play again! 'Was she very good in it?'

'Well, there was an awful lot of talking and swooning. But I was very struck with her looks –'

'Beautiful?' I have an agonised flash of jealousy, in spite of all the years that have passed.

'Not exactly, but something appealing, at any rate. I remember going backstage afterwards and saying how pretty she was. And I remember Papa turning round to me with the greasepaint still on his face, and saying that she was indeed pretty, but more importantly she was a very good and lady-like person to whom *no stain or blemish* (I remember his exact words) should attach. I remember

[342]

the words because up to then I had had no inkling that any stain *would* have attached itself to her, and it was a funny thing to have said.'

'Quite.'

'Then, when you came back from Leamington, it all started in earnest, of course.'

'What started?'

'Oh, Mama, you know – whispers from the servants, voices raised behind closed doors. Shouts. Arguments. Sounds of drawers being pulled out. Screams. Sobbing. Crashings. Boots thrown against doors. Footsteps up and down the stairs. All the stuff of domestic bliss.' He shakes his head. 'I didn't understand what was going on. Kit kept saying Papa had behaved badly and he was mean and hypocritical, and Lou said it was all rubbish and that Papa would never do anything wrong.'

I try to picture it, as it might have seemed to them, listening behind closed doors, huddling under the bedclothes, trying to make sense of it all. I'd never thought about how anxious they must have been. I'd assumed they didn't know; that Sissy and Bessie would have protected them from our arguments. But of course they were not deaf and blind.

Eddie is still staring at the fire: 'I wanted so much to ask you about it, but you were either crying in your room, or roving around with such a strange look on your face that I daren't even approach you. I thought maybe you'd gone a little mad. The servants kept saying "poor Mrs. Gibson" and "that poor creature", and wouldn't look any of us in the eye. And then, suddenly, one morning we found you'd packed and gone away. We were all in an uproar then. Poor Bessie didn't know what to do with us, nor Sissy. We were quite hysterical. Eventually Papa called us all together – captive audience, you know the sort of thing – and stood on the damned hearthrug looking all wise and noble, and said that circumstances had forced him to say things he would otherwise not have said. That he did not wish to cast scorn on you – "God knows your Mother's feebleness is not her fault" – but that for some reason known only to yourself, you'd chosen to become insanely jealous of a particular young lady and to imagine the wildest things with regard to this same person. "I need not say that the young lady in question is in every way innocent of the charges, but your mother's delusion was such that she opened every private letter addressed to me, thinking they were from this young lady – when of course they were not." And then he went on about how you'd begun to riffle through his drawers and throw his books and papers about in a foolish attempt to find such letters. And not content with these private manifestations of mistrust, you'd made his position impossible by your public accusations to friend and stranger alike, saying he was a Hypocrite and a Deceiver. "What is marriage if there is no trust? There is no marriage. After that, there was no course open to me – to us both – than to choose to live apart."'

It sounds very convincing – the Jealous Wife, the Wronged Husband, the Maligned Young Lady, the Non-existent Letters. 'What else did he say?'

'That we had to hold fast to our faith in him, and not believe anything bad that was said about him – or about anyone dear to him. Of course he meant Sissy. "I won't have disloyalty, especially to your Aunt."' He pauses, frowns, looks awkward: 'You know things were said about her, don't you? The very worst things, I mean? She didn't deserve that.'

'But didn't they realise that people were bound to think the worst when I was forced out and she stayed on? Didn't they imagine people would say that Papa preferred the slim and pretty sister to the fat and ugly one?'

'Oh, Mama! You were never ugly. You aren't ugly now.' Eddie rushes to me and gives me a kiss. A proper, manly kiss. He smells so intoxicatingly of lavender, I have to pull away for fear of fainting.

He takes my hand. 'Anyway, we weren't disloyal to Sissy – except for Kit, that is. But Miss Ricketts was a mystery to us all. Papa owned the connection – but only to point out how innocent it was: "You may hear a certain young lady mentioned in connection with me. Some of you may have been privileged to see her perform. She's a fine actress and I do my best to help her career when I can. Do not give credence to anyone who tries to say differently." Of course, I didn't know what he was getting at. I was only eleven. I couldn't understand why anyone should malign him for simply helping a young actress in her career. As far as I was concerned, he was *always* helping people. I remember the time he gave a whole ten pounds to that housemaid with a sick father in Walthamstow. I recall her crying her eyes out on the back stairs, telling Mrs. Brooks what a lovely man he was. So I couldn't understand why you'd been so angry about him helping poor Miss Ricketts and why he was so furious with you in return; so furious that you could no longer reside in the same house. We were such innocents! We only came to know the extent of the gossip because Kitty got *Yates's News* from John the coachman, and read them to us huddled up in the pantry. They were pretty brutal, you know – about the *ménage à trois*. But Miss Ricketts was never mentioned.'

I'd never read that sort of publication, of course. O'Rourke said I was better not to. He said ridiculous ideas were being thrown around. '*Ménage à trois?*' I ask Eddie. 'Did they really have the temerity to say that about *Alfred Gibson*?'

'Not in so many words. But they said you had left the family for reasons 'not altogether clear', and that Sissy was remaining with Papa, as his boon companion, with the 'ostensible purpose' of bringing us up. I remember sitting on the stone floor of the pantry and asking Kitty what 'ostensible' meant and how she glared at me from her seat on the slab. The worst thing was that they put at the bottom: "Mr. Gibson is notable for his campaigns castigating vice and immorality and for many novels in which the sanctity of the home has been much praised."'

I can see him reading that. Flying into a rage. Rushing to take up his pen and reply in any way that would clear his name; even if it meant lying about our entire life together. And yet, through it all, he managed to keep the actress out of it.

'But you met Miss Ricketts only *twice*, you say?'

'Yes, Mama, only twice, Honest Injun. And one of those times was last week, after the funeral. She said nothing then. Well, no one spoke to her. The other time was – a few years ago.' He runs his finger thoughtfully across his moustache. 'That was a damned curious thing when I think of it. I was at home doing nothing in particular – the long vac I think – when His Nibs comes rushing out of the study with a letter in his hand. Stops when he sees me and says he has an errand for me. "Take this to the address on the cover. Make sure it's handed over in person. Wait for a reply." I remember objecting – quite mildly – to being treated as a messenger, and him flaring up with anger: "Can I ask nothing of you? I educate you, clothe you, give you an allowance second to none, and you won't lift a finger to help me!" So I told him to keep his hair on, and dashed off as soon as I could. The address was 2 Pembroke Villas, South Norwood. It was for Miss Ricketts, marked URGENT.'

'South Norwood? Where's that?'

'Oh, Mama, d'you still not know London? Out beyond Peckham. Very respectable.'

'And you saw her; talked to her?' I try to read his firm, handsome face.

'For a brief moment. There was an older woman, and a younger one. I recognised them both from the play, although they looked different in their own hair and ordinary costume. The younger one read the note and wrote something in reply, sealing it up. "Thank you," she said. That was all.' He shrugs.

'Was she as pretty as you remembered her?'

'Not quite. More anxious I think. A little frown always *there* –'
He points to the place where the nose meets the forehead. 'But it
was dark, and only one lamp was burning.'

'Did she say anything else?'

'No. I was rather vexed she took so little notice of me after all
my haste in getting there.'

'And did Papa say what the note was about? Why it was so
urgent?'

'He never spoke of it again. I think he realised he had over-
stepped the mark; confusing his two lives in that way.'

'Two lives? How did he manage two lives with the Public's eye
on him all the time?'

'Mama, *I don't know*. I was at Oxford; I kept out of his way. But
when I was at home, he seemed to follow his old routine pretty
much: up early; scribbling for a couple of hours; walking; going
to the office. But apart from the reading tours, he was at home
most evenings. In fact he made a point of us all dining together
every night, seven o'clock sharp.'

'All of you?'

'When we were all there. But it wasn't how it used to be. Alfie
and I were away a lot, and Kitty was *persona non grata* – but Sis,
Lou, Georgie and Fan were the regular troops. Of course, Carrie
started to dine with us in the last few years, which much improved his mood. He seemed to come out of himself when there
was company; in fact I'd often plead with O'Rourke to stay for
supper purely to spare us the silence. One odd thing, though – he'd
started the habit of saying grace, emphasising the *truly thankful*.
He'd always drink his soup, but he didn't seem to have an appetite for much else. He'd often read, with his book propped up
against the cruet, although he never let anyone else take the liberty.
Sometimes he'd close his book and hold his hand to his side as if
he were in pain, and Sis would run about and make up little

concoctions for him at the table: three spoonfuls of this, two spoonfuls of that – all whizzed up in Seltzer water. He'd say, "Phelps trying to poison me still?" – but he'd drink it all the same, as if he wouldn't mind being poisoned.'

'It was digestive colic. His mother told me he was sometimes prostrated with the agony of it as a child. But he didn't like people to know.'

He raises his eyebrows. 'I suppose it would never have done to admit that the great Alfred Gibson – the High Priest of Hospitality – was a finicky eater.'

'Perhaps. But it was the *act* of hospitality that he loved. He never ate a great deal himself.'

'Full up with that damned seed cake, I expect!'

We laugh. And then fall silent. I want to know more about Miss Ricketts. She dances in and out of my imagination in her taunting grey silk dress. 'Did he stay with that woman at that house of hers? Did she travel with him? You must know *something*.'

'No, Mama.' He looks exasperated. 'All I can say is that she was never received at *our* house. I can't speak for what he did when he was away. I daresay he saw her in Norwood, but you know Papa – here, there and everywhere. Appearing and disappearing like blessed Abanazar. As sparing with information as if it had been gold dust. Even Sissy didn't always know his movements – whether he'd be staying at the office or not – or whether he'd suddenly been obliged to furnish three thousand words overnight before getting a cab home and collapsing on the sofa with one of his *corkers*.'

'So he maintained to you all that she was no more than a friend? A *protégée*?'

'He went into a fit if anything was even *suggested* in the other direction. We all knew, I suppose. But it was easier not to mention it. But now he's left her mother that house – well . . .' He gets up and strides to the fireplace again, gives the fender a ferocious kick. 'Oh, for Heaven's sake,' he bursts out. 'Why couldn't he have been like other men and kept a mistress discreetly? Why did he have to break up the family and put you out? And moreover make it all public? Was he completely mad?'

Mad with love, perhaps. It was all or nothing with him; I have seen that over and over again. But as I look at Eddie staring grimly down into the coals, I am suddenly too tired to make sense of it all. Eddie seems to realise this, and comes and sits by me, and takes my hand. 'I'm sorry, Mama — temper getting the better of me. Sometimes I feel I'd like to pull him out of the grave and give him a good shaking, purely to relieve my feelings. But it wouldn't change the past, would it? It wouldn't make anyone the slightest bit happier.'

'No, Eddie, you are right. I see you are still philosophical at heart.' We both laugh, and he rises, kisses me on the cheek, and picks up his (very elegant) hat. I tell him that I am so glad he has come back to me, and to be sure to come again soon.

'I will, Mother dear. Very soon. And I shall bring you a half-pound of best-quality Ceylon, and a positive Firecracker of a joke.'

25

I've slept badly. I've thought it over all night, and at breakfast I decide. 'Please get me a cab,' I tell Wilson. 'I'm going out.'

'Out? Again?' She disapproves of this 'gallivanting' of mine, although I imagine she's glad at least that O'Rourke hasn't turned up in the gig. It's a raw morning, and she insists I wear my heavy old pelisse and fur-trimmed hat.

Soon I'm trotting briskly along the new Embankment. What a wonder it is – with its wide pavements and elegant street lamps. Almost like Paris, I think. There's no sign of the wretches who once thronged the shoreline, barefoot and bent double among the rotten débris, sifting through the unmentionable for something to sell. I wonder where they have gone, these displaced women and children? *Moved on,* he would have said. *Poor creatures, always moved on.*

Now we are crossing the bridge, black smoke trailing from the pleasure boats beneath us. And where it clears for a second, I spy, in the threshing water, a leaky rowing-boat, expertly pulled by a young girl, her hair loose on her shoulders like a second Grace Darling. Suddenly there are dozens of small vessels every way I look, with tar-stained boatmen hauling at ropes or standing at tillers. The river's full of every kind of life. *Full of death, too,* he'd say. He was fascinated by it, by the ebb and flow, the cold and the darkness, the activity and noise, the desolation and pitilessness of it all. He'd sometimes go out at night with the dredger-men and watch them track dark parcels of clothing floating under the bridges or driven up and down by the tides. Once there was a woman, he said. Pale and bloated and covered in slime, but with fine hands and a silver locket around her neck. I shudder at the thought, even now. But he was always energised by such things, his face bright as lamplight, his hair practically standing on end.

We turn abruptly away from the river, and as we rattle into the suburbs I see how enormously London has changed: rows of respectable new terraces in parallel lines like furrowed fields, and here and there more substantial villas with bay windows and laurel bushes. I try to imagine the kind of house I am bound for. It's secluded, I don't doubt. South Norwood is well out of town.

We travel through Battersea, Clapham and further south; and I am becoming more and more nervous. Eventually, we come to Norwood. The cabman slows the horse to a walking pace and asks directions of a butcher's boy who is minding the horse and cart, and throwing stones into a hedge to pass the time. The boy stops and moves his hand, indicating turnings left and right, before resuming his occupation with the stones. We turn up a lane where there are no other houses. We cross several small roads and pass out to a wider road, where there is a doleful-looking church and an equally despondent inn. We turn near a railway bridge, and suddenly we are running alongside a wall with a high holly hedge, above which I can discern a shallow, slated roof. I see a name carved in the stonework: *Pembroke Villas.* There are two gateways. I ask the cabman to stop at Number Two. 'Please wait,' I say, as he helps me out.

Number Two has a blue front door. It is a small house, but immaculately kept. I pause for a moment. She may not be at home, I think. Or she may be at home but be unwilling to let me in. Or she may let me in, then send me away ignominiously. Or, again, she may be polite but tell me nothing of what I want to know. I wonder fleetingly what I would do if our positions were reversed and Wilson had arrived in the drawing room announcing

Miss Ricketts was below. Would I have been curious enough to admit her, so I could at last compare her face and figure with those of my imagination? Or would I have exercised the only power I have left, sending her card back with a withering rebuff: *Mrs. Gibson regrets that she is unable to receive a personage of whom she has no prior acquaintance.* I really cannot tell what I would have done. But then, I cannot imagine Miss Ricketts would ever have paid me such a call in the first place. And no doubt she will be equally surprised to see *me* today.

As I walk up the stone-flagged path, I feel eyes on me. I knock, boldly, and stand very upright, showing any watcher that I am not ashamed to be here. But inside I'm trembling. I've rehearsed my opening words all the way here, but I cannot remember them. My mouth is dry and my lips seem stuck together. For a moment I hope that my knock will not be answered and that I can go home swiftly with no harm done. But hardly has my hand fallen from the knocker than the door opens.

A woman looks at me. I am taken aback. She is ramrod straight and very handsome, but she is the same age as me. I realise that she must be the mother.

'Is Miss Wilhelmina Ricketts at home?' I use all the hauteur I am capable of, reminding myself that I (and no one else) am the widow of the most famous man in England.

Her face is impassive. 'What name is it, ma'am, if you'd be so good?' She seems to spread herself slightly as though she is barring the door, protecting what is beyond.

'Mrs. Gibson.'

She is very self-possessed — tremendously so — but she cannot hide the start her body gives, or the look of surprise in her eyes. 'Mrs. *Dorothea* Gibson,' I add, to clarify any doubts.

I watch her face. I see that she is considering closing the door on me, or telling an untruth to be rid of me. But, seeming to observe that I am calm and alone, she makes an instant decision.

'Mrs. Gibson – honoured to make your acquaintance.' She bows a little. 'I am Henrietta Ricketts. Please come inside.'

I step into a narrow passageway. There is a hall-stand with a looking-glass. On it are two bonnets, two cloaks and two umbrellas. On the shelf beneath the glass sit an ivory hairbrush and comb. Mrs. Ricketts ushers me into the front parlour. It is cold and dim. Thick lace obscures the window and the green chenille curtains are half-drawn. There is a looking-glass over the mantel, and a smaller one above the piano. The furniture itself is simple yet comfortable, as he always liked. There is a bookshelf containing a dozen or so volumes and, in the window, a desk. There is nothing on the desk save an inkwell.

I sit, and Mrs. Ricketts goes out. I wait several minutes. I think I hear voices raised in agitation but I am not sure. I think I hear footsteps on the stairs, but again I am not sure. In the meantime, I become very well-acquainted with the wallpaper and the three small ornaments that sit on the mantelpiece. Eventually Mrs. Ricketts returns. She has an expression both wary and anxious. 'If you would be so kind, Mrs. Gibson – there's a fire in the back parlour. I think we'd all be more comfortable there.'

I follow her out of the room. I notice to my surprise that, in spite of her elegant demeanour, Mrs. Ricketts has work-worn hands and wears a dark blue apron pinned across her skirts. The room we enter gives upon the back garden and (in contrast to the front room) is full of light. As promised, a fire roars in the grate. In the middle of the room, standing exactly in the centre of a large round carpet, stands Wilhelmina Ricketts.

To see her in the flesh nearly floors me. I thought I'd prepared myself but I have not, and I find myself standing stock-still, at a loss for words. She is so small; so very small. And young-looking; almost like a child. She is so fragile and seems so innocent – so unlike my idea of her – that I feel the breath knocked out of my body and I can only acknowledge her with the stiffest of nods.

She makes a deep curtsy in return: 'Mrs. Gibson – an honour to make your acquaintance.' She has a sweet, low voice, yet it trembles as she speaks, and I see she is frightened to death. She looks such a child that I want to put her at her ease, to tell her I mean her no harm – but then I remind myself that she is twenty-seven years old and my enemy; and if she is afraid of me, so much the better. I examine her carefully. She's not beautiful; an ordinary pale little face with light brown hair drawn back into a *chignon*, and a fringe of curls along her forehead. She is impeccably dressed, though: dark grey silk, very much as Kitty has described. Two long teardrops of jet shimmer at her ears as she moves a step towards me, then stops. She is not prepared for the sight of me any more than I am for the sight of her. She thinks me old and ugly, no doubt, and is wondering how he could ever have loved me.

There is another silence.

'Please sit down, Mrs. Gibson.' The mother takes charge, motioning me to the best chair in the room; a red plush fireside chair – no doubt the one he sat in. She takes the smaller chair beside it, pulling it close in a confidential manner which I do not altogether like. Miss Ricketts remains standing. She is not so self-possessed as her mother and twiddles nervously at a gold bracelet encircling her wrist. Its design is very familiar and, as I watch her fingers move back and forth, I realise to my horror that it is identical to one he gave to me when we were first married, except hers has a pendant 'W' whereas mine had a 'D'. My throat constricts. How could he have done such a thing? Did he think it didn't matter? Or had that first bracelet dropped from his mind as a stone into the deep? Now I hardly dare look around, fearing that I shall see a myriad objects that will betray how intimate they were, my husband and this small and ordinary young woman. I think of the hairbrush, the desk, the armchair I am sitting in – all part of a life they enjoyed and which I did not share. I wish now, most fervently, that I had never come on this fool's errand. I have seen her; that is sufficient. Now I must make my excuses and leave. But before I can collect myself, the mother speaks. 'Forgive our lack of hospitality; we are a little surprised at this visit. We keep ourselves very secluded, as you see. How did you find us? Was it Mr. Golding?'

'My son Eddie,' I say. 'He came once to deliver a letter.'

The women exchange glances. 'I remember.' Miss Ricketts' voice is stronger now. 'He was a fine-looking boy.'

'And is a fine-looking man.' I am proud of Eddie's good looks, although I do not think it is this woman's place to remark upon them.

'*Your* colouring, I think, ma'am?' Mrs. Ricketts speaks this time.

No doubt she thinks to flatter me, but I won't be so easily won over. 'My colouring *once*,' I correct her. 'Time has rendered me somewhat grey. No one, unfortunately, stays young for ever.' I give Miss Ricketts a meaningful look.

There is another awkward silence. Miss Ricketts twiddles the wretched bracelet even more. Her mother suddenly becomes aware of social niceties and rises: 'Will you be so good as to take a cup of tea with us, Mrs. Gibson?'

I can do no other than accept. Perhaps she will take some time to make it and I shall be able to make some headway with her daughter. 'Please ask the cabman to wait until I am ready,' I tell her. She nods, and as the door closes I am alone at last with the woman who destroyed my marriage.

She is still standing in the centre of the room. I take off my gloves and motion to the chair her Mama has vacated, the one that encroaches so intimately upon mine: 'Please sit down, Miss Ricketts.' But she declines such proximity and perches instead on a small footstool some distance away. She clasps her hands together firmly around her knees, as if she were a child waiting for a story. But in fact it is *she* who speaks. 'I confess that you have taken me by surprise, Mrs. Gibson. You are – forgive me – the last person I expected to see.'

'I never thought to find myself here either. But I have been remembering the many years that my husband and I spent together, and I find that you owe me something, Miss Ricketts.'

She looks alarmed. She thinks I mean money; she thinks I am come to dispute her right to what he has left her: the house and the annuity and God knows what else. He has left her too much, of course; Kitty is right. But I will not demean myself by challenging her now. 'Oh, don't fear for your ptoperty, Miss Ricketts. That is not what I meant at all. You have a quite different obligation. One that is far more important to me, and which I shall expect you to honour. If you understand the word, that is.'

She flushes. 'Mrs. Gibson, I don't imagine you think well of me. If I were in your position, I wouldn't think well of me. But I swear to you that I have always behaved honourably. Yes, *honourably*.' She holds up her head and returns my gaze without a hint of shame.

How can she look at me so brazenly, knowing what she is; what she has done? She may appear small and sweet, but I feel heat rising through my body as I contemplate the harm she has done me, the desolation she has produced with her winsome smile as she tempted my husband with the oldest of tricks and caught him unawares in her nasty net. And now she pretends she is a creature of honour! 'How can you have the *effrontery* to say that?' I cry. 'What possible *honour* is there in your arrangement with my late husband? Did he not set you up here in this – this – house? Did he not come to see you here in secret? Were you not his *mistress*?'

I cannot keep the tears out of my voice, but she flinches at the word, as if I have spat at her: 'Mrs. Gibson, I understand your feelings –'

'Do you, indeed? You are bold to presume that. Very bold.'

She colours again, and speaks quickly. 'Well, of course no one can truly know the feelings of another. But I can at least explain myself, if only – if *only* – you will allow me to.'

Explanation: that is what I have told myself I wanted from today's encounter. *The Truth*, in Kitty's words. But seeing Miss Ricketts with her genteel ways and air of innocence, now I am not so sure. What she has to say may be even more unwelcome than ignorance. I am torn; I half-raise my hand as if to prevent her speaking; yet I let it drop. I have come this far; it would be foolish to retreat now. 'Very well,' I say. 'Explain, then – if you can.'

She avoids my gaze and says nothing; she has no defence. I knew it, of course. How could it be otherwise? There is no excuse, no explanation of her conduct that can be construed in any honourable way. She smoothes the dark grey silk of her skirt in neat, regular movements as if she is playing for time, casting around for a persuasive tale that will satisfy the idiot wife. 'It is not a simple story,' she says at last. Her voice is quiet, as it has been throughout our conversation, but there is a note of steel within that surprises me. She is certainly no child. 'Whatever I did, I did by choice, Mrs. Gibson. And I did it for love. I did it for a man I cared for deeply and mourn today quite as much as you do.'

I had forgotten that she, too, might be full of sadness; that she, too, might miss him, and wake every day heavy-lidded with grief. Even so, she has no right to compare herself with me. 'I cannot blame you for *loving* him,' I say. 'Everyone who knew Alfred came to love him, after all. But your love was greedy, Miss Ricketts; you usurped the position that was rightfully mine. Did you not consider how your so-called love injured *me*?'

'Please.' She holds up her hand as grandly as if she were the Queen of Egypt. 'I said I would explain. Pray do not judge before you have heard me out.'

If I am to gain anything, I must let her speak, though it is difficult to endure. No doubt she has the skills to present a convincing case, but I need no jury to tell me what is clear as glass. Before she can speak, however, the mother chooses to make her entrance with the tea tray. She bustles about, setting out the cups, saucers and spoons, but, catching (I think) some meaningful expression in her daughter's eye, puts down the teapot and moves to the door. 'Will you excuse me, Mrs. Gibson? We've no maid today, and I have things to attend to in the kitchen.'

Miss Ricketts approaches and pours the tea. Her hand is so small and fragile that I wonder she can lift the pot, but she fills two cups with perfect precision. The tea is a clear golden colour and has an excellent taste; clearly Alfred has seen to the stocking of these particular cupboards. She then hands me slices of seed cake, cut thin and prettily arranged on a scalloped plate, but I decline. I've never really liked caraway and there is no longer any reason to pretend. We drink in silence for a while, and I wonder who will speak first. Then she turns towards me suddenly. 'I am honoured at your visit, Mrs. Gibson. I would not have expected such condescension – such acknowledgement, even. The world judges harshly in these matters.'

I cannot trust myself to speak. I merely nod. I have judged her as harshly as anybody, and wished her dead and drowned and driven to Kingdom Come on many occasions, but now she is in front of me, so sweet-faced and gentle, I am finding it increasingly hard to be hostile. It is part of her cleverness, no doubt, to win me over. But I will not be won: 'We live in the world, Miss Ricketts. We must pay the penalties if we do not abide by its rules. But I have not come to berate you for your sins. That is God's prerogative.'

She takes a deep breath, looking at me steadily the while. 'Indeed it is. Yet I believe in my heart that there is nothing I need to be ashamed of. Your husband was a good man, and Mama and I were honoured to be his friends.'

Surely she will not try to maintain with me the pious fiction he promulgated for his Public. 'Oh, I think a little more than *friendship* was involved, was it not?' I say, sarcastically.

'As I have already said, Mrs. Gibson, I came to love him. And he, I believe, came to care for me too. From the very outset he singled me out for notice.'

From the outset. Indeed, I can see it – the flirtation, the gallantry, the *whole panoply of effects* directed at this one young recipient. 'Oh, yes,' I say. 'Young ladies were two‑a‑penny throughout our mar‑ried life. But they all faded or fell from grace sooner or later. You seem to have made a more lasting impression. I wonder why that should be?' As if, of course, I didn't know.

She raises her eyebrows. 'It's a question I have often asked my‑self. I am quite an ordinary person, you know. I never dreamt that such a great man as Alfred Gibson could ever come to care for me. And indeed, when it happened, I cannot wholeheartedly say I welcomed it.'

Now she is disingenuous. 'Come, come, Miss Ricketts! What young girl wouldn't be flattered to have such a great man take notice of her?'

She lifts her eyes. 'Oh, I was *flattered* of course, I shan't deny that. After all, I'd virtually grown up with Miggs and Edward Cleverly and Little Amy. My father always had one of the novels to hand. 'Mr. Gibson will keep us company,' he'd say if we had a moment to spare. But knowing him so well on the page made it all the stranger to meet him face to face.'

'It was *Lord Royston* that brought you together?'

'Yes.' She lowers her head, and I fear she will not go on.

'He chose you to act with him?'

'No, not at all. It was chance, Fate; whatever you will. It was Mr. Lamming who recommended us – Mama and myself – and Mr. Gibson accepted his recommendation.'

'He hadn't seen you on stage before?'

'No. As I said, it was chance.' Again the lowering of her head, very pretty, very artful. But she raises it once more and looks at me. 'I was so grateful to be chosen, because – well, because

Mama and I were in such very difficult circumstances . . .' She pauses.

I remember O'Rourke saying they were always on the edge of poverty. No doubt they were always looking for opportunities to better themselves, and this must have seemed a plum to fall in their laps. 'Go on,' I say, compressing my lips.

'You see, the offer came barely a month after my dear Papa had passed away.'

'I am sorry,' I murmur, thinking of my own Papa. 'That must have been hard.'

She nods. 'It was. He'd been ill for some time and there were innumerable debts, as you can imagine – doctor's bills, rent, laundry bills, grocer's bills – and Mama and I had had to forgo most of our theatre work to care for him. In our profession, if you are out of the public's eye for the shortest time, they forget you; or the managers have some new sensation and don't want you. So when Mr. Lamming offered us the engagement, Mama was so relieved she danced me round the parlour till we were both out of breath. She said that I was bound to impress the Great Man with my skills.'

'Are you sure there was no other part of you that you hoped to impress him with?'

She looks at me in a shocked fashion. 'Mrs. Gibson,' she says, 'how could I have thought such a thing? Mr. Gibson was the most upright and moral of men.'

'That didn't stop ladies setting their caps at him. And I imagine your Mama was not averse to using the connection.'

Anger flashes across her face, and gives her small features a sudden grand and noble look, and I see for a moment how she might impress upon the stage. 'You think my Mama had a base motive in encouraging me?' she says. 'You think she was so low and scheming that she planned to loose me before him like a golden apple? No, Mrs. Gibson, all my mother wished was to earn enough to keep a roof above our heads and remain respect-able. And far from setting my cap at him, I was so nervous of meeting the Great man that the very morning we were due to begin I begged Mama to find some other actress to take the rôle. "No, you can do it, Mina," she said. "Remember what a great chance it is; how it could change both our lives."' She looks rueful. 'I didn't imagine then *quite* how much.'

Indeed, she could not have foreseen it when she accepted the rôle. Nor could Alfred, when he hired her on her reputation as an *ingénue*. And *I* certainly had no inkling as I read his weekly jokes about *the Thespian mother and daughter* while I played cards and gossiped my time away in Leamington. 'That meeting changed *my* life too, Miss Ricketts,' I say. 'But in my case, very much for the worse.'

She is instantly subdued: 'I am sorry. I fear this narrative is merely rubbing salt into old wounds. Perhaps, after all, we'd better end it here. I don't blame you for the way you feel – indeed I hardly know how you could feel otherwise – but I do not think you will ever understand why I acted as I did.'

I could depart now; I could go with my pride intact, with nothing ventured, nothing given away. But what she is telling me draws me in. I want to know; I need to understand what there was about her that drew him, too. 'No, Miss Ricketts,' I say, mollifying my tone. 'What you tell me is of interest. Please go on. Tell me the whole story, if you would be so good.'

She gives me a doubting look but, after some more agitating of her bracelet, continues. 'Of course, I didn't know what to expect from that first meeting. I put on my best blue dress and hoped I would not displease him. And when he arrived at the theatre in all his finery and addressed us *en masse* from the front of the stage, I feared I would not please him after all. He looked at us all so very sternly that I thought he might dismiss the whole pack of us on the instant. There was utter silence, I remember. Then he pulled a battered old copy of the play from his pocket and held it up: "Ladies and gentlemen, this play will be a marvel, if you only play your parts as well as I. And to play those parts well, you will need to be disciplined, hard-working and punctual. I will not tolerate sloppiness of any kind from any company member, young or old. I also look for a slavish willingness to bow to my opinion in all matters, however wrong-headed or obtuse. No doubt you've already heard that I am a positive tyrant, consumed with puffery and self-importance. Believe it, dear people, believe it! If you do, then we shall get along capitally!" And everyone laughed in a relieved sort of way, and he jumped off the stage and began to saunter about, speaking a few words to each of the assembled company, making everyone he spoke to seem – I don't know – *brighter* somehow, as if he actually gave off a kind of light. When he came up to Mama and myself, he stopped and looked me full in the face. That's when the strangest thing happened . . . I cannot really describe it.'

I can, though. I can see it as if I'd been there; Alfred looking at her in that intense way of his, and she stunned, as it were, by the force of his gaze. 'Try,' I say, quietly.

She bites her lip. 'It was almost as if the world had stopped; or rather as if *I* had stopped and the world was carrying on without me. For a moment I hardly knew where I was or who I was. I simply stood there. And he bowed, and laughed. "Ah, the Thespian mother and daughter," he said. "I am glad to see you both. I hope you will not be as much trouble to me as the genuine domestic articles have proved to be."' She looks at me quickly. 'Believe me, I had no idea what he meant by that. I'd always understood him to have the best-regulated of households, so I didn't know what to say. And he laughed again and said, 'Well, you look meek enough, at any rate.' Then Mama, seeing me so unaccountably dumb, spoke up and told him I was a good worker, and would listen and learn quicker than anyone, given the chance.

And he said that was capital, and we would get on well. And he shook my hand very firmly indeed.'

'Industry and modesty combined! Your Mama could not have chosen her words better if she'd *intended* to entrap him.' Miss Ricketts may be assiduous in excusing her mother, but I suspect she had a strategy from the first.

Miss Ricketts won't have it, though. 'Mama was simply covering up for my confusion. Actresses are not usually tongue-tied, you know; that would do us no good at all. And we're used to being looked at – even in ways we don't like. But the way he was looking at me was different: he was as attentive and observant of my appearance as if he were impressing every inch of me upon his mind's eye. And all the time I could feel this strange – draining – of my thoughts and feelings, as if he were conjuring my soul out of my body.' She shakes her head. 'No doubt that sounds fantastical –'

'Not at all.' For a moment I am almost impelled to tell her how the whole world once stopped for me all those years ago. It is on the tip of my tongue to confide in her. But the desire, thankfully, passes, and I affect nonchalance instead. 'Alfred had a similar effect on many a young girl,' I say. 'It's a kind of mesmerism – nothing more. And surely you were aware of your own effect on him? A young lady so charming, yet so shy and modest?'

'You say that again, but truly, Mrs. Gibson, I thought only of the rôle I was to play and the absolute need to be "disciplined, hard-working and punctual". He'd frightened everyone into a positive state of nerves, and I was no exception. Indeed, on the first walk-through he startled me by calling out from the stalls: "Jenny Wren, move forward. You are six and a half inches out."'

Jenny Wren. His little bird. How she must have fluttered her wings to have been noticed in that way! But he was always a stickler, even with the family plays, when he would dictate every move and position as if we were clockwork creatures; and Kitty would dispute with him as a matter of principle: *No, no, Papa, that cannot be right.* And the rest of us would sigh and sink down where we were until he had (inevitably) won and Kitty was in tears. 'He liked everything to be perfect, that's all,' I tell her. 'It had to be exactly how he saw it in his mind's eye.'

'I knew that. So I never thought him a tyrant. And as I said, he was always extremely kind to me. Like a father, in fact.'

'First friend, now father.' I smile sarcastically. 'Is there no end to his benevolent rôles?'

She shakes her head: 'You think I delude myself. But don't imagine me as the woman you see before you now. Think of me as I was then – an impressionable child.'

'Child? Even at seventeen that is stretching a point.' Although she is so slight, I can see it would be easy for certain people to forget she was fully-grown.

'You may say that. But it seemed as though I was recapturing something of the girlhood that I had lost. For over a year I'd been more of a mother than a daughter, helping to look after Papa, feed him, change his sheets and comb his poor matted hair. It was such a delight to have someone care for *me* instead; to have a man pay me fatherly attention, call me his 'Jenny Wren', give me little surprises of sweets and hot muffins, or do tricks with his handkerchief to make me laugh. And when he took time to sit with me to go over my lines, with such patience and good humour, I felt so very happy.'

I see them – oh, I see them – heads together over a script, he amusing her with a myriad different voices, she delighting to be amused. 'That play,' I say; 'what was it about? I was, as you know, in Leamington when it was performed. Living in a Fool's Paradise, you might almost say.'

She flushes a little and looks uncomfortable. 'It's about a father's love for his daughter. I suppose that was what made it so real. Alfred was the father and I was the daughter. Lord Royston loves

Alma more than life itself, but in a fit of madness he casts her aside. However, she remains faithful and true to him, and at the end they are reunited. Even though he is dying – shot through the heart – he is able to take her in his arms and beg forgiveness. It is a very affecting play.'

'So everyone says.' I half-wish I'd seen the wretched thing now.

'But I didn't realise quite how affected I'd be until rehearsals were half-way through. We'd walked through it with the book, and he'd shown us *how* he wanted us to speak and *where* he wanted us to stand, but the moment he took to the stage himself he became utterly transformed. I could hardly believe it – I, who had been brought up in the theatre! There was no stilted waiting at the end of each line, no waving of arms or grimacing for effect. He took his cues so naturally – speaking so fast and with such passion – as if the words were spilling not from the page, but from his heart. Then, at the very end, when he had to die in my arms, he held me with such desperate force and looked at me with such intensity that I could not remember a single line of my response. Tears poured from my eyes, while all the cast stood dumbly around, not sure if I were acting or not. I remember hearing him call out, "Give her some air! Smelling salts, for God's sake!" and quickly lifting me up and carrying me to the wings. He laid me down on an old sofa, and took out his handkerchief and wiped my face – and then his own, which was equally wet. Then he smoothed the hair back from my face, and took my hands and chafed them.' Tears run down her cheeks at the remembrance of it. 'Oh, Mrs. Gibson, you cannot imagine how gently he attended to me.'

Alas, I can. *My darling girl*.

'But you see, I was then obliged to tell him why I was so affected; to tell him about my own father and how the memory of his last days was still fresh with me. He said: "My dear girl, you should not be here, doing this play! How could your Mama let such a thing happen?" But I told him Mama was not to blame; that we were without means, and that if we didn't find employ﹍ment, especially now without Papa to help us, we would end up in the workhouse. "This is a very good chance for me to be seen, sir," I told him. "The world will flock to a play with Alfred Gibson in it. Further rôles may come to me if I am seen to act well." He was then kind enough to pay me a compliment on my acting, and that he would use all his influence to enable me to gain further employment. "But for *this* rôle," he said, "you must use your natural feelings as a well from which to draw. All my life I've drawn from such a well – in my writings; in my acting. And when I play Lord Royston, I plunge deep into that well. I think of someone whom I, too, have lost. Someone dearer to me than all the world."'

I cannot speak.

'So I took his advice, Mrs. Gibson. Each time we played that scene, I thought of my father, and he (I suppose) thought of the person he had lost. But now my grief did not overwhelm me; it seemed to melt and mingle into *his* grief, and we seemed to be consoling each other. And each time I took him in my arms, I felt this same unbelievable happiness: *It's a far, far better thing for me to die now, looking at your lovely face and knowing your good and pure heart, than to live one more day as a man condemned. Weep for me if you can. But do not try, in mistaken mercy, to recall me to life. Let the sweet angels who already hover over me bear their burden away for ever. All is redeemed. Now there is only love between us, Alma. Only love.* And then he'd close his eyes, and I'd feel his body grow so heavy I could hardly support it, and his head would fall upon my breast as if he had truly given up the ghost. There'd be such silence then! The whole theatre would be stunned. But when we raised ourselves, and came down to take our bows, they'd stand and applaud with rapture. Some of them wept openly. Oh, Mrs. Gibson, it was all very unsettling. I was seventeen years old, and every night I was holding the most famous man in England in my arms, and every night I was applauded to the skies by rapt and crowded audiences who came to see me do it.'

'Yet it was only acting,' I tell her, with a dismissiveness that I do not feel. After all, he had reduced me to tears on so many occasions.

'Yes, that is what I kept telling myself. Only acting, I kept saying. Immediately after the play, when half London was milling around in the Green Room congratulating us, he seemed as indifferent as if nothing special had passed between us. But something had; I knew it had. And it passed between us every time we performed the scene.' She stops and takes a deep breath. 'Every evening as I put on my costume, my whole soul longed for that moment. And I confess – yes, I confess even to you, Mrs. Gibson – that when that moment came, I no longer cared that he was someone else's father and someone else's husband. I simply wanted to be his darling Alma for ever.'

So that's how it all started. With play-acting. With the real and the imagined mingled together. With loss, death and blissful transformation. 'And Alfred,' I say, 'did he wish to be Lord Royston for ever?'

She looks away. 'I don't know. He was exhilarated, certainly. He said he'd never acted so well in his life and that he owed it all to me. "Don't worry about money, Jenny Wren. From now on, I shall be your protector."'

Ah. Now we come to the nub.

She shakes her head. 'I know what you are thinking, Mrs. Gibson, and you cannot imagine how apprehensive I was to hear that word. Even at seventeen I knew only too well what 'protection' could entail. I naturally declined his offer.'

If that is true, I am surprised at her strength of character. After all, actresses (even virtuous ones) rely on such offers to maintain themselves. But I know my husband and how little he could be dissuaded from a course of action once decided upon. 'He ignored what you said, no doubt?'

She nods. 'He said I had an 'admirable but misplaced sense of honour' and I did him a disservice to imagine his motives were other than disinterested. And when he put it that way, Mrs. Gibson, I have to say my refusal did seem foolish. I felt ungrateful, and stupid – and, to be honest, rather coarse.'

I remember how he had made me feel over Alice and Madame Brandt; how he made me feel stupid and ignorant and unworthy for doubting him in any way. I look at her and wonder how this poor girl, at seventeen, could possibly have withstood the force of his displeasure.

'He pestered me with notes, too, pleading to let him have the 'simple pleasure' of ensuring my welfare.' She shakes her head. 'It was so very, very difficult!'

'But clearly not *too* difficult, or you would not be where you are now, set up by him in this very pleasant little house.' I cast a look around at the figured wallpaper, the paintings in the gilded frames.

Her cheeks grow crimson and she lowers her head. 'I know I must seem to you a weak and immoral person to have accepted any-thing from him. But he was *Alfred Gibson*! How could *Alfred Gibson*, the great Public Benefactor, the great champion of the poor and downtrodden and the saviour of the lost, set out to ruin a girl of seventeen? A girl with no means? A girl who had so recently lost her father? A girl who trusted him with her whole heart?'

It would, of course, have seemed inconceivable. Although, sadly, I reflect that he was not averse to ruining a woman of forty-five who had no means and no father, and who had *also* trusted him with her whole heart.

She goes on: 'Every day I saw how he helped others. Almost everybody in the company had some reason to be grateful to him. The last night of the performance he ordered a splendid supper for us all, with champagne and lobsters and marbled jellies and ice-cream and everything you could ever have thought of. And the families of all the company were included – little Georgie and Fanny too – and all the stage-hands and wardrobe women and ticket-sellers. The ladies all had silver brooches from him and the gentlemen all had cufflinks. After we'd eaten, the children ran around the table in high spirits and Alfred ran after them dressed as some sort of quaint magician, giving them bonbons and toy trumpets and sugar mice. That night I convinced myself that his offer flowed from such simple kindness as I was seeing then, and it would be very ungracious not to accept.'

'What of your Mama all this time? Did she not advise you how dangerous that proceeding was?' But even as I say it, I think of Kitty and Augustus, and my own signal failure to advise my daughter when her virtue was under threat.

'Oh, you are so hard on Mama. But you have probably never known what it is to be poor, Mrs. Gibson. No doubt you have always had a home, and a husband – or father – who provided for you. Mama and I had nothing. We were only an inch away from destitution – from the streets, if you understand me. All our lives, we had prided ourselves that we were poor but honest – but you can be too poor, you know. It's not noble; it's demeaning. And now here was the most wonderful opportunity to raise ourselves out of the mire. Where would we ever find such another dis-interested benefactor again? One so understanding, respectful and respectable? One so universally renowned for his generosity and benevolence? Mama said she was sure that Alfred Gibson, of all people in the world, could be trusted: "After all, he says you remind him of his own daughter."'

I wonder which daughter he had in mind. Miss Ricketts does not resemble Kitty or Lou in the slightest, and Fanny would have been only three. I can think of someone else, though.

'So, Mrs. Gibson, rightly or wrongly, we allowed him to pay off our debts and give our landlord a month's rent in advance.

I thought it would end there, though. I fondly imagined that now he had done us some good, his philanthropy would be satisfied. The play is over, I said to myself. He will go out of our lives. My mind can settle back into a calm state, and this strange sense of being *possessed* by him will fade.'

'But he did *not* go out of your lives.'

She puts her head in her hands. 'No, it was quite the opposite. He began using his influence to secure better rôles for us, and he'd call every single afternoon to tell us what he'd accomplished. He was always cheerful, always amusing, but he'd look around our lodgings, make a wry face and say they were 'rather slip-slop' rooms, which did not reflect the genteel nature of the occupants. I told him that, on the contrary, they ideally suited our station in life. But he said that I was 'too humble' and needed to have aspirations to greatness if I were to succeed in my chosen profession. To be frank, I couldn't see what a set of rooms had to do with aspirations to greatness, but they seemed inextricably connected in his mind. Then one day he came saying he'd found an apartment near the Strand which he thought much more suitable. "I have decided to make you a present of the rent until such time as you are rich and famous – which, I am sure, with your talents and my help, will not be long." I told him we could by no means accept anything more: "You have done much for us already. Pray do not concern yourself further." But he only smiled and said, "For Heaven's sake, why? It's a paltry sum! Less than I give to many other good causes – and this particular cause gives me much more pleasure! Will you deny me that? Will you not accept a gift in the true spirit of Christian generosity?"'

'And no doubt you found him impossible to deny once more?' I begin to see a pattern now.

She flushes. 'You may not believe me, but I used to make such firm resolutions when I was away from him. You have no idea how firm I was going to be! But the moment I was in his company,

I began to weaken. And when he said how much it hurt him to know that his little Jenny Wren thought ill of him; that I didn't trust him, as if he were Jack Black himself – oh, Mrs. Gibson, it seemed so shoddy to suspect him of bad motives when he had never given the least inkling of them; when all he had done was to be kind and thoughtful about our future. So I let him help us again, determined that as soon as Mama and I could earn our keep, the arrangement would cease. I've always known how important it is for a young woman to stay respectable. The profession is not generally respected, Mrs. Gibson. We walk on a tight-rope and it's easy to fall from grace.'

'Indeed. It is a perilous profession.' And Alfred had clearly known the dangers when he discouraged Kitty from the Thespian life. He would have known that, with her thin skin and wayward temperament, Kitty would hardly survive in such a world. When I think what a wise little head Miss Ricketts had at seventeen, and what a child Kitty is still at twenty-seven, I can see why.

Miss Ricketts pours more tea in an agitated fashion. 'But if I'd thought that by agreeing to this – rental arrangement – the matter would be settled, I was wrong. Every week there were gifts of groceries, coals and wine. We protested, and sometimes sent them back – but they didn't stop. Then other parcels began to come: cashmere shawls, ivory fans, kid gloves and, finally –' she holds up her wrist '– jewellery. And in spite of all Mama had promised to me, and although we had done nothing wrong – *nothing wrong, I assure you, Mrs. Gibson* – I realised we were indeed irrevocably compromised.' She sighs. 'I believe it is a true saying that there is no gift without its obligation.'

'Especially between men and women. Especially between a rich man and a poorer woman. You cannot claim to have been ignorant of that.'

Her little chin goes up. 'But all we had done was to maintain a mutual friendship. It was very hard to be judged on that.' She sits back a little. She frowns in the way that Eddie described. It is a rather charming frown. Her face is rather charming, too, now that I have watched it for a while. Her beauty is one of expression rather than feature, a casting down of the eyelid, a softening of the mouth. It is the actress's gift.

'Go on,' I say. 'Tell me more of this *mutual friendship*.'

'You are sceptical, I see, but his behaviour at this time – even as a married man – could not be faulted. He would only call on us if Mama were there to chaperone me, and he always came so beautifully dressed, as if it were an honour to be with us. I remember how he'd sit and talk about all sorts of things – especially the *Miscellany* and the difficulties he was having with *The Red House*. He'd been struggling with it, you know, all the time he had been rehearsing the company, managing the performance, and appearing on stage himself.'

'Oh, he was never satisfied unless he had at least half a dozen things on the go.'

'Yes, I realise that now.' She smiles, and for a moment we share in a mutual acknowledgement of the habits we both knew so well. Then slowly her face changes. 'He also talked about his children. He said how much he loved them, but that he did not think they loved him in return. "Children are so ungrateful," he said.'

I think of Eddie with his nose pressed to the window. I think of Lou, always ready to defend him, Kitty, who loved him like her own soul, and Alfie, who would have gone to the ends of the earth for a kind word. How can he not have realised? Did he not see how much they cared for him? And as for me, I hardly dare ask. Yet I am impelled to, now that I have embarked on this journey. I look Miss Ricketts full in the face: 'And in all these conversations, did he not speak of his wife?'

She pauses, choosing her words. 'He explained the tragedy that had come to you; that your little girl had sadly passed away and your new babe had only lived for an hour. And that you were in Leamington to rest and recuperate.'

'Was that all?'

She hesitates again. 'He was very sad when he spoke of you, explaining that you shared his interests less and less. He said you were often too ill to accompany him to the places he loved, and that he was obliged to take his sister-in-law if ever there was a grand reception at the Mansion House or the chance to foot the light fantastic. "But a sister-in-law is no substitute for a wife."'

So that's how he presented me. A virtual invalid. A recluse. A woman who no longer shared anything with her husband — including, no doubt, her bed. Perhaps that is how he saw it; but it is not the whole truth. 'He was not exactly love-lorn, Miss Ricketts. I was often in poor health, I admit, and not as lively a wife as I should have liked to be; but Alfred had a devoted family and more friends then any man alive. And if that were not enough, he had the adulation of his Public.'

'But it seemed — I beg your pardon — as if he needed something more. Some ideal companion he had not yet met.'

Some ideal companion he had not yet met. My blood chills in my veins as I hear the drum-roll of his discontent once again, and recognise that under all his compulsive romancing and flirting, all his excessive hilarity, all the falling in and out of friendships, all the *work, work, work,* all the restless changes of his life — there was always the headlong quest for something that was forever beyond his grasp. I look at Miss Ricketts — so unremarkable and yet so surprising. And the old jealousy rises again. 'And did you, at the age of seventeen, set out to be that ideal companion?' I ask.

She shakes her head. 'I never *set out* to be anything. I did my best to cheer him up, that's all.'

She makes it sound so simple; as if no one else in the world had ever thought of it. 'And don't you think better people than you tried that very thing? Don't you think *I* did?'

She does not reply.

'You may well be silent. You can have no idea how hard I worked to keep Alfred happy. And I succeeded for twenty years, Miss Ricketts, even though he was as difficult a man as ever set foot on God's earth. But in that year – that year when you and he met in that wretched Romance – I was nearly out of my mind with grief. I had lost two children, Miss Ricketts. Are you surprised that I was in no fit state then to *cheer him up*?'

She is silent. A long time. Then, in a very low voice: 'I am truly sorry.'

'Are you? Really, Miss Ricketts, you cannot be. Because you took advantage of my absence to steal him from me. It was the greatest mistake of my life, letting myself be sent away when he was struggling with the deepest of miseries and casting around for something to fill the void. Because all the time I was resting and hoping to come back more like the pretty girl he had once married, you were working away to destroy me.'

'I swear I did not 'steal' him from you, Mrs. Gibson! I would never have done such a thing! I knew he was not free, and I respected it. And I knew that if I were to protect my own position, I needed to keep separate from him. Every time I saw him, it was a kind of agony for me, rousing up feelings that I knew I must resist. But he always seemed to take such pleasure in our company that I could not tell him to stop. "You are so much nicer to me than my own family," he said. "Your rooms are so cosy and homely. Please don't turn a poor harassed writer away."'

'And you didn't. Hardly the action of an *honourable* woman.'

'Maybe not. But it was the action of a friend. I didn't know then that I was on the slippery slope to a life of deceit – to *this* life in fact.' She gestures at the walls and furnishings in a despairing kind of way, and I see her as poor Dora Meynell, on the slippery slope, scrabbling among the moving stones: *Falling, falling, falling, until there is nowhere else to fall.*

'Well,' I say, 'public opinion will be heard. Did he not think of that when he condemned you to such a life?'

She gives a weak smile. 'He said that as far as England was concerned, he *was* Public Opinion. I was the one who had to urge him to be discreet. "Don't you think tradesmen talk? Don't you think our landlord thinks he knows why Mama and I are here? Doesn't everybody in *Lord Royston* who has seen us move from two dingy rooms to four splendid ones suspect you are at the heart of the matter? And what about your wife? Does she see and hear nothing?"'

'And what did he say to that?'

She pauses. I quail. Is what he said about me so bad that even *she* hesitates to say the words? 'I would rather know. Please tell me,' I say firmly.

She looks down, twiddles the wretched bracelet. 'He implied you frequently didn't know which hour of the day it was, and that you passed your life in a kind of haze. He said, "In the circum-stances, I hardly think she notices where I am or what I do."'

How cruel he could be. And, if he believed it, how mistaken. I turn on the wretched girl: 'And when he chose to move himself out of our bedroom for the very first time in over twenty years of marriage, did he really think I didn't notice something *then*? Or did he fail to tell you that?'

She looks embarrassed.

'Oh, he gave me some excuse, of course. He said he was restless because of *The Red House*, so I let myself believe that for a while. I even blamed my sister for coming between us. But to say I didn't *notice*!' I eye her defiantly. 'In four months, he never held a conversation with me that was more than a few words long; in four months, he never kissed me or took me in his arms. And he expected me not to *notice*!'

She is trembling a little. She seems confused and has lost her composure. 'I cannot speak for him,' she says. 'I can only speak for myself. And I swear I never set out to make you unhappy!'

'Never mind what you *set out* to do! It's a new love that makes the old one grow cold. That is why he no longer wanted *me*. Not slow, fat old Dodo, when he could have sweet young flesh instead –'

'*Flesh?*' She rises, shaking her head vehemently. 'You say you know him, Mrs. Gibson, but you judge him very badly if you can say that!'

'I, *judge him badly?*' I am on my feet too. 'How dare you say that to me! To his wife of twenty years who has toiled for him and borne children for him and seen two of them to their graves; who has stayed up with him night after night and encouraged him and comforted him through all his deepest sorrows!'

As we stand face to face I seem to tower over her. I grasp her small, thin arms and push them tight against her sides, feeling the bird-like bones beneath my fingers – so easily broken and crushed that they almost invite my violence. 'What did you give him that was so precious, if not your own body?' I cry. 'Why did he no longer wish to sleep with me, unless he had begun to sleep with you? How can you dare to tell me different?'

I have her tight in my grasp. My pulse is racing, my head thrumming. And suddenly I am shaking her. Her face advances, then retreats, her eyes wide with shock. A staccato cry escapes her lips. Serve her right, I think, shaking some more. Her hairpins shower over the floor and her long hair swirls wildly out. Her hapless voice comes in bursts: 'Please, please, please.' Now she is fading from me: a pale blur, her earrings catching the light as they dance around her little neck. She bears a strong resemblance to Madame Brandt. No, it's Miss Sarah Evans. And Sissy. It's Alice now, and Little Amy. And Madeleine Fairbright, Lillian Dawnay, it's Dora Meynell and poor Poll Lowton. Poll, poor thing, is dreadfully pale and has a livid bruise upon her forehead. *Will you kill me, Jack?* she pleads. *Have you no mercy?* But Jack's going to kill her all the same; he's going to smash her head against the parapet. He's going to squeeze and shake her until she turns blue in his arms: *Mercy?* he'll say. *Jack Black don't know the meanin' of that pertickler word!* And her head will go crashing against the stones, over and over and over and over. Until she is dead.

26

Suddenly I'm aware that Miss Ricketts is shuddering and juddering in my grasp, her eyes shut, her head lolling on her delicate neck, her whole weight sagging in my arms. I am horrified: I let her go as if she is on fire, and she drops to the ground like so much ballast. I stand and look at her collapsed figure. What have I done? She is so still; I think I have killed her. I see myself shackled, and tried at the Bailey, going to the gallows like the most notorious of convicts. I am tempted to cast myself down beside her, lie full length on the round carpet and give up the ghost as well. But I cannot do it. I must summon help. I try to call out, to bring the mother running in her pinned-around apron – but my voice does not obey me. I try to move but I have not the strength to put one foot in front of another. I stare stupidly at the door. The mother must surely come; only a deaf creature could have withstood all that fearful racket. Suddenly Miss Ricketts moves her head. Moves it a little, like a bird that has been paralysed with fright, but now lives precariously.

'Oh, Miss Ricketts!' I cry urgently, stooping over her small body. 'You are alive! Please speak. Where are you injured? What can I do?' Her eyes flutter open; and she raises herself on her elbow, staring at me as if she does not know who I am. Then she sits and staggers to her feet. Her face is flushed, her hair awry, but to my amazement, she seems unhurt. The pounding in my veins quietens a little. She puts her hand to her head, then rubs the top of her arms in a rueful manner.

'Oh, please forgive me!' I cry. 'I am a jealous woman and something evil possessed me. But you seem unhurt. Oh, tell me that is the case!'

She shakes her head confusedly. 'No, I am not hurt. A little bruised, perhaps.'

'I am so thankful.' And I *am*, because whatever she has done, she does not deserve such an attack; and the thought of the scandal that might arise has been filling me with horror. 'You will say nothing of this, I hope? I can trust you in that? Not for my sake but for *his*? I swear I will leave this house the moment I have regained my breath – and never disturb you further. Your Mama, I am sure, will see to you . . .' I am sure Mrs. Ricketts will be here any moment and I do not wish to face her outrage. I am horrified with myself: such passion and such loss of temper: *My wife the Murderess*. Maybe Alfred knew me better than I thought.

I turn to go. My legs at last are obeying me. But to my surprise, Miss Ricketts grasps the skirt of my gown to prevent me. 'No, no,' she says breathlessly. 'Please stay. I should not have spoken to you as I did. I should not have accused you of not knowing your own husband.'

'Whatever you said, there is no reason for me to behave like a barbarian.' I cast another look at the door. Still the mother does not come. Is she so habituated to hearing nothing that her aural faculties no longer function?

'I am innocent of what you think, Mrs. Gibson,' Miss Ricketts says. 'And even Alfred is not so much to blame as you suppose.'

'I daresay, I daresay.' I am too unnerved to split hairs. 'But we must leave the matter now. I am too shaken. And I am sure you are more so.'

I try again to make for the door. But she holds on to me. 'Please hear me out. Please, I beg you.'

I turn to her with disbelief. 'Do you really wish to speak with me now? After what I have done?' We are both breathing heavily, and Miss Ricketts' hair is loose around her shoulders, making her

look even younger than before. I have no idea of my own appearance – ragged as a newly-fledged bird I imagine.

'I spoke in haste,' she says. 'The subject is a delicate one. But I
believe we have to trust each other.'

We exchange looks and, from the corner of my eye, I watch
the door apprehensively. What will Mrs. Ricketts make of us
both? 'And your Mama?' I say breathlessly.

'She will not interrupt,' she says. 'I assure you we can speak in
perfect confidence.'

I wonder at this. Has her mother wrapped a muffler round her
ears and sat like a sphinx in a distant corner? But Miss Ricketts
seems in earnest, and my legs are trembling so much that I have to
sit down. She sits down too, and for a while she seems to drift into
a kind of abstraction. I wonder what she will say, what more she
can say. Suddenly she turns and speaks in a new, decisive way:
'Mrs. Gibson, have you ever come to a place in your life and wondered how you have arrived there? Knowing that, if you had been
able to see that place before you set out, you would never have
taken the path at all?'

I nod, although I am not sure what she means. We can all look
back and see we have made mistakes, I suppose.

'You see, each step I have taken these ten years has been almost
insignificant in itself, yet when all the steps are put together I find
myself at a very different place from the one I expected – on the
very edge of respectability and self-respect. Perhaps not even on
the edge, but beyond it. It was only my love for Alfred that led me
there. Only the desire to please and make him happy.'

I can understand that. We are together in that at least.

'And now he is gone and I have to make a life for myself,
somehow.'

'But he has left you money. That is something.'

'It simply makes my reputation worse. Yet the only wrong
I have done is to have allowed myself to be persuaded that our

affection – Alfred's and mine – did not matter to you. I need you to believe that.' She puts her hand on mine. It is very tender and small; it reminds me of Ada's hand.

'Why do you care about what I believe, Miss Ricketts?'

'I realise – I have been slowly realising since you first set foot in this room – that I want – and need – your forgiveness.'

'Forgiveness? For ten years of loneliness and misery? That is a great deal to ask.'

'I have been lonely and miserable, too. And now my life is blighted; I can speak to no one about what is dearest to me. I have no position as a wife or widow. The few who know of me regard me with mistrust. Some days I can hardly endure it. I should almost rather be shaken to death' – she smiles wryly – 'than linger on in this fashion.' She pauses. 'I have lived in the shadows for so long, it is hard to remember when I was last free-hearted.'

Poor girl. 'Well,' I say more gently, 'I cannot promise forgiveness, but at least I shall hear you out. What is it that you need to say?'

She makes another pause. 'I need you to understand how I became enmeshed in something I had no wish for. At first, I admit, I was delighted to be Alfred's *protégée*. New rôles came quickly and I wanted to prove I was worthy of his faith in me. But I saw it as a means, Mrs. Gibson – a means to soar free of him and make my own way, so Mama and I could be independent. But I found I could not escape him. Night after night he was there in the audience. Watching. He always joked about it, saying he had to *keep an eye on his investment* – but it was intimidating to know he was there, looking at me with those intense eyes of his. Even though I tried to put him out of my mind, I couldn't avoid seeing the faint white blur of his face, and the slight movements as he held up his opera glasses whenever I spoke. The first occasion, he even came backstage afterwards and the stage manager (knowing him, of course) let him through. *Mr. Alfred Gibson to see you!* he shouted, knocking on my dressing-room door. Everybody gawped, from stage-hands to the leading man. Everybody wanted to see him. *Enjoy the show, Mr. Gibson? Tell us, how's* The Red House *going to end? My wife swears she never cried so much in all her life!* He was perfectly polite, and smiled, answering them all with a word or two before stepping inside, and it warmed my heart to see him so loved. I remember, too, how beautifully dressed he was, his evening clothes perfect, his cloak lined with crimson satin, a carnation in his buttonhole, diamond studs down his shirt front, and the most highly polished shoes I have ever seen. He left the door politely ajar and leant up against the wall, hands in pockets, smiling round the dressing room, saying how much he loved the smell of greasepaint.

'Of course I told him he mustn't come to see me so publicly; that the world would draw the wrong conclusions. He wouldn't have it: "Oh, I am an *habitué* of the Green Room and you are my *protégée*. No one will think amiss."' She looks sideways at me. 'But you will appreciate, Mrs. Gibson, that I had a sounder knowledge of the theatrical world with its penchant for gossip, and I begged him not to compromise himself – a married man, a family man; the greatest family man in the world, in fact. "They will be talking already," I whispered. "They will be leering and joking and thinking they know something, when they know nothing at all. Even if you care nothing for *me*, please do not place yourself or your family in jeopardy by such *intimate* visits." He laughed, saying, "Is this an *intimate* visit? I did not realise! How very delightful! In that case, I am more than ever reluctant to give it up." And he took a coin from his pocket and tossed it in the air: "Heads I lose – and am banished from your dressing room for ever!" To my relief, it landed heads up, and he stared at it as if he could not believe it –'

I smile grimly. 'He would *not* have believed it. He could always make that coin fall as he wished.'

'Oh, I see – a trick.' She frowns. 'But it wouldn't have mattered which way it fell: he simply insisted that if he could not come backstage, nothing in the universe would stop him watching from the front. "I shall be at my post in the left-hand box whenever I can, armed with a dozen pocket handkerchiefs in case there is material of a lachrymose nature." I begged him not to do that – really, sincerely, Mrs. Gibson, I begged him – but he merely laughed. So I asked him at least not to be so conspicuous, but to sit well back out of sight. He wouldn't have that either: "I will not bend to you there, Miss Wren! I will not pay five shillings merely to lurk at the back of the box like an escaped convict. I will have my full entitlement!"' She swallows and looks earnestly at me. 'And he made sure of it. There he was, night after night, as if he were the worst kind of stage-door lounger.'

'So he came to gaze on you from afar,' I say. 'Was that all?'

'Oh, no, every post seemed to bring acres of correspondence. To be frank, I wondered how he had the time.'

I catch my breath. How easily she says that – and yet I can hardly bear to think how he might have used the very same loving words he used to me, as he gave her the same bracelet. The bracelet is bad enough – but his love-letters are like my own blood.

Miss Ricketts sees my consternation: 'No, no, Mrs. Gibson, they were not love letters! Admiring letters, perhaps, but nothing that I couldn't show to Mama – or to anyone. He liked to tease, as I expect you know, and it was always his conceit to pretend I had become too grand for him; that I didn't care if he had to walk back from his office with a jaundiced heart, and 'no prospect of tea and cakes *chez* Ricketts'. *I see I am a man whose usefulness is spent! Young ladies who were once grateful for the slightest word from the One and Only now cast their sights on Fame and Fortune – and merrily grind the poor devil of a hack beneath their dainty feet. Away all thoughts of cosy evenings around a roaring fire! The bird is flown. My Jenny Wren has burst from her cage and left me languishing.'* She shakes her head. 'What was I to make of such sentiments, Mrs. Gibson? It seemed he was far from 'languishing' when he turned up at our apartment with his hat at a jaunty angle and sporting the most brilliant of waistcoats. On the contrary, he always seemed in the best of spirits, full of his plans for a new weekly journal, a charity reading, a new conservatory, his intention to go abroad as soon as *The Red House* was finished, his ideas for a new serial – *a bloodthirsty murder to lift my spirits.* When he went on in this fashion, drawing myself and Mama into his confidence in the pleasantest way, he made me feel quite wicked to have ever doubted his intentions.'

So this is what he was up to all those afternoons when I would have died for a single word from him – even about conservatories. I begin to resent Miss Ricketts anew, for taking so easily what I was denied, for offering him an alternative little nesting place for him to be companionable and happy. 'So what happened to change this cosy state of affairs?'

'Oh, please – as I have told you, it was not cosy for me at all. On the contrary, I was in a continual state of dread. He was a fascinating companion – yet the one thing I was sure of, every time I saw him, was that I must separate from him; make my own way, and escape the dreadful sense of obligation.' She pauses, staring down at her hands. 'I might even have had the strength to do so. I cannot, in all honesty, say that I would not have done. But as you know, events overtook us. Well, one event, I suppose.' She glances at my uncomprehending face. 'You must know what I mean.'

I think she must be referring to something between them which she is too delicate to explain; then I realise with a sick feeling that it is something closer to home; the very worst moment of my life, in fact. My skin grows clammy even at the thought of it. Dear God, I certainly don't want to talk about it with Miss Ricketts. But she looks mutely at me, and I am obliged to answer: 'You mean that dreadful announcement, I suppose?'

She nods. 'I cannot think what possessed him. The first I knew was when I came home late from the theatre, and there was a scribbled letter thrust through our letter-box warning me that something was about to happen which might draw me into its *vile orbit*. He said he would strive – as no man had ever striven – to prevent my name being connected to this event in any way, but he had to warn me that his attempts might not meet with success. *My dear girl, you must be prepared for a blow. Believe in the power of truth. And believe me always your faithful servant and friend.* Of course, I was at a loss to know what event he was referring to, but I imagined rumours must have begun or accusations been made. And I was frightened that half London would find out where I was living, and come and stare up at my window and point me out. Yet there was nothing I could do. Mama and I had to sit tight and rely on Alfred to defend us. I couldn't even reply to his note. He'd told me I was never to write to him at home. *Letters are opened in our house*, he said. *Even private ones.*'

I redden.

'The next day, there it was in the newspaper. What he wrote about you was so shocking I didn't know what to think. I was appalled to imagine I might have unwittingly been the cause of it all, and that sooner or later, everyone would blame me for what he had done, and say that he had turned out his wife for an actress less than half his age.'

'But you were safe, you silly girl!' I cry. '*I* was the one who was exposed to humiliation. *I* was the one who lost everything that mattered – not only Alfred, but my children and my home. I lost my *whole life*, Miss Ricketts. And whatever blame may have attached to me in our marriage, I truly believe he would never have put me out of my house if it hadn't been for *you*.'

Her face falls. 'But he had never even hinted at it. And *I* had done nothing – absolutely nothing – to suggest that I wished to take his wife's place.'

I sigh. 'Women don't have to *do* anything,' I say. 'They merely have to *be*. The men will make what they will of us. Don't you see that you were simply another young creature to be endowed with

[385]

all the perfections of his imagination? You are very much in the mould – his own particular mould, I mean. The mould I never fitted once I became a wife.'

'Well,' she says with some asperity, 'I cannot say what mould I was in or how I came to be in it. But I do know that he became almost beside himself from then on, saying that he didn't know whom to trust; that his friends were giving him bad advice; that his children were rebellious and sullen; that he couldn't work. "Only Sissy keeps me going. She runs the house so wonderfully, in spite of all that is being said about her – vile rumours that I cannot even speak of to you." I did think it odd, of course, he and she and the children all in the house together, a proper snug little family. He always spoke so warmly of her, Mrs. Gibson, that I thought perhaps the *vile rumours* were true.'

'You were not alone. Half London thought that. It was brave of Sissy to face it out, but she would have gone through fire for him. And in case you are wondering, Miss Ricketts, in spite of all he had done to me – so would I.'

She turns her head and, as the light strikes her skin, I see that there are long trickles of tears coursing down her pale, downy cheeks, and dropping off the end of her chin. She makes no attempt to wipe them away. 'I didn't know that. I took his word that you rejoiced as much as he did that your *years chained in misery* had at last come to an end. I swear I would never have encouraged him otherwise.'

Ah, we are getting closer to the truth. My chest feels tight. 'So matters changed after that?'

She hesitates. 'Well, I did not turn him away.'

'Yet do you still insist nothing improper passed between you?' I watch her face, with its air of injured innocence.

'Nothing *I* consider improper. The world may have a different view, and I suspect it does. But then the world considers all loving transactions between a man and a woman to be completely carnal.'

Carnal! I have never heard that word said by a woman. I look at her sweet little mouth with surprise. Yet her assumption of innocence is absurd. Even I, foolish, good-natured Dodo with only half a grasp on the ways of the world, know this. I feel suddenly impatient. 'Come, come, Miss Ricketts. A man does not usually pay court to a woman, pay her rent and give her substantial gifts of money and jewellery, merely in order to take a cup of tea with her or watch her from the back of a theatre box. You are not green; you must have known what he wanted of you by then, however he dressed it up.'

'I did not, I swear. He never used the word 'love' to me. He never kissed me, except on my forehead. But I knew his association with me would affect his reputation. He was already being spoken of in ways he hated, and I could not add to that. So I finally took courage to write and say I would see him no more. *I shall do well now you have set me on the right path. And I have Mama to protect me.*' She bites her lip. 'He did not reply for several weeks, and I thought he was, for the first time in his life, doing what I asked. I missed him, of course; I missed him dreadfully. But I knew I would be stronger if he were not there to muddle my mind.' She shakes her head. 'Then, no sooner did I start to feel my own thoughts clear and separate from his, than a letter came. I dared hardly open it. I thought of putting it away, pretending it had never come, but Mama said, "What can a letter do?" And so I read it, forgetting that a letter was composed of words, and that he of all people knew how to use them.'

Oh, indeed, I think. Oh, indeed.

'He said he had hesitated to speak plainly before, in case he frightened his *little bird* away. He said he had a favour to ask: *It is no slight thing, but I believe you will take pity on me. Do not turn away impatiently or come to a conclusion before you have heard me out. You know I would do nothing to hurt you.*'

She stops. My breath is tight in my chest. I feel I cannot listen to this; yet I must.

'It seems – telling you now – as though I am praising myself in repeating what he said – but you must understand how it affected me. He said that no one – even those to whom he had the strongest bonds of affection – could soothe his mind and make him happy as I did. *I have rented the prettiest little house in Norwood. We can be as content and secret there as Babes in the Wood. Nothing else need change – nothing! I promise on my life! You are as sacred and precious to me as my own daughters. Until I know, I cannot work or sleep or rest. Say you will be my special angel. Say you will be there every day by my side. Say the one word that will make me live again.*'

As she speaks, as I hear the echoes of his boyish love-letters to me, and remember his earnestness and charm, his mixture of desperation and certainty, I feel as though everything within me is dissolving. I look with envy at her light brown hair, her delicate chin, the jet earrings twinkling as they lie against her neck, the well-fitting dress that shows her tiny figure to advantage.

She resumes: 'I assure you, Mrs. Gibson, I did not entirely know what he meant. Indeed, I was alarmed to think I should have the responsibility of keeping England's most famous writer in a state of continual bliss. I didn't wish to be his angel, or anybody else's for that matter.'

I am silent.

'But how could I refuse him? Even knowing that if I agreed to live in that pretty house with him, I would step outside the respectable world for ever, and lose my reputation, my profession and my chance of marriage.'

'What did your mother advise in all this?'

Miss Ricketts casts down her eyes. 'Mama said I must decide such a thing for myself.'

'But you were so young!' I burst out. 'And she of all people should have known what it would mean.' Even as I speak I recall my dereliction of duty over Kitty.

'You question her concern for me? But think what it meant for us – an end to our travelling up and down England to play at any theatre that would have us, an end to dirty lodgings and dishonest landladies, an end in fact, to all our debts and anxieties. But Mama would not tell me what course to take. All she would say was that she was sure that Alfred Gibson was an honourable man. And I remember saying, "Brutus was an honourable man." And she looked at me and said, "Whatever else, child, I don't think he will murder you in the Capitol."' She smiles grimly. 'Oh, Mrs. Gibson, believe me when I say that I simply could *not* decide what to do. I delayed answering for days. I hoped, somewhat absurdly, that matters might resolve themselves without my making a decision at all. All the time I was playing in *The Rivals* at Drury Lane, I'd be saying my lines and hearing the laughter and beginning to feel exhilarated; and then I'd see that faint blur in the box, and know he was there, and my heart would sink. Indeed, I almost wished he *would* carry me off and ravish me. Then at least I would not be responsible for my own disgrace.'

Poor child. I remember having the same thought as I lay night after night in my bedroom at Chiswick, imagining Alfred's knock at my window, and his determined arms carrying me off in spite of my faintest of complaints. 'But,' I say relentlessly, 'you agreed in the end?'

She moves the toe of her dainty shoe along the pattern of the carpet. 'What else could I do? I felt as if I were in a box-set and the walls were closing in on me, and there were no exits. I couldn't let him go on being so dreadfully unhappy. Do you understand?'

'Oh, yes. Oh, yes.' I could never suffer Alfred to be unhappy either.

'So I wrote and agreed, and he rushed round next day with a linnet in a cage, and kissed me on the cheeks most prodigiously and shook Mama's hand, and said he would never, ever break our trust in him. Three weeks later we were here.'

'Only you and your Mama?'

'He didn't want servants. Although in the end he agreed to our hiring a girl for the mornings. "Someone young," he said. "And make sure she can't read; I don't want her putting two and two together. And she's to call me Mr. O'Rourke."'

I draw my breath in sharply: 'O'Rourke?'

'That was the name on the lease and all the bills. I think someone of that name had arranged it for him.'

I feel I have been struck in the face. I can hardly trust myself to speak. The thought that Michael might have known of this house, that he might have been complicit in renting it for Alfred – that he paid the bills and saw to all the comforts that she has had and were denied to me; that he could have deceived me all these years, sympathising and pretending ignorance of this secret life – fills me with horror. It's the worst kind of betrayal. Worse even than Alfred's, in a way. I feel I am going to pass out. I fumble for my smelling salts and inhale as hard as I can. Miss Ricketts frowns. She is clearly puzzled at my distress over a simple name.

'Did he ever come here?' I say faintly. 'O'Rourke, I mean? Did he actually pay the rent? Did he collect the bills?' I see O'Rourke acting the same dutiful messenger between Miss Ricketts and Alfred as he did between Alfred and me; and Alfred thinking it as neat and symmetrical a piece of business as the identical bracelets.

'*No one* came here,' she says. 'Apart from your son, that one time. Certainly no one called O'Rourke. And no one else paid the rent; Alfred gave money directly to Mama. To be honest, I didn't think O'Rourke was a real person at all; simply Alfred in disguise.'

'Oh, O'Rourke was real enough,' I say. 'O'Rourke was his best friend – and I thought he was mine, too. If he knew about this place, he has been lying to me for years.' I think of Michael affecting ignorance of her whereabouts – *Peckham or somewhere – it might have been Timbuktu for all we knew.* Can he really have been so duplicitous?

She sees how agitated I am and tries to soothe me. 'Don't think ill of your friend,' she says. 'Alfred always liked to use names he knew; it was part of his play-acting. He used to say that when he was in the country he was a different person entirely, dressing in a loose-fitting coat and a ridiculous broad-brimmed hat pulled down over his eyes, saying he looked the picture of a *regular Oirish oncle*. He'd do the accent too.'

Her words comfort me a little. I tel myself that she is right, that it was simply a sly joke on Alfred's part. I think back to O'Rourke's protestations of ignorance, his anger at Alfred's behaviour, his fury, his despair. He would have had to be as good an actor as Alfred to have maintained such a compendium of lies all this time. And O'Rourke has always been transparent as the day, which would have made it all the more amusing to Alfred as he strolled around *incognito*, thinking how at variance his Irish *alter ego* was with Michael's own irreproachable life. I want to believe Miss Ricketts; I want to believe her so much. But somewhere in my mind I am not entirely at peace. The more I hear of Alfred's wretched dealings with this girl, the more I see how easily he bent the most resistant person to his will.

I put away the smelling salts and put on a bright face. 'I interrupted – forgive me. You were telling me about how you moved here – you and your Mama and the hired girl.'

She looks doubtful, but continues: 'Yes. And the whole house was ready for us.' She waves her hand around. 'New wallpaper, rugs, curtains, looking-glasses, all the furniture in place, the cupboards full of china and new linen. I complained he had left us nothing to do; that women in general like to arrange their own homes. He said he was sorry but he thought it would be a surprise.'

He always thought that. He always expected me to be delighted when he presented me with a new home, even though I was perfectly satisfied with the old one. 'Well, Miss Ricketts, for your information, I have lived in seven different houses with my husband, and he furnished every one of them without my help.'

She looks surprised. 'I have to admit he'd done it perfectly. And he was most particular about showing us his own room in the attic with its single bed and trouser press, saying that it would suit him when he needed a bolt-hole. But generally, he said, he had to get back home for seven sharp 'to preside over the cruet for an hour or so'. I felt reassured, as though some – tension – had been broken.'

'He'd got his way, hadn't he?'

'But apart from my leaving the theatre behind, nothing changed. Alfred would visit two or three times a week, for the afternoon, and he always found something to busy himself with – laying the fire, broiling chops, shelling peas, moving the furniture around. Once, he picked up a bonnet I was trimming and took a tablecloth for a skirt, and pretended to audition for the part of Maria Marten, and did it as well as I could (or better) so that Mama and I burst into a fit of clapping, and the girl stood in the doorway with her mouth open, till he winked at her and she fell backwards against the umbrella-stand and all the brollies rolled around on the floor. And then he took to going around the house with a hammer, looking for stray nails to knock in, or pictures that needed re-hanging. He'd make himself a paper cap and whistle the most cheerful of tunes, as if it had been his lifelong occupation, and as if he was most perfectly at home. Although sometimes it felt unreal – Marie-Antoinette playing at shepherdesses.'

I could draw the veil now, with them in chaste domesticity; I do not need to know more. Yet some demon drives me on. 'Yet all this was supposed to help his writing,' I say. 'Did he not write, after all?'

'Oh, yes. He used the room at the front – where you sat at first.'

'Ah, yes.' Such an intimate room, with its intimate desk and its intimate chair by the fire. A veritable nest of domestic bliss, with its very own little housekeeper bird.

'And I'd take in some sewing, or a book to read, and he'd scratch away, muttering to himself, laughing aloud sometimes. And when he had finished, he'd read out what he had written.'

'And you'd sit on his lap, then, would you? And ruffle his hair and give him a kiss?'

She colours, and I know I have hit home. 'Only as a daughter might,' she says.

'But you must have realised where things were tending,' I say. 'That one thing would lead to another? That he would eventually assert his rights as a man?'

'I am not foolish, Mrs. Gibson. But he had promised *on his life*. And the longer he kept his promise, the more I loved and respected him. After all, it would have been easy for him to take advantage of me.'

'Force was never Alfred's way. He always had more subtle methods of seduction.'

She gets up and walks around, her face suffused with angry blood. It makes me think of Kitty's furious perambulations, but Miss Ricketts is graceful and makes no sound as she pads across the carpet. 'You may call it seduction, Mrs. Gibson, but that's an ill word.' Her voice quivers.

'Maybe. But it was an ill thing he did. However he clothed it, whatever he said to justify his actions – he wanted you, and he got you. There you were – living in his house, sitting on his lap, kissing him. The world may rightly draw its own conclusions.'

She shakes her head. There are tears in her eyes. 'Again, I cannot tell you how wrong you are, if you think that!'

'What else am I to think? He was a man, with a man's passion, as I knew only too well. I was with child almost every year of our marriage. Do you expect me to believe that he was chaste with you?'

'It is difficult to explain,' she says. 'So easy to mock or misconstrue. I fear to tell you even now, lest you should laugh at me –

[393]

or him.' She turns to look out of the window, as if unable to look me in the face.

'I think, given the circumstances, that the last thing I would do is laugh.'

'Very well.' She comes to sit down again. She draws a deep breath. 'We'd thought, Mama and I, that having made so much effort to install us here, he would always be visiting. But we hadn't realised what calls he had on his time. Every Thursday, that wretched magazine had to be at the printers', and every Wednesday, he'd be agitated because the contributions were too long or too short or late or unsuitable for the readers — or the illustrations were wrong and no time to put them right. He'd pull his hair about and say he supposed he'd have to *do it all himself, as usual.* Sometimes he had to dash back from some public dinner or reading to see to it, bringing the proofs with him, and sitting up all night till they were done. He'd arrive at our door at four in the morning and collapse on the sofa, asking only for a brandy-and-water, saying he was going to give it all up and live in the wilds of Siberia: *The Public asks too much! It's killing me!* He used to hold up his inky fingers and joke: *Look at my life blood ebbing away!*'

I cannot help smiling. It was always thus.

'Of course, we never knew when to expect him; and so had always to be in a state of readiness. Sometimes he came by cab, mostly by train. Once or twice, when he was in a nervous state, I've known him walk all the way from London. Usually he went back to town on the last train, bundled up in that ridiculous coat, but he liked to sleep here if he could, to sit and talk with Mama and myself until the fire was nearly out. He said he always felt so comfortable with us — and that he dreaded going back to Park House, where he was *forever on the go — stretched this way and that like so much India rubber.*' She pauses. I wait, noting that the sun has shifted round and is making her dishevelled hair into a gleaming halo.

'This particular wet night — I suppose we'd been living here about a year — he complained he was exhausted with travelling and dining and talking and laughing, and would absent himself from the family hearth — *they think I'm in Ross-on-Wye*. So he took the book he had been reading from, and bade us both goodnight. He kissed me as he always did — but he seemed almost unable to release me, holding me in his embrace for a long time. He said, low so that Mama did not catch: "I wish I didn't have to part from you. I should love your face to be the last thing I see when I sleep and the first thing when I wake." Then he went upstairs, his back bowed.

'I didn't know what to do. I couldn't get the words out of my mind as I went around helping Mama lock the doors, damp down the fires and rake out the boiler. And when I tried to undress, I found myself trembling, and I went on trembling as I put on my nightgown and lay down on the bed. I lay there a long while, thinking. Thinking of what was the right thing to do. I was trying to listen to my heart, Mrs. Gibson. That is what he always said: *Listen to your heart*. I pictured him in the room above me, lying there alone. Such a good, kind man; but with no one in the world to hold him close. And I kept thinking of how sad and old he'd looked, and the little time we might have together.'

My mouth is dry. I do not know how I am sitting here so quietly. But she holds me with her words and I cannot interrupt her.

'So when I was sure that Mama was asleep, I put on my shawl and slippers, and went up the stairs to his door. I stood outside a long time, until I almost froze in the cold draughts. I lifted my hand so many times, then brought it down again. Finally I knocked, and heard his voice, rather weary, but a little surprised: "Yes? Who is it?" And I went in. He was still in his shirt-sleeves, sitting over a dying fire, reading by the light of the lamp. He didn't say a word. Nor did I. He looked at me so long that I thought I had done a terrible thing and shamed both myself and him. Then he got up and . . .' She twiddles her bracelet. Her colour is very high. 'And he said, "Have you come to stay with me tonight?" And I nodded. And he said, "You are an Angel," and kissed me on the forehead, so very, very sweetly that my heart nearly broke for love of him. And I lay down on the bed, and he covered me over and lay down beside me . . .'

She stops, and we are both silent for a while. I can hear the ticking of a clock that I have not noticed before.

She raises her eyes: 'Now what do you think of me?'

I think of her in her white nightgown. And I think of Alice laid out chastely on the bed, and the last words on the manuscript of *Ambrose Boniface*.

～ *27* ～

The afternoon light is already fading when I make my way back along the garden path to the cab. The cabman sits patiently, a rug across his knees, a muffler wound up high round his neck. I apologise for keeping him waiting, but he says his newspaper keeps him happy, 'and the orse ain't complained yet'.

I climb in and we clatter off. As we pass the gap in the holly hedge where the gate stands, I catch a glimpse of Miss Ricketts and her mother standing at the blue front door, staring stiffly ahead as if posed for a photograph. I wonder what they are making of my visit. For my part, I am in a state of incredulity. Miss Ricketts is everything I am not, and I am everything *she* is not – and yet I feel we understand each other.

We turn the corner sharply, and they are gone. Back into their strange half-life, with only each other for company. And I reflect that they are quite as cut off from society as I; and have been in that unhappy state almost as long. For over eight years they have received no letters except *his* letters, divulged nothing of their whereabouts to friend or acquaintance, and have been obliged to tell untruths to those they live among in order to keep their identities secret. *Ladies brought their cards as soon as we moved in,* Miss Ricketts told me. *But we could not return the compliment. We dared not cultivate the slightest acquaintance for fear of being found out. So to avoid the reputation of rudeness, we had to write saying that we were both in poor health and unable to go into society – which of course restricted us more.* Whereas it seemed that Alfred, in his slouch hat and voluminous coat, was considered an amusing eccentric as he tramped about the lanes.

Miss Ricketts had no option but to wait upon the hours and times of his desire, the moment of arrival that would send her into a flurry. So, in a way, she has passed the intervening years much as I have done, spinning out small domestic tasks to fill the hours of daylight. She sewed as I sewed; and she read as I read. She had extra occupations, though. Her education had been scanty, and Alfred had set about improving her mind and conversation, giving her the benefit of his very particular learning methods. Nevertheless, I doubt a young lady of her age wished to spend every day with her nose in a book, however engaging her teacher. If she had improved her conversation, with whom should she speak? If she sewed herself exceptionally fine clothes, to whom should she show them off?

Of course, she had her consolations. She could look forward to some purpose in her solitude – the anticipation of seeing him. As I know only too well, anticipation of happiness can sometimes be as gratifying as its consummation. Even during the first months of my separation, every footstep on the pavement would have me racing to the window, and every ring of the doorbell would set my heart beating as fast as a bird's. But as the months went by without even a word, I gradually had to relinquish my hopes of seeing him again. It was not easy to do so, and I am not sure whether I ever managed it entirely; however, I did stop waking with that thought in my mind, imagining what he was doing every hour of the day, and whether his journey would by chance take him past my door. I tried to tell myself instead that I was fortunate in my neglect; that now I needed have no fear that he would arrive and his gimlet eye start to anatomise the cushions, or the curtains, or the state of the fireplace; that now, at last, my life was my own. But truth to tell, I would have given anything to see him walk with his jaunty step up to my front door and rap out a cheerful rhythm with his silver-topped cane.

But even while I envy her the hope of his presence, in other ways she is to be pitied. After all, I can look back on so many happy memories; whereas what little life Miss Ricketts had known was snatched from her, as she was forced to trade the bright lights of the stage and the adulation of the audience for a life of solitary confinement. And did he really hold off from her as she implied? Perhaps she spares my feelings; perhaps she merely defends his honour, or her own. In the end, I find it does not matter; that there is no purpose in asking myself: did they do this, or that? What she has told me is what I always suspected in my heart: that he was drawn to her for the purity of her spirit; that he would have seen in this small friendless girl his own younger self, battered and put upon by the world; that he would have loved her for her struggle, and the way she kept herself gracious and true in spite of it all. And that he would have drawn strength from her admir-ation, and been flattered by her affection. It must have been an irresistible combination.

*

O'Rourke is waiting for me when I come back. He's sitting by the fire, chafing his hands, a worried look on his face. 'Dorothea, thank Heavens! Where have you been? Mrs. Wilson says you've been gone since ten-thirty, and now it's nearly half past three!'

'Half past three!' I say, affecting gaiety. 'Is it? How the time has flown.'

'So, where on earth *have* you been?' O'Rourke is standing now. He seems to possess the hearthrug like a husband.

I want to tell him how interesting it has been to talk woman-to-woman for all this time, and how Miss Ricketts is not at all the person I had taken her for – but I find I don't like to be ques-tioned in this way: 'I don't have to answer to you, Michael, do I?'

I am shocked to hear my words. I've never addressed Michael in this way in my life, and he shrinks back a little. 'No, of course not. I'm sorry; I didn't mean to pry. But I've been so concerned about you; half-mad with worry, in fact. Wilson had no idea where you were, and – well, you are not used to the outside world, Dodo. Much has changed in ten years. Even strong men are not advised to cross Hyde Park without life-preservers.'

'Oh, Michael.' I am overcome by all my old feelings of friendship. I take his dry old hands and speak more softly: 'I'm quite capable of looking after myself, you know. I may have been housebound for ten years, but my *brain* is still intact. I've only been sitting inside a London cab, and unless highwaymen with pistols have returned to the streets, I don't think I was putting myself in any danger.'

'Ah, well, you see, it wasn't so much the cab ride; it was the *destination*. That's what was worrying me. Wilson said you were *most* secretive about where you were going, and after that conversation about Augustus the day before yesterday, I feared you might be trying to intervene with his creditors. Some of these moneylenders live in the most unsavoury places, as if it went against the grain for them to spend sixpence on a half-decent abode. You take your life in your hands to go there, I swear. And a woman with jewellery, good clothes and so forth – I tell you, Dodo, if you had not come back within the next ten minutes, I would have set out and scoured all the dens in St. Giles until I found you.'

'Michael!' I squeeze his hands between mine. 'What a hero you are!'

He laughs and starts to wheeze. 'Rather a broken old one. But my heart is still true.'

I look at him sharply. I hope – oh, I hope so much – that he is not going to make a declaration. He seems to think better of it, because he laughs and says, 'I have always valued your friendship, Dodo. Let nothing come between us on that.'

'No. I hope nothing will. I hope nothing *has*. I hope we shall always be *honest* with each other.' I look directly into his pale eyes. There is no flicker of guilt or guile. On the contrary, he is puzzled.

'What do you mean, Dodo? Do you not know that already?'

'I have always believed it. But I need to know: can I still rely on you – *in everything?*'

'Why ever not?' he looks hurt. 'Dodo, what is this all about?'

'My heart has been too wrecked to bear another betrayal.'

'Betrayal? Good God, Dodo, what do you mean? What new idea is this? You pain me Dodo, you pain me. If you have no faith in me, I shall be obliged to end out friendship – and God knows what I shall do with my life then!' He looks quite haggard.

I am instantly mortified. How could I ever have doubted him? 'Oh, no, Michael! I'm sorry. I didn't wish to offend you. But I need to be sure that with you, as with no one else in the world, I can be safe and tranquil.'

'Safe and Tranquil?' He smiles ruefully. 'I could have wished for more, but let us keep it at *safe and tranquil*. You have my word on it.' He pats my arm and helps me sit down. Gyp waddles up and tries to jump on my lap; I ignore him, and he lies at my feet instead, too fat to protest. O'Rourke leans forwards to pat him. 'So your mysterious errand had nothing to do with Augustus?'

'No. Nothing to do with him at all.'

He shakes his head. 'I'm blessed if I can guess who, then.'

'Oh, you'll never guess.' I arrange the folds of my gown, and can't help a little smile turning up the corners of my mouth as I anticipate the surprise he will show. I wait a beat before I say, 'It was Miss Ricketts.'

And indeed his eyes open so wide I think they might pop out from their sockets. '*Miss Ricketts?* Dorothea, what possessed you? Where did you find her? What did you say?'

'Well, Michael, I had come to the conclusion that the very thought of her has been poisoning my mind. It's not a good thing to live with hatred, especially when it is born of ignorance. As none of you could tell me anything to the purpose, I decided I must see her myself. And Eddie gave me the courage to try.'

'Eddie? You've seen Eddie?'

'Oh yes, didn't you know?' I forget that I have not seen Michael since. 'He turned up yesterday, quite airy and genial, as if it's been his habit for years to take tea with his Mama. He's such a handsome boy, isn't he?'

'Is he? I've never noticed. In fact I haven't seen that much of him, lately. He's either been up at Oxford or out and about in town. *Spending money,* Alfred said. *Always spending money!* But to turn up so suddenly! And to suggest, moreover, that you visited that woman!' O'Rourke looks appalled.

'He didn't suggest it, Michael; I didn't say that. But at least he was prepared to discuss her. He didn't think I would spontaneously combust if I heard Alfred's name and hers in the same breath.'

O'Rourke frowns. 'He had no business to discuss her with you. He owed you more than that.'

'He owed me nothing, Michael. I have injured him badly. I didn't mean to, but I did. And yet, when he walked back into that room, he was the same lively, generous child I remember. People don't change that much, do they? Alfie has turned out exactly as I expected. He was always a *good* child – and now he is a devoted husband and father. And isn't Carrie a splendid girl! A writer, too! And such a careful mother; she always has her eye on Lucy, even when she has her mind on other things. And the child has a very strong character, she quite reminds me of Kitty!'

'*The Infant Phenomenon* reborn. Let's hope she won't drive her father to the same pitch of distraction. But,' he says, giving me the most earnest of looks, 'are you going to tell me nothing about your visit to Miss Ricketts?'

'Maybe. Maybe not.' I look at him carefully.

He looks back at me. 'This is a new mood, Dodo; you are not usually contrary. The woman's had an effect on you. I don't like it; you should not have gone.'

'So you would have stopped me if you'd had the power?'

He looks discomforted. 'Well, I would have tried to *dissuade* you, certainly. What on earth did you hope to gain?'

'The Truth, Michael.'

'And so you have it at last, do you – the Truth?' He gives me a dry look.

'I don't know,' I say. 'But Miss Ricketts has told me things – things I cannot repeat – which have given me a better understanding of her position.'

'*You* understand *her* position? That seems an odd way round, Dodo. After all, you are the injured party. And you say you cannot repeat these mysterious things?'

'It is very confidential. I may tell no one. Not even Kitty.'

'I see.' He looks exasperated, and not a little hurt; we have always been so confiding in the past. 'Then perhaps you will at least tell me how *Kitty* is getting along? I assume *that* particular topic is not *sub judice*. Will there be money to rescue her? I cannot imagine you would have gone off on your jaunt to Miss Ricketts if your daughter were about to be turned out of her house by the bailiffs.'

'Oh, yes.' I inform him excitedly of Kitty's plans for a new life: the music lessons in Fulham, and Augustus in the wine trade. 'She feels a sense of purpose now, and is convinced that Augustus has turned over a new leaf.'

O'Rourke makes a disbelieving face. 'I wish I had as much faith in that man as she has – or pretends to have. But I hope they succeed, I really do. Kitty has always been a favourite of mine. When she is in the right mood, she positively *sparkles*.'

She does, and it always warms my heart to see her sparkling away – but the sad fact is that she lacks all application. That was Alfred's great gift, *a transcendent capacity for taking trouble*, as Carlyle would say: all regularity and punctuality and determination. But Kitty was born into too much comfort; and even worse, she has shackled herself to a man who has never worked in his life. 'Oh,

Michael, I blame myself for so many of her troubles. I have given her a poor pattern to follow.'

'Nonsense! You are one of the best women I know. Even if you take it into your head to pay secret visits to ladies who are no better than they should be – and cause great agonies to your faithful friends the while.'

He tries to brush it aside, to make me feel comfortable. But I am *not* comfortable. And moreover, I shouldn't be; I have a right to criticise myself even if he does not. 'But I have never done anything in my own right, Michael. And Sissy's no better – nor even poor dear Lottie, God rest her soul. Kitty has only had to look at the three of us to see we have given up our whole lives to serve the needs of men.'

He looks at me quizzically: 'Is that so very bad? Are we men such awful tyrants?'

I look at his kind, wrinkled face, and know he has never in his life treated a woman with other than the greatest consideration. 'Oh, you are so devoted to us and protective of our every need. But that is the trouble. You treat us as children.'

He groans and rolls his eyes: 'You will be expecting The Vote soon.'

The Vote! That was the last cause I ever thought to espouse. 'I've never thought of such a thing!' I rejoin. 'Yet all the same how can it be proper for a woman to be married twenty years, then cast aside on a pittance? How can we lose the right to see the very children we have raised? Why do we have to go cap in hand for every bit of money that we need? If women made the laws, wouldn't things be different?'

'Oh, yes. I'm sure Parliament would be a nicer place – full of teapots and sewing boxes.' He laughs.

He makes light of it. All men make light of it. As if any attempt to change things is ridiculous. And I admit that I have laughed too, as Alfred poked his savage fun at Mrs. Pewgious dispensing tea, toast and emancipation in the drawing room, while her children perfected lies and larceny in the kitchen. I turn on him: 'Is it so singularly amusing for a woman to have ideas of her own? To wish to be a *person* as well as a mother? If one could be a writer, as Carrie is, or an actress like Miss Ricketts – one has some self-respect.'

'Miss Ricketts! Self-respect?' He starts, and makes as if to get up. 'How on earth can you believe *that* of her?'

'Oh, you are prejudiced, Michael. She is a young woman of taste and delicacy. And she has suffered, too. She has lost all her chances through her association with Alfred.'

'So that's what this is all about! Oh, Dodo, you are too gullible! Such women know what they are doing. She's come out well from it. And she's been clever enough to spin you some sort of tale to gain your sympathy.'

'On the contrary,' I say, beginning to warm to my theme. 'It is clear that she has lost the best years of her life confined to a little house in Norwood, waiting on Alfred's hour of arrival, playing second fiddle to all his other interests. She might have been as famous as Mrs. Siddons, you know; she might have been one of the brightest names of the century. But she'll be forgotten. No one will remember Wilhelmina Ricketts as a great actress. And of course no one will even *think* of Dorothea Millar except as a footnote to the life of Alfred Gibson!'

O'Rourke has the look of a man watching the sun set upwards. 'Well now!' he says, trying to gather his thoughts. 'Well now, Dodo, I see your appointment with Miss Ricketts seems to have turned you into something of a Radical.'

'And why not?' I say warmly. 'Alfred was a Radical; you were a Radical; and at one time every Radical in London passed through my house and held forth in my drawing room. The only surprise should be that I have waited until now to become a Radical myself!'

I hear a cough and Wilson is standing at the door. 'Sorry, madam, I heard a noise. Did you call?' She gives O'Rourke a hostile stare as if she suspects he is upsetting me, and that she will, on my nod, eject him from the premises.

I reassure her. 'No, we were becoming a little excitable, in the way of old friends. And as an old friend, Mr. O'Rourke will be staying to supper. I don't want to hear a word about lack of provisions. If we don't have sufficient, please purchase some more immediately.' I hand her the change from Eddie's ten-pound note, which she takes with a mixture of uncommon satisfaction and bad grace.

'You see,' I say, when she has gone. 'It is a revelation to me what money will do. It gives one a sense of power.'

O'Rourke looks at me miserably. 'Power! Why should a woman want power, for Heaven's sake? Why are you talking like this?'

'That's the thing, isn't it? It makes you all *uncomfortable* when a woman voices her views. Ann Baskerville once told me that she'd been called 'immoral' for daring to say Biddy Lipsom was a heroine. And Alfred wouldn't employ Mrs. Casby for writing 'a little too near the sexual side of things'. You all get so angry when we don't fit your moulds. Women aren't angels; why do you try to make us so?'

O'Rourke is dumbfounded. Poor man, it is not his fault. He rubs his hands together and tries to think of something to say. 'Men don't have things all their own way,' he says finally. 'Many's the poor devil whose life has been ruined because some woman has refused to marry him. Women have all the 'power' there, Dorothea. All the power of yea and nay.'

'One little moment of power, very early on when we hardly know how to exercise it. But once we are married . . . well, we can't say yes or no then, can we?'

He looks embarrassed; he is afraid that I am about to delve into the secrets of the bedroom. But I'm not concerned with bedroom matters; I'm thinking of *all* the relations between men and women. I see how women are so delicately poised, so dependent upon the goodwill of their husbands for their very survival. As long as Alfred was content with me, I had everything I could wish for, but once I no longer pleased him, I was cast off with no redress. 'And you know how even *patterns* of husband-hood go astray,' I cry. 'How could I have thought, when we first met, that dear, doting Alfred would be so cruel to me?'

'I don't suppose, back in those days, that "dear doting Alfred" would have thought it himself. I think it caught him by surprise more than anyone that you and he were no longer suited.'

'But could he not see – could no one see – that it wasn't fair to put me out as he did, to separate me from my children, my house, my servants – while he continued to enjoy it all unhindered?'

O'Rourke shakes his head. 'No, Dodo, God knows it wasn't fair. I suppose you could say that in general, Life's not fair.'

I turn and blaze at him as if I were Kitty. 'Then should we accept that there is no possibility of change? After all, Alfred wanted change more than anyone alive. He wanted the mean to be made generous, the debauched redeemed and the lost to find a purpose in life. In fact he wanted everyone to be in permanent good humour and sit around one great family table with a merry shout of *God Bless Us All!* How, then, could he be so adamant with me, his wife?'

O'Rourke stares at his hands a long time. 'I suppose you weren't part of his rosy fantasy, Dodo; you were reality. And he couldn't endure the reminder that life sometimes went wrong, and that even the One and Only couldn't will a happy ending for himself. And it enraged him to be so – so – how can I put it –?'

'*Powerless?*' I suddenly understand Alfred's rages, his wild behaviour. It must have been terrifying for him to find everything slipping from his grasp: his reputation, his family, his self-esteem. In those moments he was as weak as a woman. 'Is that why he did the Readings; to assert his mastery; to be up there on the platform in charge of the world once more?'

O'Rourke pauses. 'You may be right. He couldn't stop doing it. *Allow me one more tour, Mikey,* he'd say. *I have to drown Poll again for the delectation of the masses. Word has got out and the public are already forming queues.*' O'Rourke laughs, shortly. 'But as he was confident of earning such great sums I suggested he might at least pay *you* a little more each month.'

'That was hardly necessary,' I say quickly.

'Wasn't it? I thought you were all for fairness. Do you think it was *fair* for you to manage on such a fraction of what he earned?'

He has caught me out. But I would never have demeaned myself to ask. 'If he had given it freely, that is another matter, but you shouldn't have mentioned it. Wilson and I were managing well enough.'

'I saw you struggle. And he must have felt guilty about it, because he was at pains to explain himself — over three or four pages at least — saying that he was practically in Queer Street because *everyone in the world* was reliant on him and that he had no resources left to gratify a single extra demand. *I have to rent half the habitable houses in London for my multitude of ungrateful dependants, and am obliged to keep a fleet of carriages for my daughters to attend soirées where, if I am lucky, they may find a husband or two apiece who will take them off my hands. I have to pay the exorbitant wages of the whole army of servants necessitated by the continual presence of house guests who stay so long I am thinking of having their names engraved on brass plates outside the front door. Not to mention that by some strange process unknown to me, every Person of Note who comes to London seems to fetch up on my doorstep, and, being admitted, proceeds to loll about in my drawing room and read my newspapers and sleep in my sheets, and use my hot water and eat his way through my larder and drink his way through my wine cellar, as if I were a Public Hotel! I swear that last week I came across a dozen or so gentlemen whom I did not recognise in the slightest, taking walks on my lawn and picking hot-house flowers for their buttonholes while smoking Havanas from my personal store!'*

I cannot help laughing; that was such a typical tirade, but there is a truth to it too. We must have seemed such an ungrateful set of dependants — not one of us earning our bread, not one of us helping to arm ourselves in the battle of life in which he was so vitally engaged.

28

I've had a very pleasant evening with Michael. He is the best of companions. We had Wilson's best recipe for fowl, and a bottle of very good wine. (Wilson's standing with Mr. Collins has improved and she has been able to purchase a fine ham and some splendid cheese too.) We ate, talked and laughed as we have always done, putting our recent disagreements aside and resolving to be always comfortable with one another in the future, and never, ever to quarrel.

Now he has gone, I sit on for a while in the armchair. The wind outside is getting up and whistles eerily through the sashes. Strange shadows move on the walls as the curtains shift in the draught from the windows, and the fire flickers in the draught from the chimney. Whether the sounds and shapes unsettle me I cannot say, but I find that I cannot put my mind to my book. My encounter with Miss Ricketts keeps returning to me. Now I am no longer in her presence, it is more difficult to believe that I found her so congenial, and that we shared such intimate remembrances.

Yet it was a relief to find her such a ladylike person with delicate manners. I have no perverse wish to admire my rival; but at the same time I would have hated her to have been vulgar or scheming, as Kitty used to imply. I think that is why I have closed my mind to her all these years. To have discovered that Kitty was right would have immeasurably lessened Alfred in my eyes – and tainted me, too, when I think that he went so readily from me to her. This is not to say that I don't resent her for her charms, and resent him even more for succumbing to them. If anything, he was the more at fault, being so much older and wiser, and presenting himself to her as a friend and father, yet taking to some extent the liberties of a lover once she had set herself upon the path of no return.

Of course, I cannot help questioning the nature of the chaste affection she insists they shared for almost a decade. No one with a worldly mind would give it a moment's credence. But I know him well enough to think it may indeed be true; that he would not have caused such dreadful mayhem – wrecking our whole family life, setting us against each other and dividing friends and foes alike – for the simple allure of pale limbs or perfumed skin. Alfred's most powerful feelings, I have come to realise, were stirred not by the easy tumble of the bedroom, but by the recollection of a half-glimpsed face in the crowd, the sight of a small, neat figure bent over a workbox in a lighted window, or a child ministering selflessly to a father or brother. Miss Ricketts, though not a child when he met her, was very young, and had no father of her own to love her. What began in his head as fatherly may, in time, have become something else. But he would have seen no change. Love, to him, was love. He would never have examined it in more detail or asked himself whether, in pursuit of it, he was hurting others or even deluding himself. In his eyes, only coarse and envious people would misconstrue the noble nature of his affection.

They *did* misconstrue it, of course, being always ready to believe the worst in humankind, and more than usually gleeful to find fault with a man who set himself up as England's greatest moralist. Even now, in spite of her protestations, it is hard not to think that there were indeed other, deeper currents running within him; that in the dark part of his soul, when he held her in his arms and kissed her, he was desirous of doing what he would never have admitted – what he never *did* admit – and what she will never confide. But that is the part of the truth I am sure I shall never know.

What is strongly evident from her account, however, is that in all our last unhappy months together he must have been as distraught as I was, and could have seen a solution no more clearly than I could as he wrote with such agony about Arthur Grayling tormenting himself in the gloom of his green drawing room with his hopeless love for Lilian Dawnay. But whereas I cried and raged and questioned in a lunatic fashion, he became cold and ruthless, trained (as I believe only men can be) on one object, oblivious to any hurt he inflicted on anyone else; while Miss Ricketts, poor child, had no notion of all the storms that were hurtling around our house, of which she was the unknowing centre.

And I was not mad. Parcels *did* arrive, letters *were* secreted. He *did* go out to see her every afternoon wearing a flower in his buttonhole and scent on his skin. He thought I had my head in the clouds and didn't see him, sleek and smiling – whereas the truth was that he did not see *me* as I stood in my dressing gown, desperate for the slightest word. Day after day, he'd take his cane and set off at speed like a constable of the law, obsessed, possessed, in thrall. Violent as an express train rushing towards a broken bridge. And as unstoppable.

※

I'm very cold suddenly. The fire is out and the lamps are so low I can hardly see the furniture. Where is Wilson, I wonder? Why has she not come to help me to bed? I try to get up from the chair, but my limbs feel as though they do not belong to me. And where is Gyp? I call to him but there is no answering bark. Something stirs near the door; I am sure that it is not Gyp. 'Wilson?' I say in a whisper. Then the darkness seems to mould itself into a shape and there is a man standing in front of me; a dark man with some sort of beard and a hat pulled low over his forehead. I am so frightened I cannot call out. I think it must be one of the ruffians that frequent Hyde Park, and I get ready to offer all my jewels and silk dresses.

But as he steps from the shadows, I see that he doesn't have the air of a ruffian. He is wearing a rather fine suit with a gold watch chain dangling from his satin-sprigged waistcoat. I stare at the watch and the waistcoat. I know them both intimately. And when the man sweeps off his hat with a bold gesture, I know him too.

'Alfred?'

'The very same! I am glad my lady-wife has not forgotten me after all these years. I confess that Yours Truly is somewhat less handsome than of yore. A little thinner; a little more worn.' He smiles a radiant smile as if there has never been a moment's coldness between us.

'Forgotten you! Oh, Alfred, how could you think that? You were my whole life!' I try to stretch out and touch him, but I find I cannot move. Is this a dream? Is he a ghost? He looks so real, so corporeal; so like himself.

'Infinitely obliged. Compliments are always welcome, especially from the Once-Adored.' He takes his watch from his waistcoat pocket, looks at it and then spins it back into place. 'However, circumstances are pressing and time is short. I am under strict curtailment. Deadlines, my dear, always deadlines. There are Obligations, you know, even in the Place Above.'

'What do you mean?' I say, unable to take my eyes off him. His beard is speckled with grey and his hair is thinner. But he has the same mesmerising eyes.

He laughs. 'Oh, you wouldn't believe the timetabling in Heaven, Dodo! The Almighty is a stickler to the second – and if I run over my time I am doomed to the Fiery Furnace for ever.' He speaks cheerfully, as if this would be no hardship.

'Well, you never run over your time, Alfred. You are always most exact.'

'That is, of course, true. I am obliged to you again. But to business. Unfinished business. Unfinished manuscript, to be precise. *Ambrose Boniface*, to be even more precise. I have to confess myself

[413]

mortified to have left it in such a state. I have let my Public down. The only time that I have done so.'

'Save one, Alfred.'

'Ah, yes. A long time ago. A matter of some pain, now dissolved into the ether. But to the present point. *Ambrose Boniface* needs concluding. And you, Dodo, will be the one to see to it.'

'I?' I burst out into nervous laughter. 'Oh, Alfred, how? I cannot write!'

'On the contrary, I think you can. After all, who else has copied out so many of my crabbed manuscripts? Who else has read my books with such attention? Who else can quote whole passages verbatim? Who else knows every inch of my style? No, no, there is no gainsaying it! You are the very person! There can be no doubt, no *argey-bargeyment*!' His eyes twinkle.

'But you said I had no imagination, Alfred!'

'Oh, you don't believe everything I say, do you? I'm a storyteller. We are, as a species, notoriously unreliable.'

'But how did you intend to finish it, Alfred? You have left no clue.'

'It *is* a Mystery, after all.' He laughs.

'Yes, but what is the answer to the mystery? Everyone wants to know. Did Ambrose kill Mary Kincaid? Does he die too? Have you left notes? How am I to do it?' I feel all the anxiety and confusion he invariably raised in me.

'Oh, you'll find the answer if you look hard. I've every confidence in you, Dodo. You always understood me – even when you didn't think you did. Now I'm afraid that in order not to turn into a roast dinner for some undeserving demons who are even now sharpening their forks, I must be gone immediately. Forgive all impoliteness arising from circumstances of a novel nature (no pun intended). Goodbye, my dear. Yours Truly relies on you, as ever.' He flings his hands in the air – and is gone in a cloud of glittering smoke, leaving behind only a faint scent of lavender.

The room is suddenly brighter. The fire is burning, the lamps are lit, and the room is warm again. Gyp is on my lap and I hear Wilson on the stairs coming to put me to bed.

'Oh, Wilson!' I cry, as she opens the door. 'I have had such a strange experience! Alfred was here, in this room, right in front of me.' My blood is racing through my head, my heart is pounding, my whole body in a state of collapse.

She stares at me. 'You've had a dream, you mean?'

She pulls me up short. How could it have been anything else? But it was all so real that I am loath to believe it was purely a product of my imagination; the same imagination in which I was once allegedly so deficient. 'No,' I say, a little less confidently, 'he was *really here*, Wilson. In this very room, standing right there where you are now – although a kind of spirit, I suppose.'

She stares at me. 'Well, I don't believe in spirits and such-like; it's not Christian. All them mediums and whatnot, trying to cross the divide – preying on people who should know better! Mr. Gibson is gone from us, God rest his soul, and he'll never come back this side of Judgement Day.' Seeing my shocked countenance, she stops and softens a little: 'Dear madam, don't you see? You wanted to see him so much, you *imagined* him back. Now isn't that the truth?'

'Is it? Then why am I so cold?' I ask her. 'Feel my hands: they're frozen.'

She takes them in her warm, work-worn ones. 'So they are. I'll give that fire a poke.'

'It doesn't need poking.' I point at the jumping flames. 'Look! It was almost completely out a minute ago.' As if the force of his spirit had blown it out. As if it had blown the lamps out too. 'And Alfred was as real as you, I swear. He looked older, but it was still him, Wilson – still definitely him. I could even smell the scent he always used.'

[415]

She gives a big sniff. 'Well, I can't smell nothing now. You've had too much going on today, that's your trouble. Gallivanting here and there, and entertaining till all hours. You need some proper sleep.'

She tries to bring me down to earth, but I can't let it go. 'He said the oddest things,' I tell her. 'He said Heaven was run to a timetable!'

She bends to see to the fire. 'Well, that would have been his idea of Heaven, wouldn't it? Everything orderly and organised.'

I wonder whether to tell her. I can't stop myself from doing so. 'The funniest thing of all is that he asked me to finish his book for him.' I turn Gyp off my lap and get up.

She looks at me, twisting round from her position at the grate, poker in hand. 'Why is that funny?'

'Well, Alfred was a literary genius. And I have never written anything in my life – except letters!'

'I've heard it said that you write very nice letters. And you must have picked up some ideas from him over the years.'

'Oh, Wilson, there's more to it than that.'

'I daresay. But you never knows till you try. After all, young Mrs. Alfred does it, and lots of other young ladies do it – and older ones too, such as Miss Baskerville. Why not you?' She pauses. 'But did Mr. Gibson's so-called *spirit* tell you how it all ended? Because I'm blowed if I can guess.'

'He said that I'd find the answer if I looked hard.'

'*Looked hard?* Is that all he said after coming back from the Dead?' Wilson stands with her hands on her hips, looking solid and sensible – and I realise how foolish I must seem. As in the old days, when the servants would whisper about me: *Poor Mrs. Gibson. Lost her senses. Quite mad.* She's right, I have imagined it. Yet of all the encounters I could have imagined, this one is the most strange, the least like anything I should have wished for. Alfred was so odd and matter-of-fact. I never had a chance to say any of the things that have been in my mind. I didn't ask him about Miss Ricketts, I didn't ask him about Alice or Sissy or the children. I didn't ask if he was sorry for what he did to me. I allowed him to overwhelm me all over again.

I start to cry. 'Oh, Wilson, for a moment I was so happy to think he'd come back to see me!'

'That's natural enough.' She looks at me kindly. 'Believe he was really here, then. Believe it was him come back. Where's the harm?' She picks up the lamp and takes me gently by the arm. 'Come on, Mrs. Gibson dear, it's time for bed.'

When I am undressed and combed, she turns to me: 'Would you like some of your medicine? A small spoonful to calm you down?'

I think that wretched mixture will be the death of me. 'No, Wilson. I've done with it. Throw it out. I'll need all my faculties if I am to finish *Boniface*.'

'You'll try, then?'

I smile. 'Well, you never say no to Alfred.'

29

I have slept well and had no further dreams or visitations, and now the idea of Alfred coming and telling me to finish *Ambrose Boniface* seems laughable. I really cannot think I took the matter seriously.

'It's nice to have a bit of peace and quiet,' Wilson observes, when she has cleared away the breakfast things. 'Although it's nice to have company too, I suppose. When it's family.'

'More than nice. I can't tell you how wonderful it has been to see my children again.'

'Mr. Edward has turned out a fine young man.' She blushes as I catch her eye. 'And Mr. Alfred too, of course – though not quite so handsome. And the little girl is very lively – the spit of Miss Kitty – although I reckon her mother has got her measure.' She pauses. 'I suppose they'll be coming and going quite a bit now?'

'I hope so. Oh, Wilson, I really can't believe that I have got my family back.'

She picks up the tray. 'I suppose you've forgot about That There Box being emptied.' She glares at the tea-chest I brought back from the old house.

'Oh, Heavens, what a bully you are! All in good time. I really should look at the letters first.' The carpet-bag is overflowing, but I shall take a leaf out of Alfred's book and answer them all in date order. So when Wilson has finished laying the dust and has gone down to bundle up the laundry, I set about it. I open them all, and set them in piles on the table. Most of them are from acquaintances rather than friends, and they repeat the same tired old phrases of condolence that Alfred hated so much. On the other hand, my old school-friend Jenny Lockhart takes the opportunity to write several pages about her own husband, who has never loved her and never done anything to please her – and I feel that her situation over thirty dismal years is worse than mine has ever been. Miss Brougham writes too: *I fear my charitable work has lost its greatest champion. There was no one quite like your husband and there never will be again. When we worked together, I always felt in such sure and energetic hands. He had such ideas! He would not be put down on any account, and could lift the spirits of the most curmudgeonly opponent! Somehow he managed to make the impossible, possible! And above all, he made me laugh! I am sure you have had occasion, through these last ten years, to miss all that good humour. Even I, a solitary spinster, am aware that once you have known a good man – even if he is a difficult man – it is hard to live without him.*

Miss Brougham is such a dear lady – and always saw the good in Alfred. I hope now that the embarrassment between us is over, we may renew our acquaintance. I feel full of energy and set to with a will.

Then I come across another letter. The writing is unfamiliar, and rather childish.

Dear Mrs. Gibson,

Forgive me for not writing before but you know I am not much of a one with a pen. This letter is being writ for me by my brothers child aged ten who is with me in Putney learning how to be a ladys maid or at least a parler maid. She is a very good pupil and very quick and I am hoping she will get a good situation when she gets a bit older although she could never hope to have one as good as mine. I think I had the best situation a servant could ever have and I thank the Lord every day for bringing me to you. First let me say how much I cried when I heard the dredful news. I think I was nearly struck dumb. I could not believe it. I know we all has to go when our time comes but I didnt think the Masters time would have come so early, even though he worked as hard as seven men and was always on the go. The news boys in the street was shouting it out at the top of there voices saying Alfred Gibson dead, Alfred Gibson dead and everybody was coming out of there houses and saying is it true? And I could feel my heart beating fit to burst. And everybody was crying, even the little children as didnt really know who he was but knew his name like we all did.

Oh Mrs. Gibson how you must be feeling so sad without him even though you were not with him in these last ten years. I know how much you loved him, no one better and I dont think your feelings changed even though he said his did, which I dont reckon is true. Mrs. Brooks and I discussed it many a time and we think he was not fair to you and should not have done what he done and in such a crule way.

I have always felt bad that I did not come and see you but you know what the Master was like when he was crossed, and I didnt dare in case I lost my situation. I could not have bore to give up Miss Fanny and Master Georgie in particlar as they needed a mothers love and had lost you already. And I ment to write and Kitty said she would help me and so did Lou but they must of forgot and then I thought I had better not do it in case it brings up old feelings as has been laid to rest.

You may know that I have taken up my old position but not living in with Mr. Alfies little girl which reminds me of all the happy times we had. She is uncommon clever and she reminds me of Kitty. Poor dear Kitty, I am so sorry she has no children it would help settle her. I get about well on the omnibus and you are no distance from me and a good walk benefits us all, so I would be pleased to call on you at any time,

Yours in sorrow,
Signed Bessie

Dear honest Bessie! My heart fills to overflowing. I must see her. I rise hastily and nearly take the tablecloth with me in my eagerness to find a pen. I sit at the little desk and write a few words in reply. 'Come tomorrow,' I urge her. 'Come anytime. I am nearly always at home.' I call Wilson and give her sixpence to get it taken by messenger straight away.

She will come. Bessie always acts straight away. That is one of the things Alfred liked about her. *No shilly-shallying with that young woman,* he used to say. I look at the letter, written so neatly by her niece, and signed so awkwardly by Bessie, and smile to think about the day Alfred discovered that she could not read. In his typical way he had written her a list of her duties. And Bessie, having tried the capacities of the butcher's boy and the knife-grinder without success, had been forced to come to me to find out what it said. I remember how she stood in front of me, afraid she would lose her place now the truth was known: *Don't tell the Master. Please don't tell him! They all relies on me at home!* I'd told her that Alfred would never dismiss her for such a reason, and if he even dared to contemplate it, I assured her that I would not part with her for anything short of my life. But of course, no such sacrifices were required. Alfred had been mortified: 'I should have realised,' he kept saying. 'Girl like that. Eldest of ten. Busy all day. Mother's right hand. Of course, of course. But it won't do in my house. It won't do at all. And the answer is 'oblivious' – as Boodles would say! I shall apply to it straight away. Get paper, get pencils! The One and Only will teach Bessie her letters!'

And poor Bessie had been called up from the kitchen and told that she must put aside half an hour each day to work with Alfred in his study. 'It is not difficult to master,' he'd said, taking her hand enthusiastically and tracing the outlines of the vowels. 'It needs application, but I know you and I are both good at that! We shall do splendidly, have no fear!' And indeed, within months she had learnt to read perfectly and often was found eagerly digesting the latest number of his novels, and even taking a surreptitious look at the manuscript for the next one as it lay upon his desk. But she had never quite mastered the art of writing, as if her large honest hands rebelled against the dainty act of holding a pencil or a quill. I can see her now, bending over the desk, with Alfred smiling beside her. And again, standing in the kitchen doorway when I left the house for ever, and she was the only one to say farewell.

⁂

It is immensely hard work answering the letters. I am gratified that so many of our former acquaintance still think it proper to address me as his wife, but I am not like Alfred, to whom words came so naturally; who could make every correspondent feel instantly refreshed, even at second-hand, by his enthusiasm and good sense. After a morning's rigorous penmanship, I am more than eager for a different activity. All my fears of encountering old acquaintances have miraculously gone and I am anxious for another foray into the outside world. Indeed, I cannot believe how I have endured to stay cooped up in three little rooms for so very long. I will wander the streets as Alfred did, and try to see through *his* eyes. Perhaps some idea will come to me.

'I am going out,' I tell Wilson as I eat my lunch. 'I shall need a cab at two o'clock.'

'Yes, madam.' She maintains an impassive face. 'Where for, if you don't mind saying?'

'Blackfriars Bridge.'

'What on earth will you do there?' Wilson looks aghast. Perhaps she thinks I plan to jump.

'It's a good point to start. I intend to see what has happened to London while I have been out of society.'

'It's bigger and dirtier, I can tell you that,' says Wilson with feeling. 'But you're not planning to walk around on your own, are you?'

'Why ever not?'

'Any ruffian could knock into you and take your purse without you ever knowing.'

'You speak as if I have never been out on my own before. When I was first married, I'll have you know, I'd go out to the

[422]

markets in the Caledonian Road every week – and my sister and I used to take regular strolls around Camden Town.'

'Things have changed, madam. I'd better go with you. There's nothing to be done that won't keep till I get back.'

'No,' I say. 'It is kind of you. Very kind. But I want to be on my own.'

'As you please,' she says somewhat huffily. 'But take care, and call a constable if any of the riff-raff takes it in their heads to follow you about.'

⚜

There's no sign of any riff-raff when I alight from the cab. All is very respectable. There are a number of Hansom cabs and Hackney carriages rumbling along the bridge, and three police constables standing on a corner. A man with a bull terrier is leaning on the parapet, looking over.

I pay the cabman and set off. I feel excited. I try to imagine what would have gained Alfred's attention as I walk along the new embankment towards Westminster Bridge. There is a matchseller in the doorway of a public house, selling Vestas to a man in a broad-brimmed hat. Another man wears working clothes and is carrying a spade. The embankment is only recently finished, I think, and there are still piles of sand and cement along the pavement. There I see in the distance the fine new Parliament building with its splendid clock tower. It gleams, a lovely golden colour. There are laden omnibuses everywhere, mingling with the cabs and horsemen, drays and carriages, and there seems to be more mud than ever in the road. I realise soon that the weather, though not cold, is rather damp, and rain threatens. I am glad that Wilson insisted on the umbrella.

I pass Waterloo Bridge and Hungerford Bridge, where Poll Lowton was drowned by Jack Black, and I wonder, as did all the reading public, what Ambrose Boniface had in mind when he came to stare at the river every night for a month, dropping a weighted line into the tide.

As I come up to Westminster, the rain starts to fall. It is a novelty at first, those first fresh drops to one who has not felt rain for years. But it quickly begins to pelt, and as I put up the umbrella, I see that the silk is torn along one of the spokes and daylight can be seen in a long sliver. Kitty must have damaged it. But the umbrella is not much use anyway – the rain is coming sideways, pasting my skirts to my legs as I try to walk, and putting my bonnet in danger of being blown away. Unlike Alfred, I am not an all-weather walker. I need to find some shelter.

Turning my back on the river, I become aware of a number of people heading in the same direction. I see a quantity of black boots and the muddy hems of a number of black gowns as I put my head down against the wind. Suddenly, I am part of a crowd, and it occurs to me that this may be part of the riff-raff Wilson warned me about, and that I need to look out for thieves. But I cannot lift my head for the driving rain, and the thickness of the press prevents me from turning to left or right. Umbrellas wave and jostle all around me, but the crowd is strangely silent. I notice that men, women and children are all in black, and hold on to each other in a kind of comradeship. There are armbands every-where, and veils and weepers flap about in the wind and rain. Suddenly we are stopping and the crowd shuffles tighter together so that their umbrellas make a complete ceiling.

Then I see Westminster Abbey ahead. They are all going there. I make sense of their black garments, now, and their hushed voices: they are going to pay their respects to someone inside. On the instant I realise it must be Alfred. I panic; I try to turn around. But it is impossible. We are at the steps of the Abbey now. 'Let me assist you, ma'am,' says a tall gentleman, seeing my attempts to break through and thinking that I am feeling faint. 'The crowd is very close, but it wouldn't do to turn back now. We are almost inside. Let me put down your umbrella.' I let him do it, and now the cool darkness envelops us. I can hear the choked voices and, far off, the sound of muffled sobs. I am packed next to perfect strangers, with the scent of camphor and black dye strong in my nostrils. We progress down the nave. Suddenly there is a parting in the crowd, and I know we are almost there. I tell myself that I will close my eyes when we arrive and pass on, but I find I cannot forbear to look.

How I wish I had not. It's a dreadful stone slab set amongst plaques and busts and marble memorials: everything he hated. He wanted to lie in the churchyard with Alice, trees and flowers growing all around. 'I am so sorry!' I cry. 'Oh, Alfred, I am so sorry!'

A kind-faced woman takes my hand. 'There, there. Don't take on so. It's not as if he was your husband, after all.'

'But he was,' I wail. 'He was!'

People look round, eyeing me oddly. The momentum of the crowd presses me to move on, but I find myself sinking helplessly to the floor among all the wet boots and muddied hems. The kind woman calls out for air and tries to support me in her arms, but I am too heavy for her, and slip back to the flagstones with a bump. There is a murmur of disapproval and dismay. Then I am aware of the white lace edge of a surplice. A white sleeve is extended from the front, and several arms support me from behind. I am lifted and helped to a seat. The sharp tang of smelling salts brings me back to myself. The clergyman looks at me gravely out of his plump, comfortable face: 'Are you recovered, dear lady? Unaccompanied it seems? No gentleman – or servant?'

'No.'

He shakes his head. 'Not wise. Not wise at all – impressive occasion and so forth. But ladies – bless them – always more inclined to visible demonstrations of distress when confronted with the Tomb.' I cannot help but notice how his glance is drawn to my dress, my lack of mourning, but he goes on: 'Indeed, I've been obliged to administer chemical consolation to no fewer than six ladies this day alone: gentlewoman from Portland Place and laundry-maid from Stepney, to name but two.' He holds up the smelling salts.

I am calmer now that I am away from the dreadful slab. I try to explain. 'I was caught up with the crowd. I did not intend to come here at all.'

'Indeed? You are not an admirer of Mr. Gibson?' His plump face drops.

'Oh no. Quite the contrary. I am his greatest admirer –'

He rubs his hands together. 'I am glad to hear that. He spoke to everyone – rich and poor alike, and gave laughter to us all. A great man, yes. A Very Great Man.'

'Oh, yes indeed, I know that! I know everything about him. I was his wife, after all!'

He looks again at my dress, my broken umbrella, my battered bonnet. He says nothing. He thinks I am half-witted. 'Well – er – Mrs. Gibson – I suggest we get you home at once. You are very wet. I shall call you a cab. That is to say if you are able to . . . ?' He looks awkward.

'I have money.' I am so glad I accepted Eddie's largesse; it opens so many doors in life. 'Yes, please be so kind as to call a cab.'

I dread to think what Wilson will say. I suppose I shall be obliged to tell her the truth, as a child is drawn to confess to its parent, even when the misdeed might otherwise go unremarked. She will say it is my own fault. And that I am foolish and misguided and should be thankful that I did not have all my worldly goods purloined by the riff-raff and was not left lying at the roadside like poor old Jessie Jarley, a prey to mocking boys. Her anger at me will be proportional to her anger at herself for not making sure my umbrella was in sound condition.

As I expected, Wilson has insisted on strict quarantine after yesterday's outing. 'Fainting in the Abbey, and coming back in a cab soaking wet. It's a wonder you haven't caught your death.' But I tell her that I do not intend to go out today, anyhow, as I expect Bessie.

True to her character, Bessie knocks at my door at eleven o'clock exactly. Wilson has a strange look upon her face as she brings her into the room. I think perhaps she feels she should not be announcing a fellow servant, but then I realise what it is. She is jealous. Jealous of what Bessie and I share; all those years in the whirling centre of celebrity and fame. But as soon as I see the dear girl, all other thoughts fly from me. I cannot restrain myself from running to her and kissing her dear, dear cheeks. Although she is still tall, she is a little bent in the shoulders, and her honest face is wrinkled and full of broken veins. But her eyes are bright and her hands in mine are firm and strong.

'Dear Mrs. Gibson!' she murmurs. 'I come as quick as I could. How are you? Oh, my dear life, it's good to see you again!'

'Will you be wanting coffee or tea?' Wilson stands stiffly at the door, as if about to become a pillar of salt.

I look at Bessie and she says she doesn't mind, and I tell Wilson I don't mind, and Wilson goes away with her very special Look.

We sit on the sofa and talk and talk. We talk about the children. We talk about Alfred continually. 'I know he was not kind to me at the end, but he wasn't a bad man. *You* believe that, don't you, Bessie?' I say.

'Bad? Of course not! He was the best and kindest man in the world. And cleverest and funniest. And what he wrote was exactly the same. But if he had a fault, it was that he always thought he was right. And he wasn't always, was he?'

'No,' I say, laughing. 'But you couldn't reason with him. What he believed, he believed.'

'And most of the time there was no harm in it. But when anyone – poor Kitty or Alfie especially – tried to say something different, I never saw such a set expression on nobody. He'd go all pale and accuse them of breaking the Harmony of the Home. It was so unfair; I wanted to give him a piece of my mind! But the minute you'd made up your mind to go in all guns blazing, he'd make a comical face – wink or raise his eyebrows, or make some funny remark – and you couldn't help laughing, even though you was annoyed with yourself for doing it. And then he'd be kind to you when you was in tears, or notice you was tired as he passed you on the stairs, and say you needed the afternoon off, *toot sweet* (although he'd pass it off as a joke, saying, "All the better to slave away tomorrow, eh, Bessie?") and you'd love him all over again.'

Bessie tells me what I know in my heart; that I forgave Alfred because he *was* Alfred, and I couldn't stop loving him in spite of what he did to me. 'Oh, Bessie, you do me a power of good. You understand how it was. You understand my feelings. And you understand *him*. You know that Alfred was difficult to please, but that he always wanted to do right.'

'Well, it didn't take me long to catch on to his way of thinking. After a couple of months I saw how you had to manage him. I remember when Mrs. Brooks started with us, I told her that Mr. Gibson was the best master ever, always careful of your feelings and never raising his voice – but that he never liked to be crossed. "You got to work round him," I said. "That's the only way. You can't never contradict him to his face." And she, being a bit starchy at the time, said she hoped that any servant would know her place enough never to contradict her employers anyway. She was half-scandalised at first, the way I spoke to him; said it wasn't fitting. But I told her that the Master didn't like standing on ceremony, didn't like to be called Sir even, and that I'd growed up with you both and was almost part of the family, as it were.'

'Oh, you were, Bessie. You were!'

'And I told her how Mr. Gibson liked to take charge of every-thing and liked to know *every detail*, and was sometimes hard to satisfy – but how Mrs. Gibson was the sweetest-natured woman in the world, and didn't mind *what* you did as long as you was kind, and good to the children.'

'Oh, Bessie! You are too good!' We embrace again, and Wilson comes in to find us with our arms entwined.

'Coffee,' she says, putting down the tray firmly. 'And buns.'

I see that she's been out to the pastry-cook's this morning. She won't let Bessie think she doesn't look after me well enough. I want to smile, but I thank her instead: 'Mrs. Wilson is a marvel. I don't know what I'd do without her.'

'I can see that,' says Bessie generously. 'I am so glad. I worried myself near to death that you weren't being looked after properly. I *so* much wanted to come and see you, but I didn't dare ask the Master, because of all things your name was a red rag to the bull. Kitty got the address wrote out for me in the end, but you know me and writing, and I put it off and put it off and you know how things go, and then I started with Mr. Alfie, and when he said you'd be glad to see me, well, I got Rosie to write straight away. And here we are.' She folds her hands on her lap.

Wilson dispenses the coffee in a highfaluting silence. She has brought out the best cups – more than she has ever done for Michael. She has put paper doilies on the plates and makes great play with the sugar-tongs: 'Is there anything else?'

'No, thank you, Wilson. This is excellent.'

'Very unexpected,' murmurs Bessie. 'But most welcome, needless to say. I like a nice Chelsea bun.'

Wilson gives a stiff acknowledgement and retires.

I make a face. 'Poor Wilson! Her life has been turned topsy-turvy these last few days. So many visitors, so many disturbances. But what a joy to see Alfie again! And Carrie and the child. (I do like Carrie, don't you? She reminds me so much of Lottie.)'

'Oh, very like. I think that's why the Master took to her so much. She never made a big fuss about things, but she stuck to her opinions in a quiet sort of way, and he liked that. And he adored the little one. Let her sit on his lap and pull his beard and do dreadful things to his hair, just as Kitty used to.' She puts down her cup and saucer. 'And how *is* my silly Kittiwake? I hear she is a regular visitor here.'

'Only because she didn't know what to do with herself in that morbid great house with her husband always away from home. Not that the house need worry her much longer. You know, Alfred was hardly in his grave before Augustus was here demanding money.'

'He should never have brought that man home with him. What was he thinking of? One look at him and you knew that he'd do any blessed thing to keep hisself amused. And Kitty was right at that age to be taken in. Of course, after she got married and there was no going back, the Master knew what he'd done. "Oh, Bessie," he said, "I have driven Kitty away. She has done an ill-advised thing, a wrong thing – but it is my fault. I have made her choose. I have forced her from me with a heavy hand when a lighter hand might have saved her."'

'He admitted it?' I am astonished.

She nods. 'Only the once, though. But sometimes he'd go up to her bedroom and stare at it for hours. I don't think he'd imagined Kitty would ever leave him. Even when she writ to say she was married and never coming back, it was as if he didn't believe the words on the paper. I can't tell you how overjoyed he was when Mrs. Alfie brought them together again. But it didn't last. They was at loggerheads again after a few weeks. I expects she was a bit too forthright about Miss Sissy – or someone else we could name. The Master wouldn't stand for that. Said she had to be respectful, or they could not be under the same roof. She tried, I know, but bending the neck weren't easy.'

'She's taken it all very badly. She pretends not to, of course. She pretends she doesn't care – or that she hates him. But I know her, and I know she feels it deeply.'

'Well, she's proud, like him. Those two wouldn't never show weakness. But as God's my judge, she looked like death itself at the funeral. All that mountain of black! And all those beads clattering away!'

'She had to make a show of it. Even though she knew he would have hated every bit of it. She couldn't help herself any more than *he* could with Miss —' I stop. Bessie looks so kindly at me it makes me want to cry.

'The Master was the light of her life. And I always says that the ones who quarrels takes the loss the hardest in the end. It's regrets, isn't it? All they didn't say or do. She'll feel it more than the rest, mark my words. Even more than Lou, for all her snivelling.'

'All the children miss him. They realise now what emptiness he leaves behind.'

'Well, Mrs. Gibson, the whole country'll miss him. No more books, no more stories, no more magazine! What will we do every Friday without the *Miscellany*? And *Ambrose Boniface* not finished neither.'

I debate whether to tell Bessie about the strange visitation, and Alfred's peculiar demand in relation to *Ambrose Boniface*, but there is a familiar impatient jangle of the doorbell. After a brief commotion downstairs, Kitty bounds in, dressed in grey and violet, followed by Augustus in his artistic hat. When she sees Bessie, she stops dead. Then she rushes to embrace her. 'Oh, Bessie!'

'Oh, Miss Kitty!' Bessie returns her embrace.

Augustus doffs his hat and stands by the door, awkwardly. He nods at me, as if in tacit recognition of my services concerning his pecuniary difficulties, but says nothing.

Kitty frees herself slowly from Bessie's embrace and sits down. 'We came to take you to Fulham, Mama! We wanted you to come and see our new house. Augustus and I think there is no place to rival it. It is *capital*! And I know — I simply know, Mama — that we are going to be so happy there. Papa always said —' She stops and catches Augustus's eye. 'I mean, *we think* that you are happier when you earn your own bread than when you rely on other people's labours. I spent an *entire day* writing letters to everyone I know, offering my services as a singing teacher (with elocution an extra) and Augustus has been to the City and got himself the very neatest of offices in the most tucked-away corner, where he can be as industrious as a whole hive of bees. It is all so wonderful. I am so happy!' Her face clouds over. 'I mean that I am happy about this chance of a new life. I have not forgotten about Papa, of course, but he always said —' she stops again, looks at Augustus '— rather, *we both believe* that life must go on.'

'You are right. I think my trip to Fulham will have to wait for another day, though. I am entertaining Bessie, as you see.'

Augustus purses his lips, but says nothing. Bessie was never impressed by his blandishments, and he hasn't forgotten.

'Would you take a cup of coffee?' I feel I have to offer, and am surprised when Augustus accepts. 'Thanks, Ma. We've been at it like beavers the last few days. I think we deserve a chance to put our feet up.' He sits, but thankfully does not put his feet up. He picks up a book instead, and affects to read it.

I ring. Mrs. Wilson comes up, absorbs the instruction concerning coffee as if she is some kind of sponge, and goes down again. Her stiffness is majestic. Kitty, meanwhile, tells us all about her plans, and Bessie gives her warm approval: 'You can do anything if you set your mind to it, Kitty. That's what your father told me when he learnt me to read, and I've found it always to be true.'

'Do you really think that's the case?' I ask. 'For example, if I wanted to finish *Ambrose Boniface*, could I do it?'

Everyone laughs, including Augustus on the sofa. This does not encourage me to go on, but I do so all the same. 'No, suppose — just suppose — I took it in my head to do it, do you think I could?'

'Don't be absurd. No one can finish it.' Kitty knits her brow.

'Well,' says Bessie, 'it'd be very difficult. You'd have to know what happens.'

'*Do* you know what happens?' Augustus puts in slyly, as Wilson brings up another tray. 'Wilkie or one of the others would give their heart's blood for a clue.'

I shake my head: 'He didn't say.'

'What do you mean, *didn't say*? How could he discuss it with you? You never spoke to each other.' Kitty is quick to see my error.

'Your mother had a vision,' Wilson announces.

'Vision? What do you mean?' Kitty looks crossly at me. I look crossly at Wilson, but she has put down the coffee and is on her way back to the kitchen. I shall have words with her later.

'It was only a dream,' I say. 'A silly dream. Wilson should never have mentioned it.'

'Oh, do tell us!' Augustus helps himself to coffee and leans back, stirring. 'Did Alfred come back from the grave? Did he ask you to finish *Boniface* for him?'

'Well, what if he did?'

'Oh, splendid!' Augustus sips his coffee with a smile. 'The Great Man keeps us all up to the mark, even in Limbo. You will have an occupation for six months at least.'

'You cannot be serious, Mama. Simply because you dreamt something . . .' Kitty has become rather red in the face.

'You think I am incapable?'

'I never said that. But you are not practised. And if you don't know the answer to the mystery, how can you hope to attempt it?'

'Your father seemed to think I would find it out somehow. *He* at least had confidence in me.'

'I should have thought he would have asked *me* – not that I believe in this vision in the slightest. Why would he have asked *you*, of all people? He wouldn't even let us mention your *name* when he was alive!'

I see now why she is so red in the face; she is jealous. Even of a dream; even of a vision she doesn't believe in.

'Rub it in, Kit! That's right.' Augustus speaks without raising his eyes from the book. 'Make your poor Ma feel her humble position.'

'But it's absurd! Mama had some foolish dream, and she's behaving as if it's the Oracle at Delphi! I mean, *I* could finish the book if I cared to.'

'And do you care to, my sweet?' Augustus raises his eyes, now.

'I shan't waste my time in attempting to do what should never be done. No one should finish it. No one knows Papa's mind. Anyway, you know full well how busy we shall both be.'

'Ah, yes.' He closes the book. '*My path in life, No one so true should share it.*'

She glares at him. 'I don't know what you mean by that!'

'Only Shakespeare, my love, only the Bard.' His face is inscrutable. I wonder how much he has really changed, whether this new amenability is nothing but surface.

Kitty may be wondering too, as she rounds on me. 'And has it not occurred to you that you are still doing his dirty work? If you want to write, why not try something for yourself? Are you content to be his echo?' She starts to cut up a bun as if she were cutting *me* up instead.

I want to tell her that even to be his echo would be a great honour. But before I can say anything, Augustus chimes in: 'Don't throw a fit, Kitty my love. I reckon your sainted mother could accomplish the matter better than you imagine. Ma has always seen more than she lets on. I wouldn't be surprised if she hasn't worked the whole thing out already.'

'There you are!' says Bessie. 'Listen to your husband, Kitty. No one knew better than your mother what your father was thinking.'

Augustus gets up. 'What an endorsement! We'll all look forward to your literary début, Ma. Now come, my love, we have an appointment with Pickford's.'

Kitty allows him, reluctantly, to steer her to the door. 'Goodbye,

Mama. Goodbye, Bessie.' Then she turns and addresses me. 'If you really mean to do it — I daresay the singing lessons won't occupy all my day. I could help a little.'

'Thank you. I'll remember.' And they are gone.

I sit down and sigh. 'Oh, dear, Bessie, I am afraid that I am hoist with my own petard, but I couldn't let Kitty best me yet again! Not in front of Augustus. Of course I shall never take it on. It's absurd. The plot so far is too complicated.'

'It's always reminded me of that Crabtree case. In the paper.'

I laugh. 'Are you still reading those Penny Dreadfuls?' Bessie was always an enthusiast for the court proceedings at Bow Street and the Bailey, and would read out the reports of trials, the more bloodthirsty the better. Sometimes Alfred would purloin a copy from her and read it out, doing all the different voices in the middle of the kitchen. Even John the coachman would laugh.

She nods.

'And what, pray, is the Crabtree case?'

'Surely you remember. Me and Mrs. Brooks followed it for weeks. It was about this young woman down in Chatham who disappeared sudden-like, and it were thought as her sweetheart had made away with her, on account of as she had broke off their engagement only the day before, because he were jealous, you see — real, right, raging jealous, and she couldn't abide it no longer. He'd been seen going up to her house and the neighbours had heard voices raised, and seen him coming out with blood on his coat. Of course he denied he had so much as touched her. He said that he'd gone to the house to make her change her mind, but that they'd argued and he'd told her that if he couldn't have her, nobody else would — being angry and all that but never meaning to harm a hair of her head. He said that when he left her, she were alive and well and that the blood was from his own self, chopping wood that very morning. Nobody believed him, but they could never find her body, so he was let go.'

'Goodness!'

'But he knew the truth and it tormented him night and day. He knew that the girl must have run away, and hidden herself for fear of him. He knew he had lost her through his fault, through his own jealousy and rage –'

'How do you know he felt this, Bessie? Were you privy to his thoughts?'

'No, but it come out later. Three years to the day, he comes home to find her sitting by his fireside, large as life. She'd been hiding as he thought, travelling and working wherever she could, waiting to see if he would change his ways.'

'And *had* he?'

'Oh, yes, mum. In spite of everything, he'd worked hard and never complained. And warned other young men not to do as he had done, but to be trustful in love, and not lose their most precious jewel through pride and anger.'

'So he and his sweetheart were reconciled?'

'Oh, yes. And married.'

'And lived happily ever after?'

'Yes.' She laughs. 'It was just like one of Mr. Gibson's stories. Mrs. Brooks and I both thought so.'

'Indeed.' Worthless man saved by a young girl's love. 'So you think that is the clue to *Boniface*? That Mary Kincaid is not dead after all? Simply biding her time?'

'Well, me and Mrs. Brooks thought the Master would never kill Mary this soon. He thought too much of her – you can tell. But of course it's a different story, and Ambrose is a gentleman, and I'm probably wrong.'

No, I think she may be right. Alfred believed above all in the power of redemption. It will do no harm to see how he might have used this idea. It's not a new one, after all. I think of Hermione in *The Winter's Tale*. And Alma coming back from exile to love and care for Lord Royston at the last. I look at Bessie. 'Perhaps you have been sent on purpose to encourage me.'

'I would do *anything* for you, Mrs. Gibson. I feel so bad for letting you down before.'

'You didn't, Bessie. You never let me down. And you never let the children down.'

Her eyes brighten. 'It's kind of you to say so, but I wouldn't want you to think I stayed because I preferred him to you, you know. It was only – well, it was the children. And I'd never known no other life. And he said that he'd got a respectable person to look after you, and that there was no need to worry, but he'd be glad if we didn't bring up the matter again.'

'Please don't blame yourself, Bessie. I know how hard it was to go against his will. *I* gave in, don't forget. I left my house and my children. Why shouldn't *you* have given in too?'

She shakes her head. 'I let you down. I stood there in that kitchen doorway and let you go away all on your own. It nearly broke my heart.'

'Oh, Bessie!' I grasp her dear form and we both start to weep.

Wilson reappears as from nowhere. I see her over Bessie's shoulder, face implacable. 'It's time for Mrs. Gibson to take a rest, Miss Jorkins,' she says. 'She had no end of excitement yesterday and nearly caught her death of cold.'

Bessie springs away in alarm. 'Oh, my! I didn't realise.' She picks up her bonnet. 'I'll be off straight away.'

'But come again. Come regularly! Promise me that.'

'I will.' She puts her bonnet back on and shakes my hand, and is herded downstairs by Wilson, as if she is a very troublesome sheep and Wilson a sheepdog of impeccable breeding.

'I suppose you've got more plans for gallivanting,' Wilson says, when she returns.

'No, Wilson. For the foreseeable future, I shall stay at home.'

She gives a smile of satisfaction.

Stay home I shall, but I do not plan to go back to my old, idle ways. I almost feel I have Alfred's blood running through my veins. I go to the little desk, and pull a sheaf of paper towards me. I take up my pen. I hold it high up so I don't dirty my fingers. I dip it in the ink. And I start to write.

Afterword

The marriage of Charles Dickens was the inspiration for this book, and I am indebted to the great writer's numerous biographers and critics, not just for the events of his crowded and fascinating life, but for many details from his letters, conversation and behaviour which have helped me form a picture of the man.

However, *Girl in a Blue Dress* is a work of fiction, and in creating my own story of Alfred and Dorothea Gibson, I have taken a novelist's liberties as I explored an imaginative path through their relationship. I have changed many things. I have rearranged their family structures, transposed names and relationships, created some new characters and dispensed with others. I have imagined scenes and dialogues that never existed, in places where the real participants never ventured. I have struck out in new directions where the biographical material is sparse, speculative, or open to doubt – or where I was simply following the threads of Dickens's own preoccupations with things strange, romantic and melodramatic rather than realistic. At times, characters from his novels make a transmuted appearance as characters in his life.

In spite of these alterations, I have always attempted to keep true to the essential natures of the two main protagonists as I have come to understand them. Above all, in Dorothea Gibson I have tried to give voice to the largely voiceless Catherine Dickens, who once requested that her letters from her husband be preserved so that 'the world may know he loved me once'.

About the Author

Photo: Richard Battye

GAYNOR ARNOLD was born and brought up in Cardiff, and read English at St Hilda's College, Oxford. She now lives in Birmingham, where she was until recently a social worker with the city's Adoption and Fostering Service. She is married with two grown-up children and is now a full-time writer.

Thanks

I would like to thank the members of Tindal Street Fiction Group for their encouraging response to the initial chapters; and Barbara Holland in particular for reading the whole manuscript when it was finished. Thanks very especially to Alan Mahar for his original interest in the book and for continuing to have faith in it. Thanks also to Emma Hargrave and Penny Rendall for their helpful suggestions, and to John Lucas for his appreciative critique of the final manuscript.

Last, but certainly not least, I would like to thank my family for putting up with my continual ramblings about Dickens, women, and nineteenth-century life – and my husband Nicholas in particular for listening to it all with a convincing expression of intelligent interest.

Also by the same author:

LYING TOGETHER

GAYNOR ARNOLD

Stretching faultlessly from the glamour of Paris
to inner-city Birmingham, from wartime to the present day,
Gaynor Arnold's debut collection sparkles with sympathy,
style and wit. Populated by characters in search of equilibrium,
these stories explore the daily misunderstandings and
self-deceits, the secrets and lies that seep into all our lives.

Gaynor Arnold brings the same empathy and social worker's
insight to *Lying Together* that she previously shone on
the marriage of Charles Dickens in *Girl in a Blue Dress*.
This versatile and accomplished collection looks forward to
the author's next novel of 'fabulously indulgent Victoriana'
(*Observer*), to be published in 2012.

£12.99 from all good bookshops and from
www.tindalstreet.co.uk

ISBN: 978 1 806994 11 2